Darkness Past

A *WeHo* Story

Sherryl D. Hancock

PRESS

Published by Vulpine Press in the United Kingdom in 2020

ISBN: 978-1-83919-326-2

Cover by Claire Wood
Cover photo credit: Tirzah D. Hancock

www.vulpine-press.com

Prologue

Kashena Windwalker-Marshal sat in her car, a 1996 Chevy Impala. She did her best to breathe, even though the vision was still running through her head. It occurred to her that they were becoming almost painful now in their clarity. It made sense to her now, all the whispering there'd been in the tribe about her grandmother's "head pain."

Her mother, Ashani, a full-blood Ojibwa Indian, had always believed her daughter had received the gift of "sight" from her grandmother. Kashena had been getting "visions" since she was ten. At first they'd seemed like dreams, but she was awake when they happened. She'd see a car accident happen in her mind, then she'd see the accident hours later as she walked home from school. A boy had been missing in the town they were in; Kashena had told her father, a lance corporal with the Marines, that the boy was in a big tube. The boy had been found dead in a drainage pipe. Lance Corporal Timothy Marshal had quickly gotten himself and his family transferred out of that town.

Timothy did not understand or want to know about his daughter's "sight." Ashani was told never to talk to anyone about it. She was told to encourage Kashena to keep quiet about it as well. Timothy knew what could happen if Kashena was pegged as some kind of freak for her "gift." Kashena grew up in town after town as the family moved. She became withdrawn, fearing people's disdain for her Indian heritage. More often than not, Kashena would avoid contact with people before they'd ever had a chance to even get to know her.

As she grew up, Kashena, who had once been an overly tall, tow-headed child, turned into quite a beauty. She had the dark blond hair of her father's Norwegian side, and the deep blue eyes for which she'd been given her name by her grandmother. Kashena meant "She with the stars in her eyes." She also had the strong jawline and high cheekbones of her Indian heritage. By the time Kashena was fifteen, she was already five foot seven tall, two inches taller than her mother. She was also strong and lean from many hours spent running up and down whatever beach they were stationed near.

They'd been relocated to a San Diego naval base. Kashena had gone off on her own, walking along the beach, her cutoff jean shorts light against her darkly tanned legs. The black tank top she wore skimmed her lean torso, exposing a slight amount of tanned flat stomach. Around her neck was a silver chain with a silver pendant suspended from it, a symbol of the Three Fires, a union of the three tribes of the Great Lakes. It was a pendant her grandmother had given her; she always wore it. Her feet were bare, her long blond hair in a braid down her back.

She'd met another girl that day, sitting alone on the beach. The girl, an older Mexican named Marta, greeted Kashena warmly. Kashena had walked over, smiling shyly at the girl. Marta had invited Kashena to sit and watch the sunset with her. After that they'd become fast friends. And although Kashena's family only stayed in San Diego for six months, she learned something very important about herself in that time. She did not like boys—she preferred girls. Marta had been her first sexual experience, and it set her on a path she never wavered from. She hid the fact from her mother and father for years. Until she herself joined the Navy and became a Marine two years later, then a second lieutenant and platoon leader two years after that.

Only when she felt confident that she could fight her father, if it came to that, did she tell them that she was a lesbian. Her mother was speechless. Timothy was furious. He hit his daughter for the first time in her life. And she hit him back, then left the house. She didn't return to see her family for another four years, when her grandmother died. Things were strained then, but Timothy was fully aware he had no say in what his daughter did or what sex she preferred.

There was a moment of hope when she came home for the funeral, since she brought with her a man. Captain Sebastian Bach, an Airborne Ranger for the Army. He was an extremely handsome man with blond hair and eyes the color of a stormy green ocean. But Kashena had assured her parents that she and Sebastian were only friends. Sebastian did the same. Things were only slightly less strained then, but it was apparent that Kashena had her own mind about things, and wouldn't be dissuaded.

Chapter 1

Kana Sorbinno lay on her bed. She wore her usual gray sweat pants and black tank top. Her long hair was spread out on the pillow. One arm was thrown up over her head; the other rested on her ever flat stomach. She'd worked long and hard on the body she had now, so different from the body of her youth. Gone was the fat that used to make her feel ugly and horrible. She'd hated the way she looked for years—finally she'd changed it. Every hour she could dedicate to weight training and cardio workouts, she'd done. Now her body was toned, muscular, and perfect. Her five-foot-ten-inch frame was lean and strong. Her dark skin glowed with health; her black hair was shiny and thick. She was a sight to behold.

Palani Ryker thoroughly enjoyed that sight too. She'd just arrived back from a two-week photo shoot. She'd missed Kana like crazy the entire time. They'd talked on the phone every night, and a few times during the day as well, but it wasn't enough. Walking into the room that afternoon and seeing Kana lying on the bed, she was thrilled. She'd expected Kana to be at work, but apparently she'd taken the day off.

Palani put her bags down, kicking off her shoes. Walking over to the bed, she lay down next to Kana. Kana was awake instantly, her arm dropping around Palani's shoulders, pulling her closer. Their lips found each other's, and they kissed for a few minutes. Their hands touched, arms intertwined, bodies pressed together.

"I missed you so much," Palani murmured against Kana's lips.

"Yeah?" Kana queried. "Show me…" she said, kissing her again.

A while later, they lay together, their bodies still intertwined and glistening with a fine sheen of sweat.

"Mmm," Kana murmured. "I guess you did miss me," she said, grinning as she pressed her lips against Palani's bare shoulder.

"You know I did," Palani replied, sighing happily.

"Mm-hmm…"

They lay together quietly for a while. Kana's hand smoothed over Palani's perfect skin, a number of shades lighter than her own. She could never get over how beautiful Palani was. A swimsuit model, Palani was the epitome of Hawaiian beauty, with her high-cheek-boned face and wide-set dark eyes fringed with thick dark lashes. Her skin was perfect; her lips were lush, inviting. Her hair was long, dark, and silky, with brown highlights. Her body—tiny, sexy, curvy, on show in the tiniest bikinis in the swimsuit edition of *Sports Illustrated*—was the kind men dreamed about.

Kana thoroughly enjoyed the fact that men fantasized about her girlfriend, her fiancée. They could have their fantasies—none of them could have her. Palani was totally in love with Kana, and Kana with her. They'd met when Palani was married. It had been apparent from the moment they met that they were meant for each other.

Over two years before, when Kana had been shot, near fatally, it had been Palani's voice that had brought Kana back from the brink of death. Kana honestly felt that Palani's voice had saved her. All Palani knew was that she was so happy to be with Kana again. In the time before Kana had been shot, a misunderstanding had broken them up. They'd been apart for over a year—it had been a lifetime for both of them.

"Oh," Kana said tiredly, as Palani snuggled closer in her embrace, "your parents called. They want you to call them."

Palani scowled. "I don't want to call them back," she said stubbornly.

"Why not?" Kana asked, surprised.

Palani sighed. "They're just going to ask me for a date again, and I'm running out of things to tell them."

"So give them a date," Kana said in a confused voice.

They'd decided to have a commitment ceremony. Palani had felt the need to be bound to Kana so that circumstances couldn't tear them apart again.

Palani looked up at Kana in confusion.

"But, Kana, we haven't talked about a date. I was waiting for you…" Palani said, trailing off as Kana grimaced.

"Babe," Kana said, her voice chagrined, "when we talked about it originally, you were going to plan it. I just figured you were waiting… Oh, honey, I'm sorry," Kana said, seeing that she was shocking her girlfriend profoundly.

Palani shook her head, looking relieved and bewildered at the same time.

"When we talked about it before, you talked about doing it on the beach," Kana said, shrugging. "I figured you were waiting for the right time."

"I was waiting for you to tell me to go ahead with planning it," Palani said plaintively.

"Why didn't you ask me about it, babe?" Kana asked, reaching out to touch Palani's cheek, wanting to smooth away the worry she'd seen there.

Palani lowered her eyes. "I thought that maybe you'd changed your mind…" she said softly.

"Oh, honey, no," Kana said, lifting Palani's face with a finger under her chin. "I love you. I don't want anyone else, just you."

Palani bit her lip, her eyes shining in the semi-darkness of the room. "Are you sure you don't want to help me plan it though?" she asked. "It's your day too."

Kana shrugged. "As long as you don't expect me to wear anything disgusting—"

"Like a dress," Palani put in with a grin.

"Like a dress," Kana said, as if continuing her original sentence, "then it's all yours."

"I'd still like your input," Palani persevered.

"Okay. Give me options, I'll tell you what I like, alright?"

"Okay," Palani said, smiling brilliantly. "I'll get all our choices together, then you can see what you like. Since you're so much busier than me these days."

"Not for long," Kana said. "The more photos you do, the more they're going to want you again."

"I hope," Palani said.

Palani had been out of the modeling scene the entire time she and Kana had been apart. She hadn't felt beautiful without Kana at her side. Now she was re-entering the industry, trying to get known again. It didn't take long for people to forget about you in the modeling world. Fortunately, Palani Ryker was known for being the most easygoing, easy-to-work-with talent around.

It had become known around the business that Palani had come out. She'd been very publicly at Kana's side during her recovery from the gunshot that had almost killed her. Instead of hurting her career, it seemed to have enhanced it a great deal.

"Speaking of photos…" Palani said, her grin impish.

"Uh-oh." Kana narrowed her eyes. "What?"

"I got a rather interesting call while I was on location," Palani said, her tone light, but her eyes watching Kana closely.

"And what was this call about?"

"Well," Palani said, "this magazine wants to do a story on us."

"Us?" Kana echoed.

"Yes, you and me."

"Why?" Kana asked, her voice tinged with suspicion.

"They read about your being shot, and my re-emergence into the modeling field. They want to tell our story, how we got together and all that. There's also going to be a top-notch photographer doing the pictures…"

"Pictures?" Kana asked, her tone still not warming.

"Yes," Palani said, knowing all the while that Kana would have reservations about the idea. "She's really a great photographer. She captures emotion in her pictures exquisitely."

Kana looked unimpressed. "Well, I'm not a model, so they'll have to leave me out of this."

"Kana…" Palani wheedled, "they want us both. It's our story, and they want us to tell it."

"What's to tell?" Kana asked. "We met, we got together and fell in love. No different than anyone else."

"That's not true, and you know it," Palani said scornfully. "My situation was perhaps a bit common, but for me to get involved with a peace officer, and all the things we went through to be together… Then to break up like we did, and get back together under the circumstances we did, Kana…"

"Yeah, well, I don't want them sensationalizing my getting shot to sell magazines, babe," Kana said calmly. "I think I sold enough papers for the nation when all that was happening. No need to dredge it up again."

"But Kana," Palani said, "don't you think it's important?"

"Important?" Kana looked perplexed. "What's important?"

"Telling our story, showing people how two women can be in love, how gender doesn't matter. It might reach some young woman, or young man, who is wrestling with the idea of being gay. Maybe our story will show them that no matter who you are, or what you do, it's okay to be who you are, what you are, and feel how you feel."

Kana looked back at Palani for a long moment, seeing that this was indeed important to her.

"You really feel like it'll make a difference?"

"I think it would, yes," Palani said. "It's a big magazine, very high in readership."

"What magazine?" Kana asked.

"*Cosmopolitan.*"

Kana stared back at her, shocked. She'd expected it to be an alternative lifestyle periodical, not some mainstream magazine.

"You're kidding, right?"

"No," Palani said.

Kana thought about the idea for a few minutes, while Palani watched.

"I'd have to talk to Midnight," Kana said, finally. "I don't want any bad publicity for her from this."

Palani nodded, understanding that Kana would protect Midnight Chevalier at all costs. It was her job, after all.

"How long do you have before you give them an answer?" Kana asked.

"Two weeks."

"Okay, I'll talk to Midnight," Kana said. "But I'm warning you, I'm not playing any games with these people."

"I know," Palani said. "I'll make sure we have final say on what is printed, both pictures and text."

Kana realized that Palani did indeed want to do this. Kana didn't like the idea of her face being out there with people pinning the word "lesbian" to it. She'd always been discreet about her sexual preference, feeling that it wasn't anyone's business but her own and whoever she was involved with. Unfortunately, when she'd been shot, Midnight Chevalier, a friend for over twenty years and the Chief of Police of San Diego PD where Kana worked, was running for Attorney General.

Midnight's competitor in the race, a low-life greasy politician type, had dredged up the fact that Midnight was at Kana's bedside. Allegations of Midnight being gay and being Kana's lover surfaced. Midnight had squashed the rumors with a press conference. In that press conference, Midnight Chevalier had stated that while she wasn't gay, Kana was a very close friend and a twenty-year veteran of the police department and therefore deserved the press's respect, rather than condescension.

Kana agreed with Palani that this article could indeed be important to people who might be confused about their sexuality. She just wasn't sure she wanted to become some spokeswoman for gay activism.

A week later, Kana was driving the Lincoln Navigator she drove as a bodyguard for Midnight. Tiny was in the passenger seat, and Midnight was in the center of the back seat. They were just leaving the garage when Kana finally got up the nerve to ask Midnight about the story.

"Midnight, I have something I need to talk to you about," Kana began.

Midnight glanced up from the papers she was reading, sensing her old friend's hesitation. It wasn't like Kana at all.

"What's up, K?" she asked.

"There's this thing," Kana said, trying to think of a way to put it. "It's something Palani wants to do."

Midnight said nothing, her glance skipping to Tiny, who was looking over at Kana. He merely raised an eyebrow.

Kana took a deep breath and plunged ahead.

"It's a magazine article, on Palani and me. They want to write about how we met and all that..."

"Okay..." Midnight said, her tone leading.

"Well, I'm just worried about how that's going to look." Kana grimaced.

It went against her grain to appear embarrassed by her sexuality, but she also knew that in working as Midnight's bodyguard she was more closely scrutinized by the public. Midnight had worked hard to get where she was; Kana had no intention of ruining that for her.

"What are you afraid of, K?" Midnight asked, canting her head to the side.

"Of embarrassing you," Kana said, her look direct.

Midnight looked at Kana for a moment, then she shook her head.

"Kana, there is no way you can embarrass me. You're one of my very best friends. The question is, do you want to do it?"

Kana took another deep breath, then nodded. "I think Palani's right. She said she thinks it's important that people see that we're regular people. That anyone can be gay, anyone can have feelings they don't understand, it happens."

"I think she's right too," Midnight said. "I know how much happier you've become since realizing who you were. If you want to do it, Kana, then do it."

"You don't think it will reflect badly on you and the office?" Kana asked, still unsure.

"Kana," Midnight began, her voice ever patient, "as far as I'm concerned, a story about you and Palani is no different than all the press Rick and I get, being in love and all that. It's about time they have someone else to watch," she said with a wink.

"Oh, great..." Kana said, rolling her eyes.

"You honestly thought this would bother me, didn't you?"

"I wasn't sure," Kana said.

"You're my family, K," Midnight said, putting her hand on Kana's arm. "I love you no matter what. Nothing you can do or say will ever bother or embarrass me. Palani is the best thing that ever happened to you. I want you to share that with other people, okay?"

"Okay," Kana said, grinning.

Kana let Palani know that night that she'd talked to Midnight and that she was willing to do the article.

"If they really want to do it," Kana said, not sounding enthusiastic about the prospect.

They were in their living room. Kana was sitting on the couch, her long legs stretched out in front of her comfortably. Palani was standing at the counter going through the mail. It was something they did frequently when they were both home.

"They do want to do it, Kana," Palani said, moving to sit on Kana's lap and handing her the mail that was addressed to her.

Kana opened the few envelopes she'd received, glancing at the bills and setting them aside. "The whole picture thing makes me nervous," she said, looking up at Palani.

"That's because you don't like people seeing your true self."

"No," Kana said, shaking her head. "I don't like putting myself out there at all."

"Because of work?" Palani asked, knowing that it was possibly a valid reason.

"No," Kana said. "Hell, they photograph me behind Midnight all the time." She made a face. "I'm not exactly undercover or anything."

"Then what is it?" Palani asked, touching Kana's cheek fondly.

Kana looked at her, tilting her head to the side.

"Look at you," Kana said, taking Palani's face in her hands gently. "You're such an incredibly beautiful woman—tiny, delicate, perfect. Me, I'm… not," Kana said, shrugging her shoulders simply.

Palani sighed, then pinned Kana with a look. "No, you're not tiny, you're not delicate," she said softly. "But you're something that not many women can be, Kana. You're a combination of strong and beautiful. You have this incredible strong physique, combined with this beautiful proud face," she said, her hands tracing Kana's face. "Kana, you have qualities that no one can touch. Your strength, your pride—your very nature emanates through your eyes."

She sat back, her eyes scanning Kana in assessment. "My thinking is, once they take one look at you, they'll forget all about me."

"Not likely," Kana said, sitting up and capturing Palani's lips with hers.

They kissed for a while, then got up to make dinner together. The feeling of worry nagged at Palani. She was afraid that any negative comments made about Kana's appearance would hurt Kana. The last thing Palani wanted to do was expose Kana to the highly appearance-critical modeling world. Palani honestly felt that Kana was incredibly beautiful in her own way. On top of that, Kana had style in the way she dressed, and she had a presence that could not be ignored. Palani only hoped that Kana would be perceived the way that Palani perceived her. It was a thought that kept her awake nights after the decision to go forward with the article was made. She hoped it wasn't a mistake.

***

Kashena Windwalker-Marshal was sitting at her desk in the office she shared with her best friend and partner, Sebastian Bach. They worked together at the Sacramento Attorney General's office. They were in charge of security for the Sacramento office, as well as backup bodyguards for Midnight Chevalier. Kashena was just finishing up a report when her cell phone rang.

"Marshal," she answered.

"Kashie, hi," came a voice from the past.

Kashena was silent as she did her best to block the rush of feelings that started immediately.

"Hello," she said, her voice calm.

"You're still mad at me, right?" the caller said knowingly.

Kashena sighed. "I don't have the energy to be mad at you anymore, Linda. What is it you want?" she asked, getting straight to the heart of the matter.

Predictably, Sebastian's head snapped up at the name she used. He knew all about Linda, and how often he had to put the pieces back together whenever she showed up.

"Damn, Kash, don't be mean," Linda said, sounding offended. "I was calling to tell you I'm coming to town."

"Okay," Kashena said calmly, avoiding looking at Sebastian, who was now glowering at her.

"I want to see you, Kashie…" Linda said, her tone softer now.

Kashena closed her eyes, wincing at the sensation hearing that caused.

"I don't think that's a good idea," she said, her voice not betraying her feelings.

"Come on, Kash," Linda cajoled. "You know you want to see me."

"Do I?" Kashena asked, her raised eyebrow reflected in her tone.

"Don't be like that, Kashie," Linda said, her voice dropping an octave. "I need to see you..." Her voice trailed off suggestively. Kashena was silent for full minute, prompting Linda to say, "Kash? Babe, you're going to see me, aren't you?"

Kashena blew her breath out. "Look, I'm at work. I can't talk right now."

"Baz is there, right?" Linda said, her tone taking on an edge.

"Yes, he is," Kashena said.

"And he still hates my guts, right?"

"He's still not fond of you, no."

"Are you still a lesbian, Kash? Or has he told you you're not allowed to be one anymore?" Linda snapped.

"I think this conversation is over," Kashena said callously.

"Don't hang up," Linda added hastily. "Please, Kash, I'm sorry. The guy just pisses me off."

Kashena nodded on her end, but said nothing.

"Kashie? I just want to see you, okay? That's all, please?"

Kashena curled up her lips in self-disgust as she felt her resolve start to give. "Call me when you get into town. We'll talk then."

"Okay," Linda said, knowing that was the best she was about to get.

As soon as Kashena hung up, she knew Sebastian was going to be all over her. And he was.

"Why did you even talk to her?" he asked, his tone berating.

"Don't start with me, Baz," she said, shaking her head. "Just because you've never been addicted to a woman in your life, doesn't mean all of us are so damned lucky. Okay?"

"Yeah, well that bitch is worse than heroin," he said.

"I agree with you," Kashena said, "but she's a habit I can't seem to break."

"Did you forget you're living with someone?" Sebastian asked.

"Did you forget Carrie isn't exactly the love of my life?" Kashena countered, thinking of the little redhead who was currently residing in her house, not actually going to school like she was supposed to be, failing all of her college courses.

"And Linda is? That irresponsible little twit?"

Kashena sighed. They went through this every time. Sebastian hated Linda with a passion.

"Well, don't expect me to pick up the pieces this time," he said.

"Uh-huh," Kashena said, sounding unaffected.

"I'm serious."

"I know."

He stared at her, his eyes narrowed. She stared back at him undisturbed.

"Goddamn it!" Sebastian snapped.

Kashena grinned.

"It sucks that you know I'll always be here for you, you know that?" he said, irritated.

"I know," she said, doing her best to quash her grin.

"Don't grin at me, Marine," he said, his tone low.

"No, sir," she said, her voice low like his.

He gritted his teeth. "I mean it."

"I know," she assured him, her lips still tugging in a grin.

"I need a drink." He glanced at his watch.

16

"It's only ten a.m., sir," she replied, smiling now.

"And I care because?"

"Special Agent Supervisor, Attorney General's office, Department of Justice, law enforcement… Ringing any bells?" she asked.

"Just shut up, will ya?" he said, still doing his best to be mad at her.

"Sir, yes sir."

He gave her another pointed look, then went back to work.

***

Linda Rose was nothing but trouble. She had been since the day Kashena had met her.

Kashena and Sebastian had been on patrol four and a half years before. They'd gotten a call about a woman who was drunk and disorderly at a bar. At the bar, they'd encountered five-foot-two-inch Linda Rose, wearing a black cat suit, a long flowing scarlet cape, and knee-high black boots. She was a sight to behold, and drunk off her ass. She had long black hair that hung to her waist, and dark, almost black, eyes.

When they walked in, she was standing on the bar itself, dancing to the music from the jukebox. Sebastian and Kashena grinned at each other. Another wild one.

"Why don't you come down?" Sebastian suggested to the girl on the bar.

Linda shook her head at him playfully, but her eyes were sharp with suspicion. She was also wavering dangerously on too-high heels.

"Come on down," Kashena seconded, reaching her hand up to help Linda down.

Linda looked at Kashena. Their eyes connected, and Linda put her hand in Kashena's immediately. In Kashena she sensed a savior, whereas in Sebastian she'd sensed a destroyer. As she climbed down from the bar, Linda's heel caught on the edge and she fell. She was tiny, so Kashena was easily able to catch her and keep her from hitting the floor. That cemented Linda's estimation of Kashena.

The bar owner was determined to press charges, since Linda had broken a number of things while up on the bar. So they had to arrest her.

"Please don't," Linda had begged Kashena, ignoring Sebastian altogether. "I'll be good, I promise."

Kashena had only shaken her head. "I'm sorry, hon, we have to," she said soothingly. "Just relax and it'll all be over soon, okay?"

"No!" Linda had screamed, the alcohol in her veins suddenly making her scared and violent.

She took a swing at Sebastian as he moved in to subdue her—she actually connected with his jaw, but he didn't even flinch. He did, however, narrow his turbulent green eyes dangerously. Linda backed up into Kashena in terror. Kashena put her arm out, stopping Sebastian.

"I'll take care of it, Baz," she said, moving Linda out of his reach and turning to face her, putting her body between Linda and Sebastian.

"Listen, honey," Kashena said, her tone reasoning, "we have to take you in. We don't have a choice now, okay? And I have to cuff you or I'll lose my job. You don't want that, do you?"

Linda shook her head slowly, her eyes wide.

"I'll cuff you, but I'll sit in the back with you on the way to the station, so you won't be scared, okay?"

Linda nodded.

"Kash, that's not a good idea," Sebastian cautioned from behind her.

Linda trembled at the sound of his voice. Kashena glanced over her shoulder at him.

"I'll be fine." She looked back at Linda. "You won't try to hurt me, will you?"

Linda shook her head vehemently.

So, Kashena rode in the back of the patrol car with Linda in cuffs. By the time they got to the station, Linda was asleep, lying against Kashena's shoulder.

"Real dangerous," Kashena said to Sebastian with a grin.

They booked her, and Kashena carried her into the cell to dry out.

She thought nothing of the incident until a week later. Linda Rose showed up at her desk at the station and waited most of the night for her to come back from patrol. Kashena wouldn't have even known about her being there, but the patrol sergeant called her on the radio to tell her about it.

"You're not going to do anything…" Sebastian had said, his voice trailing off.

"Why not?" Kashena asked. "She was drunk, Baz, not high. How many times have I seen you drunk?"

Sebastian curled his lips in disapproval, but said nothing else.

Kashena collected Linda from her post at Kashena's desk and ended up taking her home that night. Linda never left. She stayed with Kashena for six months. It was the most passionate, turbulent, exciting six months of Kashena's life up until that point.

It came crashing down when Linda flirted with Sebastian, suggesting they do something to tame his inner beast. She'd been serious, and he told Kashena about it. Kashena questioned Linda about it, and Linda became incensed, saying that she was a "free spirit" and couldn't be caged. She left the following day, disappearing for three months.

When she reappeared she was very definitely high and drunk. She also had a man with her. She drunkenly begged Kashena to let them stay with her. Kashena refused. They left, and Linda had come back by herself the next day. She begged Kashena to let her come back. Crying and telling Kashena how much she'd missed her, loved her, needed her. "I just want to be in your arms again. I feel so safe there, please, Kashie…"

Kashena asked about the man that had been with her. "He's just a friend. We were really high, I just didn't want him getting hurt without me. But I came back to this Godforsaken town for you, Kashie, because I need you, please?" she begged again.

She reached out, touching Kashena's face, moving in to press close to her, and Kashena found, to her shock, her resolve was weakening. She'd missed the little fireball. So it had gone—they'd gotten back together. Much to Sebastian's disgust.

Four months later, while on the job, Sebastian suggested that it was highly possible Linda had slept with the man she'd brought to Kashena's house, and perhaps lots of others.

"And what was she on, Kash?" Sebastian asked. "Is she using needles? Do you really want to get AIDS from that scumbag?"

Kashena scowled at the scumbag comment, but she also knew Sebastian might be right. So Kashena talked to Linda and suggested that they both get tested. The next day, Linda disappeared again.

Sebastian suffered with Kashena as she got tested. He was terrified that Linda had left because she was HIV positive and couldn't face Kashena with that information. It made him sick to think he could lose his best friend, but he resolved to stick with her through whatever came. Thankfully the test came back negative, but not before Kashena drank herself into a stupor for three days. If it was possible for Sebastian to hate Linda more, he managed it.

In the end, Linda showed up every so often with a truckload of excuses and apologies. Kashena realized early on that she was addicted to Linda. Sebastian neither understood it nor liked it. But he was always there when Linda left Kashena in ruins again. Kashena did, however, put one important condition on sleeping with Linda again: she had to have a negative result on an HIV test every time. Sebastian had insisted on that, and Kashena had agreed with him.

***

Two weeks later, while they were in Sacramento, Midnight called Kana into her office. Kana walked in, surprised to see a woman sitting in the chair in front of Midnight's desk.

"Kana," Midnight said, standing and gesturing to the dark-haired woman, "this is Sierra Youngblood. Sierra is the new head of the criminal division. Sierra, this is Kana Sorbinno. She's in charge of my security team throughout the state."

Kana walked forward, extending her hand to the woman as she stood and turned to Kana. Sierra extended her hand as well, smiling warmly.

"It's great to meet you," Sierra said, her voice soft.

"You too," Kana said, her eyes searching the other woman's.

Kana sat down; Sierra did the same. Midnight also sat, her eyes on Kana, having noticed Kana's look.

"K, Sierra is having a problem with a previous client," Midnight began. "When she was with the District Attorney's office, she prosecuted a case where the victim's brother was a bit over the top with his interest in the prosecution's investigation."

"And in me," Sierra said distastefully.

"Now he's apparently calling her again, here," Midnight said.

Kana looked at Sierra. "Has he threatened you?"

"He's always suggesting that I just 'give in,'" Sierra said, her eyes staring into Kana's.

Kana lifted her chin slightly—she knew exactly what Sierra was saying. The gaydar was working just fine.

"When you refused?" Kana asked, knowing Sierra had, and why.

"He got really angry," Sierra said. "The next night someone tried to break into my house."

Kana's eyes narrowed. "Did you file a report?"

"I called the police," Sierra said. "They came, but he was gone by then. He may have heard me on the phone, I don't know."

"Did they lift any prints?" Kana asked Sierra.

"Yes," Sierra said, "but he has no criminal record, so there was no way to know if it was him."

"So what do you need from us?" Kana asked

"I was hoping I could at least get someone to take me home," Sierra said. "My husband is in the military and he's currently overseas. I have a ten-year-old son—I'm more afraid for his safety. I think that if this man sees that I have someone escorting me home, he might back off."

"It's possible," Kana said, her mind working.

Kana looked over at Midnight. "Who do you want me to pull for this?"

Midnight pursed her lips in thought.

"I'd like—" Sierra began, then stopped.

Kana and Midnight looked at her.

"What, Sierra?" Midnight asked. "You'd like what?"

Sierra was silent, looking at Kana pointedly.

Kana nodded, knowing what Sierra was getting at.

"I can take care of it," Kana said, looking back over at Midnight.

Midnight's gaze went between the two women, then back to Kana as she nodded.

Later that afternoon, Kana showed up at Sierra's office.

"You ready to go?" she asked, leaning against the doorjamb.

Sierra glanced up. "Yes, certainly," she said, getting up and turning off her computer.

Kana led Sierra out to her Navigator, opening the door for her. When she turned on the vehicle, the radio played R&B music. Sierra looked surprised.

Kana grimaced, reaching over and turning the radio down.

"Sorry," she said, grinning. "My girlfriend was in the car this morning. That's her stuff."

"Oh." Sierra smiled. "I know how that is. I had a girlfriend once that was really into the classics, and God only knew what would blast forth from my stereo when I turned on the car some mornings."

Kana chuckled, nodding.

On the way out of the garage, Kana picked up her cigarettes, then glanced over at Sierra.

"Do you mind?" she asked, holding up the cigarettes.

"No, go ahead," Sierra said.

"Thanks," Kana said, shaking out a cigarette and putting it in her mouth and lighting it.

Sierra watched with a bemused smile on her lips. She'd seen Kana a number of times in the office. Kana was always dressed stylishly, without being either too trendy or too feminine. She carried an air of authority about her that was impossible to miss. Kana, much like Midnight Chevalier, was an anomaly in a political office like the Attorney General's office. It was actually very refreshing to see and experience.

Sierra had worked for the Attorney General's office for eight years. At thirty-five, she was one of the youngest women promoted to Chief Deputy Attorney General ever. She knew that she never would have had this opportunity if Midnight Chevalier hadn't become Attorney General. Jeffrey Cook had been the previous Chief Deputy AG in charge of the criminal division. When he'd retired two months ago, Midnight had held interviews for the position. Sierra had applied but hadn't really expected to get it, basing her expectations on the previous administration's attitude that experience didn't count as much as what other men in the division would be comfortable with. Sierra couldn't count the times she'd been told, "No man will work for a woman, especially not in the criminal division." She couldn't think of a more ridiculous reason not to promote her, yet it happened time and time again.

At one point she'd finally threatened to sue for sexual discrimination, and she'd been promoted to a Deputy Attorney General IV. She had a Yale law degree, having been admitted to Yale Law with a perfect LSAT score, something unheard of. After Yale, she'd put her time in at the District Attorney's office as a Deputy District Attorney in the second chair. She'd made first chair, main prosecuting attorney, in a record year. In a courtroom, she was in charge—no one could beat her as long as she had half a case to prosecute. Defense lawyers had started making a record number of plea bargains when they'd heard that Sierra Youngblood was prosecuting. She was that good.

In Sierra, Midnight had seen someone like herself. A woman who had the smarts to get where she wanted to be, but held back by conventions and what Midnight privately called "man thinking." There had been no competition once Midnight had interviewed Sierra. She knew who she wanted running her criminal division, a lawyer who knew how to get the job done. And if, in fact, men didn't want to work for a woman, as far as Midnight was concerned they didn't belong working for the AG's office anymore, since the Attorney General was a woman too, and they indirectly worked for her.

"So, your girlfriend," Sierra commented after a few minutes, "is that your partner?"

Kana nodded, glancing over at Sierra.

The woman had said her "husband" was overseas. Had she read this wrong? She'd sensed that Sierra Youngblood was gay, but married? It wasn't unheard of. Palani had been married before she'd realized she preferred women. Kana was curious now but knew there was no real way to ask. So she decided to let the conversation wander in that direction.

"What branch of the service is your husband in?" Kana asked.

"Marines," Sierra said. "He's in the Middle East right now."

"That must be difficult, having him gone," Kana said casually.

Sierra smiled. "Not so difficult. It actually gives me a little bit of breathing room."

"Breathing room?" Kana asked, her senses working overtime to detect a hint of something else.

"My husband can be a bit stifling," Sierra said.

"I've heard they can be like that," she said, grinning. "One more reason I never wanted one."

"A husband?" Sierra asked, her eyes twinkling humorously.

"Yeah…"

"That and the fact that you prefer women, right?" Sierra said, chuckling.

"Yeah, that too."

"Well, I took the chicken way out," Sierra said, her tone more serious.

Kana nodded slowly, serious now too. "Happens a lot."

Sierra nodded too, with an almost pained look. "Sometimes I wish I hadn't, but I did get my son, Colby, out of the bargain."

Kana thought about Palani and her desire for a baby. "Then it was worth it," she said. "Does your husband know?"

Sierra nodded. "I discovered I was at the very least bi my senior year in college. I explored it for four years but never found a woman I wanted to be with. Jason, my husband, came along and basically swept me off my feet. But he'd known then that I was seeing women as well as men. He said he was okay with it. I guess he really wasn't," she said with a grimace.

"Why do you say that?" Kana asked.

"Well, after we were married, he started letting his facade fall, making comments about women on women being 'hot,' stuff like that," she said with a wry look. "By the time I had Colby, he was saying that gays were really just sick people. Now he won't even acknowledge the fact that I am gay. It's like he's wiped it from his mind."

Kana winced. She knew what it was like to have to pretend she wasn't what she was. She'd done it long enough with her family and friends, hiding her realization that she was gay for a full five years before finally telling the people she loved.

They were silent for a while, each lost in her own thoughts.

"Thank you for doing this," Sierra said quietly.

Kana nodded. "No problem, but can I ask why you wanted me to do it?"

Sierra was silent for a moment, then she shrugged. "I feel more comfortable around women—I always have. I knew that you were gay, so I guess I just gravitated toward someone like me. Does that make sense?"

"Yes, it makes sense," Kana said, still feeling the effects of what Sierra had told her. It was like watching a tragedy on TV—you really felt for the person, even if there wasn't anything you could do.

Kana dropped Sierra off at her house, telling her if there were any more problems, she was to let Midnight or Kana know.

"Does the house have a security system?" Kana asked.

"Yes," Sierra answered.

"Use it. I'll get you the cell number for the Special Agent Supervisors in charge of security here in Sacramento. If anything happens, day or night, you can call them. They'll respond quickly. Okay?"

Sierra nodded. "Thank you so much," she said, smiling.

"You're very welcome," Kana said, smiling too.

On the flight home to San Diego, Kana found herself thinking about Sierra's situation. It was something she couldn't imagine dealing with. When she got home, she hugged Palani tight, once again extremely happy that she had found the love of her life. During dinner that night, she told Palani about the new Chief Deputy Attorney General.

"Her husband knew she was bi, and married her even though he apparently hates gays?" Palani asked in disbelief.

"A lot of men think they can change us," Kana said, picking up her beer and taking a drink. "Since she's bi, he probably figured he could make her forget the other part about wanting women."

"Doesn't work that way," Palani said.

"No," Kana said. "I think she is fortunate that she never found a woman she really connected with, or it would be harder for her now."

Palani nodded. "I know. That's how it was for me, when I had to go home to Matthew. I realized suddenly how little he and I had in common, and how much our marriage was lacking. It was awful."

Kana looked pained. "I know, I remember what you told me about that. I'm just sorry I insisted you go home to him to keep things stable until the divorce."

Palani put her hand out to touch Kana's. "Don't start feeling like that again, Kana. What happened with Matthew wasn't your fault. It was his bad judgment, not yours. You were only trying to protect my interests."

It had been at Kana's insistence that Palani had stayed in the same house with her husband. Palani had a hard time sleeping without Kana beside her, so she'd started taking Halcion to help her sleep. Matthew Ryker had foolishly decided that the best way to keep his wife was to get her pregnant. And as such had gotten her pregnant while she was deeply asleep on Halcion. Since Palani wasn't, to her knowledge, having sex with Matthew, she couldn't explain to Kana how she'd gotten pregnant. She'd told Kana repeatedly that she wasn't sleeping with him. So when Palani ended up pregnant, Kana assumed Palani had lied to her. That had been the cause of their breakup.

In the end, Palani had not only found out about Matthew's duplicity, but it had been the final straw that had ended their marriage for good. She'd lost Kana, the only woman she'd ever been with and loved deeply. She also lost the baby that had separated them. Palani's brother, Sampson, a huge Samoan man, had come over from Hawaii to talk some sense into Palani about getting a divorce. Palani had, out of sheer frustration, blurted out that she was in love with a woman. Sampson had backhanded her, causing her to fall down a flight of stairs. She'd lost the baby then.

It was still a source of angst for Kana. She felt that if she'd been with Palani then, none of that would have happened. If she'd trusted Palani enough to stay with her long enough to find out the truth, Palani would now have the baby she'd wanted so badly. Palani felt that it was for the best, since they intended to get married now and have Kana's brother, Natano, donate the sperm for the baby they would have. To Palani's way of thinking, this was better because the baby would be of Kana's family and of her. That was best.

Kana and Palani spent the rest of the evening talking about other things. Palani was leaving on a two-week photo shoot in two days. They wanted to spend as much time together as they could.

That was why the next day, when Palani told her they were having dinner with Jerry, Palani's model friend, and Jerry's girlfriend, Jane Anne, Kana wasn't pleased.

"Do we have to?" Kana asked, glancing over at Midnight, who was grinning.

"Please, K?" Palani pleaded. "Jerry's still having doubts about filing against that photographer who assaulted her. I know you can remind her why it's important."

Kana rolled her eyes. "What am I, the law enforcement consultant to the modeling industry now?"

"Honey…" Palani beseeched. "Please?"

Kana sighed heavily. "Okay, okay, I'll go, but I have to be home early. We fly out first thing in the morning."

"I know. It'll be an early night," Palani promised.

In the end, it wasn't an early night. Things were really tense between Jerry and Jane Anne. For that reason, Jerry had a lot to drink and got very talkative.

Jerry talked them into going over to Bourbon Street, a local gay bar, "just for one drink." One drink turned into two and three. When the waitress spilled a drink on their table, she apologized profusely for it. Kana assured her it was okay.

"That's so sweet of you to say," the waitress said, smiling brightly at Kana.

After the waitress walked away, Kana looked over at Palani, who raised an eyebrow at her comically.

"What?" Kana asked, already grinning.

"She was flirting with you," Palani said, laughing.

"She was not," Kana said. "Not every woman that's family flirts with me."

"Like hell they don't," Palani said, narrowing her eyes at Kana, her grin still in place.

Kana rolled her eyes, shaking her head. She eventually abandoned any hope of getting home at a decent hour. Once she did that, she allowed herself to have a good time.

At one point, Kana and Palani danced. Since discovering that Kana could indeed dance, quite well, Palani always wanted to dance with her. Kana had a very natural rhythm, combined with the style she had in the way she dressed and looked. With Palani, the stunningly beautiful, petite, perfect woman that she was, as Kana's partner, people tended to stare. Palani loved it, because she knew that, contrary to what Kana thought, many women in that particular bar wanted Kana for their own. And Kana was all hers. It was one huge ego boost.

Jerry watched as they danced, a sour look on her face. Jane Anne, being very butch, didn't dance. It was one of those things that had always bugged Jerry. Since she was drunk, it seemed to bug her more.

Jerry had thought Palani a lucky girl for a long, long time. Palani had met and fallen in love with Kana the first time she'd even tried a relationship with a woman. Kana was not only beautiful, but she had an innate sense of style and a presence that made her the center of attention whether she wanted to be or not. Kana was also sexy—Jerry had just started noticing that recently. It bothered her normally that she was finding herself attracted to Palani's partner, but in her drunken state she felt like commenting on it. It wasn't a good idea.

"You know," Jerry said, leaning across the table and grabbing Palani's hands in hers, "you are so lucky."

Palani nodded slowly, not sure where Jerry was going with that comment. She knew her friend was very drunk and so was trying to keep up with Jerry's conversation, which had been all over the place that evening.

"Why is she lucky?" Jane Anne asked, narrowing her eyes at her girlfriend.

"Because," Jerry said, gesturing drunkenly at Kana, "she has an incredible, sexy girlfriend that every woman in this place is dying to nail."

Jane Anne's eyes narrowed further as she flicked a glance at Kana. Kana shook her head. She, too, knew that Jerry was drunk and that she'd just said the wrong thing in front of Jane Anne.

"Jerry," Palani said, standing up and pulling Jerry with her. "I think we need to go to the bathroom. Let's go."

With that, Palani all but dragged a stumbling Jerry to the women's bathroom at the back of the bar. At the table, Kana looked at Jane Anne.

"She's had way too much, you know," Kana said, by way of explanation for Jerry's comment.

Jane Anne looked irritated. "She also needs to learn to keep her damned mouth shut," she snapped.

Kana sat back, not willing to get into this with Jane Anne. She sensed there was a lot of underlying tension between the two women. The last thing she wanted to do was get herself stuck in the middle of it.

The waitress came by. "You need anything?" she asked Kana, her smile bright.

"You sell muzzles here?" Kana asked, grinning.

The waitress giggled. "Sounds kinky."

Kana laughed, shaking her head. "Let me get a shot of tequila. Jane Anne, you want anything?"

"A shot," Jane Anne said. "Make it a double."

The waitress looked at Jane Anne, then back at Kana, widening her eyes slightly. Kana nodded, winking at the girl to tell her it was alright. The waitress walked away. Kana and Jane Anne sat in silence. Jane Anne was stewing, and Kana wasn't about to prod her. She'd been in enough fights at this bar; the last thing she wanted was to get into one with Jerry's girlfriend over some perceived slight.

Meanwhile in the bathroom, Palani was trying to talk to Jerry.

"I'm sorry," Jerry said. "I shouldn't have said that to you about K. I'm sorry…"

"It's okay, Jerry," Palani was saying. "I know you've had a lot to drink."

"Still," Jerry continued, "I know better than to say stuff like that. And now Jane Anne is pissed at me too. God, I'm so sorry!" she wailed.

"It's okay," Palani said, grinning. "Besides, it can't hurt Kana's ego at all, right?"

Jerry rolled her eyes. "No, just put me in the doghouse for a week or so."

"Well, we leave day after tomorrow, Jerry, so it'll be a short stay in the doghouse."

Jerry straightened up at that thought. Jane Anne couldn't be mad at her while she was gone. She smiled, and then looked in the mirror to fix her makeup, glancing at Palani in the reflection as she did.

"You're not upset, are you?" Jerry asked, her tone worried.

"About what?" Palani asked as she too checked her makeup.

"About me saying that about Kana?"

"Why would I be upset?"

"Well, we're friends. I didn't think you'd want me thinking your girlfriend is hot, you know?" Jerry said, her look leery.

Palani shrugged. "You're right, just about every woman in this place wants her. The point is, I have her, so it doesn't bother me, no."

Jerry smiled, happy to see her friend so secure in her relationship. "Good."

The night ended shortly after that. Jane Anne didn't speak to Jerry again the short time that they stayed at the bar.

Chapter 2

Kashena was lying on her bed, wearing a jog bra and sweat pants. It was mid-morning on a Saturday. Carrie was at school for a change, so it was nice and peaceful in the house. So peaceful that Kashena picked up on the slightest creak of the boards on her hardwood floors. She instantly knew someone was in the house.

Sitting up in a flash, her hand hovering near her holstered weapon on the nightstand, Kashena was shocked to see Linda standing in the doorway to her bedroom.

"Jesus!" Kashena exclaimed, moving her hand away from her gun and running it through her long blond hair. "Are you fucking nuts?"

"No," Linda replied, grinning. "Just persistent as hell."

"I'd call it being a pain in the ass, not to mention trespassing," Kashena replied, her voice low.

"Ah, c'mon, babe," Linda said, flipping her dark hair over her shoulder. "Stop playing games. You know you missed me, like I missed you."

"I don't recall missing you," Kashena said, her tone serious.

Linda looked back at her for a few moments, then walked toward the bed.

"I think you did," she said, her voice dropping an octave, her look meaningful.

"Don't even start," Kashena said, holding her hand up in a halting gesture.

"Why not?" Linda asked, her expression still seductive.

"I'm living with someone," Kashena said.

Linda said nothing, toying with a lock of her hair. Finally, she nodded. Kashena thought it was acceptance of the situation. She thought wrong.

Linda moved to the bed and straddled Kashena's hips. Before Kashena could react, Linda leaned down and kissed her on the lips, her hands cupping Kashena's face. For a full minute, Kashena couldn't even think—her mind was so blurred by the excitement of the kiss. Then suddenly she realized, this was Linda, and Linda always did this to her.

Putting her hands on Linda's shoulders, Kashena set Linda away from her. Apparently Linda was ready for that, because she grabbed Kashena's forearms, holding on to her.

"Kashie," she said, her voice low and husky, "why are you fighting this? You know we're meant for each other; you know we're good with each other. Why are you avoiding me?"

Kashena looked at her for a full half-minute before answering. "Maybe it's shit like the five hundred dollars of my money you walked off with last time you left," she said sharply.

Linda took a deep breath. "I know, Kash, and I'm sorry I did that. I'll pay you back."

"With what? Your looks?" Kashena asked sarcastically.

"Damn, you've gotten really bitter lately, haven't you?" Linda said, canting her head to the side.

Putting her hands on Kashena's shoulders, she slid them downward, her thumbs brushing over Kashena's nipples. Kashena gasped involuntarily, trying desperately to fight Linda's effect on her.

"I think," Linda said, her tone conversational, as her thumbs brushed back and forth, making Kashena shudder at the sensation, "that this little girl you're living with isn't as good as me."

"Stop…" Kashena said, trying to will herself to make her stop, but even her voice held no real conviction.

"She doesn't do you like I can, does she, Kash?" Linda asked, her lips moving to Kashena's neck, her hand sliding lower.

"Linda… no…" Kashena said, a moan escaping her lips moments later.

"Mmm," Linda murmured against her ear. "You need it, don't you?"

"No…" Kashena said, her voice a moan.

Minutes later they were making love. Kashena had never been able to resist Linda when it came to sex. Linda was one of the very few women that had ever actually gotten Kashena to have an orgasm every time. It was something Linda knew, and used. She was an addiction, Kashena knew that.

Linda was right about Carrie. Carrie had never managed to satisfy Kashena the entire time they'd been together. It wasn't that she hadn't tried, she had, but Kashena knew that it took a lot, and most women just didn't have either the stamina or the right touch. Linda did, in spades.

Afterwards, Kashena lay on her back, already disgusted with herself for her weakness. She'd thought for sure that this time she'd be able to resist Linda. She'd refused to see her for the entire week that Linda had been in town. Just when she thought she was finally conquering the addiction she had for the black-haired vixen, she was once again snared. And it felt like shit.

Linda lay on her side, her hand caressing Kashena's now bare stomach. She reveled in the feeling of power she had at that moment. She had known that she needed to force the issue with Kashena. On the phone Kashena had sounded so different, so cold. Linda was afraid she'd truly lost her hold on Kashena. She hadn't. Kashena was hers, and she would always be hers.

In her heart, Linda felt that Kashena was her soul mate. The problem was, Kashena was very stable and responsible. It was something that was comforting for a while, but at times it became constricting. That's when she had to get out. She knew Kashena didn't understand it, but apparently she didn't mind it too much. When she came back, Kashena took her in, every time. The sex with Kashena was always the best. No one was as good as Kashena.

Kashena didn't realize she'd dozed off until she heard the uttered "What the fuck?" from the doorway.

She started awake, recognizing Carrie's voice. Sitting up, she realized where she was and what had happened. She instantly felt like shit. Carrie had caught her in bed with another woman. Jesus!

"Carrie…" she began, unable to form any way of explaining her actions.

Carrie held up her hand and gave her an icy look. "Don't!" she exclaimed, her eyes on Linda, who sat up, her expression arrogant. "Who the fuck are you?" Carrie asked viciously.

"I'm the person whose spot you've been filling for the past few months," Linda said, her tone confident.

"Linda, shut up," Kashena snapped, not in the mood to deal with a catfight.

She'd pulled her sweats and shirt on. Standing, she moved toward Carrie. Carrie backed up against the door, staring up at Kashena. Her hands were up between them, as if to ward Kashena off.

"Carrie," Kashena said softly, "I'm sorry…"

Carrie shook her head. "No, I'm sorry," she said, looking near tears.

"Carrie, please…" Kashena moved to hold the girl, feeling like hell.

Carrie's arms came up again, blocking her from doing so. Kashena dropped her arms, stepping back. Carrie looked up at her, then lashed out with her open hand and slapped her.

"I hate you for this," she said softly.

Turning, Carrie walked out of the bedroom, leaving the house in tears. Kashena leaned against the wall, her head back against it, her eyes closed. It wasn't that she loved Carrie, she didn't, but the girl had been with her all this time. This wasn't how she wanted to end things. It wasn't right.

Linda watched the scene from the bed, wise enough to stay out of it after Kashena had told her to. In truth, she felt fully vindicated in what she'd said. Carrie wasn't meant for Kashena—Linda was. All Carrie had been was filler. The sooner the girl realized that, the better off she'd be. No one could be to Kashena what she was—that was just fact.

"Kash…" Linda began.

Kashena shook her head. "Don't say anything right now," she said seriously.

"What's wrong?" Linda asked, thinking the scene had gone fairly smoothly.

Kashena looked at Linda, her face disbelieving. "I just became the asshole I never wanted to be."

With that, Kashena walked out of the bedroom. Walking through the house, she picked up her cigars and strode out to her backyard, lighting a thin cigar the moment she got outside.

Linda got up from the bed, pulling on her shirt and nothing else. Walking out onto the back deck of the house, she saw Kashena sitting at the edge smoking. Standing and watching her for a while, Linda realized how much she really had missed Kashena.

The woman was so damned beautiful, with her long straight blond hair reaching halfway down her back and her deep blue eyes. She had the proud bone structure of her Indian heritage, but the lean strength of a warrior woman. Muscle cut against Kashena's rich gold-colored skin, flexed when she lifted her cigar to her lips, rippled across her back.

It excited Linda no end to know that Kashena could kill with her fingers, fight any man and win. To know that Kashena could and would protect her, because she loved her. It was a major high to have such an effect on a woman like that, to have her under her control. Linda knew she had the power to get Kashena to do anything. Maybe she'd stay this time; maybe she'd finally get Kashena to beg.

As she moved behind Kashena, Linda saw her tense. Ignoring the tension Kashena was exuding, Linda sat down behind her, her legs on either side of Kashena's hips. She slid her hands up Kashena's chest from behind and laid her face against Kashena's back. She felt Kashena suck her breath in with a great deal of satisfaction. Kashena was hers, always had been, always would be. No one could change that.

***

Kana sat in her Navigator, smoking and watching people walk by. She saw Palani and Jerry emerge from the airport terminal. Getting out of the Navigator, she tossed her cigarette away, blowing smoke out in a long stream as she opened the back and walked toward her girlfriend. Leaning down and kissing Palani on the lips, she took her suitcase from her, then reached for Jerry's.

"Thanks, Kana," Jerry said, looking surprised.

"Get in," Kana told the two women. "It's cold out here and the heat is on in the car."

Jerry and Palani complied. Kana put their luggage in the back and closed up the car. As she got in, an officer walked up.

"You know you can't stay parked out here," he said, his tone authoritative.

Kana held up her badge and lit another cigarette.

"Oh, sorry, ma'am," the officer said, inclining his head.

"No problem," Kana said, getting into the Navigator and starting it up.

"I'm sorry it's so late, babe," Palani said. "The sky phones weren't working, and things at the airport in New York were crazy when we got on the plane."

"It's okay, hon," Kana said. "I was awake anyway."

"Still…" Palani said. "Having to stay dressed and everything…"

"It's okay," Kana repeated.

"But definitely thanks for this, Kana," Jerry said from the back seat.

"You're welcome, Jerry," Kana said.

"I missed you so much," Palani said, taking Kana's free hand and squeezing it.

"I missed you too, babe," Kana said, smiling over at her. "How was the shoot?"

"It was okay. Freezing, but okay," Palani said.

When they got to the apartment Jerry shared Jane Anne, Kana got out. She opened the back and to Jerry's surprise gestured for her to precede her. Kana carried Jerry's suitcase up three flights of stairs and deposited it at her door. She waited politely while Jerry unlocked the door, letting herself into the apartment.

"Thanks again, Kana," Jerry said warmly, reaching up to hug Kana quickly.

Kana was surprised by the hug, but put her arms around the slight blonde and hugged her back.

"You're welcome," she said, smiling.

Back in the Navigator, Kana looked over at Palani.

"So why wasn't Jane Anne there to pick Jerry up?"

Palani grimaced. "They're fighting again."

Kana shook her head as she put the vehicle into gear. "They fight more than anything these days."

"I know," Palani said, sounding worried. "I don't know what I'd do if we fought like that."

Kana grinned. "Babygirl, if we fought like that, we wouldn't be together. It's as simple as that."

Palani looked over at her with wide eyes.

"Babe," Kana said, her tone explanatory, "I deal with enough stress at work. I won't do it in my personal life too."

Palani nodded, understanding what Kana was saying. She'd just been surprised by Kana's comment.

"You're right," Palani said. "I wouldn't want to do that either. I'm just glad we rarely fight."

It was true. Since they'd gotten back together, their fights had been very few and very minor.

Once home, Palani did some of her unpacking while Kana lay on the bed. Palani glanced over and saw Kana watching her.

"What?" she asked with a grin.

Kana shook her head. "Nothing," she said, grinning too. "I just like watching you move."

"Oh really?" Palani moved to the bed.

"Oh yeah…" Kana said, smiling as she sat up.

Palani leaned over and kissed Kana on the lips. Kana's hands were on her hips immediately, lifting her off her feet and setting Palani down on her lap.

"Mmm..." Palani moaned as Kana's hands removed her shirt.

Things between them were getting heated when the phone rang.

Kana growled, even as she reached for the phone. She was on call 24/7.

"Hello?" she answered.

"Kana..."

"Jerry?" Kana queried, hardly able to identify the voice—she was crying.

"Yes," Jerry said softly. "Can I talk to Palani?"

"Sure," Kana said, giving Palani a long look as she handed her the phone.

Palani talked to Jerry for a few minutes, telling her to stay where she was. She hung up, reaching for her shirt.

"What's going on?" Kana asked, knowing something had happened just from Palani's side of the conversation.

"Jane Anne hit her," Palani said, sounding worried. "She's at a coffee shop down in PB. I'm going to go get her."

"Like hell you are," Kana said, getting up. "Where's she at? I'll go get her."

"Kana..." Palani said, not wanting to put Kana out any further that night.

"Palani, PB isn't a place I want you in at night, okay? I'll go get her and bring her here."

Palani stared back at Kana, feeling her heart swell. Kana could always be counted on when someone needed her. It was one of the things Palani loved most about her.

Twenty minutes later, Kana walked into the coffee shop where Jerry sat huddled in a booth. Jerry wore no makeup, and she was dressed in sweat pants and a T-shirt. Still she looked tragically beautiful. Kana, dressed in black jeans, a white shirt, black boots, and her long black leather jacket, her hair flowing down to almost her waist, was quite a contrast. Kana walked over to Jerry and stood next to her table

"Jerry," she said quietly.

Jerry's head snapped up, her eyes indicating surprise.

"Kana?" she said tearfully.

Kana held out her hand to Jerry. Jerry took it, letting Kana gently pull her out of the booth. She was surprised when Kana pulled her into her arms and hugged her gently.

"Where's Palani?" Jerry asked.

"At home," Kana said. "I'm taking you there."

"To your house?" Jerry asked as she let Kana lead her outside.

When they got to Kana's Navigator parked just outside, Kana turned and looked down at Jerry.

"You're our friend, Jerry," Kana said. "You need us, and we're going to be here for you."

Jerry's eyes filled with tears as she nodded.

Twenty minutes later, Kana walked into her and Palani's house, leading Jerry. Palani was there immediately, taking Jerry to the living room and sitting her down on the couch. Kana left them alone to talk, going into her and Palani's bedroom and changing her clothes. Palani found her lying on their bed two hours later.

"How's Jerry?" Kana asked as Palani climbed into bed with her, laying her head on Kana's chest.

"She's sleeping," Palani said. "She's really worn out."

"Did she say what happened?"

43

"That she and Jane Anne were fighting again, and that Jane was drinking. Things got heated. Jane Anne hit her."

Kana drew a deep breath, shaking her head. "It's not good that she's moved up to violence."

"I know," Palani said. She was silent for a while, then glanced up at Kana. "K? Is it okay if I let her stay for a little bit?"

Kana looked down at Palani. "Of course it's okay, babe."

Palani smiled up at her. "Jerry was really surprised to see you at the café."

"Why?" Kana asked

"Because she thinks that you think we're all about drama."

"Who's we?"

"Models," Palani answered.

Kana shook her head. "I don't categorize anyone by their profession."

Palani smiled softly. "I love you," she said.

Kana pulled her up, kissing her lips. Minutes later they were making love as quietly as possible. Hours later they were lying asleep. Palani lay on her back; Kana lay on her stomach, her arm across Palani's chest, her leg thrown over Palani's. It was a striking picture that they made. Palani so delicate and classically beautiful, and Kana with her long dark hair, strong, proud features, and her skin darker than Palani's. Kana had her head bowed slightly so her lips were at the hollow of Palani's neck.

There was a white sheet over them, but only half covering them. Kana's lean muscled back and shoulders were bare, as well as one tawny muscular leg, a complete contrast to Palani's smooth, delicately shaped leg next to it. Jerry couldn't help but stare at them. She'd awoken in a strange house and had wandered to where she thought the bathroom was. The door was ajar—she'd opened it but saw that it was their bedroom. She'd been mesmerized by the sight of Kana and Palani. She'd just realized what she was doing and was turning to go when Palani stirred slightly and opened her eyes, widening them when she saw Jerry standing there looking at them.

"Jerry," she whispered. "What's wrong?"

"Nothing," Jerry replied in a whisper. "I'm sorry, I got confused and thought I was headed to the bathroom, but... you two just look so gorgeous together," she said, indicating the way their bodies were positioned. "You should seriously have Chez take this picture for the magazine layout in *Cosmo*."

Palani shook her head. "Kana would never go for such a risqué shot."

"It's not risqué," Jerry said. "It's art. You two look like this incredible sculpture. Have Chez take it in black and white. It would look fantastic, even the contrast of the white sheet against Kana's dark skin. I'm telling you, it would be amazing."

Palani thought Jerry was probably right, but she was fairly sure Kana would never even consider it. It was worth asking about though. One never did know until one asked.

***

Kashena knew she was pushing it, and she knew she needed to slow down. Linda wanted to celebrate their being back together. Her idea of celebrating was going out every night of the week and staying out until 1 or 2 a.m., then coming home to make love for hours. It was a pace Kashena couldn't keep up with.

Finally, after two weeks, she told Linda they weren't going out that night.

"Why not?" Linda asked, shocked.

"Because," Kashena said, leaning back against the couch, "I need some sleep for one thing."

"Sleep is overrated," Linda joked, walking over to the couch and straddling Kashena's waist. "Besides, my favorite DJ is at 21 tonight. We have to go."

"Babe…" Kashena said, brushing Linda's hair back. "I can't, not tonight. I need to get some sleep. This pace is killin' me."

Linda pouted, her eyes downcast.

Kashena hadn't mentioned how it was costing her a fortune to go out every night. Between cover charges, drinks, and dinner, things were starting to add up. Kashena made decent money, but she had a mortgage and a few other bills to be concerned with. Linda didn't understand that because she had no responsibilities, not even a job.

Linda lifted her head, a triumphant gleam in her eyes. Kashena knew she wasn't going to like what came out of her mouth next, and she didn't.

"Well, I'll just go to 21 alone then," Linda said matter-of-factly.

Kashena narrowed her eyes at Linda. "Can't just stay home one night, huh?"

"I'm enjoying myself, Kashie. I'm young and I'm going to enjoy life while I can," Linda said dramatically.

"I'm sure one night would ruin your life," Kashena said, moving Linda off her lap and getting up.

"You can go with me, Kash…" Linda said in a leading tone. "You just want to stay home. I'm not a homebody like you."

Kashena turned around, looking at her in disbelief. "For two weeks we've been going out every night. Two weeks, Linda. When is it going to be enough for you?"

Linda looked back at her thoughtfully. Finally she shrugged and got up, leaving the room. Kashena stayed in the living room, not willing to follow her girlfriend. After a few minutes she started cooking dinner, doing her best not to worry about what was going on down the hall. An hour later, as Kashena was sitting down to eat, Linda came out. She was dressed up, her hair flowing around her shoulders. Kashena knew that Linda was going out without her.

Kashena ignored her, continuing to eat and read the report she'd brought home from work. Linda moved around the kitchen, using a fork to pick out some meat and vegetables from what Kashena had made. It wasn't long before it became obvious that Linda was waiting for Kashena to comment on her going out. It made Kashena more determined not to comment.

When she finished eating, Kashena got up, rinsed off her plate, and put it in the dishwasher. She refilled her wine glass, her eyes avoiding contact with Linda's. Then she went down the hall to the bedroom. Linda heard the TV in the bedroom a few moments later. Kashena was in for the night.

Linda debated her options. She knew if she went out, she'd have to beg her friends to buy her drinks. Her friends got tired of that really quickly. Part of her thought that she'd be smarter to stay home and assuage Kashena's ego for a night. Then another part of her rebelled against being "kept." Who did Kashena think she was? Linda was her own person—no one told her what to do and when to do it! This was bullshit! Just because Kashena didn't want to go out, didn't mean she couldn't. And she would. She would show Kashena that she couldn't boss her around.

With that Linda left the house, borrowing the keys to Kashena's car on the way out, as well as a few twenties out of Kashena's wallet. She wouldn't mind, would she?

Linda got in about 2:30 a.m. Bumping into a table in Kashena's room was her first mistake. Although she suspected that Kashena was awake already. Kashena turned over, glancing at the clock, then back at her. She said nothing, never a good sign.

Linda climbed into bed next to Kashena a few minutes later, having dropped her clothes in an untidy pile on the floor. She snuggled against Kashena and sensed the tension in her right away.

"I missed you tonight," Linda whispered.

Kashena didn't respond. Instead she turned over on her side, putting her back to Linda.

"Kashie," Linda said, sliding her hand over Kashena's waist, "please don't be mad. I just wanted to have fun."

Again, Kashena didn't respond.

Linda sighed, turning over on her back to stare up at the ceiling. "I just don't feel like I'm your partner, you know? You're always telling me what we can do and can't do. I hate that. I don't want to feel like you own me, Kashena. Is that wrong?"

That had Kashena turning over to face her.

"Own you?" Kashena asked. "You think I feel like I own you?"

"Yes," Linda said, her voice tearful. "You're always saying 'we can't do this' or 'we can't do that.' I feel like you're the boss around here."

Kashena stared at her, then shrugged.

"Tell ya what, babe," she said evenly. "You get a job and start paying for shit around here, and I'd be happy to let you tell me what we can and can't afford, okay?"

"Don't be a bitch," Linda growled.

"Then don't fucking push your luck."

Linda was shocked by Kashena's harder-than-stone tone of voice. Usually Kashena would do anything to keep Linda with her longer. This time she wasn't doing that. Linda found that it made her want to stay more. But she had to push.

"I'll go out anytime I want to," Linda said impudently.

"Better start taking your own money," Kashena said, her voice icy, "or I'll arrest your ass for theft."

Linda stared back at Kashena like she'd never seen her before. And before she could formulate a reply, Kashena's hand was on her cheek, her thumb under Linda's chin, keeping their eyes locked.

"And," Kashena continued, her tone still angry, "you ever touch the keys to my car again, and I'll kick your ass all the way into next week. You got that?"

Linda swallowed a few times, shocked to feel herself getting excited. This was a side of Kashena she hadn't seen in a long, long time. This was the forceful, experienced woman she'd gotten attached to.

Without a word, Linda was kissing Kashena, wrapping her body around her, begging forgiveness with her body, her mouth, her hands. Kashena remained tense for a long time, but she finally gave in. The lovemaking that night was wild and passionate, something it hadn't been in a long time. Linda fell asleep curled in Kashena's arms, feeling like she'd just rediscovered gold.

Kashena fell asleep knowing their relationship had just stepped up to a dangerous level. She'd been ready to beat the crap out of Linda for not only stealing from her, again, but for taking her car too. What was worse, she'd realized that Linda had indeed been drinking and then driving Kashena's prized possession. It showed total disregard for her, and Kashena knew it. It didn't bode well. Squashing the thought, Kashena fell into a restless sleep.

***

Kana glanced at Palani, rolling her eyes. Palani hid her smile behind her hand. They were waiting for the writer who was doing the story on them. It had already been an experience in exasperation. Apparently the writer wanted the pictures done first, and the photographer wanted the story done first. Kana said as far as she was concerned they could just skip the whole thing. Of course, the editor of the magazine had been quick to negate that idea.

"This is an important story—it must be told!" she said, with far more flair than Kana felt was necessary. "We'll do it according to how you two feel," the woman went on to say.

"I don't feel like doing it," Kana said, her tone even.

"But Ms. Sorbinno…" the editor began, alarmed.

"Relax," Kana said. "My girl wants to do this, so we're doing it. But I have a job, so I need you people to get on the ball."

"Certainly, Ms. Sorbinno. So sorry this has caused so much hassle."

Kana couldn't believe these people. She knew they were kissing ass because Palani had just been chosen for the cover of not only *Sports Illustrated*'s swimsuit edition, but also for *Vogue*, *Cosmopolitan*'s chief competitor. But no one had the exclusive that *Cosmo* had, the story of how Kana and Palani came to be. Somehow, they'd suddenly become a hot commodity.

Between Kana being so high profile, being with Midnight Chevalier all the time, and Palani re-emerging in the modeling field and becoming bigger than ever, they were a hot couple to know. With the world focusing on California and whether Proposition 8—a much-debated proposition that eliminated the options for same-sex couples to get married in the state—would remain in effect or be struck down in the Supreme Court, Kana and Palani's planning to have the commitment ceremony was also a very current topic.

Kana had no idea what to do with the newfound fame. All she knew was she didn't like it. Palani was used to being photographed and asked about her life. Kana didn't want anything to do with it. She was used to her life being private.

The following day, Kana and Palani met with the writer of the story. The photographer was there as well, snapping candid pictures. Fortunately, the woman writing the story, while not gay, was very family friendly. She was highly intrigued by what Kana did and how she and Palani actually got together. It was the first question she asked.

"You two met when Kana was an officer with San Diego Police Department, didn't you?" the reporter asked.

"Yes," Palani said. "Kana was a sergeant with homicide."

"Homicide?" the reporter queried. "How exactly did you meet?"

Kana looked at Palani and waited for her to answer.

"Kana came to question my husband about a murder," Palani said.

"That's right, you were married when you two met, weren't you?"

Kana nodded, thinking, *here it comes.*

"Yes, I was," Palani said.

"And when did you two start dating?" the reporter asked.

"After I pursued Kana and begged her to date me," Palani said, looking at Kana and smiling.

The reporter looked at Kana. "You didn't want to date Palani?"

"She was married, and not even sure she wanted women," Kana replied simply.

"Not sure she wanted women?" the reporter echoed, looking at Palani.

"I knew I was missing something in my marriage," Palani explained. "I had a good friend who was gay, and I saw how she and her girlfriend were together. I wasn't sure if that's what I was looking for, but when Kana kissed me the first time, believe me, I knew."

The reporter grinned. "Kana's a good kisser?"

"Kana's good at everything," Palani said, biting her lip and smiling.

Kana rolled her eyes and shook her head.

"What's wrong, Kana?" the reporter asked.

"Would you want your sexual abilities printed in a magazine?" Kana asked the reporter.

"Only if it was a report that I'm good at everything," the reporter replied, chuckling.

"Well, I don't think I want it in a magazine," Kana said.

"So, you two started dating while you were married?"

"Yes," Palani said. "I wanted to see Kana, and she agreed reluctantly."

The reporter nodded, understanding that Kana had not wanted to interfere with Palani's marriage. "So what happened next?"

"We fell in love," Palani said, her eyes glowing. "Kana was who I knew I was meant to be with."

"And that's when you left your husband?"

"Kana wanted me to ease out of my marriage. She knew how Matthew would react if I was leaving him for a woman."

"And did he find out?"

"No," Palani said, her tone softening. "He did decide to find another way to keep me in the marriage."

"How?"

"Palani…" Kana warned.

Palani looked at Kana, and Kana shook her head slightly. Palani understood what Kana was telling her.

"I'm sorry, I can't really talk about that. Suffice it to say, it almost ruined Kana and me."

"You two broke up?"

"Yes, for a year," Palani said sadly.

"But you got back together," the reporter said.

"Yes, when Kana was shot," Palani said with a stricken look.

"This was a little over two years ago, right?" the reporter asked, looking from Palani to Kana.

Kana nodded, as did Palani.

"You almost died, isn't that true, Kana?"

"Yes," Kana said, looking at Palani. "I was dying. Palani pulled me back."

"Pulled you back?" the reporter asked, an excited light in her eyes.

"Her voice," Kana said, taking Palani's hand and looking into her eyes. "She was crying and begging me not to leave her. How could I go?" Kana asked, as if it were truly a question.

Palani smiled back at Kana, tears gathering in her eyes.

"And who asked who to marry her?"

Palani bit her lip, smiling shyly. "I asked Kana to marry me."

"You did?" the reporter asked, shocked.

"Kana didn't believe in same-sex marriage," Palani said.

"Really?" the reporter asked.

Kana shrugged. "I don't shove my sexuality down anyone's throat."

The reporter, Tina Castle, was known for her liberal views, and therefore the liberal slant to any story she wrote. She found it interesting that Kana Sorbinno was against a right gays were fighting heavily for.

"So you don't think gays should get married?" Tina asked.

"I didn't say that," Kana said. "I just didn't feel like it was something I needed to do to prove that I love Palani. There are a lot of people that don't feel marriage means anything. That it's just a piece of paper and a ring. I'm no different than people who dodge marriage their whole lives."

Tina nodded again. "Would you say that you're a liberal or a conservative?"

"Conservative," Kana said.

"Yet you live a lifestyle that the conservative side of the nation, Republicans, don't recognize as either legal or legitimate."

"I don't base my political beliefs and practices on my sexuality," Kana said. "While the liberal Democratic party supports my right to get married to another woman, they also support things I find incomprehensible."

"Such as?" Tina asked, sensing that Kana Sorbinno was far from the typical.

"Such as the legalization of marijuana, the creation of more government aid programs, the lack of control on the welfare systems, the abolition of the death penalty—I can go on and on."

"And you disagree with the Democratic stand on these?"

"Completely," Kana said.

"What about you, Palani?"

"I have to say that a lot of my opinions have changed since I got together with Kana," Palani said. "I've learned a lot more about law enforcement than I ever knew. I understand more about why certain laws are in place, and most importantly how it feels to have someone try to kill the person you love most with total disregard."

Kana sat back, watching the reporter make notes to herself. She wasn't sure if things were going as expected or not.

"So, why did you agree to marry Palani if you didn't believe in gay marriage?" Tina asked.

"I never said I didn't believe in it," Kana said, her eyes narrowing slightly. She didn't like the woman putting words into her mouth. "I said it wasn't something I ever wanted to do. The reason I agreed to it, however, is simply because Palani wanted it so much. When you love someone, you go out of your way to give them something they want."

"And did I hear correctly that you two are planning on having a baby?"

"Yes," Palani answered.

"Who will you have father the child?" Tina asked.

Palani glanced at Kana, unsure if she wanted to answer that. Kana gave her a nod.

"Kana's brother is going to donate the sperm. That way it will be Kana's family DNA combined with mine."

Tina looked surprised. "Your brother won't want custody of a child that is his?"

"My brother wouldn't know what to do with a child," Kana said with a grin. "He's better with things like puppies. They can be put outside when they're bad, whereas children can't."

Tina chuckled at that description.

"Can I ask you questions about Attorney General Chevalier?"

"That would depend on the questions," Kana replied.

"Fair enough. During the election, Midnight Chevalier made a very moving speech defending you and telling people that you were to be respected for your time in law enforcement, rather than being crucified for your sexuality. How did you feel about that?"

"I wasn't even aware of that speech until weeks later," Kana said, "but when I found out about it, I'd have to say it made me proud to know a woman like Midnight. She's someone who is able to separate business from personal. Yet she's unfailingly loyal to both her friends and the people she works for."

"The people she works for?" Tina asked guilelessly.

"Currently, the citizens of the state of California," Kana replied, a quirk to her lips.

"Currently?" Tina asked, surprised by the word.

"Well," Kana said, "I think Midnight could be the first female president of the United States if she put her mind to it."

"You think that much of her?"

"I think more than that of her," Kana replied.

"So you two are close?"

"Yes," Kana said. "Midnight and I have worked together since I was eighteen years old. She's one of the very best friends I have."

"Is that why you act as her bodyguard?"

"No," Kana said. "I act as her bodyguard because she felt I was one of the best people for the job. I protect her back, literally and figuratively."

Tina grinned.

"If you could say one thing to young people who may be wrestling with the idea that they might be gay, what would you say?" Tina asked, looking at Palani.

"I'd say that you should always follow your heart, no matter what," Palani replied, her eyes on Kana, her smile soft.

"Kana?" Tina queried.

"I'd say that they shouldn't let anyone tell them who they are," Kana said simply.

They were done with the story then. Kana was relieved. The photographer had been snapping shots throughout the interview, and Kana was ready to swat the woman.

"I'd like to get together with the two of you tomorrow morning, if that's possible," the photographer said cautiously.

She'd been warned by the editor of the magazine that under no circumstances was she to irritate Kana or Palani. This story was too important.

Kana glanced at her watch. "It's only eleven o'clock. Can't we do this now?"

The photographer looked nervous suddenly, but Palani stepped into the uncomfortable silence.

"Kana, she has to have good lighting, plus they need to schedule hair and makeup people…" Her voice trailed off as Kana's eyebrow went up. "I know, I know," Palani said. "This isn't stuff you're used to, but you want our photos to look good, don't you?"

"Frankly, my dear…" Kana began, her tone sardonic.

"Kana," Palani beseeched softly, "I want everyone to see how beautiful you are. With the right lighting and camera angles—"

"We can fake it," Kana cut in, her look sour.

"No," Palani said. "With the right lighting and camera angles, the camera will capture who you are, inside and out."

"You truly have magnificent features," the photographer put in, her dark eyes assessing Kana.

Kana looked cynical.

"I have photographed some of the most beautiful women in the world," the photographer, Chez Grace, said, "and rarely do I meet someone with such raw beauty. Without all the need for makeup, hair, and the right clothes. Ms. Kana, you have a style that is part of your soul—you are truly beautiful. Please let me photograph you so the world can see this."

Kana looked back at the photographer, not sure what she actually wanted to believe. She knew this story was major to the magazine, but she imagined a world-famous photographer had to lie to get someone to take pictures. Glancing at Palani, she saw complete joy in her girlfriend's eyes.

Palani was thrilled beyond words that Chez, who was usually quite quiet and introspective, had seen fit to tell Kana all that she had. It was what Palani truly felt about Kana, and now someone else had told Kana the same thing. It substantiated it, and proved that it wasn't just her love for Kana that made her believe this.

Kana sighed. "I have to make sure Midnight has nothing going on in the morning, but what time are we talking?"

"Say six a.m.?" the photographer said.

Palani nodded, while Kana glowered.

"Okay, maybe you're used to this, but that early?" she asked, her tone indicating her shock at such an early start time.

"Morning light is soft, it is perfect," the photographer pronounced.

Kana exhaled deeply. "Hell, Midnight won't even be finished with her coffee by then," she said with a grin.

Palani smiled. Kana was already regaining her sense of humor—that was a good sign.

The photo session went well. Kana surprised Palani by agreeing to some more artistic shots, including the shot Jerry had suggested. There had, of course, been the caveat that Kana and Palani have all final approval on what photos were actually published. It was understood that Kana would not allow anything to be put out to the public that might embarrass Midnight in any way. Also surprising was that the photographer readily agreed to their reviewing the photos. Palani tended to think it was because she had every confidence that the pictures would be incredible.

Chapter 3

Sierra was in Los Angeles, at the Attorney General's legal offices. It was a meeting of the Deputy Attorneys General for the criminal division. She was anxious to get home to her son; it had been two days, and the meetings just seemed to drag and drag. Glancing at her watch as she listened to another long-winded attorney giving his summation of a recent case, Sierra prayed he'd be done soon. It was already four thirty. If she was lucky she could make the airport by six thirty and be home by eight that night. Unlike the rest of the deputies, she wasn't staying the night and traveling back in the morning. She had responsibilities at home.

The attorney wrapped up fifteen minutes later, and Sierra gave her last words on the meeting. Everyone left, talking about the new division head. Sierra Youngblood didn't mince words; she was a lot like Midnight Chevalier. Many in the division felt that was why she'd received the position she had. Others had their own ideas but wouldn't speak of them in public. It had already been seen that Midnight Chevalier didn't appreciate anyone denigrating her decisions. Her rebuttals were always swift and cutting. No one wanted to be on the end of one of Midnight Chevalier's diatribes.

Leaving the meeting, Sierra hurried to her rental car parked across the street at one of the daily lots. Her bags were already in the trunk. All she needed to do was get through the LA traffic and get to the airport. *Easier said than done*, she thought as she got in the car, tossing her purse on the passenger seat. She was just turning the key in the ignition when she glanced through the windshield, catching a glimpse of red. Her eyes widened as she stared at the red rose that was under one of the windshield wipers. Glancing around frantically, she felt a chill go through her. It couldn't be...

She got out of the car. With shaking hands, she reached for the rose. There was a note tied around its stem. Her eyes darted around her surroundings, fearing he'd jump out of the darkness and attack her. Opening the note, she read it slowly.

"We'll be together soon," it said in scrawled handwriting.

"Oh God," she whispered to herself, tossing the rose away from her and jumping into the car.

Locking the doors, she started the engine with a roar and threw the car into reverse. Unfortunately, the cars were parked rather close together—she ran into a car behind her before she realized just how close. Terrified, she looked around, hoping someone would come to find out what had happened. Luck was with her—three people turned in her direction and started toward her. Two of them were deputies that worked for her.

"Are you alright?" one woman asked, reaching for Sierra's elbow.

"Are you hurt?" the man asked.

Sierra was already near hyperventilating from the fear, so she nodded.

Within an hour, Sierra had told the police what had happened, including receiving the rose and who it was from. The police had called Kana Sorbinno at Sierra's request.

Kana was at the hospital an hour after she was called, thanks to Joe Sinclair's personal jet.

"But how?" Sierra asked, her eyes wide as Kana walked up.

"Don't worry about it," Kana said, smiling. "Let's get you home." She took Sierra's elbow gently.

Less than an hour after that, Sierra was on a small jet bound for Sacramento. Joe Sinclair had greeted her and explained that a friend had bought him the plane for his birthday. "So don't be too impressed," he said with a grin.

Kana was sitting with her, but Sierra still hadn't really recovered from the shock.

"Look," Kana was saying, "I think this is more serious than we originally thought. Sierra," she said, putting her hand on the younger woman's. "I think you need full-time security."

"Security?" Sierra asked, her tone disbelieving.

"Yes," Kana said. "Someone to travel with you, at least until we feel this guy is no longer a threat to you."

Sierra wasn't sure how to take that. What did security mean? A person with her night and day? How would that work? Her mind was going in a million different directions. Then it came to a screeching halt as Kana mentioned a name.

"I've only got one person I can use in Sacramento right now, but she's good. Her name is Kashena Marshal."

"I'm sorry, who?" Sierra asked, sure she'd just heard wrong.

"Kashena Marshal," Kana repeated, wondering if Sierra was still in shock. "She's very good. She's been law enforcement for over six years, and most of that doing bodyguard work. Before that she was—"

"A Marine," Sierra said, staring straight ahead.

"Yeah…" Kana said, looking at Sierra oddly. "You know her?"

"I knew her a long time ago in college," Sierra said, sounding somewhat haunted. "She rescued me once."

"Rescued?" Kana asked, curious now.

Sierra nodded, but she was too caught up in memories to explain.

Sierra had been a junior at the University of San Diego. She'd been young, idealistic, and full of hope. Her entire tribe had raised the money for her to go to this private college. She was going to be a tribal lawyer. Or she thought she was. Whatever she did, she knew she'd help her tribe get whatever they needed.

In order to better understand the world's version of Indian history, Sierra had taken an American Indian Studies course. She was sure it would be an interesting class, and it was. More so because of the blond Marine who joined the class two sessions into the course. In her Marine uniform of khaki, and her hair pulled back severely in a bun, Kashena Marshal exuded power and strength. She also displayed an air of dignity when she talked about "her people."

The professor of the class, of course, asked her how she'd come by her knowledge of Indians.

"Simple," Kashena answered, her voice strong and proud. "I am Indian. One half Ojibwa. I've spent a great deal of time on the reservation with my grandmother."

Sierra was taken aback. Kashena didn't look Indian, with her blond hair and deep blue eyes. Once she knew, however, Sierra started to see signs of Indian blood in Kashena. Her bone structure, her skin that got darker as the long summer wore on. And something about her spoke volumes about the quiet dignity of a people whose time ended violently at the hands of white men.

At one point in the class, Indian names were discussed, and Sierra's own name was examined. The professor, who had a love/hate relationship with his extremely bright pupil Kashena, asked her what her Indian name meant.

Kashena looked back at the man, then glanced at Sierra, her eyes connecting with the only other Indian in the room as she answered.

"It means 'She with the stars in her eyes.'"

Sierra felt a connection then. Simply two spirits uniting over common ground, was how she explained it to herself. After class, Sierra felt the need to say something to the usually aloof, solitary Marine, so she stopped Kashena on her way out of the room, still fumbling for something to say.

"What is your family name?" Sierra finally blurted out.

Kashena looked back at the older girl, her deep blue eyes reflecting amusement at Sierra's obvious nervousness.

"Windwalker," she said simply, starting to move past the smaller girl.

"Wait!" Sierra exclaimed, before she even knew what she'd say next.

Kashena turned to her, her stance for all intents and purposes a "parade rest," like she'd just been given an order.

"Yes, Ms. Youngblood?" she queried, her voice amused.

This served to only further befuddle Sierra. "I, well, can we, I mean, can I invite you to coffee sometime?"

"Coffee, ma'am?" Kashena asked, her voice holding an odd note.

"Yes," Sierra said. "You do drink coffee, don't you?"

"Quite often, ma'am, but I don't really think that would be appropriate."

"Appropriate?" Sierra asked, perplexed.

"For appearances, ma'am."

"Whose appearances?" Sierra asked, getting irritated that this was becoming so difficult.

"Yours, ma'am, considering," Kashena answered, her eyes glittering with subdued humor.

"Considering what?" Sierra asked, already deciding she didn't like this conversation.

"Considering that you're a young attractive female, and I'm gay, ma'am."

That answer stopped Sierra dead in her tracks. Gay? Why hadn't she known that? She stared up at Kashena with such shock evident on her face that Kashena grinned. Before Sierra could recover and ask why that mattered, Kashena had turned on her heel and strode away.

The next time the class met, Kashena acted like nothing had happened. Sierra had no idea what to say to her, so said nothing at all.

A month went by, and Sierra did her best to forget about the conversation. Kashena didn't speak to her, so Sierra did the same, assuming she'd in some way offended the other woman. She'd come to realize what Kashena had been saying that day. Being seen with a gay woman would make people question Sierra's sexual preference. She'd been dating men since she'd gotten to school, since things had been so restricted on the reservation, especially with her parents being so prominent. She wasn't gay, everyone knew that, but Kashena had been being cautious for her benefit. Or had she? Sierra wasn't sure.

After finals, Sierra and some friends went to a party at one of the fraternity houses off campus. That night she drank way more than she should have, and a guy that had been trying to get to her for months finally made his move. He took her up to his room in the fraternity house. They were making out when Sierra suddenly realized she was far too drunk to be doing this. She didn't really like the guy; it was the alcohol that had made her say yes.

"I can't do this," she said, pushing at him.

"Sure you can, baby, sure you can," the young black man said.

"No," she said, firmer this time. "I don't want to do this."

"It'll be good, I promise you it will."

"No!" she yelled, pushing at him again and starting to panic.

He was over her, his weight holding her down. His hands were pulling at her clothes now—he wasn't getting off her.

"Stop!" she cried again. "I said no!"

"What are you, a cocktease?" he sneered.

"No, she's a woman who just told you no, three times," came a voice from behind them. "I know because I counted," Kashena continued, her voice a slow drawl.

Sierra didn't think she'd ever been so relieved in her entire life. The man didn't move.

"Get off her, now," Kashena said, walking into the room.

"Who do you think you are?" the guy asked, glancing behind him, obviously not feeling too much of a threat.

"I said," Kashena began, putting her foot on the bed and grabbing a handful of his shirt and hair as she hauled him to his feet, "get off her."

Sierra shifted herself to the head of the bed, away from him. But his attention was on Kashena now. He whirled on her, his eyes blazing.

"Who the fuck do you think you are, bitch?" he asked viciously. "All up in my business and shit. Get out of here."

"Fine," Kashena said, holding her hand out to Sierra.

Sierra jumped off the bed and reached for Kashena's hand.

"I meant you get the fuck out," the man said, reaching for Sierra as he did. "Shorty's stayin'."

Kashena used Sierra's hand to pull the smaller girl behind her and away from him.

"No, Shorty is leaving with me," Kashena said. "And if you're smart you'll back up off me."

65

"You think you can take me, dyke?" the man said, his stance hostile.

Kashena's eyes narrowed, her hand releasing Sierra's. She balled it into a fist and slammed it into his jaw before he could even blink. He sunk to the floor, unconscious.

"I think I just did," Kashena said, her voice perfectly calm.

Turning, Kashena took Sierra's hand and led her out of the room, down the stairs, and out of the fraternity house before anyone could stop them. Kashena put Sierra in her car and drove her back to the college where the women's dormitories were. Once there, she parked her car and opened the door for a now quiet Sierra. Kashena put her hand out to Sierra and noticed that the smaller girl's hand was shaking as she reached out to take it.

Leading Sierra up to the dorms, she glanced down at her. "What room?" she asked gently.

"425," Sierra said, her voice shaky.

Kashena led her inside and to the elevators. A few minutes later they were in Sierra's dormitory room. Kashena looked around. It was decent, definitely better than the barracks she stayed in on base at Camp Pendleton. There were two beds, which let Kashena know that Sierra had a roommate. All the more reason to get out of there fast.

Glancing at Sierra, who now stood near the window looking out, she noticed the girl's shoulders were shaking. It was Kashena's natural reaction to comfort her. Stepping over to Sierra, Kashena put her hands on Sierra's shoulders. Sierra immediately turned and leaned against Kashena, crying in quiet sobs. Putting her arms around the smaller girl's shoulders, Kashena did her best to comfort her. Finally, when Sierra quieted, Kashena sat down on the bed, still holding her. She looked down at Sierra, tipping her face up to hers with a finger under her chin.

"Thank you," Sierra whispered, her eyes shining with tears again.

Kashena nodded. "You're okay now."

"But if you hadn't been there..." Sierra began, her tone becoming hysterical again.

"Shhh," Kashena said, putting her hand up to brush the tears off Sierra's cheek. "It's okay."

Sierra shook her head, her lips trembling as she looked like she was going to cry again.

Kashena did the only thing she could think of. Leaning down, she kissed the other girl.

As their lips met, Sierra tensed momentarily. Their lips parted for a second, as Kashena sensed Sierra's hesitation, but then she kissed her again, and this time there was no hesitation. Kashena pulled her closer, deepening the kiss as she heard Sierra sigh. Sierra's hands came up to touch Kashena's face tentatively. Kashena buried her hands in Sierra's long jet-black hair. Things were very definitely heating up when they heard a voice right outside the door, a woman talking to someone else, calling "Goodnight." Kashena broke the kiss, standing up and straightening her clothes before the girl could even open the door.

"Sierra I just had—oh!" the girl at the door exclaimed, seeing Kashena standing there.

Sierra turned around, looking at Sally, her roommate, and seeing that she was still staring at the staunch-looking Marine standing in their dorm room. They'd had conversations about Kashena Marshal a couple of times. Sierra had talked to Sally about her. And here she was, standing in their dorm room. Sally glanced at Sierra, who stood up, her glance at the Marine furtive.

"Sally," Sierra said, her voice shaky, "this is Kashena Marshal. Kashena, this is Sally, my roommate."

Kashena inclined her head to Sally. "Nice to meet you, Sally Sierra's roommate," she said wryly.

"I, uh, yeah, you too," Sally said, sounding surprised.

Kashena turned to Sierra, giving the other girl a slight bow. "You're in good hands now, so I'll take my leave, ma'am," she said, her tone formal.

Sierra looked up at her, her mouth open to say something. Kashena shook her head slightly, telling her silently not to say anything, her eyes sparkling with amusement. With that, she walked past Sierra to the door that Sally still stood in front of. Sally stared up at Kashena open-mouthed as well. Kashena canted her head to the other girl, then her eyes went to the door behind Sally.

"Oh!" Sally exclaimed, moving away from the door so Kashena could get out.

Kashena quirked a grin as she opened the door. She spared a glance for Sierra, who was still looking shell-shocked. White teeth in a sardonic smile, then Kashena was gone. Sierra stood staring at the closed door for a full minute, unable to believe what had just happened. Kashena had kissed her. That in itself had been shocking, but more shocking still, she'd liked it.

Kana took Sierra to pick up her son at the sitter's, then took her home. Her son, Colby, asked Kana a million and one questions all the way home.

"Are you really a police officer?" he asked first, his dark eyes wide.

"Yes," Kana said, smiling.

"Can I see your badge?"

"Sure," Kana said, unclipping her badge from her belt and handing it to him in the back seat.

"What's a Special Agent in Charge?" he asked, touching the lettering on the badge.

"Special Agent in Charge means I work too hard and no one likes the decisions I make," Kana said, glancing at Sierra with a grin.

"It also means that she's the boss," Sierra added.

"I thought that other lady was your boss," Colby said. "The one with red hair."

"Midnight Chevalier is my boss," Sierra said. "But Kana is Midnight's bodyguard, and the boss over all the other security officers that work for the department."

"You're a bodyguard?" Colby asked, his eyes wide again.

Kana nodded. "Yes, I am."

"Cool..." Colby said.

Sierra laughed; Kana chuckled. Kana got them to the house and went inside with them. She spent the evening there. Sierra made them dinner, asking Kana to join them. Kana accepted graciously. After dinner, Kana walked around the perimeter of the house, checking windows and doors from the outside. She also checked the connections for the security system to make sure there were no breaks.

At nine o'clock, Sierra put Colby to bed, then walked back into the living room. Kana was on her cell phone, hanging up just as Sierra walked back into the room.

"If you want me to stay tonight, I can," Kana said.

"I wouldn't want you to have to do that," Sierra said. "I know you have someone you want to get home to," she said with a soft smile.

"Palani's gotten used to sleeping without me there," Kana said.

"Yes, but that's when you're protecting the AG, not for someone like me."

"Sierra," Kana said, her face serious, "Midnight wants to ensure you feel safe. If that means me staying here tonight, I will, okay?"

Sierra nodded. "Thank you," she said. "I appreciate your help, I really do. But I think we'll be fine tonight."

Kana assessed her for a long moment. Finally she nodded.

"Okay," she said, pulling out her cell phone again and dialing a number.

Sierra could only hear Kana's end of the conversation, but she listened intently.

"Kashena, it's Kana… I'm fine, thanks… Look, I have a new assignment for you… Well, I need you to handle some personal security… right… It's for our Chief Deputy Attorney General, Sierra Youngblood," she said, her eyes trailing over to Sierra.

Sierra silently held her breath, wondering if Kashena would remember her name, if nothing else. Nothing in Kana's look told her Kashena had said anything to indicate recognition. Sierra was surprised to feel disappointment at that fact.

"Well, I need you to take over first thing tomorrow," Kana was saying. "Chief DAG Youngblood has a conference to attend back down in Los Angeles next week, and I'd like you to coordinate with her on that… Great, thanks, Kashena… No problem. I'll talk to you sometime tomorrow."

Kana hung up.

"Special Agent Supervisor Marshal will meet with you sometime in the morning to coordinate your next trip and set some guidelines for your protection, okay?"

"Okay," Sierra said, hiding her nagging disappointment well.

Kana left a little while later, after once again cautioning Sierra not to open the door to anyone and to make sure that the alarm system was on when she went to bed and when she left in the morning. Sierra assured Kana she would.

That night, lying in her bed, Sierra couldn't sleep. She tossed and turned, wondering if Kashena would recognize her in person. The idea that the woman who'd thrown her emotions into such turmoil so many years ago was now going to be protecting her sent her mind in a hundred different directions. Was it good that she didn't remember her? Maybe it was better; otherwise there might be a lot of mutual unease that would just make life more stressful for both of them. It was a good thing. By the time she woke up the next morning, Sierra had convinced herself that she hoped Kashena wouldn't remember or recognize her.

Three hours later, sitting in her corner office on the sixteenth floor, Sierra felt her heart stop as Kashena walked in. She looked the same, but different. She wasn't wearing the uniform she'd worn all the time in college. She was dressed nicely in stylish black slacks, low black heels, a rich plum-colored blouse tucked into her slacks, and a black jacket over it. On her hip she wore a fairly nasty-looking gun, and there was a gold badge, similar to Kana's, clipped to her belt. Her hair was pulled back in a bun, much as it had been years before. There was also no recognition in her deep blue eyes. Once again Sierra found herself disappointed. Squashing that emotion, she smiled at Kashena.

"Chief DAG Youngblood," Kashena said, striding forward and extending her hand to Sierra. "I'm Special Agent Supervisor Kashena Marshal. SAC Sorbinno assigned me to you for protection. It's a pleasure, ma'am."

Sierra took Kashena's hand, shaking it firmly. Kashena's look was direct, but without a hint of recognition in her eyes whatsoever.

"I—" Sierra stammered. "Thank you, Agent Marshal. I appreciate your time."

Kashena nodded as Sierra gestured for her to sit down in the chair in front of her desk.

"I'd like to go over your schedule," Kashena said, reaching into her jacket and pulling out a notebook and pen.

Sierra sat down behind her desk, still trying to decide how she felt about Kashena not recognizing her. They went over her schedule for the next morning, and then Kashena left, promising to be back at five to pick her up and take her home. After Kashena left, Sierra did everything she could to avoid thinking of Kashena. This was not going to be easy at all.

***

In Los Angeles, Kana and Palani had agreed to attend a party to celebrate the release of their story in *Cosmo*. It was being held at the trendy W Hotel. They'd invited their friends from Kana's law enforcement family, also known as "the Gang," to the party. As Kana made her way back to the table that the Gang had taken over, she caught a few looks from people. She merely looked right back at them, raising a dark eyebrow in question. She sat down next to Palani and handed her a glass of wine, as well as handing her friend Cat a beer, then took a drink of her own beer.

"Tough crowd," Kana said, grinning.

"They probably recognize you," Palani said.

"Huh?" Kana asked.

"*Cosmo*, K. You two are kind of the point of the party…" Cat put in, leaning past Palani.

"Oh, shit," Kana said out loud, causing a few people to turn and stare.

Cat laughed. "It's a bitch being famous, isn't it?"

"Fuck you," Kana growled quietly.

Cat only smiled.

"Stop instigating," Elizabeth told her girlfriend in a whisper.

"Why?" Cat asked. "I'm having fun."

"All we need is for Kana to cause a scene," Elizabeth whispered.

The party had many of fashion's elite in attendance, as well as a number of people from England that Elizabeth happened to know

"Like the Gang isn't causing that anyway," Cat replied.

Elizabeth sighed. She felt uncomfortable being around people from London again. It was too close to home, and there were still so many people that didn't know about her current relationship with another woman. Oddly, the girl who loved to shock people was afraid to do just that now. She knew people were whispering, and it made her want to leave. She hadn't been sure about this party in the first place, knowing people she'd known back in England would be there, but everyone was going, and Midnight herself had called her. Rick was her uncle, her mother's brother. Midnight had always been Elizabeth's favorite aunt, so when Midnight asked, Elizabeth couldn't say no. So here she was, wishing she was somewhere else.

Cat sensed that Elizabeth was uncomfortable, and she knew exactly why. It bothered her that Elizabeth was embarrassed to be seen with her. It also irritated her. She'd tried to tell Elizabeth that being openly gay wasn't always going to be easy. Things had gone easy for them with Elizabeth's mother, Deborah, who'd been accepting of the relationship. So had Midnight and Rick, only wanting to see the ever wayward Elizabeth settled and happy. But Elizabeth wasn't settled. She was restless and it was affecting her relationship with Cat.

They'd gotten together a little over two years ago. A previously very heterosexual Elizabeth had been drawn to Cat. Catalina Roché was a narcotics officer who worked under Elizabeth's brother-in-law,

Dave Dibbins. They worked for San Diego Police Department, the department Midnight was formally the chief of, before she'd become Attorney General. Cat had been the one to get Elizabeth off the cocaine that had started ruling her life. It had been Cat who had helped her through withdrawals and befriended her to help keep her clean. Cat had also been the one to support her when she'd wanted to start a restaurant and bar.

Elizabeth's restaurant, Catalina's, was becoming very successful, as was the bar/nightclub, Cat's Bet. While she was thrilled that she was a success at her very first business venture, Elizabeth was becoming increasingly stifled by day-to-day details. She'd always been a free spirit, moving from one place to the next, one party to the next, and suddenly she was living with someone, running a business, and becoming, in her mind, sedate and boring.

Dawn was just breaking when the party broke up. The Gang retired to the rooms the magazine had reserved for them. Cat prowled around the room she and Elizabeth had. She was too keyed up to sleep. The room they were in was incredible, with backlighting behind glass mosaic mirrors, a sculptured headboard in muted gold, and marble vanities in the bathroom. It was just beautiful.

"This place is incredible," Cat said, glancing at Elizabeth.

Elizabeth was lying on the bed, looking wholly uninterested.

"Guess this isn't a big deal for you, huh?" Cat asked, sitting on the damask-covered bed.

"I grew up in places like this," Elizabeth said.

Cat narrowed her eyes slightly, sensing something.

"So you're bored," she said.

"What?" Elizabeth said, shocked.

Cat tilted her head to the side. "That's it, isn't it? You're bored."

"It's one night in a hotel, Catalina," Elizabeth said tiredly.

"I don't mean the hotel, Bet," Cat said, her eyes searching Elizabeth's.

"Catalina…" Elizabeth said, her voice placating.

Cat shook her head. "Never mind," she said, standing up and putting her tennis shoes on. She'd already changed into sweats and a T-shirt.

"Where are you going?" Elizabeth asked, worried suddenly.

Cat picked up her cigarettes, her lighter, and her jacket. "I need some air."

With that she walked out of the room.

Down in the outside café space, Cat sat down, ordering a drink as she pulled a cigarette out of her pack.

"But miss, it's six a.m.," the waiter said, shocked.

Cat looked back at the man, a cigarette hanging from her lips. "And I care because…?"

The waiter hurried away, and a minute later set a drink down in front of her. Cat reached into her jacket pocket and pulled out a twenty, tossing it on his tray. She sat smoking and drinking her drink. Even without makeup and in sweat pants, she looked good. Kana noticed that as she walked toward her.

"Aren't you supposed to be asleep?" Kana asked as she sat down at the bar next to Cat.

"Aren't you?" Cat asked, grinning.

"Needed to smoke," Kana said.

"Me too," Cat replied, holding up her pack.

Kana suspected it was more than that. She'd sensed an undercurrent between Cat and Elizabeth the entire trip. Kana shook out a cigarette and lit up.

"Can I get you something, miss?" the waiter asked.

"Coffee and Baileys," Kana said.

The waiter didn't bother reminding Kana that it was 6 a.m. Cat winked at him.

"So what's really up?" Kana asked once she had her coffee.

Cat sighed, shaking her head. "Got me," she said.

"But there is something wrong, isn't there?" Kana asked.

Cat took a long drag of her cigarette. Blowing out smoke, she nodded. "But I'm goddamned if I know what it is for sure."

"What do you think it is?"

"I think Elizabeth is embarrassed to be gay now."

Kana nodded. "Well, you have to realize that we're suddenly around a lot of people she knows."

"I know," Cat said, "but Jesus…"

"Maybe she needs time to get used to the idea," Kana suggested.

"K, we've been together two years already. I think that's plenty of time, don't you?"

"Cat, she didn't grow up around the same kind of people we did. They have different ways of thinking, and the last thing they are is open minded."

Cat took another long drag of her cigarette, not looking happy.

"Give her a chance," Kana said. "She might come around yet."

"And if she doesn't?" Cat asked sourly.

Kana didn't answer, only looking pained. Finally she shook her head. "I'm sorry, Cat. I wish I could help."

"It's okay," Cat said. "I always land on my feet."

Kana knew that for a fact. She and Cat had been a couple a while back. Unfortunately, Kana had still been deeply in love with Palani, so Cat had taken the brunt of the rejection every time Kana felt heartsick. In the end, it had been Cat who had stepped aside so Palani could have Kana back. Kana still felt she owed Cat for that. Cat didn't feel that Kana owed her anything. Life was a gamble—you took a chance and sometimes you won, other times you lost. Being with Kana had, however, made Cat crave a long-term relationship. Whereas her previous relationships had been short lived, she wanted something that would last.

"Well, I better get back to my girl," Kana said after she'd finished her coffee.

Cat smiled. "So when are you two getting married?"

Kana smiled. "Whenever Palani can get it planned."

"Ah," Cat said. "I am getting an invitation, I hope."

"Of course," Kana said, standing. "Don't stay down here too long."

"Yes, dear," Cat said, grinning sardonically.

Kana walked away, glancing back as Cat ordered another drink. Kana headed up to her and Palani's room on the fifth floor. As soon as she got inside she went to the phone.

"What's wrong?" Palani asked as Kana called the front desk and asked for Catalina Roché's room.

Kana just shook her head.

Elizabeth answered on the third ring.

"Your girlfriend is downstairs drinking at six in the morning," Kana said. "I think you need to get down there and talk to her."

Elizabeth was silent for a few seconds. Breathing a sigh, she said a soft "Okay."

Kana hung up.

Ten minutes later, Elizabeth walked out onto the patio where Cat sat. She looked around and saw Cat sitting in a chair, smoking. She was singing along with the song playing in the background—T'Pau's

"Heart and Soul." The chorus hit home, talking about giving heart and soul and not making her beg for more.

Elizabeth watched as the song continued. Cat turned her head, looking directly at her , and sang the line about having lost her way and trying to find something in her lover's eyes. It went straight to Elizabeth's soul, and she felt immediately guilty, although she didn't know quite why.

Elizabeth walked over and sat down next to Cat. Cat finished the cigarette she had in hand and reached for another one. Elizabeth noticed a number of butts in the ashtray in front of Cat. She was chain-smoking, not a good sign.

"Can we talk?" Elizabeth asked gently.

Cat nodded, looking straight ahead, her face a cool mask.

"Things have just been crazy lately," Elizabeth said, her tone reasoning. "The restaurant is doing business hand over fist, and the club is getting more and more popular... Plus you've been working so much lately..."

Cat gave a short laugh. "We've been three people down on a six-man team, Bet. Of course I've been working a lot. That's not about us."

Elizabeth had no idea what to say.

"I think we're just..." Elizabeth's voice trailed off as she saw Cat's gaze sharpen.

"Bored," Cat supplied. "But don't say 'we,' Bet. I'm not bored."

"That's not what I was going to say," Elizabeth snapped, then pulled herself up short, knowing that getting mad at Cat wasn't going to help.

In her heart, Elizabeth knew it was true. She was restless, and she didn't know what to do to fix that. If she talked to anyone, they'd just tell her that was what a relationship was about. Living with one person day in and day out. Elizabeth just didn't know how to handle that. What she did know was that she didn't want to get into a big nasty fight with Cat.

It would be far too easy for her to run fast and loose in Los Angeles, and that would only get her into trouble again. Her aunt was the California Attorney General now—any headlines involving her niece would reflect badly on Midnight. The last thing Elizabeth wanted was to face her uncle's wrath if she did anything to hurt Midnight's image. Elizabeth had witnessed Rick in his fury a couple of times, and she knew she didn't want that turned on her.

"Please, Cat," Elizabeth said, putting her hand on Cat's arm. "Can't we just go back to the room?"

Cat looked at Elizabeth's extensively manicured hand, then at her own hands. She had two broken nails, no polish on at all, and her hands had cuts on them from a barbed-wire fence the week before. Far from what Elizabeth's hand looked like. Maybe Kana was right. They were so different. Was that ever going to change? Cat didn't think so, and she wondered how long it would take to tear them apart.

Sighing, Cat stubbed out her cigarette, drank the last of her drink, and tossed another twenty on the table. She got up, taking Elizabeth by the hand and leading her to the elevators. Inside the elevator, Cat turned to Elizabeth and kissed her, pressing her back against the wall of the elevator. At first Elizabeth responded, but as the bell rang for the floor they were on, Elizabeth pushed her away.

"Someone might see," she said, her voice hushed.

Cat's lips curled in a sardonic grin. Shaking her head, she walked out of the elevator and headed for their room. Inside, she tossed her jacket aside, kicked off her shoes, and went to bed. Elizabeth climbed into bed after her, but Cat's back was to her, her arms curled around the pillow under her head. Elizabeth knew with a sense of dread that this was the beginning of the end for them. It made her heart ache. She lay there crying silently, knowing that this was her fault and there was nothing she could do to make it right.

***

"When will you be back?" Linda asked plaintively.

"On Friday," Kashena said, not for the first time.

"Why can't Baz take care of this?"

Kashena sighed, pausing as she was putting her laptop into its case.

"We've already talked about this, Linda," she chastised. "And complaining about it isn't going to change anything. Baz already has a security assignment. I have to take care of this."

Linda pouted, not liking that Kashena would be gone so long.

"What am I supposed to do while you're gone?" she asked, her voice still whiney.

Kashena had to squash the irritation she was feeling. The last thing she needed this morning was this.

"I don't know," Kashena said. "What do you do all day when I'm at work?"

"Hang out with my friends," Linda answered. She didn't like the direction of this conversation.

"So do that," Kashena said, then narrowed her eyes as she saw an excited light in Linda's eyes. "But not in my house."

"But Kash…" Linda began.

"No," Kashena said. "Don't even start with me on this, Linda. I don't want those people in or around my house. Do you understand that?"

"God, I'm living here with you!" Linda exclaimed. "You'd think I could have some friends over every now and then."

"Get a new set of friends and we'll discuss it," Kashena replied.

"You don't trust my friends?"

"Not as far as I could throw them," Kashena said unapologetically. "Wait, let me qualify that—I could probably throw some of them way farther than I'd trust them."

"Kash!" Linda cried, sounding offended.

"Look," Kashena said, holding up her hand to fend off another diatribe. "They're not welcome in my house. That's the end of it. You want to hang out with them, go to their place."

Linda crossed her arms in front of her chest. "So I'm like a prisoner here."

Kashena rolled her eyes at Linda's dramatic statement. "No, prisoners aren't allowed out. I'm encouraging you to go out, just don't bring any criminals back with you."

"My friends are not criminals!" Linda yelled, jumping off the bed to face Kashena.

Kashena looked down at Linda, unimpressed with her declaration. Glancing down, she saw that Linda's hand was balled into a fist. Her eyes moved back to connect with Linda's, her face still impassive.

"Do it," Kashena said evenly.

"Do what?" Linda asked, her tone still angry.

Kashena's lips curled into a sardonic smile. "Whatever you think you're going to do with that fist you've made."

Linda stared back at Kashena, sensing the threat Kashena didn't verbalize. Kashena's deep blue eyes narrowed as she waited for Linda to act. Linda swallowed a couple of times, feeling nervous suddenly. Kashena had never been violent, although she was certainly capable of doing a lot of damage if she ever was. Linda finally drew her courage up, shaking her head.

"You wouldn't hit me," she said. "I know you wouldn't."

"Just remember the term 'reciprocating force,'" Kashena said with a pointed look at Linda's still balled-up fist.

Linda actually took a step back this time, her chin coming up as she unclenched her hand. Kashena nodded as if Linda had just conceded defeat, because in truth she had.

Zipping up her laptop case, Kashena went back into the bathroom to do a last check for anything she might have forgotten. When she walked back into the bedroom, she saw that Linda had moved to sit in the middle of the bed. She looked a bit stunned. Kashena almost felt sorry for her. Linda was finding that Kashena wasn't nearly as pliable as she used to be.

Picking up her laptop case and looping it over her shoulder, Kashena leaned over and kissed Linda on the lips.

"I'll be back Friday," she said softly.

Linda nodded, her eyes lowered.

Kashena stared at her, trying to determine if Linda was putting on an act now or not. She kissed the girl again, bringing her hand up to cup Linda's cheek. This time Linda responded by wrapping her arms around Kashena's neck, kissing her back. When their lips parted, Kashena smiled.

"That's more like it," she said, winking at Linda.

Linda smiled.

Kashena left the house five minutes later, bound for Sierra's house to pick her up so they could head to the airport.

They'd only driven together one other time, the first day Kashena took over security for her. Sierra had ended up having to take the rest of the week off to take care of her son, who was home sick. When Kashena drove up to Sierra's house, she got out of the state-issued Suburban she was driving. She walked up to Sierra's door and rang the bell.

Sierra answered a few minutes later, looking harried.

"God, I'm running so late!" she exclaimed. "I'm so sorry, Agent Marshal, but I haven't even dropped my son at day care yet. He was still not feeling well this morning... I'm so sorry."

"It's okay," Kashena said. "We can drop him at day care before we go to the airport." She glanced at her watch. "We're still ahead of schedule. Are these your bags?" she asked, indicating the luggage in the entryway.

"Yes," Sierra said.

"Okay, I'll go get these in the car. You just do what you need to do."

"Great, okay," Sierra said, smiling. "Thank you."

"No problem," Kashena said, looping Sierra's garment bag over her arm and picking up the matching suitcase.

Fifteen minutes later they were headed toward her son's day care. Not before Colby had to interrogate Kashena. He wandered out to the Suburban and stood looking up at her with dark eyes like his mother's.

"Who're you?" he asked.

"I'm Special Agent Supervisor Kashena Marshal."

"Are you my mom's bodyguard?"

"Yes I am."

"Can I see your badge?"

"Sure," Kashena answered, smiling as she unclipped her badge and handed it to the boy.

"This is like that other lady's badge," Colby said, running his finger over the badge's surface.

"Which other lady?" Kashena asked.

"The one that brought my mom home last week."

"Oh, that was SAC Sorbinno."

"Yeah, her," Colby said. "Do you have a gun too?"

"Yes," Kashena answered.

"Can I see it?" he asked excitedly.

Kashena lifted her jacket aside, showing him the holstered weapon.

"That is so cool…" he said, his eyes bright.

Sierra came out of the house then, her eyes searching the area. She saw her son.

"Colby, do you have your backpack and overnight case?" she called to him.

"No, Mom!" he called back.

"Come get them. Hurry up, please!"

Colby turned and ran toward the house. Sierra waited for him, then locked up the house after he came out with his backpack. Sierra was carrying a small suitcase.

Kashena opened the passenger door of the Suburban for Sierra, then opened the rear passenger door for Colby. As he climbed in, Kashena nudged him.

"Hey," she said, "can I have my badge back now?"

Colby grinned, his eyes twinkling mischievously as he handed back the badge.

Kashena narrowed her eyes at him, then grinned back. Sierra was watching from the passenger seat, smiling too.

After they'd dropped Colby at day care, they headed for the airport.

"I really am sorry I was so late," Sierra said, feeling bad that she was now causing them a time crunch.

"Don't worry about it," Kashena said. "I always build in an extra hour or so for variables."

"Such as Chief Deputy AGs that can't get their shit together in the morning?" Sierra asked with a grin.

"Yeah, like that," Kashena said, grinning back.

Sierra nodded. "I see."

Sierra was still trying to get over the fact that after all these years, Kashena Marshal was now her protector again. It still bothered her that Kashena didn't seem to remember her at all. She kept waiting for Kashena to suddenly realize who she was, but she didn't. Sierra knew it was going to drive her crazy.

Kashena pulled up to the terminal area, waving down an airport police officer.

"I'm Special Agent Marshal, from the AG's office. I need to park in VIP parking. Can you open the gate, please?" Kashena said, showing the man her credentials.

"Yes, ma'am," the officer said. "Do you need a skycap for the bags?"

"That would be great," Kashena said.

"I'll send one right over. What airline?"

"Southwest."

"You got it, Agent Marshal," the man said, then waved her around to the side.

Kashena parked the Suburban in the VIP lot and got out. She pulled the bags out of the back. The skycap came and took the bags, telling them to meet him up front.

Twenty minutes later they were checked through a special security gate. Sierra watched, fascinated, as Kashena took out her gun, removing the ammunition clip and then pulling back the slide to remove the chambered round. The security officer looked at a piece of paper Kashena handed him as well as her credentials. He nodded, handing her back both. Kashena then reloaded and holstered her weapon. Glancing up, Kashena saw Sierra watching with interest. She smiled and nodded toward the gates. Sierra followed her through.

"So what was all that about?" Sierra asked when they were seated at the gate.

"I have to carry my weapon on the plane, so they have to check my gun letter and credentials to make sure I'm legal."

"Gun letter?" Sierra asked.

"Yeah," Kashena said, pulling the paper out of her jacket and handing it to Sierra.

The letter was printed on the Attorney General's letterhead. It stated that Kashena Marshal was a sworn peace officer who needed to carry her weapon in the commission of her duties. The letter was signed by Midnight Chevalier herself.

Sierra handed back the letter, smiling. "I didn't realize what all it took to do security work."

Kashena chuckled. "Well, off-duty peace officers are required to carry their weapon while in the state, so it's not just the security work."

"Oh," Sierra said.

Their flight was called for boarding shortly after that. Sierra was surprised to note that as a peace officer, Kashena was allowed to board before other passengers.

"Another perk to the job," she told Sierra with a wink.

The flight to Los Angeles was uneventful. Sierra noticed that Kashena was very watchful of everything around them. It made her feel very safe. So safe, in fact, that she was able to sleep on the plane for the short one-hour flight. Kashena touched her lightly on the hand to wake her.

"Deputy Youngblood," she said softly. "We're landing."

Sierra sat up, realizing with a start that she had been leaning against Kashena's shoulder. Sitting back, she smoothed her hair nervously, then glanced at Kashena. Kashena caught her glance and simply smiled. Sierra felt relieved—she had been worried that the other woman would give her an odd look, or at least frown at her.

Once off the airplane, Kashena took charge again, carrying both her laptop case and Sierra's small carry-on bag. She touched Sierra on the elbow to get her attention, then nodded toward the baggage claim. The two of them headed there, Kashena's eyes scanning their surroundings constantly. At the baggage claim, Kashena handed Sierra her carry-on, and then stood by to grab their suitcases off the carousel. She then led the way to the rental car agency.

Once there, Kashena handled the paperwork for the rental, then led Sierra out to the car. Kashena opened the passenger door for her, then got in on the driver's side, starting the car and turning on the air conditioning. Getting out, Kashena put the bags into the trunk, then got into the car again.

"I have the map to the hotel where the conference is," Sierra said, having pulled the map out of her purse.

"Great," Kashena said, smiling.

She took the map, glanced at it, looked around them, then looked at the map again. Then she handed it back to Sierra. Putting the car into gear, she drove out of the parking lot. Sierra was amazed to note that she didn't glance at the map again.

"Have you been to this hotel before?" she asked ten minutes later when Kashena had taken the three different freeways listed on the map.

"No."

"You mean, you're following this map by just looking at it once?" Sierra asked, sounding amazed.

Kashena grinned. "I'm part Indian tracker," she joked.

Sierra laughed softly. "I guess you are. I'd have been hopelessly lost by now."

Kashena looked over at her. "I don't believe that," she said seriously.

Sierra felt her breath catch. Did Kashena remember her? She waited for Kashena to say something else, but she didn't, just turned back to her driving. The disappointment Sierra felt was almost crushing. She sighed, turning to look out the passenger window at the LA landscape of concrete and steel. What she didn't see was Kashena's glance over at her, brows furrowed.

"Everything okay?" Kashena asked.

Sierra nodded, still looking out the window.

There were a few long minutes of silence, during which Kashena turned on the radio, scanning the stations until she settled on a soft-rock station. Finally, Sierra turned her head to look at Kashena.

"Agent Marshal?"

Kashena grinned. "You can call me Kashena, or Kash if you want to."

Sierra smiled. "Okay, Kashena," she said, then hesitated, not sure if she should even ask what she wanted to so desperately.

Kashena waited in silence, glancing over at Sierra a couple of times.

"You don't remember me, do you?" Sierra blurted out before she lost her nerve.

A slow smile spread across Kashena's lips, her deep blue eyes sparkling in the sunlight.

"I remember you," she said softly.

"You do?" Sierra asked, unconvinced.

Kashena nodded. "The University of San Diego, Indian Studies class..." she said, her voice trailing off.

"A particularly foul frat house room," Sierra finished.

Kashena nodded again in agreement.

Sierra narrowed her eyes at Kashena. "So if you remembered me, why didn't you say anything?"

"Why didn't you?" Kashena asked with a smile.

Sierra pressed her lips together. "Good point," she said, laughing softly.

Kashena smiled again.

"I was sure you didn't remember me," Sierra said, grimacing.

"Of course I remember," Kashena said. "You almost cost me my military career."

"What?" Sierra asked with alarm. "How?"

"That whole scene in the frat house."

"Rescuing someone isn't acceptable to the Marines?" Sierra asked, aghast.

"Punching a civilian in the face isn't acceptable to the Marines," Kashena clarified.

"Oh," Sierra said. "What would they have expected you to do?"

"Subdue him through non-violent means."

Sierra canted her head. "And you could have done that?"

"Of course," Kashena said.

"So why didn't you?"

Kashena grinned. "Because he pissed me off."

"You broke his jaw, you know."

"I know," Kashena replied. "I felt it crack."

Sierra's mouth dropped open, her eyes widening. "I'll make a note to myself not to piss you off," she said, smiling.

Kashena laughed at that. "I'm in better control of myself these days."

"Good to know," Sierra said lightly, her smile wide. "So what happened to you after that?" she asked. "I never saw you around school after that semester—after that night, even."

"I shipped out right after that," Kashena said, seeing Sierra's relief and raising an eyebrow at her. "Did you think it was because of you?"

Sierra hesitated, then shrugged. "I didn't know for sure."

Kashena nodded slowly. "Well, now you do."

Sierra dropped her head, smiling. "I just figured I was a really bad kisser or something," she said, surprising herself by bringing that up.

Kashena surprised her further by laughing. "Not that bad, no."

Sierra bit her lip, not daring to look at Kashena, afraid her face would reflect what she was thinking.

They were both silent for a few minutes. Then Sierra looked over at Kashena.

"So did you end up finishing your degree?" she asked.

"Yep, bachelor's in American History with a minor in American Indian Studies. And apparently you not only finished your degree, but went to law school too," Kashena said, smiling.

Sierra nodded.

"And you got married…" Kashena said, her eyes dropping to the wedding ring Sierra wore.

"Yes," Sierra said. "To a Marine, in fact."

"My condolences," Kashena said, shaking her head.

Sierra laughed. "Why do you say that?"

"Because I've lived with male Marines 24/7. I wouldn't wish one on my worst enemy."

"It does have its challenges," Sierra said with a grin.

"I'd imagine," Kashena said, rolling her eyes.

"So what about you?" Sierra asked. "Did you get married or anything?"

"Uh, no," Kashena said. "I'm still gay."

Sierra laughed, looking embarrassed. "I didn't mean that," she said. "I just meant, well, you know, women are having commitment ceremonies all the time now."

"Not this woman," Kashena said.

"No?" Sierra queried. "Against gay marriage, or just haven't found anyone you want to marry?"

"Well, commitments are a thing, but I've never felt the need to be committed," Kashena said with a wink.

Sierra laughed out loud at that. "Well, I'm sure you have any number of women who'd happily work on changing your opinion."

Kashena glanced over at her, tilting her head. "Now what makes you think that?"

"Uh…" Sierra said, realizing she'd just revealed a little more than she'd meant to. Kashena waited in silence for an answer.

The silence stretched as Sierra debated with herself over how much to tell Kashena. Finally she sighed.

"Well, you're, um… you," Sierra stammered.

"Me?" Kashena repeated.

Sierra blushed furiously, squeezing her eyes shut. No matter what she said, she just backed herself into another corner.

"Sierra?" Kashena queried, saying her name for the first time.

"I meant, well... damn, look at you! And the way you kissed..." Sierra said, mentally wincing at how dumb she sounded.

Kashena grinned. "I only kissed you that one time."

"And I still remember it like it was yesterday," Sierra said matter-of-factly.

"And I wasn't even that good a kisser then," Kashena added.

"So you kiss even better now?" Sierra asked, her tone challenging.

"Gods, I hope so!"

Sierra couldn't help but laugh. It seemed that no matter what she said to Kashena, nothing seemed to really faze her. It was comforting to know.

As the car slid to a smooth stop, Sierra realized they were in front of the hotel. She was surprised. She hadn't even noticed when they got off the freeway; she'd been too involved in the discussion with Kashena. The woman was far too distracting.

They walked inside and located the room where the conference was taking place. People were already milling around. Kashena got Sierra through the crowd and up to the table to sign in for the conference. After walking Sierra into the conference room, Kashena found Sierra's assigned seat.

"Okay," Kashena said, turning to Sierra. "I'm going to go get us checked into the hotel and take the bags up to our room. Unless I miss my guess, they arranged a room with two beds, assuming that as I'm your bodyguard and female too, for security purposes it would be better if we're in the same room. Is that going to be okay?"

"Of course," Sierra said. "As long as you don't mind."

"I sleep with women all the time," Kashena said, grinning. Then she grimaced, realizing that her off-color joke may not be appreciated by the Chief Deputy Attorney General.

Sierra laughed, however, nodding her head. "True. So will you come back here?"

"Yes," Kashena said, glancing at her watch—it was 9:30 a.m. "I'll be back here in two hours for the lunch break." Reaching into her jacket, she pulled out a card and handed it to Sierra. "If you need to leave before that for any reason, just page me and I'll be right here."

"Okay," Sierra said, holding on to the card.

Kashena left then.

True to her word, she was back at eleven thirty, waiting outside when the conference let out for lunch.

Sierra hadn't even seen her when suddenly Kashena appeared at her elbow.

"What would you like to do for lunch?" Kashena asked. "I've checked out the area—we're looking at Chinese, chicken, burgers, pizza, or something here at the hotel."

Sierra was impressed at how organized Kashena was. She never missed a beat.

"What would you like?" Sierra asked.

"I'm easy, I can eat anywhere."

"Any places with a decent salad?" Sierra asked.

"As a matter of fact, I saw a salad place too," Kashena said, smiling as she escorted Sierra out to the car.

They ate lunch companionably, then Kashena took Sierra back to the conference. Like clockwork she was there when the conference ended for the day at 4:30 p.m.

"What's next on your agenda?" Kashena asked as she fell into step beside Sierra.

"Honestly," Sierra said, "I'd like a cool bath and to relax for a little bit."

It was quite warm in Los Angeles. Even though it was early spring, the humidity was high, making it seem even warmer than eighty-five degrees.

"Alright," Kashena said amiably. "Let's go."

She led Sierra up to their room, opening the door and gesturing for Sierra to precede her inside. Sierra noted that Kashena's clothes hung on one side of the small closet, leaving more than half of the closet for Sierra. Kashena had set Sierra's suitcase on one of the beds and hung her garment bag in the closet. Sierra went about unpacking. When she went into the bathroom, she found that Kashena's personal items were set neatly to one side. Shaking her head, Sierra smiled. Kashena was meticulous, that was for sure.

Walking back out into the room, Sierra saw that Kashena was standing at the window looking out. When she heard Sierra, Kashena turned around, smiling.

"While you take your bath and relax, I'm going to go down to the fitness room."

"Okay," Sierra said.

"When I get back, we can figure out what you want to do for dinner." Kashena walked over to the dresser and opened the drawer she had put her clothes in, pulling out some items.

She went into the bathroom and emerged five minutes later, her hair in a ponytail, and wearing a black jog bra and black pants. Sierra did her best not to stare open-mouthed, but there was no way she couldn't look. As she suspected, Kashena's body was in perfect shape. Not one ounce of fat showed on her body—everything was lean muscle, no bulk whatsoever.

Kashena caught Sierra's look and smiled.

"What?" she asked, sitting down to put on her shoes.

"I just want to know where I have to go to buy a body like yours."

Kashena laughed. "I work my ass off to have this body, I'll have you know."

Sierra sighed. "That's what I was afraid of," she said. "I can't just buy one?"

"Not that I know of," Kashena replied, grinning.

"Damn…" Sierra said, shaking her head remorsefully.

Kashena left the room a little while later. Sierra went about taking her bath, her mind continually wandering back to the visceral pleasure of seeing Kashena's long, lean form. She sighed and did her best not to think about it. She was quickly becoming obsessed.

In the end, Kashena was gone for an hour and a half. She came back with a sheen of sweat on her skin. Sitting down, she unlaced her shoes and kicked them off, then got up and set them next to the boots she'd worn that day. Sierra was lying on her bed lazily flipping through TV channels. She'd put jeans and a blue blouse on. She looked comfortable. Her long black hair was back in a braid.

"I'm going to take a shower," Kashena said. "Any thoughts on dinner?"

"Pasta," Sierra said.

"That's the only thought?" Kashena asked with a grin.

"Wine," Sierra added, making Kashena laugh softly.

"You got it, Deputy," she said, smiling.

A half hour later, Kashena emerged from the shower, dressed and her hair back up in a clip. Sierra watched as she took her folded gym clothes and put them in her suitcase, then sat down to put on her boots. Sierra went into the bathroom to touch up her makeup. A few moments later, Kashena walked into the bathroom, reaching around Sierra to pick up the silver chain and pendant that hung on the side of the hair dryer. Watching in the mirror's reflection as Kashena put on the necklace, Sierra remembered it.

"Do you always wear that?" she asked.

Kashena nodded. "I've worn it since I was a kid. My grandmother gave it to me."

Sierra turned around and looked at the pendant, lifting it so she could get a better look. It was the size of a dime. Colored enamel pieces separated it into four areas, white, yellow, red, and black, with a green emerald in the middle. It took Sierra a few moments to recognize the symbol.

"The Council of Three Fires," she said, glancing up at Kashena to see if she was right. She touched the center stone. "Balance," she said, remembering a little about the symbol.

The Council of Three Fires was made up of Ojibwa—otherwise known as Chippewa—Ottawa, and Potawatomi Indians. It was an alliance formed by the three tribes that had been documented as far back as 796 AD.

Kashena smiled. "My grandmother was an elder in our tribe."

"Ojibwa, right?" Sierra said.

"Good memory, Chief."

"But do you remember—" Sierra started to say.

"Kumeyaay," Kashena answered, naming the tribe Sierra was from.

"Very good," Sierra said, winking.

They left for dinner a little while later, finding that the hotel restaurant actually had a good menu, including pasta like Sierra wanted. They decided to stay at the hotel and eat. True to her request, Sierra had pasta as well as two and a half glasses of wine. Kashena drank decaffeinated coffee and had a salad.

"Not hungry?" Sierra asked when Kashena ordered.

"I never eat much at night," Kashena replied.

"That's another reason you look so good," she said, smiling.

Kashena grinned, her eyes sparkling humorously.

"What?" Sierra asked self-consciously.

"Good wine, huh?" Kashena asked, her grin widening.

"I am not drunk," Sierra said, attempting to look offended, but her smile spoiled the effect.

"Yeah," Kashena said, nodding. "That's right up there with 'But ociffer, I'm not as think as you drunk I am.'"

Sierra laughed, shaking her head. "I've never said that."

"Right," Kashena said.

Dinner proceeded, and Sierra found that Kashena was a great dinner companion. Their conversation was interesting without being too heavy. Kashena had a way of expressing herself without denigrating other people's opinions. She also talked using her hands, and her facial expressions were often very animated. More and more, Sierra found herself simply watching Kashena as she talked.

When they were finished with dinner, they lingered over coffee. Kashena had suggested that Sierra have some to help counter the wine. Sierra agreed to drink the coffee as long as Kashena would tell her about Marine basic training.

Kashena talked; Sierra listened and watched.

"Needless to say," Kashena said, wrapping up her story, "once I was out of boot camp my parting shot was to write him a note letting him know that his wife did indeed prefer women."

Sierra laughed. "Shame on you!"

"Hey," Kashena said, as the check came and she reached for it, "he deserved it."

"What are you doing?" Sierra asked as she watched Kashena pull out her credit card and put it in the leather holder with the check.

Kashena shrugged. "It's commonly called paying the check."

"Kashena…" Sierra began, her tone chastising.

"I'm paying for dinner, deal with it," Kashena replied with a smile.

"But that bill is way over per diem rate," Sierra said, reaching for her purse.

"Don't even think about it," Kashena said, putting her hand on Sierra's.

Sierra looked back at Kashena, her emotions warring. For one thing, Kashena's hand was still on hers, and Sierra felt like her nerves were holding their breath, waiting for more. Sierra was sure she made at least twice what Kashena made a month, and it wasn't right for her to have to pay for dinner. Then again, she didn't want to offend Kashena by either pointing that out or insisting on paying at least her share.

Kashena watched the emotions play across Sierra's face, knowing that Sierra was thinking about the fact that as a chief deputy she made much more money, and should therefore pay. The per diem rate for dinner was only eighteen dollars. The bill was easily four times that. Kashena didn't care—she wanted to pay, and she did. Simple as that. She also realized that this was difficult for Sierra, so she gave in a little bit.

"I'll let you pay next time," she said.

Sierra smiled, relieved that she didn't have to feel as concerned now. Little did she know that Kashena had no intention of eating in such an expensive restaurant when Sierra was paying. It was her way. She knew it was antiquated, what would be considered chivalrous, but she didn't give a damn. The waiter, who'd been eyeing both women all night, took the check and came back a few minutes later with the credit card receipt. Kashena added the tip and signed the receipt, pocketing her credit card. Standing up, she waited for Sierra to get her purse and stand, then gestured for Sierra to precede her out of the restaurant. The waiter watched them go, sighing to himself. Two beautiful women, and a good tipper, the blond one.

Back up in the room, Sierra decided to take a shower to "clear" her head. Kashena grinned knowingly. By the time Sierra emerged from the shower, Kashena had changed into her comfortable clothes. She wore plaid flannel pants and a dark gray jog bra. She was sitting on the bed with her knees up to her chest, one arm draped casually over one knee. In her other hand she held her cell phone. The most amazing thing of all to Sierra was that Kashena's hair was down. It flowed around and two inches past her shoulders in a silken dark-gold curtain.

Sierra stood staring at Kashena while she talked on the phone. Her eyes were fixed on Kashena's face, framed so beautifully by her hair.

Kashena smiled, noting the dumbfounded look, but assuming it had to do with the alcohol in Sierra's veins rather than anything she was actually seeing.

"My charge is out of the shower, Baz," she said, winking at Sierra. "I need to go sober her up. I'll talk to you tomorrow."

She laughed at something the other person said, then said goodbye. Sierra sat down right by where Kashena's feet were planted on the bed. Kashena put her phone down and draped her arms over her knees, her eyes surveying Sierra's face.

"That shower didn't help much, did it?" Kashena asked.

"It helped," Sierra insisted. "I feel really, really good right now."

Kashena pursed her lips as she attempted not to grin.

"I'm not drunk!" Sierra insisted.

"Right…" Kashena nodded, sounding unconvinced.

Sierra narrowed her dark eyes. "You know…" she said in a warning tone.

"No, what?" Kashena asked with an indulgent smile.

Sierra made an impatient noise in the back of her throat, causing Kashena's grin to widen.

"Stop it," Sierra said, her voice a whine now.

"Okay, I'll stop," Kashena said placatingly.

Sierra gave her an assessing look. "Do you have any idea how much more beautiful you are when your hair is down?"

Kashena was caught totally off guard by the comment. Her mouth dropped open, then she started to shake her head.

"And don't think that this is the alcohol talking," Sierra warned. "I thought you were beautiful in college too, only I never saw you with your hair down."

"True," Kashena said. "You only ever saw me in uniform then."

"And with your hair up every time I've seen you recently too," Sierra put in accusingly.

"It's more professional."

"Well, I like it down," Sierra said petulantly.

Kashena nodded, her lips tugging at the corners.

"You're still writing this off to alcohol, aren't you?" Sierra asked.

Kashena slowly expelled a deep breath and nodded again.

"Okay," Sierra said, her tone changing slightly, "how about this? Remember I told you that I remembered that kiss you gave me like it was yesterday?"

"Uh-huh."

"Well, what I didn't tell you is that after you disappeared on me, I went about dating women for the next four years or so."

"You did?" Kashena asked, shocked in spite of herself.

"Yes," Sierra said.

"And apparently you swung back the other way," Kashena replied knowingly.

"Yes," Sierra said, sitting forward, her eyes staring directly into Kashena's. "Because no one made me feel like you did with one kiss."

Kashena stared back at her, unable to think past what she'd just heard. Then reason kicked in.

"How many women did you date?" she asked.

"A lot."

"How many?" Kashena repeated.

"I don't know, maybe ten or so," Sierra said. "That's not the point. The point is that no matter what they did, no matter how hard they tried, how pretty, how butch, how smart they were, none of them did for me what you did."

Kashena pursed her lips, her mind churning. Finally she shrugged, sitting back against the headboard of the bed.

"It was the excitement of the unknown the first time," she said.

"No," Sierra said. "It was you."

Kashena shook her head, unconvinced.

Sierra stared at her for a long moment. Then, without warning, she moved forward, up between Kashena's knees. Bringing her face within an inch of Kashena's, Sierra stared into the other woman's eyes.

"It was you," she repeated, moving to lightly touch her lips to Kashena's.

Kashena pulled back, searching the other woman's eyes, then she moved in again, her lips taking possession of Sierra's. Sierra moaned immediately, her hands moving into Kashena's hair as Kashena cupped her cheek gently, her other hand moving to the back of Sierra's head. The kiss was passionate and excited, and there was no denying the fire that ignited between them. They kissed for a long time, hands grasping at each other. When Kashena broke the kiss, her breath coming in heated gasps, Sierra moaned unhappily. She lowered her head to Kashena's ear.

"Please don't stop, Kash," she whispered, her voice husky. "I want you so much…" Her voice trailed off as she kissed Kashena's ear.

Kashena's hold tightened as she guided Sierra's face back to hers and kissed her again. There was no stopping then. Kissing and caressing, they grew more and more excited. Kashena slid her hand under the camisole top Sierra wore over silk bottoms. Sierra groaned heatedly. She pulled the top over her head, tossing it aside, desperate for Kashena's hands on her bare skin. Minutes later, the bottoms followed the top and Sierra lay naked against Kashena. At that point, Kashena had only caressed her skin; as if inflamed by her nakedness, however, Kashena finally began touching more sensitive spots.

Sierra cried out as she felt Kashena's hands slide across her nipples. Her body responded wildly, aching and tightening at the same time. Sierra was still lying over Kashena, who was half sitting up against the headboard.

"Come here," Kashena murmured as she lifted Sierra's body, sliding it upwards a few inches.

Sierra was sure she was going to explode when Kashena's mouth closed over a hardened nipple.

"My God, my God…" Sierra groaned, pressing her body closer to Kashena's mouth. "Please, please…" she chanted, feeling her body go wild with sensations.

Kashena's hand slid down Sierra's back as her fingers closed over her other nipple, her mouth still sucking at the first. Sierra stopped breathing as she waited in heated anticipation for Kashena to touch her. She felt Kashena's hand slide further down, over the backs of her thighs. She trembled in anticipation. Suddenly, she felt Kashena's fingers slip between her legs and touch her. Cool fingers against moist heat, and Sierra was exploding, crying out over and over again. It went on and on, subsiding slightly, then coming back again in waves. By the time it was over, Sierra was trembling against Kashena, resting her head against the top of Kashena's.

As she did her best to catch her breath, Sierra felt Kashena's hand at the bottom of the long braid she wore. She felt tugging, then the braid was loosened. Kashena's fingers slid through the long tresses, releasing it from the braid. Sierra's hair fell almost to her waist.

"I always loved your hair," Kashena said, her voice reflecting awe.

Sierra pulled back, looking down at her. "Why?" she asked softly.

Kashena picked up a handful of Sierra's jet-black hair, caressing it gently between her fingers. "Because," she said, her eyes connecting with Sierra's, "it's the hair of our people, this rich black silk."

Sierra felt a tug at her heart. Kashena was one of her people, Indian like her.

Leaning down, Sierra kissed Kashena, her lips saying without words what her heart was thinking. Kashena buried her hands in Sienna's hair as they kissed. Sierra's hands slid over Kashena's skin, making Kashena shudder. Slowly but surely, Sierra worked up the confidence to touch Kashena as Kashena had her.

Sierra moved her lips down to Kashena's neck, hearing Kashena suck in her breath sharply. Spurred on by that, Sierra kissed Kashena's neck again, sucking at her skin.

"God…" Kashena said, her voice a moan.

Sierra moved lower, kissing down to Kashena's breast, which was still covered by her jog bra. She slid her hand over Kashena's nipple, hard through the material. Getting brave, Sierra pulled the material up. Kashena assisted her further by pulling the top off. Sierra's mouth hovered over her nipple. Kashena's hand was at the back of her head, applying slight pressure, her body arching against Sierra in silent pleading. When her mouth closed over Kashena's nipple, Kashena's body arched higher and she gasped deeply. Sierra continued moving her mouth over Kashena's nipple, her other hand caressing the other nipple.

"Sierra... Sierra..." Kashena murmured, her body straining against Sierra's.

Sierra felt a sense of power and excitement building in her. Feeling Kashena's reactions to her touch only excited her more. Kashena had been the object of so many fantasies years before, and now it was really happening. Moving her hands to the waist of Kashena's pants, Sierra pushed at them. Kashena obliged her by lifting her hips, and moments later both the pants and Kashena's underwear were on the floor. Sierra slid her tongue over Kashena's nipple again, gliding her hand downward, as she felt Kashena's hands touching her again. Sierra felt aroused beyond anything she'd ever felt before. As she touched Kashena for the first time, feeling the excitement she had created, an overwhelming sense of complete ecstasy washed over her. Kashena cried out, arching against her, and Kashena's fingers slid deep inside her, making Sierra come yet again, their voices mingling in their release.

Afterwards they lay together, neither of them moving, just lying together, absorbing the sensations they'd just felt and caused. Sierra's head rested on Kashena's chest. Kashena's hand was in Sierra's hair, the other hand still at the back of Sierra's thigh. One of Sierra's hands rested on Kashena's hip, the other on Kashena's shoulder.

"Do you realize," Kashena said breathlessly, "that there are experienced lesbians who can't make me come?"

Sierra lifted her head. "Really?" she asked, surprised.

Kashena nodded, an astounded look on her face. Sierra bit her lip, happy at that thought. She rested her head against Kashena again.

It was a long time before either of them spoke again. Sierra broke the silence first, glancing up at Kashena.

"Kash?" she queried softly.

"Hmm?"

"You never really said… Do you have someone in your life?" Sierra asked, her voice still soft.

Kashena opened her eyes and looked down at Sierra, still amazed at what had just happened between them and at how much Sierra affected her. Finally she nodded.

"I have someone living with me."

Sierra's eyes widened.

"It's not really serious," Kashena felt compelled to add. "I mean, she shows up for a few months, usually screws me over in the process, and leaves again."

Sierra felt immediate dislike for a woman she didn't even know.

"Why do you let her do that to you?" Sierra asked.

Kashena laughed softly. "Now you sound like Baz."

"Baz?"

"Sebastian Bach. He's my partner and my best friend."

"And he doesn't like this woman either?" Sierra said.

Kashena grinned, noting that Sierra had said "either," meaning she already didn't like Linda too.

"He hates her with a passion," Kashena said.

"I like him already."

Kashena laughed. "He'll be happy to hear he has another ally in the war against Linda."

"That's her name?"

"Yes."

Sierra nodded. "So, how long have you known Baz?"

"About ten years," Kashena said. "We met in the military."

"Was he a Marine too?"

"No, he was an Army Ranger," Kashena said.

"I thought the branches of the service never got along," Sierra said.

"Which explains why the first time we met, we had a knock-down, drag-out fight."

"You fought with him?" Sierra asked, her tone shocked.

"Yep," Kashena said. "And when he could hold his own against me, I decided he wasn't such a bad guy."

Sierra laughed, shaking her head. "That's crazy."

"That's military," Kashena replied.

"I guess…" Sierra said. "But now he's your best friend?"

"Yep," Kashena said. "He knows me better than anyone."

"So I should definitely align myself with him," Sierra said, grinning.

"Uh-huh…" Kashena smiled.

They were both silent then, falling asleep a little while later. Sierra's last thought before she drifted off was that she'd never felt so good.

Kashena and Sierra woke at the same time the second morning of the conference. Sierra woke to the sensation of Kashena's warmth next to her. When Kashena felt Sierra stir, she opened her eyes, looking down at the other woman. She was half convinced that Sierra would quickly remember and regret the night before. That thought was squashed when Sierra kissed Kashena on the lips softly.

"Good morning to you too," Kashena said, smiling.

Sierra snuggled closer to Kashena, enjoying the feel of being with her.

"It's crazy," she said, her face buried against Kashena's neck.

"What is?"

"How good this feels," Sierra said, sighing.

Kashena smiled, unaccountably pleased that Sierra felt that way.

The alarm on the nightstand went off, and Sierra groaned audibly. Kashena reached across Sierra, turning the alarm off.

"Can't we just skip the conference this morning?" Sierra asked petulantly.

"The AG will be here," Kashena reminded her.

"Damn," Sierra said, grinning.

"Do you want me to take the first shower so you can rest some more?"

"I don't want to rest," Sierra replied, her eyes sparkling mischievously.

"No?" Kashena asked with a smile.

"Uh-uh," Sierra said, moving to kiss her again.

Minutes later they were making love. The alarm went off again; Kashena reached blindly for it as she and Sierra continued to kiss. Eventually, she yanked the plug out of the wall. Sierra laughed softly, then gasped when Kashena's lips touched her body again.

Afterwards, they lay together, trying to catch their breath.

"Okay, I'm taking a shower," Kashena said, after reaching over to check her watch that lay on the nightstand.

"We could take one together and save time," Sierra suggested.

Kashena kissed her lips again. "If we take a shower together, honey, we'll never get downstairs."

Sierra bit her lip, liking that Kashena had just called her "honey" and also liking that she seemed to be enjoying their new intimacy as much as Sierra herself was.

In the end, Kashena took her shower, and Sierra took hers right afterwards. Even so, Sierra was ten minutes late for the conference. Twenty minutes into the session, Kashena walked in quietly, setting coffee and a bagel down in front of Sierra. Sierra glanced at Kashena, smiling brilliantly up at her. Kana, who'd just entered, escorting Midnight, caught the look. Her lips quirked in a grin, which Midnight saw.

"What?" Midnight asked.

"Nothing," Kana replied, schooling her features.

Midnight narrowed her gold-green eyes at Kana, but everyone had noticed her entrance by that time, so she wasn't able to question the big Samoan any further.

Minutes later, while Midnight was talking to the group, Kashena walked into the lounge just outside of the conference room. Kana was sitting in one of the chairs. Tiny was on his phone over near the bar.

"So how's it going, Marshal?" Kana asked warmly.

"It's going alright," Kashena said, sitting down across from Kana.

Kana gave her a considering look. "The chief deputy told me you rescued her once, back in college. Is that true?"

Kashena canted her head, sensing a slight undercurrent in the question, but nodded. "She had a rather ardent admirer that didn't want to take no for an answer."

"Seems to be a problem for her," Kana said, smiling.

Kashena chuckled. "Women like that just seem to attract them."

Kana's phone rang. Excusing herself, Kana stood up, moving toward the window to talk. Kashena sat in her chair, wondering if Kana suspected what had taken place between her and Sierra. She hoped not. It wasn't exactly professional to be sleeping with the person you were protecting. Not unheard of, just not professional. Besides the fact that it was a same-sex issue, Sierra was also married. She was also a Chief Deputy Attorney General. Kashena felt the prickling of guilt starting, even though Kana said nothing more about Sierra.

Later in the morning, Kashena was standing looking out the window of the lounge when a vision hit her. It was vivid, and she inhaled sharply at the pain that shot through her head as the vision was burned into her brain. Throwing up her hand in front of her face, as if to block the vision, Kashena withstood it, bracing herself with a hand on the window.

Kana glanced over, seeing Kashena suddenly put her hand up almost defensively. She strode over to Kashena, who was now panting and looking like she was in severe pain.

"Are you okay?" Kana asked, her tone worried.

Kashena nodded, although she looked anything but okay.

"Tiny!" Kana called.

Tiny walked over, his eyes on Kashena.

"What's wrong?" Tiny asked, his eyes going from Kashena to Kana.

"I don't know," Kana said. "Marshal, are you okay?"

Kashena nodded again, one hand at her stomach, the other still shading her eyes. She wavered then, and Tiny picked up the smaller woman in his arms, even as Kashena protested the necessity.

"I'm okay," she said, her voice weak.

"Yeah, we can see that," Tiny said, grinning. "What's your room number?"

"424."

"I'll take her up," Tiny said to Kana. "You stay here, and let the chief deputy know I'll stay on her detail until Marshal feels better."

Kana nodded. "Will do."

"Wait…" Kashena inserted feebly.

"Not likely," Tiny said, striding toward the elevators.

Two minutes later he was opening the door to Kashena and Sierra's hotel room. The maid hadn't been into the room yet. Tiny noted that only one bed looked slept in, but he said nothing. He carefully laid Kashena down on the bed, moving back to look down at her. She looked pale.

"What happened?" he asked.

Kashena shook her head. "I just have a migraine. I'm okay."

Tiny sensed there was more to it than that. "Well, rest," he said. "I'll take care of Chief Deputy Youngblood today."

Kashena started to protest and caught Tiny's stern look. Finally she nodded. "Okay."

"Good," he replied with a grin.

He left the room a few minutes later, after closing the curtains to shut out the light, and turning on the air conditioner.

Kashena lay on the bed, feeling sick to her stomach. She kicked off her boots and put her arm over her eyes, lying there until she fell asleep.

She woke to the feeling of someone touching her cheek. Opening her eyes and moving her arm slightly, she saw Sierra kneeling on the bed next to her, looking very concerned.

"SAC Sorbinno said you almost collapsed," she said, her voice worried. "Are you okay?"

Kashena put her hand out, touching Sierra's arm. "I'm okay," she said. "It's just a migraine."

"SAS Ako said it came on rather suddenly," Sierra said.

"Happens like that," Kashena said. "It has since I was little."

"Is there anything you can take for it?"

"I have some herbs that I got from the healer," Kashena said, grimacing. "I just didn't want to get up and deal with them."

"Where are they?" Sierra asked.

"In my bag."

Sierra got off the bed and went to the closet where Kashena's suitcase was.

"The side pocket," Kashena told her.

"Found it," Sierra said, pulling out the black pouch and opening it.

"Don't you worry you'll get arrested for marijuana?" Sierra asked with a grin. The herbs closely resembled the plant.

Kashena chuckled. "I've been questioned before, trust me."

"I'll bet," Sierra said. "So what should I put these in? Tea?"

Kashena smiled, liking that Sierra knew about herbs. "That's usually how I take them, yeah."

Sierra walked into the bathroom and used the coffee pot there to brew the herbs. A few minutes later she knelt next to Kashena, holding a cup.

Kashena sat up slowly, feeling her stomach lurch. Taking the cup from Sierra, she took a drink.

"I used sugar," Sierra said. "I figured that would help."

"It does," Kashena said. "The healer never does worry about taste."

"If it tastes good it doesn't work," Sierra said with a smile.

"Exactly," Kashena said, laughing softly.

When she'd finished the medicine, she handed Sierra back the cup. "Thank you," she said, touching Sierra on the cheek gently.

"You're welcome." Sierra smiled.

Kashena lay back down, and Sierra put aside the cup then sat next to Kashena on the bed. She smoothed her hand over Kashena's hair.

111

"Mmm…" Kashena murmured. "My mother used to do that when I got these as a kid."

Leaning against the headboard, Sierra turned to face Kashena and continued to stroke her hair soothingly. Kashena closed her eyes, sighing softly. It felt good to have someone take care of her for a change. Kashena was always the care-taker, and for once she was being cared for.

She reached her hand out to touch Sierra's waist. Sierra moved down on the bed, lying next to Kashena and continuing to soothe her. Kashena dozed, feeling the effects of the herbs. When she woke half an hour later she felt better. Sierra was still lying with her, her hand on Kashena's shoulder. Squeezing Sierra's waist slightly, Kashena opened her eyes. Sierra smiled at her.

"I can see that you feel better," she said. "I was really worried about you."

"I know," Kashena said, smiling, "and I appreciate that. It's nice for a change."

"Your girlfriend doesn't worry about you?" Sierra asked, surprised.

"Linda worries about herself. She doesn't have the capacity to worry about anyone else."

Sierra made a face, but she didn't want to attack Kashena's girlfriend, sensing it wasn't the right thing to do at this point.

"Do your migraines always come on so suddenly?" Sierra asked.

Kashena hesitated, then nodded. "I used to get them all the time when I was young, and then they eased up a bit for a while. Now they seem to be back."

"No cause has been determined?"

Kashena didn't answer, her look once again hesitant.

"What is it?" Sierra asked.

Kashena blew her breath out slowly, making a decision in her own mind. "I get these visions…"

Sierra's eyes widened instantly. "You have the sight?" she asked, her voice awed.

Kashena grinned. It figured that Sierra would know exactly what she was talking about.

"Yeah," she answered. "My grandmother was the tribe Seer."

"And you inherited her gift."

"Yeah," Kashena said wryly. "Lucky me."

"So what did you see?" Sierra asked.

Kashena's face became serious. "I'm not totally sure, but it wasn't good."

"What was it?" Sierra asked, worried.

"Two eagles in a bloody battle," Kashena said, her tone grave.

"And what do you think it meant?"

Kashena shrugged, doing her best to be casual. "Eagles are a symbol of pride."

"And strength," Sierra added.

"And the Marines," Kashena countered.

Sierra looked shocked, but then nodded. "Are your visions usually about you?"

"Not always," Kashena answered. "I just don't know this time."

"What do you think it means?" Sierra asked, sensing that Kashena had a definite opinion on that.

Kashena didn't answer for a long moment, then she sighed. "I'm afraid it means I'm in for a battle."

Sierra nodded slowly. She didn't want to ask if Kashena meant with another Marine. She didn't want to push her luck. Kashena had already accepted a lot of things about her that Sierra had been sure would be a problem. She didn't want to find out just how much Kashena could deal with.

"What happened to Marshal?" Midnight asked Kana that afternoon at lunch.

Sierra had been worried sick about Kashena and had insisted on skipping lunch to go up and make sure she was okay.

"I don't know," Kana said. "One minute she was fine, the next she looked like she was going to throw up or pass out or both."

Midnight looked perplexed. "What did she tell you it was?"

"She said it was a migraine," Tiny put in.

"They come on that fast?" Midnight asked.

"Not that I know of," Kana said, shaking her head.

Midnight nodded, her mind churning the thought over. She always worried when one of her people was down for any reason. It was her nature. Anyone loyal to her earned her loyalty in return. Along with that came her concern.

"K, go up and check on her, will you?" Midnight asked when they got up from lunch a little while later.

"Chief Deputy Youngblood is up there now," Kana said cautiously.

"So?" Midnight asked. "What difference does that make?"

"I, uh," Kana stammered, then nodded. "I'll go up."

"K," Midnight said, putting her hand on Kana's arm, "what's going on in your head?"

"Just a hunch," Kana said in a mysterious tone.

"About?"

"About Kashena and Chief Deputy Youngblood," Kana replied.

Midnight looked back at her for a moment, then it occurred to her what Kana was saying. "You mean you think…"

"I don't know," Kana said, unwilling to say anything at this point.

"So go find out," Midnight said.

Kana's eyes searched Midnight's.

"I'm curious," Midnight said, shrugging, her eyes averted from Kana's.

Kana narrowed her eyes, then nodded.

Five minutes later, Kana knocked on the door to Kashena and Sierra's room. Sierra answered a minute later.

"SAC Sorbinno," she said, smiling up at Kana.

"I was just checking on Agent Marshal," Kana said, by way of explanation.

"Of course," Sierra said, opening the door wider. "Come in."

Kana walked into the room and noted the same thing Tiny had: only one bed was unmade; the other still looked like it hadn't been slept in.

Kashena caught Kana's look at the other bed and knew that the other woman knew. Kashena had changed into her comfortable clothes and was sitting up on the bed, her knees up to her chest, her arms draped over her knees.

"How are you feeling, Marshal?" Kana asked, nothing of what she suspected in her voice.

"Better," Kashena said, inclining her head. "Thanks for checking."

Kana's eyes connected with Kashena's. "Midnight wanted me to make sure you're alright."

Kashena's eyes widened a little as she nodded slowly. Kana nodded too, then turned to Sierra.

"Chief Deputy Youngblood, will you be coming back down to the conference?"

Sierra looked surprised by the question, then glanced at Kashena. It was all Kana needed to see. They were definitely involved. Kana waited in silence for Sierra's answer, seeing Kashena drop her head out of the corner of her eye. Kashena knew that had been telling. Sierra's concern for her bodyguard outweighed her concern for propriety.

"I—" Sierra stammered. "Yes, I'll be right down."

Kana glanced at Kashena again.

"I'll wait outside for you," Kana said, turning and walking from the room.

Sierra stared after Kana, then looked at Kashena in askance.

"She knows," Kashena said.

"How?" Sierra asked, looking shocked.

"She's good," Kashena said, amazed at Kana's instincts.

Sierra nodded slowly.

"Well, I guess I better get down there," she said. "Are you okay?"

"Yeah," Kashena answered. "Just make sure you stay with Kana or Tiny."

"I will," Sierra assured her.

They looked at each other. Sierra wanted to touch her, to kiss her or something, but somehow she was worried Kana Sorbinno would sense that too. Somehow Sierra knew it wasn't a good thing that Kana had figured them out. Now she was worried.

Kana was silent on the ride down in the elevator. Sierra did her best not to appear nervous.

That evening, Kana sat with Midnight and Tiny in Midnight's hotel room.

"So they're involved?" Midnight asked.

"Definitely," Kana said.

116

Midnight nodded, her mind working. "Think anyone else figured it out?"

"I doubt it," Kana said. "I just happen to know Sierra's story, and I saw how she reacted when I said Kashena was going to protect her."

Midnight nodded again.

"What are you going to do?" Kana asked, her voice even.

Midnight canted her head to the side. "What do you think I should do?"

Kana looked surprised at the question, then shrugged. "I guess that depends on your opinion of the situation."

Midnight narrowed her eyes slightly. "What's yours?"

"Mine doesn't matter," Kana said.

"It does to me," Midnight countered.

"Why?"

"Because, Kana, you understand lesbian relationships better than I do. Do you think it's going to be a problem?"

"Which part?" Kana asked, putting her hand on the table between them. "The part where she's married? To a man? The part where she's a Chief Deputy Attorney General for your criminal division, therefore very high profile? Or the fact that Kashena is her bodyguard and should therefore be objective where her charge is concerned?"

Midnight looked surprised at Kana's diatribe. She glanced at Tiny.

"What about you?" she asked.

Tiny looked pensive. "I don't know how much we have a right to interfere."

"They both work for Midnight, Tiny," Kana said.

"True," Tiny said, "but it's their private lives."

"They're conducting it while at a state conference."

"Not in the conference room, they're not," Tiny countered.

Kana narrowed her eyes at him. He narrowed his back at her.

Midnight grinned—they were like two kids sometimes.

She sighed then. "I made Sierra my chief deputy because I trust her judgment. I'm just going to have to trust that she'll use good judgment where Agent Marshal is concerned."

Kana nodded, not looking convinced.

"We need to be extremely careful," Kashena told Sierra that night.

"In terms of what?" Sierra asked.

"In terms of us," Kashena said. "If Kana knows, you can bet the AG knows now too."

Sierra nodded. "Do you honestly think they'll say something?"

"I think if we're not careful to be professional in public they will."

"I can't imagine you ever being anything but professional in public, Kashena," Sierra said.

Kashena smiled. "You might make it difficult."

"Why?" Sierra asked, her eyes shining.

Kashena leaned down, kissing her lips, then moved in closer to deepen the kiss. She pulled back when they were both breathless.

"That's why," Kashena said.

"Ohh…" Sierra replied, smiling brightly. "I think I like that."

"Having power?"

"Having power over you," Sierra said, her dark eyes sparkling.

"We'll see about that," Kashena said, kissing her again.

They stopped talking then, but Sierra had understood what Kashena was saying. This wasn't something they should be public about. Both their jobs could be in danger if they were.

Chapter 4

Things between Cat and Elizabeth only got worse after they got back from Los Angeles. Elizabeth spent all hours at her restaurant and bar, both named after Cat. She came home later and later. Cat sensed something was going on but didn't have the desire to fight with her about it. Cat worked more and more, taking every case she could get her hands on. Before long she was exhausted, and it showed.

Kana and Cat had lunch one day, since they hadn't seen each other in a couple of weeks. Kana noticed Cat's fatigue right away.

"What the hell are you doing to yourself?" she asked, having heard that Cat was overdoing it, and able to tell just from the way she was acting.

"Nothing, K, I'm just working," Cat said, leaning back on Kana's patio and smoking.

"Yeah," Kana said as she lit a cigarette, "and I'm supposed to buy that, right?"

"Yeah, you are," Cat said, grinning.

"Take off the shades," Kana said seriously.

"It's bright out here."

"Take them off, Catalina."

Cat stared at her, shaking her head. Kana leaned forward with a menacing look, her hand pointedly placed on the table between them. Cat looked at Kana's hand, a half grin on her lips.

"Think you're faster than me, K?"

"I think if you don't take those shades off now, we'll find out," Kana said ominously.

Cat sighed. "I look like shit, okay? I know that."

Kana narrowed her eyes. "Why are you overworking yourself?"

Cat shrugged. "There's a lot of bad people out there, K."

"Don't pull that shit with me," Kana said evenly.

Cat said nothing, merely leaning back and taking a long drag of her cigarette.

"You and Elizabeth are still having problems?" Kana guessed accurately.

Cat looked considering, studying her nails, then shrugged. "Everyone has problems."

"You know, you're starting to piss me off," Kana said.

Cat stood up, dropping her cigarette and stubbing it out with a sandaled foot.

"I'll leave then. I don't want to stress you out," she said, her voice sincere.

Kana tossed away her cigarette and reached up as Cat walked by. Grabbing Cat's hand, she pulled her down onto her lap. Cat's chin came up, her lips pursed in defensiveness. Kana gently took off Cat's sunglasses. She gave Cat a pained look when she saw how tired the other woman was.

"Ah, babe…" Kana said, shaking her head.

Cat took her sunglasses out of Kana's hand and put them back on.

"It's no big deal, K," Cat said dismissively. "I just need some sleep."

"Yeah, about a week's worth," Kana said.

Cat smiled weakly. "Thereabouts."

Kana shook her head, knowing that Cat wasn't going to talk. Cat reminded Kana a lot of Midnight, especially when the AG was younger. If she didn't want to talk about her feelings, she didn't, and that was that.

"Stay," Kana said, reaching up to touch Cat's cheek. "Have lunch—you look like you need it."

Cat grinned. "You saying I'm too thin for you now?"

Kana's lips quirked. "I'm saying you look like you've lost weight, and I want you to get it back."

"Yes, ma'am," Cat said, her eyes sparkling.

Fact was, Cat was losing weight. She rarely ate anymore. Nothing appealed to her. Her appetite had always centered on whether or not she was happy. Fortunately, when she was unhappy she didn't eat, rather than the other way around. These days, if she was a depression eater she'd weigh three hundred pounds. She'd actually dropped fifteen pounds, which was considerable on her small frame.

At the office she was a source of worry for her teammates. Christian, Stevie, Kevin, and Jeanie had all noticed her weight loss and the fact that she was working too much.

"Think she's even sleeping at all anymore?" Stevie asked Christian one morning, when they got in at 7 a.m. and noted Cat seemed to have been there for a long time before that.

Christian shook his head. "Doesn't look like it."

"Think Dave's noticed?" Stevie asked.

"Dave's not as alert as he normally would be. I don't think Dave junior is even sleeping through the night yet."

Dave Dibbins had a one-year-old son. A child that had been born at the height of a vicious winter storm the year before. Almost the entire Gang had been present for the birth, since they'd all been at Joe's for Thanksgiving dinner at the time. As their supervisor, Dave was usually quite aware of everything going on in the two narcotics units he supervised. Christian just doubted it right now because Dave looked tired consistently these days.

"Should we mention it?" Stevie asked, glancing across at Cat.

"And have her pissed at us for the rest of the year?" Christian asked.

"Good point," Stevie said, rolling her eyes.

"We'll just keep an eye on her," he said.

"When she crashes it's not going to be pretty."

"No doubt," Christian said, his lips twitching in concern.

Cat had become friends with Christian when they had been working on the same undercover case. Informing Christian that she was bisexual had been one of the first things she'd done. Neither of them had known the other was a cop, though, until Cat had gone to arrest him. She had worked for the San Diego Sheriff's Department at the time. He'd shown her his San Diego Police Department badge then. The following day, Cat had gone to Christian's house to have him sign some paperwork to finish up her case. That was when she'd met Stevie.

The three of them had spent the afternoon and evening together, ending up in bed. Cat had joined Rogue Squadron shortly after that. The three of them hadn't been together since then, since Cat got involved with a then-single Kana soon after. The experience had, however, cemented her friendship with Stevie and Christian. They were constantly on their guard to protect her.

Later that morning, Kyle called down to Dave and asked him to send one of his narcs upstairs. Dave asked Cat to go, since she was closest to his office at the time.

"Lucky me," Cat said, grinning.

At Kyle's door, she knocked.

"Come in," Kyle called.

Cat walked in, looking around. Kyle Masterson had been promoted to chief when Midnight Chevalier had become Attorney General. Previously he'd been the assistant chief. Midnight herself had recommended Kyle for the job of chief. She trusted him to maintain the department she'd worked so hard to improve. In being promoted, Kyle had remained in the office he'd occupied as assistant chief, not wanting to move into Midnight's territory. He'd yet to hire another assistant chief. He was thinking about promoting someone in-house, but hadn't had time to make a decision yet.

"You wanted to see a narc, Chief?" Cat asked, glancing at the woman sitting in front of Kyle's desk, then looking again.

The woman smiled; it was a world-famous smile. Sable, that was the name she went by and had for years now. A very popular rock star, Sable had been in the charts for many years. She was consistently compared to Melissa Etheridge, not just for her hard-edged style, but for the fact that she was openly gay. Sable fit her name perfectly, with her rich mane of chestnut-brown hair, warm chocolate-brown eyes, and richly tanned skin. She wore brown leather pants, dark brown leather boots, and a black camisole top. Her body was toned and cut with muscle. Cat couldn't believe she was actually standing in front of the woman.

She hid her shock well, however—she merely inclined her head to Sable, then looked back to Kyle.

"Ms. Sands," Kyle said, "this is Sergeant Catalina Roché. She works in one of the narcotics units."

Sable extended her hand to Cat, her eyes meeting Cat's very directly. Cat looked back at the superstar, extending her hand as she stepped forward.

"Narcs don't look like they used to," Sable said, her voice rich and husky. She smiled, her eyes still staring into Cat's.

"Well, we still have some that look like they used to," Cat said, smiling, "but it's not only a boys' game anymore."

Sable didn't reply, just stared at Cat, thinking what a beautiful woman she was. Cat didn't look away, keeping her eyes on the other woman's. The rock star was the first to break the look, glancing over at Kyle, who'd watched the exchange quietly. Cat looked at Kyle too, and he merely raised an eyebrow slightly, then gestured for Cat to sit down.

When they were seated, Cat waited for Kyle to explain why she was there.

"Ms. Sands had an incident late last night," Kyle said, looking from Sable over to Cat. "And I'm tending to think it was drug related."

Cat nodded slowly, her face serious. "Is this the shooting I heard about?"

"Probably," Kyle said, nodding. "Ms. Sands' bodyguard was shot. It's believed that they interrupted a drug deal."

"Believed?" Cat queried.

"We drove up on it," Sable said.

Again Cat nodded, not convinced, but willing to concede the point right then.

"Cat, I'd like you to go with Ms. Sands to the scene and see what you can come up with from there."

"You got it," Cat said.

Ten minutes later, Cat led Sable out to her dark blue Chevy Blazer.

Once in the car, Cat reached for a cigarette. "Do you mind?" she asked the other woman, holding up the pack of cigarettes.

"No," Sable answered. "As long as you don't mind if I smoke too."

"Not a problem," Cat replied.

As Cat started the Blazer, Linkin Park blared from the stereo speakers. Cat reached over, turning down the stereo.

"Linkin Park?" Sable asked.

"Yeah." Cat grinned. "My partner got me into them."

"Partner?" Sable said, her tone almost hopeful.

"Yeah, you know—narc, cop stuff," Cat said. "He loves this stuff."

Sable nodded, looking disappointed.

"Besides," Cat added with a grin, "my girlfriend doesn't like the hard stuff."

"Girlfriend?" Sable queried.

"Uh-huh."

"So you are gay?" Sable asked, nodding as if confirming something to herself.

"Uh-huh," Cat replied.

"But you have a girlfriend," Sable said, shaking her head ruefully.

"At this point," Cat said, slightly irritated.

"Really?" Sable asked. "Problems?"

"Enough," Cat said wryly. "So," she said, changing the subject before things got too personal, "where did this happen?"

"Downtown," Sable said. "I think it was at the corner of Broadway and Market."

Cat nodded, driving out of the lot and heading toward downtown.

"So tell me what happened."

"We got turned around when we left the Sports Arena last night," Sable said. "We were trying to get back to the Intercontinental. We had just stopped at a light when my bodyguard noticed two men hassling another man. He told the driver to hold on and got out to see what he could do. When he got out, one of the men turned and shot him."

Sable's voice was tremulous, and Cat couldn't help but touch her hand in empathy.

Sable nodded, doing her best to regain her composure.

"What did the two men look like?" Cat asked.

"They were black, both of them tall."

"What were they wearing?"

"Both of them had on jeans and dark shirts, T-shirts."

"Any colors?" Cat asked.

"Colors?"

"Yeah, you know, bandanas, wrist bands, something," Cat replied.

"Yes," Sable said. "They both had red bandanas—one had it sticking out of his pocket, the other had his under a baseball cap."

"Shit…" Cat muttered under her breath.

"What?" Sable asked.

"We've been hearing noise about the Bloods trying to move in on some of the drug business here, but this is the first proof."

Sable nodded.

Cat looked over at her, her eyes narrowing slightly. "You weren't the one making the deal, were you?"

"No," Sable answered, looking shocked that Cat was asking.

"You aren't lying to me?" Cat asked.

Sable looked at Cat, her rich brown eyes steady and unaffected. "Sergeant, if I get any narcotics, I don't buy them myself, nor do I go to street-level dealers."

Cat grinned. "This narc didn't just hear the part about 'if you get narcotics.'"

"Good," Sable replied, chuckling.

Cat chuckled too.

They drove to the spot where the shooting took place. Cat parked the Blazer and got out, telling Sable to stay in the vehicle. Then she went about checking out the area. She also talked to a few people nearby. Sable found herself watching Cat's every move, fascinated. Cat was wearing jeans that fit perfectly on her petite shape, and a cropped navy blue camisole top. She also wore brown dress boots with a two-inch heel, and a brown belt that matched. On the belt at her hip sat a brown leather holster, with a nasty-looking gun in it. Something about the power a woman with a gun presented intrigued Sable no end. Cat walked back to the Blazer and got in.

"Everything okay?" Sable asked.

Cat nodded, reaching for another cigarette as she started the Blazer again. "I'll tap a few of my sources and see what I can come up with."

Sable sighed in relief, then she looked over at Cat.

"I don't suppose I can take you to lunch?"

Cat considered for a moment. "I'm not really supposed to accept gratuities."

"I want to take a hot-looking cop to lunch," Sable said, her smile unrepentant. "That's a crime?"

"No…" Cat said.

"Then let me take you to lunch."

Cat sighed, taking a long drag on her cigarette, then she nodded.

Lunch ended up being at the Hotel Intercontinental in Sable's suite of rooms.

"Jake'd kill me if he heard I had lunch out in public while he wasn't around to protect me," Sable explained.

Cat suspected more than that, but she said nothing. Sable ordered lunch, including wine for both of them.

"I can't drink," Cat told her.

"Alcoholic?"

Cat laughed, shaking her head. "I'm on duty."

"Oh," Sable said, smiling.

Their lunch arrived in what had to be record time. Sable had the waiter put the food out on the penthouse terrace. She also tipped him heavily.

Sable's hand slid over Cat's arm as she gestured to the terrace. Cat controlled the shudder that went through her at the contact. She was rarely affected by other women—usually she did the affecting. Sable, however, was so legendarily sexual that there was no way to avoid it.

While they ate, Sable talked about life on the road, and how it got too lonely sometimes.

"I'm sure you have no trouble finding someone to spend time with," Cat said, rolling her eyes.

"I have a problem finding someone to hold my interest," Sable said.

"And what does it take to do that?" Cat asked, knowing she was edging closer to the line.

"A lot," Sable said pointedly.

Cat nodded slowly, not even going to go into that with her.

"So what kind of nightlife does San Diego have?" Sable asked, sensing that Cat was backing up again.

"Some," Cat said.

"I don't suppose I could get you to show me," Sable asked.

"Uhhh…" Cat said hesitantly.

"Strictly platonic," Sable added.

Cat grimaced, knowing that she shouldn't.

"Please?" Sable pleaded, taking Cat's hand in both of hers.

Cat sighed. "Okay, but strictly platonic."

Sable nodded, doing her best to look sincere. Cat caught the effort and narrowed her blue eyes. Sable merely smiled, her expression not innocent in the slightest.

"What about tonight?" Sable pressed, before Cat could change her mind.

"I can't tonight," Cat said. "I have a case."

"A case?"

"Yeah, you know, a narcotics case," Cat said.

"Oh," Sable said, smiling. "What about tomorrow night?"

Cat looked pensive.

"Is your girlfriend going to be around?" Sable said.

"No," Cat said, grimacing. "She works nights a lot."

"Doing what?" Sable asked.

"She owns a restaurant and bar in Del Mar."

"Which one?"

"Uh, Catalina's," Cat said, her tone a bit chagrined.

"She named her place after you?"

Cat nodded, looking embarrassed.

Sable looked duly impressed.

"So, what about tomorrow night?" Sable asked, undaunted.

Cat blew her breath out in surrender. "Okay, tomorrow night."

"Say eight?" Sable pressed.

"Yes, eight."

Cat left the penthouse room a little while later, promising to call Sable if she couldn't make it. Sable half expected her to call that night, but she didn't. She was relieved—she was actually looking forward to going out with the feisty little blonde.

She'd been telling the truth when she'd said she had a hard time finding someone who could hold her attention. Sable believed that

Cat might be the exception to that rule. It was definitely worth finding out.

Sable glanced at her watch as Cat drove up.

"Don't hassle me, I had a rough day," Cat said as she got out and opened the door for the other woman.

"You're only five minutes late," Sable said, shrugging.

"Uh-huh," Cat replied, unconvinced that the superstar wasn't secretly annoyed.

Sable watched as Cat walked back around the front of the car to get in the driver's side. She looked good—she was wearing a rich blue halter top that had just a touch of glitter to it, black slacks that hugged her body, and black leather heeled boots. Her hair was a cascade of rich gold waves, and her makeup was darker than it had been the day before, making her pretty face even more enchanting.

Shaking her head, Sable cautioned herself. This woman was not only not bowled over by Sable's fame, she was also attached. Not that being attached ever meant anything to Sable. When she wanted something she took it, regardless of what it cost. That's how she'd attained her fame, by going after and taking what she wanted. If it meant kissing ass, fucking this person or that person, then so be it. It had also meant a lot of hard work on her part. Her voice, body, and sex appeal were her assets, and she used them to the maximum.

Getting in, Cat glanced at Sable. The star never ceased to amaze. She was dressed in a rich gold-toned leather bustier and miniskirt. On top of that she wore a leopard-print leather duster jacket, and black thigh-high boots. Her rich chestnut hair was loose and wild, hanging to her waist. Her brown eyes were rimmed in gold shadow, with black liner and sooty black lashes, rich auburn blusher, and lips the same shade. She was an incredible-looking woman, there was no doubt about that.

"Have you eaten yet?" Sable asked as Cat put the vehicle in gear.

"Today?" Cat queried with a smile.

"You haven't eaten all day?"

Cat shrugged. "Happens a lot."

"Shouldn't happen at all."

"You're not old enough to be my mother, honey," Cat said, with a wink.

"How old do you think I am?" Sable asked.

"I have no idea, but I know it's not old enough to be my mother."

"How old is your mother?"

"Forty-seven."

"How old does that make you?"

"Thirty."

"Okay, you're right, I'm not old enough to be your mother," Sable said, grinning. "But I am old, so don't give me any lip."

Cat laughed, shaking her head. "You don't look anywhere near forty."

"Well, I am, but don't tell anyone," Sable said, winking at her.

"People don't know?"

Sable narrowed her eyes at Cat. "You don't know anything about me, do you?"

"I know some stuff about you," Cat said, "but I'm not a rabid fan or anything. I mean, I don't know your birthday, sign, favorite color, biggest crush, or how old you were when you lost your virginity."

"November nineteenth, Scorpio, black, Angelina Jolie, and fifteen," Sable replied, her brown eyes sparkling. "Your turn."

"Uh…" Cat began, looking thoughtful. "August fourth, Leo, blue, Angelina Jolie is safe, and fourteen."

"Ah… you're a Leo, huh?"

"Yep," Cat replied.

"Like to be in charge?"

"Usually am."

"Take care of everyone else?" Sable asked, her voice softer this time.

Cat took a deep inhale, then released it and nodded.

"Does it make you tired?" Sable asked, tilting her head to the side.

"It has its moments."

"Ever have anyone take care of you?"

"Don't let many people get that chance," Cat replied.

Sable noted that Cat sounded a bit touchy now. She knew she didn't want to push on this.

"Let's go have some dinner," Sable suggested. "You need to eat and so do I."

Cat nodded. "What do you feel like?"

Sable grinned rakishly. "I'd tell you, but you'd probably kick me out of your vehicle."

Cat chuckled at that. "Maybe," she agreed. "What do you want to eat?"

Sable raised an eyebrow at Cat, which made Cat laugh.

"Okay, what restaurant do you want to have dinner at?" Cat qualified.

"You choose," Sable said. "You know San Diego better than I do."

"What kind of food do you like?" Cat asked.

"Anything."

"Seafood, Mexican, Greek, Italian?"

"Greek sounds good," Sable said.

"I know a great little Greek place, not too flashy, but fantastic food. Sound good?"

"Sounds perfect."

Cat drove down to Chula Vista, pulling into the parking lot behind a restaurant named Zorba's. At the door, Cat was greeted by a dark-haired woman, who hugged her warmly.

"Katrina, this is Sable Sands," Cat said, gesturing to Sable. "Sable, this is the owner, Katrina."

"It's nice to meet you," Sable said, smiling at the shorter woman.

"Welcome," Katrina replied.

As promised, the food was excellent, and Sable found that Cat was great company as well. They drank ouzo together, a Greek licorice-flavored liquor. Cat stopped at one shot, long before Sable did, however, since she was driving.

They talked about Sable's upcoming tour in Europe, and a little about Cat's work, although Cat was hesitant to talk about narcotics work too much. She knew the limits and how dangerous it could be to talk too much. While she felt Sable was probably fairly trustworthy, Sable also talked to a lot of people.

"So why can't you tell me about the case you worked last night?" Sable asked, not for the first time.

Cat sat back, sighing, as she signaled for the check.

"It's hard to explain," she replied, hoping that this time Sable would accept that.

"Try," Sable said, reaching across the table and touching Cat's hand.

"If I tell you about who I'm working right now," Cat began, "and you happen to say something in passing to someone else, and they tell someone else… it could get around to the people I'm working, and then I'm dead."

Sable stared back at her in shock. She was waiting for Cat to laugh or at least tell her she was joking. It became evident very quickly that Cat was not kidding at all.

"Fucking A," Sable said, her voice reflecting her surprise.

Cat shrugged as the check came. She automatically reached for it, but Sable was faster, picking it up and handing the waitress the check and a credit card with a wink.

Narrowing her eyes, Cat canted her head to the side.

"You didn't think I was letting you pay?" Sable asked, sounding truly astounded.

Cat opened her mouth to answer, but then smiled instead. In truth, she was used to being the one in charge in her relationship. Elizabeth always let her take care of things like the check. Not that Elizabeth didn't pay many of the expenses in the household—she certainly contributed through the profits she made on the restaurant and nightclub. Cat staunchly refused to let Elizabeth use her trust fund or her father's money, which was considerable, to pay for daily living.

Cat and Sable left the restaurant and headed to Bourbon Street, a popular gay bar in San Diego. Cat was known there, since she was there frequently with her friends, or on occasion with Elizabeth. Naturally everyone was shocked to see Cat in the presence of a superstar.

Standing back, Cat watched Sable work the crowd that gathered around her. Cat was watchful, naturally taking on the role of a bodyguard. When a taller butch woman with short dark hair was insistent that Sable have a drink with her, her hand on Sable's arm, Cat intervened.

"Let's ease off the lady now," Cat said, stepping between Sable and the other woman, her hand on the taller woman's arm.

"Step off," the butch woman growled.

Cat slid her hand down to the woman's wrist, tightening her hold and applying pressure at the pulse point.

"I said," Cat repeated, her tone all cop now, "ease off the lady."

When the dark-haired woman tensed, her other arm balling into a fist, Cat tightened her grip further.

"If you don't think I can break your wrist with one hand, you can try me," Cat said, her voice dangerous. "I can also put a fairly nasty hole in you with the nickel-plated Beretta in the holster at my ankle."

The taller woman brought her chin up at the threat, but could also easily sense that Cat was serious.

"Back off, Jackie," one woman said from the butch woman's side. "She's a cop."

"A cop?" Jackie queried, looking surprised.

"A cop," Cat repeated.

Jackie, who'd already let go of Sable's arm, since the pressure Cat was exerting on her wrist was causing her arm to tingle, stepped back.

"Good choice," Cat said, her smile icy as she escorted Sable to the bar.

While they stood at the bar ordering their drinks, Sable glanced around them. She could see people looking at them, and pointing at Cat and talking. It was obvious the story of what had just happened was circulating around the bar—no one else approached Sable, other than to smile at her.

"You're handy to have around," Sable said, her hand on the small of Cat's back.

"Uh-huh," Cat said, feeling Sable's hand but not mentioning it.

Sable lowered her head slightly, her lips right next to Cat's ear. "Are you always so forceful?" she asked, her voice husky.

Cat felt the involuntary shiver go through her; it was a natural reaction to the feeling of such a sexy woman so close to her. Turning her head, Cat looked directly into Sable's eyes.

"Always," she replied, her lips quirking.

"Mmm…" Sable murmured, feeling her pulse quicken.

Cat turned back to the bar, taking the drinks the bartender handed her with a wink.

"A friend of yours?" Sable asked Cat as they made their way to a table.

"She dated my ex," Cat replied with a shrug. "So she kinda knows me now too."

Sable thought that the bartender looked more than interested. In fact, a number of women seemed interested in both her and Cat. When a song came on that Sable liked, she grabbed Cat's hand and pulled her out onto the dance floor. She found quickly that Cat could definitely move. Everything about the way she danced was sensual, and Sable found her mind wandering to what Cat would be like naked and in bed. She knew she was quickly becoming obsessed with the beautiful blond cop. It was Sable's nature to form quick attachments. When she felt a connection, she felt it and went for it.

They'd been at the club for about an hour when Cat heard a very familiar voice behind her.

"Fancy meeting you here…"

Cat turned around, a bright smile already on her face. "What has you out of your love nest?"

Kana grinned, nodding toward Palani, who was talking animatedly with Jerry at the bar.

"Ah, the little woman," Cat said, smiling.

Kana looked at Cat, then at Sable, raising her eyebrow slightly.

"K, this is Sable," Cat said.

"I know who she is," Kana said, a smile on her face. "Nice to meet you. My girlfriend loves your music."

Sable extended her hand to Kana, sensing the presence that everyone did with the big Samoan woman. She tilted her head to the side. "Your girlfriend, but not you?"

Kana grinned unrepentantly. "I'm more of a classic rock kind of girl."

"I see," Sable said, nodding.

"Sable, this is Kana Sorbinno," Cat said, finishing the introductions as Palani and Jerry walked up.

Sable's eyes widened slightly at seeing the beautiful dark-haired model, because she recognized her immediately. Hell, she'd had enough fantasies about the cover girl. Then it clicked. She looked back at Kana, then at Palani again.

"You're Palani Ryker," she said, then looked at Kana. "And you two were on the cover of *Cosmo* last month."

Kana rolled her eyes, as Palani gasped.

"Oh my God, you're Sable Sands!" Palani exclaimed.

"I know," Sable said, grinning.

"I love your music so much," Palani said, all smiles now.

"So your girlfriend says," Sable replied. "I'm glad to hear that. I happen to love your pictures—you are an exquisite-looking woman."

Kana exchanged a look with Cat, a smile tugging at her lips. She knew women all over the world were in love with Palani's looks. This was nothing new. What had Kana curious was the fact that this very publicly gay rock star was out with Cat. Had she missed something?

"Cat," Kana said, putting her arm around the smaller woman, "let's go to the bar."

"Uh-huh," Cat murmured as Kana steered her toward the bar.

Sable, Palani, and Jerry got engrossed in a conversation, even though Sable's eyes kept wandering back to where Cat and Kana stood talking. She saw Kana touch Cat's cheek at one point, her look sympathetic, and she knew the two of them had been intimate at one time. It was obvious. By the time Kana and Cat came back to the table, Jerry was dancing, and Palani was sitting down with Sable. Kana took Palani's hand and led her to the dance floor, leaving Sable and Cat alone.

"So was that about your girlfriend?" Sable asked Cat as she sat down.

Cat nodded. "K just wondered if Bet and I have broken up."

"Her name is Bet?"

"Well, it's Elizabeth," Cat replied, "but I've always called her Bet."

Sable was surprised to feel a stab of jealousy for a woman she'd never even met. "So why didn't we go to her club?" Sable asked. "Or doesn't she know you're out with me?"

"She knows," Cat replied. "We didn't go to her club because it's not a predominantly gay club. I thought you'd feel more comfortable here."

"I would, or you would?" Sable gave her a pointed look.

Cat returned her look. "If you want me to take you there, I will."

Sable didn't answer, looking at the dance floor and watching Kana and Palani dance.

"Your friend can really move," Sable commented.

"Yeah, K's pretty good," Cat agreed, noting that Sable had avoided the part about going to Elizabeth's club, but not commenting on it.

Sable looked over at Cat, her eyes narrowing slightly. "You dated her, didn't you?"

Cat nodded.

"And you let that go?" Sable asked, gesturing toward Kana.

"I never had her heart," Cat said, smiling wistfully. "Palani always did."

Sable remembered what she'd read about Kana and Palani being separated for a while. "Did you love her?" she asked out of curiosity.

"I came pretty close to it," Cat said, "but it's hard to really love someone you know will never truly love you back."

"So do you love Elizabeth?"

Cat looked across the table at the other woman. Eventually she shrugged and nodded. "I love her."

"You don't seem too sure of that," Sable asked, having noted the slight hesitation.

"I'm sure of it," Cat said. "But I'm beginning to wonder how sure of us she is."

Sable was surprised by that. "Why wouldn't she be sure of the two of you?"

"Because Elizabeth was straight before she met me," Cat replied, not sure why she was telling a virtual stranger about this.

"So you think she's not sure she's gay?"

"Well, I'm not really gay," Cat said. "I've always been bi."

That surprised Sable even more. "Really?"

"Yeah," Cat replied, knowing that Sable had thought her a lesbian.

Sable nodded, processing that information. "But you're sure of your relationship with her?"

"I knew I wanted to be with her," Cat said, "and I know now that I prefer to be in an actual relationship with a woman."

"Why's that?" Sable asked.

"Because in relationships, women are better able to share themselves. Men are too preoccupied with other things."

Sable liked that answer. "So you're basically a lesbian now?"

Cat smiled. "Well, I'm in a relationship with a woman," she said. "That's not to say that if I was single again and the hottest man alive offered, I wouldn't take him up on it."

"Have you had the hottest man alive?" Sable asked, her tone derogatory.

"I've had one that's pretty damned hot," Cat said, grinning.

"And was he as hot in bed?" Sable asked, sure of the answer.

"Oh yeah," Cat said, her blue eyes sparkling.

Sable's mouth dropped open. She was shocked. In her limited experience with the opposite sex, she'd had the man considered the "hottest man alive" by *People* magazine, and he'd been a total waste in bed.

"So who was this?" Sable asked.

"One of the men I work with," Cat replied.

"So why didn't you stick with him?"

"Well, for one thing he's married," Cat said, surprising Sable again. "And for another, I respect the hell out of his wife."

"You respect his wife?" Sable asked, not sure if she was ever going to understand Cat at all.

"Yeah," Cat said. "She's also on my team. She's a damned good shot too."

"Is she pretty?" Sable asked, her grin evil.

"Gorgeous, and," Cat added with a mischievous wink, "good in bed too."

"Oh my God, you had them both?" Sable asked. "Do they know?"

"Of course they know," Cat said, shrugging as she drank the shot she'd brought back from the bar. "They were both there at the time."

Sable's eyes widened further, even as she smiled. "You are a bad girl, aren't you?"

Cat grinned. "I do what feels good at the time."

"Mmm," Sable murmured, thinking that sounded far too good an opening to ignore.

Standing up, Sable took Cat's hand, pulling her up out of the chair and leading her to the dance floor. A slow song had just started, and Sable took that opportunity to get close to Cat, her hands on her small waist, pulling her closer. Cat kept her head to the side, allowing herself to feel the music for a little while. Sable wore an intoxicating scent, very sexy, and Cat was feeling the shot she'd just had.

Closing her eyes, Cat let her body move with the music. She felt Sable's hands slide farther around her waist, pulling her even closer. There was only two inches difference in their heights, so their bodies melded perfectly. Hair brushed Cat's cheek as Sable lowered her head. Cat felt the soft slight wetness of Sable's lips on her neck. She sighed, allowing herself to enjoy it. When she felt the gentle suction of Sable's mouth, and her thumb brush over an already hard nipple between them, Cat gasped. Lifting her head, she looked up into Sable's eyes.

That's when Sable kissed her.

Warning bells started to go off in Cat's head, but they were quickly overtaken by the sheer sensuality of the kiss. It was obvious Sable was very used to kissing women. Her lips were strong and demanding, but had just the right amount of sensual softness to them to make Cat feel absolutely weak. When Sable's hand slid through her hair, tightening on a handful of the silken strands, Cat was sure she was going to come right there. The kiss intensified, and Cat could only respond, forgetting where they were, that she had a girlfriend, that anything existed. This was pure sexuality, and she reveled in it for the moment.

Reality kicked in as the song ended, and Cat broke the kiss, trying to calm her pulse as she stepped back from Sable's embrace. Glancing up, she felt a brief sense of satisfaction to note that Sable looked just as affected by the kiss as she was feeling. Again, reality closed in. When they walked back to the table, Cat kept going and went to the bar, ordering a shot of Cuervo 1800.

"After that kiss, I'd need one too," came Kana's voice from behind her.

Cat turned around to look up at Kana, shot in hand. She tossed back the shot; after that she felt calm enough to look at Kana again.

"Saw that, huh?" she asked, grinning as she felt the alcohol soothe her frayed nerves.

"The whole bar saw it, Cat," Kana said, her smirk humorous.

"Great," Cat said, shaking her head. "What am I doing? Am I trying to fuck up my relationship or what?"

Kana looked considering, then shrugged. "I think you're having a really rough time right now, and Sable is one hell of an outlet."

Cat nodded, her expression contrite. "Not what I should be doing."

Kana shrugged. "I'm not here to judge you, babe."

"Okay, but it's crazy," Cat said.

Kana said nothing, merely looking back at her.

"You're not helping," Cat said sourly.

Kana shrugged again, grinning. "And?"

"Fuck you," Cat said, grinning too.

"You're not driving home, right?" Kana asked.

"I'm fine," Cat assured her.

"How many have you had?" Kana asked, her eyes narrowed.

"Three shots total, K," Cat said. "I'm fine, really."

Kana narrowed her eyes further. She rarely trusted someone who said she was "fine," but she also knew Cat was extremely responsible about such things. Finally she nodded, and they headed back over to the table.

An hour later, Cat found herself walking into Cat's Bet with Sable. She wasn't sure exactly how she'd been talked into going to her girlfriend's club, but here she was at the front door. The doorman knew her and opened the doors for her and Sable with a smile and a "Hey, beautiful." He always flirted with her—he knew she was dating the owner, but he always flirted with her.

The club was crowded as usual. It was an upscale, happening place, with style and a lot of beautiful people. Cat looked around, spotting Carmella, Elizabeth's hostess, who kept an eye out for anyone important entering the club. Carmella spotted Cat as well and made her way to the best table in the bar, near the dance floor, clearing it for Cat and her guest.

"Hello, Catalina," Carmella murmured in Cat's ear, her Mediterranean accent clear and rich. "It's lovely to see you again."

"Hi, Carmella," Cat said, smiling, then gesturing to Sable. "Carmella, this is Sable Sands."

"I know Miss Sands," Carmella said, her smile brilliant as she extended her hand to the other woman. "I like your music very much."

"Thank you," Sable replied automatically, as she glanced around the place. Cat's girlfriend was no slouch in the style department, at least not where her club was concerned.

"I will let Ms. Endicott know you are here," Carmella told Cat, smiling again at Sable as she walked away.

"They always clear the way for you here?" Sable asked as they sat down at the table cleared just for them.

Cat shrugged. "The owner's girlfriend," she said, sounding unimpressed.

A waitress appeared, and Cat ordered a double shot and a Corona. Sable ordered a shot of Jägermeister and a Hefeweizen. Their drinks had just come when a beautiful woman with long golden hair and deep blue eyes walked up. She was dressed in a black Halston dress and strappy heels. Around her neck she wore a gold Byzantine chain with a sapphire and diamond heart. Her skin was tan and smooth, and as far as Sable could see there wasn't one flaw to her. Gorgeous, was all Sable could think.

"Finally made it to my club, I see," the woman said, her English accent clear and sophisticated.

Cat smiled, standing up and turning to Elizabeth.

"Yes, honey, finally," she said, leaning down to kiss her girlfriend's lips softly. "Bet, I want you to meet Sable Sands."

Elizabeth extended her hand to the other woman, her eyes looking directly into Sable's. Sable took Elizabeth's hand, reading in the other woman's eyes something akin to suspicion.

"Thank you for letting me borrow your girlfriend to act as tour guide," Sable said with a slight edge to her voice. "You've got a great place here."

Elizabeth nodded, a polite smile on her lips, even as her eyes narrowed slightly. She glanced at the table and saw the shot glass of tequila, a double, and a Corona. Elizabeth's eyes slid to Cat, searching hers.

"Come dance with me," Elizabeth said, taking Cat's hand and pulling her toward the dance floor. She glanced back over her shoulder. "You'll excuse us, won't you?" she asked, her tone holding no sort of question to it.

On the dance floor, a slow song was playing. Elizabeth moved in close, her arms wound around Cat's neck, her hands burying themselves in Cat's long hair. They moved together well; it was obvious they were intimate. Sable watched from the table, knowing she was being reminded by Elizabeth Endicott who Cat belonged to. It both amused and rankled her.

"You smell like her," Elizabeth said, her lips close to Cat's ear.

"We danced at Bourbon Street," Cat replied.

"How close?" Elizabeth asked sharply.

Cat sighed. "Bet, would I have come here if I was trying to sneak around on you?"

Elizabeth pulled back, looking Cat in the eyes. "If you smelled another woman on me, wouldn't you wonder?"

Cat bit back the comment on the tip of her tongue about being more likely to smell a man on her than another woman. Someone like the Puerto Rican bartender that had been hitting on Elizabeth since she'd hired him. A man Elizabeth quite frequently closed down the bar with. Something that bugged Cat no end.

"I didn't come here to fight with you, Bet," Cat said, taking a step back.

Elizabeth tightened her hold on Cat's hair in sudden desperation. "I'm sorry, Cat, I didn't mean… I'm sorry," she said, pulling Cat back to her. Cat was tense.

"Please, babe, I'm sorry," Elizabeth whispered. Her lips touched Cat's ear, her neck. "I love you. I'm just jealous." Her lips moved over Cat's neck. "I can't compete with someone like Sable Sands. I love you…"

Their lips connected then, and Elizabeth moved in, pressing her body against Cat's. Cat moaned softly, wrapping her arms around Elizabeth's waist, pulling her impossibly closer, deepening the kiss.

Cat bit gently at Elizabeth's bottom lip, making Elizabeth moan and tighten her hand in Cat's hair. The club melted away as they kissed, reconnecting on a physical level, reassuring each other that they were still in love, still together.

Sable watched from the table, ordering a double shot of Jägermeister and watching them dance. When they kissed, Sable knew she'd lost whatever ground she'd gained with Cat that night. She also knew that she wasn't ready to give up yet. There had been too much of a connection there, and Sable never ignored a connection. Never.

***

"What's this from?" Linda asked, her fingers brushing over a red mark on Kashena's upper arm.

Kashena lifted her arm listlessly, glancing at the mark Linda was touching. Then she shrugged. "I don't know, caught it on something in the airport."

Linda's eyes searched Kashena's face. "You look tired."

"I feel like shit," Kashena answered, an edge to her voice. "That might be why."

"Jesus, you don't have to be nasty about it."

Kashena sighed, snuggling farther under the blankets. "I just want to sleep, okay?"

"Okay," Linda said, disappointed.

There was something she'd been dying to talk to Kashena about since she'd gotten back from her trip to LA, but there hadn't been a right time. Now Kashena was sick. A woman who was never sick was sick the one time Linda wanted to tell her something important. *Figures!* Linda thought snidely. *Probably caught something from that lawyer.*

Linda knew about Sierra—of course she knew. Kashena was never one to lie. The first day Kashena had gotten back, Linda had noticed she was quieter than normal. She'd also seemed unexcited to see her again. It had been bothering Linda a lot to note that Kashena wasn't nearly as possessive and desirous of her as she'd been in years past. But now this!

"You seem awfully quiet," Linda had commented while they were at the grocery store the day Kashena arrived back.

Kashena had just shrugged. "I'm tired," she'd said simply.

"Those conferences running really late into the night now?" Linda had snapped, her temper flaring.

She'd called the hotel looking for Kashena one morning, and another woman had answered. Linda had hung up, but something inside had told her there was something wrong. She'd asked Kashena about the other woman in her room, of course, and Kashena had said that Sierra was the lawyer she was protecting and that naturally they were sharing a room; it was safer that way. *Safer for what?* Linda had wanted to ask, but she knew when not to push.

At the grocery store, however, Kashena had been far too preoccupied. Once they got back to the car, Linda had turned to Kashena and just said it.

"Tell me you're not fucking her."

Kashena looked over at her, her deep blue eyes unreadable. "Was that a question?"

Linda narrowed her eyes. "Are you fucking her?"

"Are you fucking that guy that was at my house while I was gone?" Kashena countered.

"What guy?" Linda asked far too quickly.

"The one I smelled in my bedroom when I got home."

Linda glowered at the other woman. It drove her nuts that Kashena seemed to sense everything.

"Are you fucking the lawyer, Kash?" she'd asked again.

Kashena's look had been direct. "Let's just say I'm doing the same thing with the lawyer as you're doing with some guy in my bedroom when I'm not there."

That had been it, and Linda had been smart enough to shut up then.

Leaving Kashena in the bedroom, Linda went into the living room, turning on the TV and engrossing herself in an episode of *Saturday Night Live.*

Over the course of the next three days, Kashena didn't get better. The second day, she was sweating and writhing around so much in the bed that Linda opted to sleep in the guest room. On the end of the third day, Sebastian showed up at the house.

"What are you doing here?" Linda asked when she opened the door.

"Checking on my partner," he said, his storm-green eyes narrowed.

"She's sick," Linda said, shrugging.

"I know, she called me," Sebastian said. "Now get out of my way so I can go see her." He pushed past her.

Linda followed him into the bedroom. She got worried the minute she saw the expression on his face as he looked at Kashena.

"What?" she asked, her gaze sliding from him to Kashena then back again.

Sebastian didn't answer, striding over to the bed and putting his hand to Kashena's cheek.

"She's burning up," he said sharply. "Didn't she take anything?"

Linda gave him a wry look. "You know Kash doesn't take medication."

"Did you think to call the healer?" Sebastian snapped.

Linda looked guilty instantly.

"Why doesn't that surprise me?" he asked, his tone anything but a question.

Straightening, he opened Kashena's bedside drawer, pulled out her address book, and tossed it to Linda. "It's under H."

"For healer?" Linda asked.

"For Hilea," he replied with a denigrating look.

Taking off his jacket, he tossed it aside. He unbuttoned his shirt and pulled his shirt tails out of his jeans.

"What the hell are you doing?" Linda asked as he kicked off his shoes and climbed into bed behind Kashena.

"Relax, babe," he said snidely. "We need to get this fever down, and the best way to do that is adding body heat to hers so it'll break. And the longer you stand there gaping at me like an idiot, the longer I'll have to do this, so could you get your ass on the phone?"

"Why aren't I doing that and you making the call?" Linda asked suspiciously.

As soon as Sebastian wrapped his body around Kashena's and she felt his heat surrounding her, she tried to jerk away from him. Fastening arms of steel around Kashena as she fought against him, he looked up at Linda.

"Think you're strong enough to handle her, sweetheart?" he asked sarcastically.

Linda curled her lip in disgust at him, knowing he was right. Kashena was damned strong, and it was obvious she didn't want Sebastian's heat anywhere near her.

"I hope she manages to nail you in the balls," Linda spat angrily.

"Wouldn't be the first time, honey," he said with a wink. "Now make the goddamned call, will you?"

Sebastian spent an extremely uncomfortable two hours holding Kashena, sweating like crazy and doing his best to control her thrashing. At one point she quieted, and he hoped the fever was breaking. He made the mistake of loosening his hold on her, and regretted it a moment later. Her elbow rammed up and back, slamming into his rib cage and, he was fairly sure, cracking a rib.

"Fuck!" he yelled as he grabbed her arms tightly again, doing his best to protect his now aching rib.

Linda ran in to see what happened and saw the way he was holding his arm out away from his side, even as he was still holding Kashena's arm. She smirked, seeing the already darkening bruise.

"Watch it," he warned her, "or I'll make you lie here, and she'll probably manage to kill you." His tone held no concern at that thought—he actually looked like he relished the idea.

"Fuck you, Sebastian," she snapped.

"Not in this lifetime, honey."

Linda glared at him, hating him more every time she had to deal with him. She knew he couldn't stand her, and that he was forever berating Kashena for getting back together with her. Soon he may be stuck with her, and wouldn't that just be too bad for him. Bastard.

The healer arrived an hour later. Walking in, she saw Sebastian lying in bed holding Kashena. She smiled. She'd met Sebastian a number of times over the years that he and Kashena had been friends. She very much liked the big man, and had named him "animikii akamaabi," which in Ojibwa roughly translated to the "thunderbird who waits in watch." She knew that Sebastian was Kashena's protector. Whereas Hilea called Linda "animoons animishimo," which translated into "the puppy who dances away." The healer had no use for Linda; she felt Linda would only drain the life force from Kashena given the opportunity.

"Hilea, aaniin," Sebastian said, inclining his head respectfully to the healer in greeting.

"Aaniin, animikii akamaabi," Hilea said, returning the greeting with a smile.

Sebastian had taken the time to learn a few words of the Ojibwa language. It showed his respect for his best friend's heritage.

Linda looked on, her lips twitching in irritation that, as usual, Sebastian was running the show and showing off. Damnit, she was Kashena's lover—didn't that count for anything? The damned healer hadn't even acknowledged her presence!

"She's had a fever," Sebastian was telling the healer, "and I can't seem to break it."

The healer nodded. "I will fix something," she said, her dark brown eyes glowing.

"Miigwech, nenaandawi'iwed," Sebastian replied.

The healer left the room.

"What did you say to her?" Linda asked, her tone sharp, as it always was with Sebastian.

Sebastian looked back at her, derision curling his lips. "I just said thank you."

"All that for thank you?" Linda asked suspiciously.

"It basically translates to 'Thank you, healer,'" he said impatiently.

"Well, excuse me for not speaking Indian."

"It's Ojibwa," he reminded her, not sure if she ever even remembered what tribe Kashena was from.

"I know that, asshole," Linda snapped, turning and stalking out of the room.

151

Sebastian chuckled to himself, glancing down at his partner. "You're with such a charmer, honey," he said, even though he was fairly sure she couldn't hear him.

He was worried sick about her, even if it didn't show. The fever hadn't broken, and that bothered him—it meant her body was trying desperately to rid itself of some illness. Kashena was rarely, if ever, sick, so when she was, she got really sick. He didn't like that Linda had apparently not been worried at all. Kashena herself had called him three days before to say she was sick and wouldn't be in. She hadn't called since then; however, Sierra Youngblood had called three or four times asking if she was better. He'd finally decided he'd better come check on her. He was glad now that he had.

Ten minutes later, Hilea came back carrying two small cups. Handing one to him, she gestured for him to drink.

"Me? But Hilea…"

"It is for your pain," she said, motioning to his side, which was now black and blue from where Kashena's elbow had caught him.

"Miigwech," he said, inclining his head and taking the cup, then downing it like a shot.

He couldn't help the grimace that followed. The herbs tasted horrible, but he knew that Hilea believed in them being pure. Hilea chuckled at the face he made, then gestured to Kashena.

Sebastian sat up, gently lifting his partner with him. Kashena groaned, struggling against his hold again.

"Easy, Kash. Hilea is here. You need to take some herbs," he said soothingly.

Kashena groaned again, shaking her head.

"It's okay, babe. I'll help you." He smoothed back her hair.

Taking the cup from Hilea, Sebastian gently placed Kashena's head back against his shoulder. Holding his hand to her forehead, he brought the cup to her lips.

"Drink, babe," he said softly in her ear.

Kashena did as he told her, grimacing as he had at the taste of the herbs.

"Just a little more, Kash... come on," he said when the cup was near empty.

She drank the rest, then sighed, relaxing against him. He knew it was somehow a psychological relief for her to have the healer there. It was Kashena's deeply held belief that the healer could take care of anything. She'd been brought up to believe in the power of others' gifts, so knowing the healer had come to take her fever away made her relax into the deep sleep her body badly needed.

She slept for five hours, during which time Sebastian hovered close by. He'd pulled on his shirt but hadn't bothered to button it. Naturally, when Kashena woke, the first thing she saw was the dark nasty bruise on his rib cage.

"What happened?" she asked, her voice gravelly.

"You," he said, grinning.

"Oh God, Baz..." Kashena began, horrified at having hurt him. "Did I..."

"Yeah," he confirmed. "You probably cracked it," he said, winking at her. "Exactly what I'd expect from a Marine."

"Oo-rah," she said, her tone far from enthusiastic.

"There's my partner," Sebastian said with a wide smile. He kissed her on the forehead. "I'm leaving you in the care of your girlfriend now. I need to take a shower. I don't think I've sweated this much since those twins in Rome."

"Ugh!" Kashena said, pulling the pillow over her head. "Thanks for the visual."

Sebastian chuckled. "Anytime, honey, anytime."

Kashena lay in bed, feeling drained and still tired. Linda wandered in a few minutes after Sebastian left.

"Well, I'm glad he finally left," she said, lying down on the bed.

Kashena didn't say anything. The last thing she wanted was to get into a discussion with Linda about Sebastian. Linda noted Kashena's silence and pressed.

"He was so mean to me, Kash…" she said in a pouting tone.

"Linda," Kashena said tiredly, "let's not do this."

"Do what?"

"You hate Baz, he hates you. I already know this, okay?"

"But he was mean to me," Linda whined.

"He was worried about me," Kashena said, a sigh in her voice.

"So was I," Linda said sharply, "but he didn't have to be a total asshole."

Again Kashena didn't answer, too tired to have this discussion with her girlfriend.

Linda was silent for a while, snuggling against Kashena.

"Kash?" she queried a little while later, just as Kashena was drifting off to sleep.

"Hmm?"

"I think we should get married," Linda said matter-of-factly.

"What?" Kashena asked, fully awake now.

"Well," Linda said, biting her lower lip, "you've always wanted a commitment from me, and you know I always come back to you… So maybe if we got married, I'd stay."

"Being married doesn't make anyone stay where they are, Linda," Kashena said, already wondering how she was getting out of this.

Linda was right—previously, Kashena would have been thrilled at the prospect of settling down with Linda. But too much had happened. Linda had abused their relationship far too often. Also, a particular black-haired woman had been in her thoughts and fevered dreams far too much. Kashena knew that the last thing she really wanted right now was something heavy with Linda to tie her down.

Linda noted Kashena's silence and found herself getting quite irritated at it.

"You don't want to?" she asked incredulously.

Kashena sighed. "Linda, I'm way too tired to have this conversation right now. Can we just not?"

"I see," Linda said, her face a mask of fury. "It's the lawyer, right? She makes a shitload of money, and that's what you want."

Kashena stared at Linda, unable to believe the girl had been dumb enough to use this tactic.

"If I was interested in money, Linda," Kashena said dryly, "why the hell would I date you?"

"Don't be a bitch," Linda snapped.

"Then drop this conversation," Kashena countered calmly, closing her eyes again.

"It's her, isn't it?" Linda sounded like she was near tears. "She's taking you away from me…"

Linda couldn't believe it—she was actually losing her hold on the one woman she was sure would always love her. This wasn't happening!

"You love me, I know you do," Linda said fervently. "I'll fight her for you if I have to."

"That wouldn't be wise," Kashena said quietly, her eyes still closed.

"Why not?" Linda asked.

"Because as her bodyguard, I'd be the one kicking your ass if you touched her."

Linda was stunned into silence. She had absolutely no idea how to respond to that. Kashena was basically threatening her. And she was telling her to stay from her new woman. Oh shit!

Kashena took Linda's silence as an opportunity to go back to sleep. Linda lay next to Kashena, thinking of ways to hold on to her. She'd never been so unsettled before in her life.

The following day, a Friday, Linda announced that a friend of hers had invited her to go to Tahoe for the weekend and that she'd decided to go. She was hoping Kashena would ask her not to. Kashena didn't. Linda left two hours later.

Sierra was sitting in her office when her phone rang.

"Attorney General's office," she answered automatically, her mind on the brief she was reading over.

"Chief Deputy Youngblood?" asked a male voice.

"Yes?"

"This is Agent Bach," Sebastian said in a businesslike voice. "I thought you'd want to know that Agent Marshal is doing better now."

Sierra sighed softly. "Wonderful," she said, smiling.

There was a slight pause on the other end of the line.

"I also thought you might want to know that her girlfriend has left her alone for the weekend," Sebastian said then, his tone still informational, as if reading off a script.

Sierra bit her lip, remembering that Agent Bach was Kashena's best friend. Therefore he'd more than likely know about Kashena and her. He was telling her that Kashena's girlfriend, the one he didn't like, was not at the house and Kashena was alone.

"Thank you, Agent Bach," she said, her voice as businesslike as his. "I will very definitely utilize this opportunity."

"I was hoping you would," Sebastian said, his grin evident through the phone line.

Sierra laughed softly.

A few minutes after their conversation, Sierra received an email from Special Agent Supervisor Sebastian Bach. It read simply, "That security code you needed is 926543." Sierra committed the numbers to memory, knowing it was his way of giving her the security code to Kashena's house. She couldn't believe he was encouraging her this much, but it was obvious that since he hated Linda, he wanted Kashena to have anyone else. She had no idea that Sebastian had seen the glow in his partner's eyes when she'd told him about the encounter with Chief Deputy Youngblood. He recognized that glow, and he fully intended to fan it as much as humanly possible.

Kashena was lying on her bed, one arm thrown up over her eyes. She'd gotten up and taken a shower, which had tired her out. She'd managed to throw on a black tank top and her black sweat shorts with the Marine emblem on them. Now she was trying to gather the strength to get back up and dry her hair. Knowing that her hair took forever to dry since it was so thick, a gift from her Indian heritage, wasn't helping her get into the mood to get back up.

Sierra walked into Kashena's bedroom, having first knocked on Kashena's door for five minutes, then finally using the security code Sebastian had given her to get into the house. She'd checked a number of other rooms first and had no luck in finding Kashena. Kashena sensed a presence immediately, and her hand moved toward the gun on her bedside table, then moved away just as quickly.

"I'm sorry," Sierra said. "I didn't mean to startle you."

"It's okay," Kashena said, smiling. "How'd you get in?"

"I had an informant," Sierra said, suppressing a grin.

"Baz?" Kashena asked.

"Uh-huh," Sierra said, smiling as she walked over to the bed.

Now that she was here, she wasn't sure how to act. She'd been desperately worried about Kashena being so sick, but she'd known that Linda would be at the house and wouldn't have dared call there to check on Kashena. Calling Sebastian had been a safe alternative, but she'd really wanted to see Kashena. However, standing in her bedroom, staring down at the woman that had haunted her every waking moment and a number of her sleeping ones as well, it was impossible to think of something to say.

Kashena sensed Sierra's hesitation. Dropping her arm, she patted the bed next to her. Sierra sat down, her eyes searching Kashena's face.

"How are you feeling?"

"Still tired as hell," Kashena said, "but at least the fever's gone."

Sierra grimaced. "Agent Bach said you had it for four days."

"Yeah," Kashena said. "Apparently he spent the last day of it trying to sweat it out of me."

Sierra nodded. "He said he paid for that." Canting her head, she asked, "What did he mean?"

Kashena looked embarrassed. "It means I cracked one of his ribs trying to break his hold on me."

"Are you serious?" Sierra asked, her eyes wide.

"Yeah," Kashena replied, grimacing. "I tend to fall back on Marine reflexes when I'm in a stressful situation. My elbow caught him in the ribs."

"Ouch," Sierra said, wincing.

"Yeah, and he didn't even smack me for it," Kashena said, chuckling.

"He doesn't strike me as the type of man that would strike a woman for anything."

"Only in hand-to-hand combat," Kashena replied with a wink.

"Oh yeah…" Sierra said, remembering what Kashena had told her about how she'd fought with Sebastian the first time they'd met.

They were silent for a few minutes, Kashena closing her eyes again while Sierra looked around at Kashena's room. It had a very earthy feel to it, the décor was rich dark woods, with rusts, golds, and greens for the bedding and curtains. The room wasn't overly decorated—it seemed to closely match what Sierra had seen of Kashena's personality so far. Very straightforward, easygoing, yet connected to her roots.

Glancing down at Kashena, she saw that her eyes were closed. Instinctively, Sierra reached out and brushed a lock of blond hair off her cheek. Kashena opened her eyes, staring up into Sierra's.

"Do you need anything?" Sierra asked softly.

"A way to will my hair dryer into my hand," Kashena said, gesturing to her still-damp hair.

"I can get it," Sierra offered, standing and walking toward the bathroom.

By the time Sierra returned with the hair dryer, Kashena had sat up. Sierra looked for and found a plug for the hair dryer, plugged it in, then handed it to Kashena. After about five minutes of watching Kashena try to dry her hair, it was obvious to Sierra that it was too tiring for her. Sierra gently took the dryer out of Kashena's hand and continued drying her mane of blond hair. It felt good to run her hands through Kashena's hair again, even if it was only to help dry it.

Glancing down at Kashena, she saw that the other woman had her eyes closed and a pleasured look on her face.

Kashena was thoroughly enjoying having Sierra's hands in her hair; it was both relaxing and soothing. By the time Sierra switched off the hair dryer, Kashena was feeling so relaxed she just wanted to sleep again. Wrapping her arms around Sierra's waist, Kashena lay back against the pillows, pulling Sierra down with her.

"How long can you stay?" Kashena asked, her eyes already closed.

"As long as you want me to," Sierra replied, elated that Kashena wanted her to stay.

Kashena snuggled down farther on the bed, lying on her back and holding Sierra half over her.

"Mmm," Kashena purred. "But that would be all weekend."

"I said as long as you wanted me to."

"Mmmmmm," Kashena sighed this time, turning onto her side and pulling Sierra against her. "I'll take it."

Kashena was asleep minutes later. Sierra lay in her arms, thinking once again how good this felt. Kicking off her shoes, she got comfortable. She was surprised when she started awake later and found that it was dark outside. Feeling Kashena's arms still around her, Sierra smiled, feeling like a human-sized teddy bear for the other woman. She glanced at her watch and realized she needed to make a couple of phone calls.

Carefully extricating herself from Kashena's embrace, she walked into the other room, taking her purse with her. She got on her cell phone and called her day care, and then talked to Colby. She'd already arranged for him to stay with a friend of his from school for the weekend, in the hopes that Kashena would let her stay around. Sierra had sensed that Kashena needed looking after, and the fact that her girlfriend had obviously abandoned her during this time made Sierra dislike Linda even more.

After all her arrangements had been made, Sierra decided to check and see if there was anything she could make Kashena for dinner. She'd seen that Kashena had lost some weight and knew that in order to get healthy again, Kashena would need to eat. Checking out the refrigerator and pantry, she saw that apparently Linda didn't bother shopping either when her girlfriend was sick.

She went back to the bedroom. Kashena was still asleep. Sierra pulled a pad of Post-it notes and a pen out of her purse, scribbled a quick note saying she'd be "right back," and stuck it to the lamp next to Kashena's bed. Grabbing her shoes, she walked out of the room.

An hour later she was back with three bags of groceries. She was in Kashena's kitchen making homemade chicken soup when Kashena walked in.

"What are you doing?" Kashena asked, sounding far from upset.

Sierra turned to see that, in fact, Kashena had a pleased smile on her face.

"Making you some dinner," she replied.

Kashena walked over to stand behind Sierra, looking down into the pot that Sierra was stirring.

"Smells good," Kashena said, putting her hands on Sierra's waist and kissing her temple.

"Why don't you go relax, and I'll bring you some in a few minutes?" Sierra said.

When Kashena didn't reply, Sierra turned to look up at the taller woman. She caught the soft smile on Kashena's lips.

"What?"

"Thank you," Kashena said simply, putting her fingertip under Sierra's chin, leaning down, and kissing her lips softly.

"You're welcome," Sierra replied, smiling up at her.

Kashena gave her a squeeze, then walked out of the kitchen. Sierra found her twenty minutes later, sitting in the living room with the TV on. Handing Kashena a bowl of soup, Sierra moved past her to sit down on the couch. They ate in companionable silence, watching a documentary on Spanish galleons. When they were finished, Sierra got up and took Kashena's bowl from her, taking it back into the kitchen. She washed the dishes quickly then went back into the living room.

"You don't have to do all of this, you know," Kashena said as Sierra moved past her again.

"I want to," Sierra answered simply.

Kashena took Sierra's hand and pulled her down next to her. She moved then, putting one leg up on the couch, the other planted on the floor. Pulling Sierra closer, she held the smaller woman against her. Sierra snuggled back into Kashena's embrace, thrilled by Kashena's action. Resting her head against Kashena's shoulder, Sierra felt like this was where she belonged. She didn't know how she knew that, but it just seemed so right. She could feel Kashena's heartbeat against her temple and was so comforted by it she felt a sense of unreality. It was like she was somehow destined for this, and finally it was here.

They spent hours lying there together. At one point, Sierra glanced up at Kashena and saw that she was getting tired again. Sierra moved to the other end of the couch, and, taking Kashena's hand, she tugged her over to her. Kashena lay down, resting her head against Sierra's stomach, her arms around Sierra's waist. Sierra stroked Kashena's hair, soothing her to sleep.

They spent the entire weekend in much the same manner. Sierra found that she thoroughly enjoyed taking care of Kashena. And

Kashena, who usually couldn't stand to be taken care of, realized she enjoyed Sierra's attention thoroughly. It was a warm, comfortable weekend for them both. They hated for it to end.

Chapter 5

Cat wasn't sure what was happening. What did she know was that something wasn't right with this meeting. She'd been contacted by one of her confidential informants and told that a new player to the drug scene was in town and wanted to meet her. What she'd been told and what had generally checked out was that the man was well connected and was running fairly high-end narcotics, pharmaceutical grade. Usually that would indicate a connection with a medical doctor, and that could turn out to be a big drug ring, so it was definitely worth the meeting.

However, this meeting wasn't going as planned. They'd originally said to meet at an upscale restaurant, but when she arrived, they wanted her to drive somewhere else. Now they were at a random La Jolla park, and the guy kept directing her farther and farther from anything populated. Losing patience, she yanked the wheel, turning her Blazer into a dirt area, irritation clear on her face.

"Okay, what the fuck, dude?" she snapped, playing the irritated dealer to the hilt. "I got shit to do. What's this about?"

The man's thin lips twitched. He was dressed in a suit, but Cat had already detected that he wasn't comfortable in it. She knew it was common to check a prospective dealer out using a decoy, so she assumed that was what was happening in this case. Playing the annoyed party for having her time wasted was her role. She watched as the man reached into his inner pocket. She tensed, wondering if he was going for a weapon, dipping her hand toward her ankle where her weapon was concealed, but when the man brought out a simple cell phone and handed it to her, she relaxed. Taking the phone, she put it to her ear.

A man's voice on the phone said, "I appreciate you taking time out of your day to assist me with this little project…" The voice trailed off as he chuckled in a creepy way.

Fear crawled up her spine like an electric worm, and Cat felt the driver's door being yanked open—she nearly fell out of the truck, it happened so fast. As she turned to look at who had opened the door, she was struck by a fist. It dazed her.

"What, I…" she began, trying to get clear and reach down to grab her weapon.

"Don't try it, bitch," the man who'd obviously struck her said, holding a knife dangerously close to her face.

He grabbed her arm roughly and walked her to the passenger side of the Blazer. The man in the suit was standing next to the vehicle now, pointing a gun at her. Every internal alarm Cat had was going off. With a sudden move, she turned on the man behind her, yanking her arm out of his grip and bringing her other arm up to attempt to dislodge the knife. He was not as close as she'd thought—she hadn't realized he'd kept her at arm's length, apparently expecting something like what she was trying. The knife sliced through her shirt and cut her arm. Then she felt the blow to the back of her head from the butt of a gun, sending her to the ground. She scrambled to get up, but she was kicked viciously and repeatedly in the stomach. She curled into a ball to protect herself but was hauled to her feet and turned to the face the man in the suit.

"You shouldn't have tried anything, bitch," the man gritted out as he smoothed back one side of his hair with his free hand, the gun shaking with his obviously adrenaline-fueled anger.

"Okay, I think I'm done now," Cat said, reaching into her jeans pocket and pulling out her badge. She held it up, noticing as she did that her arm was bleeding profusely, blood dripping down onto the dirt.

The man behind her laughed and reached forward with his knife, slicing at the wrist of the hand that held the badge. The gold of the badge glinted as it fell into the dirt. It was the last thing Cat saw before she was knocked to the ground with a slam of the man's arm.

Cat woke in a daze. Her vision swam darkly as she did her best to focus on where she was. She attempted to rub her eyes but realized with a shudder that her arms were tied behind her back. Fighting back the panic that tried to creep up on her, she squeezed her eyes shut, then opened them again to attempt to get them to focus. She rubbed her face against the mattress that was under her. She felt the wetness of blood as her cheek stung.

Rolling to her side, she tried to move her hands; there was a little give in the rough rope that held them. Thanking the dance classes that had kept her agile over the years, she bent her knees and brought her legs up behind her, trying to hook a boot heel in the ropes. It took a few tries and a lot of ignoring the burning pain of the cuts to her arm and wrist, but she finally managed to get her heel to the ropes. Between wriggling her hands and pushing with the boot heel, she managed to almost get one hand free.

Stopping to rest, she looked around her. The room was sparsely furnished, but she couldn't miss the wide baseboards and crown molding. *Not your usual dive. This guy is connected… but to what?* As she thought it, the door to the room opened, and the man who had been in the suit walked in. She recognized the slicked-back hair and the thin lips, but he was dressed in jeans now.

"Knew that suit didn't fit you," she said conversationally, even as she kept trying to wriggle her hand free behind her. Fortunately she was facing the door, so he couldn't see her hands.

"So fuckin' smart, huh?" the man sneered.

"Smarter than you think," Cat replied mildly. "So what's the deal?"

"Shut your mouth, that's the deal," the man snapped, obviously annoyed.

"Come on, man, this ain't no shakedown. What are you guys about?" Cat asked, endeavoring to give herself time, but also wanting to try to gain some clue as to why she was taken.

Laughing in the least humorous way Cat had ever heard, the man stepped closer, his eyes moving over her in a way that made Cat want to cringe. She just about had her hand loose—she wished she could use her boot heel again, knowing the leverage would help, but she didn't want to tip him off. Just as she started to feel a sense of hope, because her hand was nearly free, a second man walked into the room. Cat felt a sense of dread as the men looked at each other, then over at her again.

"He just said hold her," the second man said to his companion. "He didn't say we couldn't have any fun while we did it."

The look of lust was clear on the first man's face as he looked back over at Cat again. He moved toward her, reaching for her, and Cat backed up, yanking hard on the ropes, desperate to free her hand. She fell off the bed with a thump and a yelp, but her hand was suddenly free. As hands reached for her, she yanked at the ropes to free her other hand, and it came free right as the thin-lipped man grasped her shirt, ripping it open. She kicked out, catching him in the knee; he went down with a yell. The second man was there then, grabbing her and dragging her up off the floor. She swung her fist at him, missing his face but dislodging his hands.

"Fucking cunt!" the man yelled, grabbing at her again. Cat tried to evade him but tripped over the man on the floor, who grabbed her foot. Instead of falling, though, she lifted her foot higher, stomping on the man's arm.

She turned to run to the open door. She was tackled—she reacted like a wild animal, punching, kicking, doing everything she could to get away. He had her on the ground, punching her in the face, and she did everything she could to block him. In the background Cat could hear someone yelling—it was jumbled, but she heard "… the fuck… doing?!" She did her best to turn her head to see who was speaking, and that was when the man on top of her landed the blow that knocked her out again. The room faded to black.

When she came to again, it was night. The room was dark, and this time her hands were tied over her head. Her head was aching wildly, and her arms hurt. Moving around, she felt her boots were still on and her jeans still fastened. At least these men didn't go in for raping a woman who was unconscious… at least not so far. She did her best to clear her aching head and listen for anything that would give her a clue as to where she was. Closing her eyes, she let her mind go silent and listened. She could hear a TV on somewhere in the house; she heard talking, but only in murmurs. Somewhere closer she heard a sliding glass door open… Was that waves she heard? The beach? What kind of drug dealer was this? Was he holding her in his own home? Maybe she was imagining the sound of waves…

Later, someone came in; he said nothing to her but gave her some water, leaving shortly after. A few hours later, she wasn't sure how many, someone came in to take her to the bathroom. She was surprised when she was allowed to go into the room alone. But when she looked around the room, she realized why—the only window was tiny, over the shower. Even so, she made a point of running the water as she quietly climbed into the shower to open the window slightly. She did hear waves! She also smelled that salty sea air and felt somehow relieved. Looking in the mirror in the bathroom, she saw the damage from her captors. She didn't care—it was worth it to keep from being raped. She just hoped she had convinced them she wasn't worth the trouble she'd give them. Her head was throbbing as she did her best to clean her face off. Her mind was racing as she did. To her way of thinking, some rich doctor wasn't going to kill her… at least she hoped not, but why kidnap her? It was that nagging thought that kept her awake long into the night. Something wasn't right.

The next day someone came into the room with a phone. He handed it to her, his face warning her not to say too much. Cat didn't care—this was her chance! Sitting up to take the phone, her vision swam. She took slow deep breaths to try and steady herself.

"Cat?" Kyle said, sounding worried. "Cat, is that you? Are you alright?"

"In some sense of the word," Cat replied, hearing how gravelly her voice sounded.

"We'll get you back, don't worry," Kyle said. Cat knew he was drawing out the call, hoping to get enough time to trace it.

"10-4," Cat drawled laconically. "Hate the beach anyway."

The guy who'd handed her the phone snatched it away, slamming his fist into her face as he did. Cat saw stars, and then her vision went dark.

Cat woke to the feeling of someone sitting on the bed. Her brain said fight, but her body refused to respond. Her head was aching; she couldn't even open her eyes. She heard the click of a knife locking into place and braced herself for what was to come. Maybe they were just going to kill her now, she thought, but then she felt the rope at her wrists being tugged. Forcing herself to open her eyes, just as she was lifted up, she saw that it was Kana and let out a moan of relief.

"I've got you, babe, I've got you," Kana said soothingly.

Cat passed out again, dropping her head against Kana's shoulder.

When Cat woke, feeling groggy and out of it, she saw that Kana sat beside her. As the big Samoan noticed she was awake, she reached out and touched Cat's hand. Cat smiled softly, even as she looked around expecting to see Elizabeth. Her heart fell as she looked back at Kana.

"She's not here," Cat said. It was a statement, not a question.

Kana took a deep breath, expelling it slowly and shaking her head.

Cat closed her eyes, feeling tears sting the backs of her eyelids. When she opened them again, Kana looked pained.

"Where is she?" she whispered sadly.

"Cat..." Kana began.

"I don't want to know, do I?"

Kana didn't answer, dropping her eyes from her friend's. Cat nodded, closing her eyes again. Silent tears slipped down her cheeks.

"At least tell me you got the bastards," Cat commented, her tone edged with sadness.

"We did," Kana said, nodding, "but they're not talking, and we don't know who ordered this. We're still looking into it though. Don't worry."

Cat nodded. Part of her really didn't care. Her world was crashing around her at this point anyway—what difference did it make?

Elizabeth arrived at the hospital with a sense of dread. She knew she was in trouble and there was really no way out of it. She hoped that no one realized that she hadn't been alone on the trip to San Francisco, but she knew that her aunt had ways of finding out anything she needed to know. Elizabeth paused at the doors to the hospital, trying to gather her courage. She had no idea what she'd face inside. Part of her wanted to run away, but she knew that she wouldn't get away with that either. Drawing up the courage that had gotten her through numerous scandals in her life, she walked through the automatic doors.

She was directed to the ICU. There she encountered the Gang—Cat's friends and Elizabeth's own family. Meeting stares and inquisitive looks with a haughty look of her own, Elizabeth proceeded to the room she'd been told Cat was in. Once again she paused before pushing open the door. The first thing she noticed was Kana, the big, dark-haired Samoan sitting in a chair next to the bed. She also noted the dark, angry look Kana shot in her direction. Then Elizabeth looked at the woman lying in the bed, and all thoughts of the trouble she was in fled. She couldn't believe what she was seeing. Cat's face was battered and bruised; Elizabeth gasped involuntarily at that sight. She could also see that Cat was crying, which told Elizabeth that everyone did indeed know where she'd been and with whom.

When Kana stood up suddenly and walked toward her, Elizabeth stepped back, terrified that Kana would actually strike her. The look on the darker woman's face was so filled with anger that Elizabeth could feel it coming directly at her. Bracing for what was to come, Elizabeth was truly surprised when Kana walked past her and out of the room, closing the door behind her.

When Elizabeth looked back over at Cat, she saw that her eyes were open now. She felt a sudden rush of shame for what she'd been doing while the woman she loved had been being brutalized. Cat turned her face away from her, but guilt and shame drove Elizabeth to walk over to the bed, wanting to somehow make it up to Cat.

"Cat…" she began, reaching out to touch Cat's hand, wanting to offer some kind of explanation but not sure what she would say.

"Don't," Cat growled, pulling her hand away.

Elizabeth's lips trembled. She knew she was in the wrong, and there wasn't much she could do to change it right now. She just hoped she could make up for it somehow.

"Cat, please…" Elizabeth began again, thinking if she could just lie her way out of this…

"Get out," Cat said, her voice as cold and hard as her heart suddenly felt.

"Please—"

"Now," Cat said, her voice unchanged.

"If you'll just let me explain—" Elizabeth whispered.

"Get out!" Cat roared, coming half up off the bed in her vehemence. "Now!"

Elizabeth jumped in response to Cat's anger.

"Catalina, please!" Elizabeth cried, terrified now, knowing she'd screwed up badly this time.

"She said to get out," Kana said from the door, her look immovable. "Get out, now. Or I'd be more than happy to remove you."

The last was said in a low threatening tone, and Elizabeth didn't doubt Kana for a moment. She hurried out of the room past the glaring Samoan. Out in the hallway, Elizabeth encountered her aunt and uncle. There was a closed look on Midnight's face. Glancing at Rick, Elizabeth saw his disapproval clear in his deep blue eyes. She ran from the hospital, unable to handle the overwhelming sense of failure she was feeling.

Kashena was in the office when she got the call. She answered it while she reached for her coffee; it was going to be a long day with Baz in San Francisco guarding Samantha Cobb.

"Ma'am, this is Sergeant Ross from the San Francisco Police Department. I'm calling about Special Agent Supervisor Sebastian Bach?"

"What'd he do this time?" Kashena asked, thinking Baz had irritated some suit at the courthouse.

"Ma'am, I'm sorry to say that he's been shot."

"What?" Kashena felt the blood draining out of her head as her hands grew cold instantly. "Is he... I'm... Is he okay?" She gripped the phone tighter as the man paused. Baz couldn't be dead—she would know... she'd feel it, right?

"No, ma'am, he's in critical condition. I understand you are in contact with the Attorney General. We need to inform—"

"I'll do it." Kashena said, reaching for her jacket. "Is Deputy Attorney General Cobb alright?"

"I, um, yes, ma'am," the sergeant stammered. "She was not hit. Agent Bach shot the assailant."

"Is he dead?"

"Yes, ma'am," the officer replied, sounding pleased.

"Good," Kashena murmured. "Thanks." As she hung up, she put her Bluetooth in her ear and strode out of the office toward the elevator, her mind racing. She dialed Midnight's direct number, knowing that she was in San Diego dealing with the attack of one her former officers.

Because of that, Kashena was surprised when Midnight answered the phone on the third ring.

"Chevalier," was the brisk, distracted greeting.

"Ma'am, it's SA Marshal."

"Marshal, what is it?" Midnight asked, sounding immediately focused on the call. Kashena appreciated that.

"It's Bach. He's been shot."

"What?" Midnight sounded as shocked as Kashena felt. "Is he okay?"

Kashena fought back the tears that wanted to clog her throat. "I... Ma'am, he's in critical condition."

"Oh, Jesus…" Midnight breathed. "Are you with him?"

"Headed there now, ma'am."

"By car?"

"Yes, ma'am."

"No, go to the airfield. I'll have one of the aviation staff waiting for you—they'll fly you there. Did you hear if Deputy AG Cobb is alright?" Midnight asked, her mind racing.

"She is, ma'am, and thank you," Kashena said, happy for the help. She'd wondered about asking the aviation unit but wasn't sure if it would be misuse of state resources.

"Go check on our boy, and find Deputy AG Cobb. I'm sure she's freaked," Midnight said, her tone both authoritative and supportive. Kashena took heart in it. In less than half an hour she was on a plane heading to the Bay area. When it touched down, she was met by an agent from the San Francisco office, who drove her directly to the hospital.

Kashena hit the doors to the hospital at a dead run, lifting her jacket aside to show the security guard her badge as she passed him. Inside she ran straight up to the front desk. She pulled her badge off her belt and showed it to the nurse.

"Agent Sebastian Bach was brought into Emergency—I need to know where he is and who can tell me how he is."

The nurse looked startled but responded quickly to the authority in Kashena's voice. She tapped at the keys on the computer in front of her.

"Mr. Bach is in surgery right now. There's a waiting room on the sixth floor. The doctor will find you there when Mr. Bach is out of surgery."

"Thank you," Kashena said crisply, and strode toward the elevators.

When the elevator didn't come fast enough, she located the door to the stairwell and jogged up the six flights of stairs. She was doing her best to work off the tension she was feeling. All she'd been told was that Sebastian had taken a round in the chest and he'd been airlifted to San Francisco General.

In the waiting room, Kashena saw Deputy Attorney General Samantha Cobb. She was being set upon by reporters asking her what had happened. The attorney looked frantic as she was assailed with questions.

Kashena walked up, pushing her way through the reporters.

"Alright, back up," Kashena said, moving to stand in front of Samantha. "The Attorney General's office has no official statement at this time."

As she pushed the reporters back, Kashena blocked anyone from getting to Samantha again. When the reporters finally retreated, Kashena turned around to look at the much smaller woman.

"DAG Cobb," Kashena said, "are you alright?"

Samantha stared up at the blond woman.

"Who are you?" she asked.

"Special Agent Supervisor Kashena Marshal," Kashena said, pulling her jacket aside to show Samantha her badge. "Are you alright? Were you injured?"

Somehow, knowing that this was Sebastian's best friend, and knowing that she was most likely worried sick about him but asking after her instead, made Samantha lose her composure. Bursting into tears, she shook her head.

Kashena was surprised by the attorney's tears. She knew that Sebastian and this woman had been at odds on a number of things. But she also knew that Sebastian had a soft spot for the headstrong, opinionated attorney.

Sensing that Samantha Cobb was sincerely upset by the incident, Kashena did her best to comfort the other woman. She was careful to keep her gestures professional, however, considering there were a number of people around them, including the reporters.

Kashena got a call from Kana an hour after she got to the hospital.

"Have they told you how he is yet?" Kana asked without preamble.

"Not yet, ma'am," Kashena answered.

"Call me as soon as you hear anything."

"Thank you, ma'am," Kashena said. "I hope your friend is okay."

"She will be. Bach will be okay too," Kana assured Kashena.

"I hope so, ma'am."

Kana hung up at her end, shaking her head. Things were getting weird, and she didn't like that they were happening at the same time.

"Is he okay?" Midnight asked.

Midnight, Rick, Kana, and Rogue Squadron were all still at the hospital in San Diego. Everyone else had gone home, planning to come back the next day to see Cat, although she'd already said she didn't want to see anyone.

"They haven't told Kashena anything yet," Kana said, looking worried.

"You're not thinking these incidents are related?" Midnight said.

Kana shrugged. "Probably not," she said. "But it's too much of a coincidence for my liking."

Midnight nodded. "I know what you mean."

Back in San Francisco, Kashena found a private waiting room for herself and Samantha. Sierra called her on her cell phone a few times. Kashena waited until she was safely able to talk before she called Sierra back.

"Is he okay?" Sierra asked first thing.

"I don't know yet," Kashena said, shaking her head, starting to feel the effects of what was happening.

"I wish I could be there with you," Sierra said, her voice soft.

Kashena blew her breath out, closing her eyes. "I wish you could be too."

Sierra was silent for a moment. "Kashena, do you want me to come there?"

Kashena hesitated. Yes, she wanted Sierra there—she knew that Sierra understood what this meant to her, her best friend being shot. She wanted someone to hold her hand and tell her everything was going to be alright. She wanted Sierra to be that person, but she knew it was impossible.

"It's too risky," she said finally. "There are reporters here. If they see you here they might get suspicious."

Sierra was silent at her end. "Okay," she said softly, feeling both disappointed and sad that she couldn't be there when Kashena needed her most, and wishing desperately that things were different.

"I'll call you as soon as I hear something," Kashena said.

"Okay," Sierra answered again, trying her best to hide her feelings.

It was another four hours before the doctors came out to talk to them.

"Agent Marshal?" the doctor said, walking over to Kashena.

"Yes?" Kashena asked, her heart in her throat.

"Mr. Bach is in recovery right now," the doctor said. "We removed a nine-millimeter bullet from his chest wall. He lost a lot of blood, and there was some damage to a corner of his heart, but we've repaired that and feel that his prognosis is good."

Kashena was sure she'd faint from the relief. It was Samantha Cobb who fainted instead. Kashena caught her before she hit the floor. She carried her over to the couch in the room and laid her down. A nurse came to her aid with smelling salts; it took a moment before Samantha jerked her head away from the smell, waking as she did.

"What happened?" Samantha asked, her voice tremulous.

"You fainted," Kashena said.

"Oh…" Samantha said. "Sebastian is going to be fine, right? That's what the doctor said?"

"Yes," Kashena said, smiling. "Yes, that's what he said."

"Oh, thank God," Samantha said, moving to sit up.

"I think you should stay down, Deputy AG Cobb," Kashena said, as she saw the other woman sway slightly.

"Samantha?" came a voice from behind them.

Samantha opened her eyes and saw her husband, Jeffrey, standing in the doorway to the waiting room. Kashena stood, stepping aside. Jeffrey walked in and stood next to where Samantha lay.

"Are you alright?" he asked, sounding mildly concerned. "Were you hurt in the attack?"

Samantha sat up with an effort. Kashena noted that her husband made no move to help her.

"No, I'm fine," Samantha replied. "I simply fainted a little bit ago."

"Fainted?" Jeffrey queried. "Why?"

"She's been through a bit of a shock, Mr. Cobb," Kashena put in when Samantha couldn't come up with an answer.

Jeffrey looked at Kashena in speculation.

"She watched her bodyguard gunned down in front of her," Kashena said.

"Yes, he did his job well," Jeffrey agreed.

"His job?" Kashena repeated incredulously.

"Jeffrey," Samantha said, putting herself between Kashena and her husband, "I think I need some coffee. Could you get me some, please?"

Jeffrey looked hesitant. He glanced at Kashena, whose look had turned to stone. Finally he nodded, walking out of the waiting room. Samantha immediately turned to Kashena.

"I'm sorry for what my husband just said," she said sincerely. "Jeffrey tends to forget his manners in stressful situations."

Kashena raised an eyebrow at the smaller woman. "I see," she answered simply.

Samantha grimaced, knowing that Jeffrey would only stick his foot in his mouth repeatedly where Sebastian was concerned. Kashena, being Sebastian's best friend, was likely to tell Sebastian what Jeffrey had said. The fact was, Jeffrey had never considered Sebastian anything but hired help, nor would he change his mind now. As far as Jeffrey was concerned, Sebastian had served his purpose in keeping Samantha from being hit in the attack.

It showed the polarization of the differences between her husband and Sebastian. Something that had been slowly but surely becoming clearer in the time that she'd known Sebastian Bach. She had no idea how she was going to handle Jeffrey being there. She was worried sick about Sebastian, and now here was her husband. It was going to be difficult no matter what happened.

**

"What do you mean he's not dead?" the man snapped at his companion. "You told me that man was the best in his field!"

"I'm sorry, sir," the man replied to his temporary employer. "He was, but I guess Bach was better." He rubbed his hands on his pants nervously, wondering if he'd still get paid for the job; he was supposed to have split it with the now-dead hitman.

"Well, it should keep them guessing for a bit, regardless," the man who'd ordered the hit reasoned. "At least for the moment. They'll have more than they can take soon..." he finished with an evil smile.

**

As Samantha had suspected, the next two hours were extremely tense, with Kashena leaning against the far wall of the waiting room, as far away from Jeffrey as she could get. Unfortunately, it wasn't far enough not to hear repeatedly the comments that Jeffrey made. He had no idea why Samantha didn't want to leave the hospital.

"There's nothing you can do," he said snidely. "You're not a doctor, for God's sake."

Samantha glanced over at Kashena to see if the woman had heard. Indeed she had, because her dark blue eyes narrowed as she stared across the room, pointedly looking away from Jeffrey.

"Jeffrey," Samantha began quietly, "I need to make sure he's okay."

"Why?" Jeffrey asked, his voice louder than necessary.

Kashena turned to look at the man, her lips pursed in consideration. She was evaluating whether or not wiping the floor with him would be construed as assault. Given that he was a lawyer, it might be considered an environmental improvement.

Samantha noticed Kashena's look and hoped the other woman wouldn't say anything. In truth, however, Samantha was getting fed up with her husband's attitude.

"He saved my life, Jeffrey," Samantha said, her voice louder this time in her rush to defend Sebastian. "I think that warrants a great deal of respect and appreciation."

Jeffrey actually had the temerity to give a sarcastic snort.

"He's paid to protect you, Samantha. That's what he did."

Samantha saw Kashena's chin come up slightly and her body tense. She bit her lip, not sure what was going to happen now. She refused to try and run interference for her husband again—he didn't have any sense of propriety or even courtesy at all, and it was making her mad.

"Jeffrey," she said sharply, "go home."

"What?" he asked, sure he hadn't heard her right.

"I said, go home, Jeffrey," Samantha said, standing and gesturing toward the door.

"What are you talking about?" he asked her, standing too, his look perplexed.

"I want you to leave," Samantha clarified.

"Why?"

"Because you're pissing me off, that's why," she snapped. "You're an inconsiderate snob, and I'm tired of listening to it tonight. So just go home."

Jeffrey's mouth dropped open in shock. He glanced at the blond woman standing at the far wall, her lips curling into a smirk. It annoyed him. He turned his gaze to his wife.

"I think you've been keeping far too much company with the lower classes, Samantha," he said condescendingly. "You're starting to talk like them."

"Better them than you," Samantha replied with an angry look.

She turned away, walking over to where Kashena stood and then sitting down in a chair, her arms crossed in front of her chest. Jeffrey stared after her, shocked. He narrowed his eyes at Kashena, a sneer on his lips. Turning on his heel, he strode out of the waiting room.

The room was silent. Samantha sat doing her best to calm down.

"Very nice," Kashena murmured in approval, a grin in place.

Samantha glanced up at the other woman and saw her smile. Laughing softly, she shook her head.

"I'm just sorry you had to listen to him this whole time," she said.

"Fortunately, Marines are known for their self-control," Kashena said, grinning still.

Samantha laughed again.

At one point during the night, alarms started going off at the nurses' station. Samantha and Kashena heard them, and through the windows of the waiting room they saw two nurses and a doctor running down the hall. Kashena pushed off the wall, striding to the door. Samantha was right on her heels. When they reached the scene of the commotion, all three medical personnel were trying to calm Sebastian down

"Sir, you have to lie back down!" the doctor was yelling as the nurses tried to push Sebastian back toward the bed.

"Move or I'll kill ya," Sebastian told the doctor, refusing to budge at either the nurses' insistence or their attempts to move him.

Kashena pushed her way through and past the doctor, knowing what needed to be done. Samantha stood in the doorway looking terrified. Sebastian's blood was dripping on the floor from where he'd ripped the IV out of his arm.

"Baz, calm down," Kashena said, standing in front of her partner. "Samantha is fine. You need to lie back down."

"She's okay?" Sebastian asked, not sounding convinced.

"She's right there," Kashena said, pointing to the doorway.

"I'm fine, Sebastian," Samantha assured him, moving to help Kashena coax him back to bed. "Please lie back down."

Sebastian stood where he was, his eyes scanning Samantha from head to toe. Reaching out, he touched her cheek as if checking to see if she was real or an illusion. Then he closed his eyes, weakening instantly as the adrenaline left him. Kashena reacted quickly, levering his body against hers and moving him toward the bed. After helping him to lie down, Kashena moved back, letting the doctor and nurses reconnect what they needed to.

To Kashena's surprise, Samantha moved to the other side of the bed and took Sebastian's hand in hers, her eyes watching him worriedly. Kashena nodded slowly to herself. Samantha's actions said a lot, and it comforted her somehow that Sebastian's sacrifice hadn't been for nothing. Samantha Cobb actually cared about him, and really did feel that it hadn't been his job to give up his life for hers. It wasn't just words.

Once the monitors and IVs were hooked back up, the nurses left. The doctor looked at Kashena and Samantha.

"It's usually against hospital policy for anyone to be in the recovery room," he said, "but it's obvious to me that we'd have been in serious trouble here if it hadn't been for your presence."

Kashena grinned, glancing at Samantha, who laughed softly.

"Just make sure he rests," the doctor said, smiling.

"No problem," Kashena said.

Sebastian was asleep from the moment his head hit the pillow. Kashena and Samantha alternated sitting in the one chair in the room over the next few hours. At one point, Samantha glanced around the room, perplexed. Then she rolled her eyes.

"It's too quiet in here for him," she said. "That's what's wrong."

Kashena laughed out loud, realizing that not only was Samantha right, but she knew Sebastian pretty well.

"He does need his music," Kashena agreed.

"His chaos," Samantha added.

"Yeah," Kashena said, smiling. "Maybe we can smuggle him in a radio once he's in his own room."

"I think that would make him feel more comfortable."

"Roger that," Kashena said.

Things between the two women changed in that moment—they became friends. Kashena liked anyone who cared enough about Sebastian to know his habits. Samantha respected Kashena for her friendship with Sebastian and her obvious concern for his wellbeing.

Dawn was breaking when Sebastian stirred again. Opening his eyes, he located Kashena leaning against the wall, a cup of coffee in hand. He also saw Samantha sitting in the chair next to his bed, her hand in his. She was asleep.

Giving her hand a little squeeze, he whispered her name. She woke immediately.

"You're still here?" he asked, his voice gravelly.

"Can't go anywhere without my bodyguard," Samantha said, smiling at him.

"You still have work," he said, his tone concerned.

"A day or two away isn't going to compromise any of my cases."

"If you say so," he replied, looking both pleased and surprised by Samantha's response.

Samantha simply smiled. Kashena walked over and looked down at her partner.

"Still alive?" she asked blithely.

"Currently," he replied with a grin.

"Roger that."

Sebastian chuckled softly. His eyes were already closing again. He was asleep moments later.

"I'll be back," Kashena told Samantha.

Walking outside, Kashena went out to the smoking area. She wasn't inherently a smoker, but she found that smoking the cigars she did calmed her nerves more often than not. Standing in the quad, she leaned against a nearby wall and lit a cigar, staring up at the sky, which was clouded over and looking like rain.

"Agent Marshal?" a blond man queried, his English accent clear in the quiet quad.

Her head came up, deep blue eyes assessing the man walking toward her purposefully. He looked somewhat familiar, but in a way she couldn't put her finger on.

"I'm Marshal," she answered.

The man extended his hand. "Joe Sinclair," he said, smiling at her.

Kashena took his hand. Not only did he look familiar, his name sounded familiar too. She waited in silence for him to tell her as she shook his hand.

"Midnight sent me," he said. "She's asked me to take over for Agent Bach while he recovers, at least until we assess any further danger to the Deputy AG."

Kashena nodded, her eyes not giving anything away.

"Can I see your badge?" she asked, her tone and look direct.

Joe grinned, rubbing the bridge of his nose with his index finger.

"That's gonna be tough—it's at home in a redwood shadow box. Perhaps this will help," he said, reaching into his pocket and pulling out a business card as well as his cell phone.

He handed Kashena the card, pulled out his phone, and dialed a number. He then handed the phone to Kashena. Leaning back against the wall, he reached for a cigarette, his light blue eyes on her as he lit it.

The phone was answered on the third ring.

"Chevalier."

"Ah," Kashena stammered, not having expected to be connected with the AG herself. "Attorney General Chevalier?"

"Yes," Midnight said, smiling at her end. "Agent Marshal?"

"Yes, ma'am."

"I assume Joe just got there?"

"Yes, ma'am," Kashena answered again.

"I've sent him to keep an eye on Deputy Cobb, until things settle down a bit," Midnight said. "I've also sent one of my people to keep an eye on your charge while you're there with Agent Bach."

"I—" Kashena stammered, suddenly realizing she'd left Sierra without protection in her haste to get to Sebastian. "I'm sorry, ma'am, I—"

"It's okay, Kashena," Midnight said. "I want you to be able to be where you're needed right now. I just want to make sure we cover all our bases while we're at it."

"Yes, ma'am," Kashena said, grimacing still, feeling like she'd let both the AG and Sierra down.

"Kashena," Midnight said, her voice softening. "See the guy standing in front of you?"

"Yes, ma'am."

"He's been my partner for over twenty years. If something happened to him, and it has, I would and have dropped everything to be there for him. So relax, okay? I know where your head is right now. I want to make sure you're able to stay with Bach as long as you need to, while Sierra is protected too."

Kashena blew her breath out, ever amazed at the woman she worked for. Was there no end to the understanding Midnight had? She was very much a cop's cop—of that there was no doubt.

"Thank you, ma'am," Kashena said finally. "I promise to get back on the job as soon as I feel Baz is stable."

"I've assigned Christian Collins to Sierra. Joe can give you his cell number. Just let him know when you're ready to take over again," Midnight said. "And Marshal?"

"Yes, ma'am?"

"Make sure you take care of yourself while you're at it," Midnight said, knowing full well how often she'd failed to eat or take care of herself when one of her people had been in the hospital.

"I'll do my best, ma'am," Kashena said.

"All I can ask for," Midnight replied. "Put Joe on, will you?"

"Yes, ma'am," Kashena said, handing Joe back the phone.

"All clear?" Joe asked into the phone, laughing out loud the next minute. "I figured the direct route was fastest," he said, his eyes on

Kashena. "You got it. I'll give you an update once I make contact with DAG Cobb. Let me know what happens down there."

Joe hung up his phone a moment later, pocketing it again as he took a long last drag of his cigarette.

"Any questions you want to ask?" Joe asked her.

"Christian Collins?" Kashena replied.

"My cousin, a narc, and a very good cop," Joe said. "And you can trust him to keep her safe."

Kashena's eyes narrowed slightly. She was wondering if Joe knew the nature of her relationship with Sierra Youngblood. His look gave nothing away, however.

"I hope you understand," Kashena said, gesturing to the cell phone in his pocket. "I had to check."

"I would have been worried if you hadn't," Joe replied. "How is Agent Bach doing?"

"They said he's stable," Kashena said, sounding immensely relieved. "The bullet nicked his heart but didn't do a lot of damage, thankfully."

Joe nodded, remembering countless times he'd been relieved to hear a good prognosis on one of his friends. From what Midnight had told him, Kashena and Sebastian Bach were best friends. Much like he and Midnight had been forever. He understood her concern, and her need to be at the hospital at this point.

"Can you take me into Agent Bach's room and let Samantha Cobb know I'm cleared?" Joe asked with an engaging smile.

Kashena chuckled. "I can do that, yes."

***

Sierra was doing her best to focus on her work, but her mind kept going to Kashena in San Francisco. She ached to be there with her, to help take away some of the stress of what she must be going through. The idea of Sebastian being shot, when she knew how close he and Kashena were, was beyond her comprehension. What Sierra did know was that she wanted to be there for Kashena. It felt like she was failing Kashena, and that wasn't sitting well with her at all. She'd considered throwing caution to the wind and driving to San Francisco, regardless of what Kashena said, but the sensible part of her knew that she needed to be cautious, not only for herself, but more importantly for Kashena. The idea that she'd put herself in danger, possibly giving her stalker a chance to get to her, was a concern, but more because it would get Kashena in trouble if something happened to her. She chuckled at herself, amazed at how quickly she'd become so enamored of the Special Agent. *Worrying more about her than your own skin!* she chided herself silently.

She'd just made a point of refocusing her thoughts on the brief she was reading when there was a knock on the door. She called for the person to come in. She figured it was her secretary again—oddly enough, Amanda had checked on her repeatedly since they'd received the news about Sebastian Bach being shot and Kashena going to San Francisco to be with him. Sierra suspected that Amanda had an inkling of what was going on between them.

When she looked up, she was surprised to see a man standing in the doorway. He was very handsome, in a dark, dangerous-looking way.

"Chief Deputy Youngblood, I'm Sergeant Christian Collins. AG Midnight Chevalier asked me to look after you while Agent Marshal is in San Francisco."

Sierra noted his English accent. She was surprised by his statement but nodded all the same.

"Is Kashena okay?" she couldn't help but ask, addressing her chief concern.

"She's fine, I'm sure," Christian said. "But AG Chevalier feels that she'll need to be with Agent Bach for a while, and she wants to make sure you're safe in the meantime."

Sierra's mind raced as she weighed her options.

"So, if you can give me an idea of your agenda," Christian said, "I can make plans accordingly."

"I want to go to San Francisco," Sierra blurted out, having made the decision in an instant, her true desire winning out over all her internal arguments.

"I'm sorry?" Christian queried, sounding surprised by the outburst.

"I want to go to San Francisco," she repeated, feeling more sure about it this time.

She waited in silence to see if he'd question her. To his credit, he merely nodded. "I'll make arrangements. When would you like to leave?"

"As soon as possible," she replied.

Christian nodded again, then turned and walked out of the room.

An hour later they were driving to her house to pick up a few things.

"You said 'Sergeant,' didn't you?" Sierra asked after a few minutes. "You don't work for DOJ, do you?"

"No, ma'am," he said. "I work for San Diego PD."

"Do you do bodyguard work there?" she asked, thinking that didn't sound right.

"Narcotics work," Christian answered, then glanced at her, seeing her perplexed look. "I'm a close friend of Midnight's—she trusts me to do the job right."

Sierra blinked a few times. Midnight Chevalier did things very differently than the previous AG would have.

Christian smiled. "Midnight's best friends with my cousin, Joe. He's over in San Francisco watching over Agent Bach's girl."

"I see," Sierra said, still trying to understand.

Christian's phone rang. He hit the hands-free.

"Collins," he answered.

"Hey, it's Mace," said a man's voice.

"Hey, man, how's Cat?"

"She's good, man. Doctors say she can go home in a couple of days."

"But what home?" Christian asked, an edge to his voice.

"Kana and Palani's," Kevin answered.

"I was hoping you'd say that," Christian said, breaking into a smile.

"Yeah, you know K. She takes care of her own."

Sierra listened, perking up at the mention of Kana Sorbinno's name.

"Indeed she does," Christian replied. "Thanks for the update, man. Did you get anything out of those guys?"

"Nah, not really," Kevin said. "But Cat says that they asked a lot about Elizabeth."

"Really?" Christian asked. "Family business, then."

"Sounds like it."

Christian nodded, not looking happy in the slightest. "Well, keep me up to date. Keep an eye on Cat when K heads back out with Midnight too, will ya? And check on my girl every so often too, huh?"

"You know I will," Kevin replied. "All for one."

"One for all," Christian replied with a grin.

"Later, man."

"Later," Christian said, then hung up the phone.

Sierra had questions swirling in her head. The people that surrounded Midnight Chevalier had long been a curiosity of hers. So much had been said about Midnight's "people"—so much, but so little. Sierra remembered the report about Midnight's friend and now bodyguard, Kana Sorbinno, being shot during Midnight's campaign. The subsequent stories about Kana being gay and Midnight being "more involved" than just a friend. Followed closely by Midnight's well worded speech about love knowing no gender, and how anyone that paid attention could see, however, how in love she was with her husband. Since then, many people had been curious about the people who seemed to both shield and stand behind Midnight Chevalier. This was a chance she couldn't pass up.

"So, can I ask who Cat is?" she asked tentatively.

"A member of my team," Christian answered, reaching for his cigarettes and glancing at her. "Do you mind if I smoke?"

"Not at all," she said. "What happened to her?"

"She was attacked, actually the same day Agent Bach was shot."

"Oh my God, is she okay?" Sierra asked.

"Yeah," Christian said. "It sounds, though, like they may have been after Liz, Cat's girlfriend."

"Girlfriend?" Sierra queried in a slightly odd tone.

Christian gave her a measured look. "Yeah, Liz and Cat are dating. Liz is Midnight's niece."

Sierra nodded, surprised by that but knowing she shouldn't be. Midnight Chevalier had already stated quite publicly that she didn't care about things like that. Love knew no gender.

"So that's what you meant by family business?" Sierra ventured. "Because they might have been after the AG's niece?"

"Yeah," Christian said.

"But you're not related to Midnight Chevalier, are you?"

Christian grinned. "Well, no, but neither is ninety-five percent of her family."

"I'm sorry?"

Christian laughed at that. "What Midnight considers her family is a group of us who have become her extended family. Either because they've been with her from the beginning of her law enforcement career, or by family ties with those members, or by being the lovers, wives, girlfriends of the aforementioned."

"And you're a family-tie member?" Sierra asked.

"Yeah," Christian said. "So's my wife, in a few ways."

"A few ways?"

"Long story."

"I see," Sierra said, not wanting to be a pest.

His phone rang again; he answered it.

"Collins."

"What's a good-looking guy like you doing way up in Sacramento?" came the husky reply.

Christian's smile was brilliant. "Talking about my beautiful wife, as it happens."

"Oh shit, what are you saying about me?" Stevie replied, laughing.

"I was just trying to explain to Chief Deputy Youngblood the intricacies of our family."

"Oh God," Stevie replied. "That ought to have her confused for a week or two. No one understands us, babe, you should know that by now."

193

Christian glanced over at Sierra. "Oh, I dunno. She seemed to be grasping the concept pretty well."

"You get into the whole Donovan, Mace, Erin, Jeanie thing yet? Or the Joe, Rick, and Midnight thing yet? Hmm? Or better still, my sister, Kyle, and Midnight? That's when it gets complicated, babe."

Christian rolled his eyes. "No, I hadn't gotten into all that," he said, glancing at Sierra and seeing her eyes on him expectantly. "But it looks like I'm gonna end up explaining it all now."

"Oops, sorry," Stevie replied, not sounding like she was. "So you obviously got up there okay?"

"Yeah," Christian replied, "and I'm headed to San Francisco on a 2 p.m. flight."

"Huh?"

"Chief Deputy Youngblood wants to go to San Francisco," Christian replied, his eyes staring straight ahead.

"Oh," Stevie replied, sounding perplexed but not questioning further. She knew her husband and that he was purposely not explaining.

"Hey, Mace said that this thing with Cat might have been family related," Christian said, his tone serious now. "Promise me you'll be careful out there."

"I will be, babe, you know that. Dave isn't even sending us out alone right now."

"Mace having to cover both you and J?"

"No, Dave's going out with me. Mace is going out with Jeanie."

Christian nodded, looking comforted. "Good."

"We'll be fine, babe, don't worry."

"Good." Christian said again, his expression serious.

"I'll let you go. I know you're trying to juggle driving, smoking, and talking to me all at the same time."

Christian laughed—his wife knew him well. "You got it."

"You be careful up there, too, okay?" Stevie said, her tone softening.

"Always, love, always."

"I love you," she said seriously.

"And I you," he replied, his smile gentle.

Sierra knew she was seeing a man deeply in love with his wife. It made her heart ache. She missed Kashena desperately. She hoped Kashena wouldn't be too angry with her for showing up in San Francisco, but she just felt she needed to be there. That was the beginning of the realization. She didn't miss Jason at all, and he'd been gone for eight months. Kashena had been gone less than two days, and she missed her presence keenly.

She was risking having Christian Collins report to Midnight Chevalier that one of her Chief Deputy AGs decided to make a run to San Francisco because she missed her girlfriend. To her credit, she'd insisted on using her own credit card to pay for both her plane ticket and Christian's, as well as for the rental car. She had no intention of filing a claim to get the money back either. This trip was personal, not business. She would have done it sooner, but Kashena had warned her to be careful and not travel at all while she was unprotected.

All Sierra knew was that she needed to see Kashena, and she needed to be there when Kashena needed her.

Back in San Francisco, Sebastian had finally ordered Kashena out of his room.

"Go get a hotel room and get some sleep, Kash, or I'm going to kick your ass," he'd threatened.

"Oh, there's a threat I'm going to take seriously," Kashena said, rolling her eyes as she stifled a yawn.

"See?" Sebastian said, his look pointed. "Go get some sleep. I'm not goin' anywhere."

Finally Kashena had acquiesced and left the hospital, going to a hotel nearby. As soon as she got into the room, however, she called the hospital to tell them where to get ahold of her in the event that Sebastian needed her. She took a shower, washing and drying her hair. Not bothering to get dressed, she slid under the sheets of the bed and was asleep a minute later.

"I just need to know what room she's in," Sierra cajoled.

"I'm sorry, ma'am, we can't give out that information," the woman at the counter said for the third time.

"Maybe I can help," Christian said, stepping up to the counter and holding up his badge. "This is a police matter, miss," he said, his smile warm and sexy. "I'm sure you can understand that it's important that we speak with Ms. Marshal."

The young woman behind the counter stared open-mouthed at the outrageously handsome man standing in front of her. Badge aside, she'd give him anything he wanted, just anything.

"Oh," she said, finally finding her voice again. "I see. Well in that case…" she said as she tapped at the keys of her computer. "It says here that Ms. Marshal is in room 1022."

"Is there an adjoining room?" Christian asked.

"Yes, room 1023 is an adjoining room."

"Is it available?" Christian asked, his smile brilliant, light blue eyes intense.

"Yes, sir," the woman said.

"Excellent," Christian said. "Can you book that room? And can we get a key to Ms. Marshal's room as well?"

"I…" The woman hesitated, wanting to say she couldn't give out keys to other people's rooms, but looking up at Christian, she saw him smile again and figured *why not?* "Certainly, sir. Your name?"

Minutes later Christian had secured a key for his room as well as one to Kashena's. As he escorted Sierra to the elevator he muttered, "Won't be using this hotel as safe house anytime soon."

Sierra laughed softly. "You charmed her into that."

Christian widened his eyes, his lips twisted in a grimace. "That's my point."

Sierra nodded, realizing that had they been out to hurt Kashena, it would have been easy. That was very dangerous.

At the door to Kashena's room, Christian handed her the key and her overnight bag.

"I'll be next door if you need me," he said, his voice casual.

Sierra looked back at him for a few seconds. She'd been wondering how she was going to approach seeing Kashena again with Christian looking on ever since they'd left the hospital. When they'd arrived in San Francisco, Christian had driven her over to the hospital without even asking if that's where she wanted to go. The hospital staff had told them that Agent Marshal had gone down the street to the hotel. Sierra hadn't been sure if Christian knew exactly why she was in San Francisco until that moment in the hotel hallway.

She nodded, appreciating both his discretion and his lack of apparent judgment on the situation. He quirked a grin and walked over to his door, opening it and waiting for her to do the same. She went into Kashena's hotel room, closing the door quietly behind her. She immediately saw Kashena lying asleep in the bed. Leaning back against the door, she stared at the woman who'd haunted her every thought for quite a while now.

She set her bag down and kicked off her shoes. Sitting on the bed, she touched Kashena's cheek gently. Kashena was awake immediately, her deep blue eyes widening when she recognized Sierra.

"What? How? Wait, where's Collins?" Kashena's words tumbled out over themselves.

"Relax," Sierra said, smiling. "He's next door. He brought me here."

"Why?" Kashena asked, looking perplexed.

"Because I asked him to," Sierra answered.

Kashena drew in a breath, her eyes reflecting concern and caution.

"Please don't be angry with me," Sierra said, lying down next to Kashena and reaching up to touch her cheek again. "I needed to be here with you."

Kashena propped herself up on her elbow and looked down at Sierra, her eyes searching. Finally she leaned down to kiss Sierra's lips softly.

When their lips parted, Sierra said, "You know, it never occurred to me that Linda might have come…"

Kashena gave a short sarcastic laugh. "Linda doesn't do anything that doesn't have anything in it for her."

Sierra pressed her lips together, determined not to comment on how wrong that was.

Kashena kissed her again. Any thought Sierra had about Linda was gone moments after that. Kashena's hands held her face gently as they kissed. She lay back, gently pulling Sierra with her and over her. They continued to kiss, reveling in being close again

Sierra pulled back, looking at Kashena and seeing how exhausted she looked.

"How much sleep have you had?" she asked.

"Not a whole lot in the last forty-eight hours."

"And here I just woke you up," Sierra said, grimacing.

"I'm glad you did. I want you here," Kashena said, reaching up to kiss her again.

Minutes later, Kashena removed Sierra's clothes and they made love. Lying together afterwards trying to catch their breath, Kashena held Sierra to her, her lips against Sierra's temple.

"I want you here," Kashena said, her hands tightening around Sierra, indicating which "here" she meant.

Sierra smiled, her cheek against Kashena's shoulder, her body still half over Kashena's. "I want to be here too."

"Here?" Kashena echoed.

"All the time," Sierra answered.

Kashena smiled tiredly. Rolling to her side and taking Sierra with her, Kashena kept her arms around the smaller woman. She fell asleep holding Sierra to her, feeling Sierra's lips and breath on her neck. She woke later that night, feeling Sierra stir.

Brushing her lips against Sierra's forehead, she caressed her skin, hearing Sierra sigh. Kashena smiled in the darkness, wrapping her arms tighter around Sierra and feeling her snuggle closer.

"Kash?" Sierra said softly after a few minutes.

"Hmm?"

Sierra was quiet, hesitating. Maybe this wasn't the time to mention this.

Kashena pulled back, looking down at Sierra in the dim light of the hotel room.

"What's up, babe?" she asked softly.

Sierra raised her head. "I got a letter yesterday," she said cautiously.

Kashena nodded slowly, waiting for the rest.

"Jason got his orders. He's coming home," Sierra said in a rush, as if saying it quickly would lessen the impact.

Kashena's arm, wrapped around Sierra's shoulders, dropped away as Kashena looked back at her.

"When will he be stateside?" Kashena asked evenly.

"Next week," Sierra said, already sensing Kashena pulling away.

Kashena nodded again, accepting what she was hearing.

"It's going to be so difficult," Sierra said.

Kashena rolled to her back, her hand that had been on Sierra's waist sliding away as she stared up at the ceiling.

"What's difficult? He's your husband," Kashena said, her tone matter-of-fact.

Sierra propped herself up on one elbow, reaching out to touch Kashena's stomach. "I meant in terms of my feelings," she said softly.

Kashena gave her a cynical look.

"I want to see you, Kashena. I need to."

"It's not going to be that easy, Sierra," Kashena said wearily.

"I know that," Sierra said, "but I need to see you."

"You will see me," Kashena said. "I'm still going to be your bodyguard."

Sierra stared back at her, her lips trembling. "Please don't do this," she pleaded. "I've never felt this way. I feel so much for you, so much I don't understand, but so much I need. Please don't pull away now."

Kashena winced at the sheer desperation in Sierra's voice. Her own thoughts were in turmoil. She'd known Sierra was married, and to a Marine, no less. But somehow she'd never stopped and thought about what would happen when he came back. And now it was happening, and now she felt sick. Her automatic thought was to back off, to keep her emotions shut down; it was easier that way. But Sierra's dark eyes staring down at her, begging her not to pull away, were tearing at the iron-clad control Kashena was so proud of.

Exhaling slowly, Kashena pulled Sierra down to her and kissed her softly. Her thumb brushed gently over Sierra's lips, silently telling her not to say any more. They kissed for a long time, caressing and touching. No more was said about Jason's arrival home, but it was a looming cloud on the horizon.

***

After a week at Kana and Palani's, Cat was feeling a bit smothered. The first few days at the house, Kana had been extremely attentive, even coming into the room she was staying in and lying down behind her, holding her. Cat had spent a great deal of time listening to the radio and just lying on the bed, trying to get her mind around everything.

She thought about what had happened, and the time in the hospital. Kana had been ever present, but Elizabeth hadn't attempted to return after Cat had ordered her out. She hadn't been there for her when Cat had needed her—Cat's mind frequently veered away from that thought. The idea of Elizabeth in a hotel in San Francisco with some man... Jesus, she'd smelled the man still on Elizabeth when she'd come to the hospital. *How could she?* That was the question that kept circling in Cat's head. After everything that they'd been through, to have Elizabeth let her down when she needed her most. It was the ultimate betrayal. It made her sick.

"I need to drive," Cat said, one evening after a week of lying in bed "recovering."

Kana looked up from her laptop. Palani looked back from the stove where she was cooking dinner.

"Uhhh…" Kana hemmed. "Your Blazer is still at forensics," she said, grimacing.

Cat nodded, looking resigned.

Kana stood up and grabbed her keys off the counter. "We can take the Navigator."

"K," Cat said, holding up her hands. "I want to drive. I need to breathe… I appreciate it, but I really don't need company."

"I won't say a word," Kana said, grinning. "And if you decide to stop off and get plowed, I'll drive you home."

"I don't want to talk," Cat clarified.

"We won't talk," Kana said.

"I need to crank my music."

"I'll get my ear plugs."

Cat sighed. "Okay, you can come, but I drive."

"You drive," Kana said.

Kana walked over, leaning down to kiss Palani on the lips. "We'll be back, babe."

"I'll keep dinner warm," Palani said, smiling up at Kana. "Be safe."

With that Kana and Cat walked out of the house.

Cat plugged in her iPod. She carried it everywhere she went. Fortunately, it had been left in the Blazer and had been retrieved by Kana the day after they'd rescued Cat. For the next two hours, Cat drove at breakneck speeds, the window down, her music blaring. Both she and Kana smoked.

Cat's selection of music ran the gamut of genres, going from Möt-ley Crüe to Nelly to Evanescence and up into old favorites like Jour-ney, Quiet Riot, and Def Leppard. Kana could see that some of the songs meant more to Cat than others. One of the songs, Matchbox Twenty's "Disease," seemed pretty accurate at that point.

What Cat loved about Matchbox Twenty was how Rob Thomas' lyrics seemed to talk right to your soul. "Disease" was all about how hard it was to leave someone who you knew was bad for you, like a disease.

It was an addiction of sorts, one that was almost impossible to break. And Cat was dealing with that. She was handling everything, and she was doing it alone. It worried Kana no end. The following week she needed to get back on the road with Midnight. Kana was concerned that Cat would simply continue in the state she'd been in, a limbo between life and non-life. Cat was operating in a kind of haze, and the last thing Kana wanted her doing was going back to work in that mode. It would get her killed. At that point, Kana wasn't sure if Cat cared.

Like the song said, her world was coming down on her. Cat had put her faith, love, and trust in Elizabeth, and Elizabeth had betrayed it totally. Kana knew that wasn't something Cat was going to just get over. She wasn't talking about it either, and Kana was fairly sure that wasn't going to help matters any.

A solution presented itself two days later. Kana was on her way to the airport with Midnight and Tiny when her cell phone rang.

"Sorbinno," she answered.

"Is this Kana Sorbinno?" asked an unfamiliar voice.

"Yes," Kana answered, glancing over at Midnight.

"Ms. Sorbinno, this is Sable Sands. I was told that you could put me in contact with Cat."

Kana's mouth actually dropped open, then she grinned.

"And how did you come by my number, Ms. Sands?"

"I contacted Chief Masterson, to ask about Cat. I heard that she'd been hurt. He told me she was staying with you."

"I see," Kana said, still grinning. "Well, as it happens, I can tell you anything you want to know."

"I want to see her," Sable said in a no-nonsense voice.

Kana was surprised, pleasantly so, by the rock star's straightforward approach. "When?"

"I'm in town right now," Sable said.

"I'll give you my address. My girlfriend is home."

An hour later, Sable walked into the bedroom Cat was staying in. Cat was lying on the bed, wearing gray shorts and a black tank top. Her long blond hair was pulled up into a ponytail, and she wore no makeup. The fading bruises on her skin were still evident, but not as terrifying as they'd originally looked the week before.

Cat heard the door open and glanced up. Her eyes widened as she moved to sit.

"What are you doing here?" she asked Sable.

"I was in town and heard about what happened," Sable said, by way of explanation.

"You were in Europe," Cat replied, her tone circumspect.

"And now I'm in town," Sable said smoothly as she walked over to the bed and sat down, her gaze trained on Cat's face.

Cat dropped her eyes from Sable's, not liking the searching look the other woman was giving her. Sable touched her cheek gently; Cat flinched, not in physical pain, but emotional pain. She'd been holding in so much, and having someone touch her so tenderly right now was too much. She pulled back, moving away from Sable's hand.

Sable nodded, as if understanding or at least accepting Cat's response. Kicking off her sandals, she sat on the bed, her back to the headboard.

"This is Evanescence, isn't it?" Sable asked about the song on the radio.

Cat nodded.

"Amy has an incredible voice," Sable said.

Again Cat nodded, moving to lean against the headboard too.

The ended up sitting there listening to music for the better part of two hours. Cat had her iPod plugged into the Bose Wave radio in the room, so all her favorites were playing. It gave Sable some insight into her state of mind. The songs were angry, heartbreaking, and sad. Linkin Park's "Don't Stay" came on, and Sable was surprised by the vehemence with which Cat sang the words. They spoke of wanting the other person to stop wasting her away, like Liz throwing her love away with both hands.

The song ended, and Cat closed her eyes, swallowing a few times. Sable said nothing, only watching. Another song started, and Cat seemed calmer again.

"So," Sable said conversationally, "your chief tells me you're on leave for another two weeks or so."

Cat nodded, not looking pleased about the idea.

"Ever been to Europe?" Sable asked, her tone so casual it took Cat a minute to realize what she'd just asked.

"Have I what?"

"Been to Europe," Sable repeated, her rich chocolate eyes staring directly into Cat's. "I want to take you there."

205

Cat's mouth opened as if to say something, then she shook her head, like she didn't understand. "Why?"

Sable shrugged, looking around her. "I think you could use a change of scenery."

Cat looked perplexed. "Why are you doing this?"

"Because I'm an extremely eccentric rock star, haven't you heard?" Sable asked with a wry smile.

Cat narrowed her eyes.

"Just come with me," Sable said before Cat could level some kind of accusation at her. "No strings, no hassles, I swear."

Cat had to admit it was tempting. Right now everything was weighing on her. Elizabeth had come to Kana's house the day before. When Cat refused to see her, Elizabeth had attempted to force her way past Kana. That had been a mistake. Kana had yanked her back by a handful of hair. Cat had interceded then, not able to allow Kana to hurt Elizabeth, regardless of what the girl had done. Kana had ordered Elizabeth out of her house. Elizabeth had pleaded with Cat to talk to her. It had been an ugly scene. One Cat wasn't anxious to go through again.

Three hours later, Cat was on Sable's private Gulfstream jet on her way to New York to make a connection to Europe. It was a surreal experience to say the least.

Cat lay sleeping. It was four in the afternoon in Rome, but her body was still on California time, and it was stubbornly refusing to adjust to the nine-hour difference. It was 1 a.m. in San Diego at that point.

Sable walked in, her eyes sweeping the open, airy room. She located Cat lying on the bed, her arms thrown up over her head. Smiling, Sable put down her keys and walked over to the bed. She glanced in the gilded mirror on one wall and took in her appearance. She looked damn good for a forty-year-old woman. She wore a black miniskirt with a chain that looped down her flat belly, black strappy high-heeled sandals, and a rich copper silk blouse. Her long mane flowed down her back, and her makeup was, as usual, perfect and exotic. It took a lot of work and money to look this good, but she knew she did.

Kicking off her sandals, she lay on the bed next to Cat. Thus far their relationship had remained platonic. It had been four days since they'd arrived in Rome, and Sable had no intention of pushing Cat into anything. She knew that the attack Cat had sustained, combined with the subsequent betrayal by her girlfriend, was not going to be something she'd get over quickly.

There was no denying, however, her attraction to the beautiful blond cop from San Diego. She'd thought of her constantly since the night they'd gone out. Sable had made it a priority to contact the department to check on the status of the case of her bodyguard being shot, simply because she wanted contact with Cat. Cat had only called her back twice, telling her nothing had turned up on the men who had shot her bodyguard, but she was still checking.

Then had come the day when Sable had called from Paris to check in with Cat. One of her co-workers had answered her line and had subsequently transferred her call to Dave Dibbins, who'd ended up telling her that Cat had been hurt. Sable had asked to speak to Kyle Masterson at that point. Kyle had been the one to tell her that, no, Cat wasn't at her apartment, she was staying with a friend. He'd given her Kana's cell phone number.

It had been Cat who'd told Sable why she was staying with Kana and Palani rather than with her girlfriend. Sable had been circumspect about the breakup. It was obvious Cat was still hurting over it, and Sable had no intention of pushing her luck.

Propping herself up on one elbow, Sable watched the younger woman sleep. As if sensing her there, Cat stirred, turning over on her side to face Sable and opening her eyes.

"Hey," Cat said tiredly.

"Hi there," Sable said, smiling. "Time change still nailing you?"

"Uh-huh," Cat said, rubbing her eyes, looking very young without makeup. "How did your, um, thing go?"

"My thing," Sable said, grinning at Cat's word, "went fine."

"It was a TV show, right?"

"Yes," Sable said. "Kind of like your Billboard Top Forty type of thing."

"Ohh," Cat said, nodding.

Sable smiled, touching Cat's cheek impulsively. "You are so beautiful," she said softly.

Cat smiled slightly, looking tired still. "I'm glad you think so," she said, her tone unconvinced.

"I do." Sable brushed her thumb back and forth over Cat's jawline. "You don't think so?"

"I'm no judge," Cat said, shrugging.

Sable narrowed her eyes. "Don't let her betrayal change your feelings about yourself, Catalina."

Cat swallowed, wincing. "I just don't feel too beautiful right now, Sable."

"Well, you are," Sable said, her voice strong.

Cat still looked unconvinced.

"Why don't we do something today?" Sable said, glancing at her gold Cartier watch. "It's still early enough to get out and do something."

Cat nodded and moved to sit up; Sable's hand on her arm stopped her. Turning to look back at Sable, Cat found herself caught in a kiss.

Sable's lips were gentle, searching, yet sensual at the same time. She felt Sable's hand slide through her hair, her other hand at Cat's waist. When their lips parted, Sable looked back at Cat.

"I want you to know," Sable said huskily, "that just because I haven't come on to you since you've been here, doesn't mean I don't want you."

Cat gazed back at her, then a smile tugged at her lips. "I didn't figure you brought me here as a public service, Sable," she said, her tone holding a hint of her former spark.

Nodding, Sable laughed.

In the end, Sable took Cat shopping. She had an intense desire to dress Cat in the most exquisite clothing she could find. They went through shop after shop, and Sable encouraged Cat to try on anything she liked.

Cat came out of the dressing room in the private showroom of a very fashionable Rome boutique. She was wearing a black silk mini-dress that was backless and had a plunging neckline. On her feet she wore Jimmy Choo high heels. Sable was floored. Cat noticed the look on her face and grinned.

"You like it?" Cat asked, her eyes sparkling.

Sable stood up and walked toward Cat, as Cat turned back to look in the mirror. Sable came up behind her, putting her hands to Cat's waist, then sliding them down over her slim hips and down her thighs. Cat stared in the mirror, her breath catching when Sable's hands touched the bare skin of her legs. Sable's hands continued to travel downward. She kneeled so she could slide her hands all the way down to Cat's ankles, her eyes watching Cat's in the mirror. Sable leaned forward, and her lips touched the skin at the back of Cat's knee. Her tongue slid upward; Cat closed her eyes momentarily.

There was something very erotic about the situation. A dressing room that, while it was private, the staff had a key to, a dress... heels... Sable's hands were traveling up her legs now, her thumbs on the insides of Cat's thighs. Cat gasped as they slid up past the material of the short skirt.

Minutes later, Cat's hands were braced against the mirror and there was no thought of anyone or anything but what Sable was doing to her. It was an extremely erotic experience, one Cat could never have imagined. That was Sable's style: expect the unexpected.

***

Kashena went back to guarding Sierra a week and a half after Sebastian came home. During that time, she had only talked to Sierra on the phone, and even then they were very careful. Kashena wasn't convinced that Christian Collins wouldn't carry tales back to the AG, and she didn't want to find out by way of experience. By this time, too, Sierra's husband, Jason, had been home three days.

The morning Kashena reclaimed her job as Sierra's bodyguard, Christian had already driven Sierra into the office. So Kashena was able to drive her home. Once in the Suburban Kashena was using to drive Sierra in, Sierra turned to her, very aware of the cameras in the garage.

"Can we go somewhere?" she asked Kashena.

Kashena looked over at her for a moment, then nodded.

She drove them to her house, knowing Linda was out. Linda had been out a lot lately. Kashena was fairly sure she was ready to move on again, and Kashena was more than ready for Linda to do just that. Things between them had been barely civil since Kashena's rejection of Linda's idea of them getting married. Linda was just biding her time, Kashena suspected, until something better came along. For that reason, Kashena was sure to keep her available cash and credit cards locked up. She didn't trust Linda not to clean her out before she left. She wasn't allowing that to happen.

"Is this okay?" Sierra asked as they got out of the car.

"Yeah," Kashena said. "She's not here."

Sierra wanted to ask if that was permanent, but she knew it wasn't her place to ask. Kashena had every right to continue seeing Linda, especially now that Sierra's husband had come home. Sierra was determined not to bother Kashena about the other woman in her life.

Walking inside, Kashena tossed her keys on the counter and reached into the refrigerator for a beer.

"Do you want some wine?" Kashena asked, aware that was what Sierra drank.

"Sure," Sierra said, smiling.

They took their drinks and went to sit out on Kashena's back patio. It was a few minutes before either of them spoke. Kashena lit a cigar, feeling tense. She wasn't sure if this was the speech about needing to stop seeing each other because of hubby coming home. It wasn't something she was ready to hear just yet.

Sierra glanced across the table at Kashena, who looked for all intents and purposes totally relaxed.

"I've missed you so much," Sierra whispered, her tone reflecting how hard it had been to be away from Kashena.

Kashena looked across the table. There was mild surprise in her eyes, but it didn't show on the rest of her face.

"I've missed you too," Kashena said, her voice soft.

Sierra put her wine glass down, stood, and walked around the table. She knelt in front of Kashena, staring up at the other woman. Reaching out, she took Kashena's hand in hers. Kashena tossed her cigar aside and took Sierra's other hand. With that, Kashena pulled Sierra onto her lap, her lips finding Sierra's immediately.

They kissed for what seemed like hours, neither of them wanting to stop long enough to move into the house. In the end, they made love on the back patio, while Kashena thanked the spirits that she'd been wise enough to make the patio private and unviewable from the outside.

Afterwards, they hastily adjusted clothing, and then Kashena led Sierra inside. They sat on Kashena's couch. Sierra leaned her head against Kashena's shoulder, snuggling into her embrace. Kashena sensed Sierra's mood, feeling her turmoil.

"Are things bad at home?" she asked softly.

Sierra shrugged, taking a deep breath and blowing it out in a quiet sigh.

"I don't want to talk about it," Sierra said. "About him," she qualified.

Kashena nodded, realizing that it was probably difficult for Sierra to split her loyalties. "Then how's work?" Kashena asked with a grin.

Sierra smiled, appreciating that Kashena didn't push about Jason. The fact was that things were awful, and she didn't want to dump all of that on Kashena.

"Well, I've got three capital cases in pre-trial, another starting trial tomorrow. I've got three DAGs out with the flu, and a serious legal support issue."

"Sounds like a lot."

Sierra sighed. "It is a lot," she agreed, "but I'll deal with it."

"I know you will," Kashena said. "If anyone can handle all of this it's you." She got up and poured Sierra another glass of wine. Kashena handed it to her and sat down again. "So, the DAGs that are out, are they the ones in pre-trial?"

"One of them is," Sierra said. "He's one of my best, and I'm scrambling trying to help his legal assistant get everything together in his absence."

"Can you replace him?"

"Well," Sierra said, looking considering, "I can, but he's so intimately acquainted with this case. A lot of what lawyers do is think on their feet. When a witness doesn't answer the way you expect them to, you need to be able to fall back and regroup. You need to find a new angle to get at the point you're trying to make. It's much easier to do that when you're highly familiar with your case."

Kashena nodded. "But what are you going to do if he can't get back in time?"

Sierra took a deep breath and released it in a whoosh. "I guess I'll end up trying the case myself."

"Oh, that defendant will be hating life then," Kashena said, grinning.

"You think so?" Sierra asked with a smile.

"Oh yeah, siccing my girl on them is probably the nastiest thing Midnight Chevalier could do to a defendant."

Sierra bit her lip, her eyes shining. "Your girl, huh?"

Kashena looked back at her, smiling softly. "Yeah," she said quietly.

"Yeah," Sierra echoed, snuggling back against Kashena.

They talked for another hour, then Kashena saw Sierra glance at her watch.

"I better get you home," Kashena said, moving to stand.

"I guess so," Sierra said, sounding a bit forlorn.

When Kashena dropped Sierra off, Jason was out working on the lawn. He stopped the mower and stared at Kashena. Kashena merely looked back at him from behind her sunglasses. He was a classic Marine—flat-top blond hair, darkly tanned skin, ruggedly handsome, but not too handsome. His bare chest was on display; he was well muscled with tattoos on both arms.

As Kashena drove away, Sierra walked past Jason, trying to move out of arm's reach. It didn't work. He pulled her to him, crushing her against his sweaty torso. His lips smashed down on hers. She had a flash of what kissing Kashena had been like, just an hour or two before. So different. Kashena's kisses were soft, sometimes intense, but never crushing like this. She felt like her lips were being flattened against her teeth. She wanted to shove away from him—he was getting sweat and grime on her beige suit—but she knew he'd just complain about it, so she didn't.

"Who's the broad?" Jason asked when he let her go.

"That's my bodyguard," Sierra said, not liking that Jason thought of all women as "broads."

Jason gave snort of sarcastic laughter. "Some skinny little broad is going to protect you? From what? Flies?"

Sierra looked back at him, unable to believe she'd ever found him charming. Of course, he was much more coarse since he'd come back from the Middle East. It was apparent he'd gotten used to the way women were treated in that part of the world.

"For your information," Sierra said tightly, "Kashena is an ex-Marine."

"Bullshit," Jason snapped.

"No, not bullshit," Sierra replied. "She was a second lieutenant and led her own platoon."

Jason curled up his lips in disgust. "So she fucked some general and got herself made a second lieuy, so what?"

"I seriously doubt that," Sierra replied scathingly, "since she's a lesbian."

Jason's mouth fell open in shock, and Sierra took the opportunity to retreat inside the house. She was already castigating herself for telling him that. She knew it was something he wouldn't let go. He couldn't stand gays, and what if it was too telling that Sierra knew that about her bodyguard?

Sure enough, ten minutes later he came inside, leaning on the counter as she was cooking dinner.

"So how do you know she's a homo?" he asked crudely.

Sierra turned around, staring at him, disbelief on her face. Finally she shook her head and turned back to her cooking, ignoring his question. Suddenly she could feel him behind her. The smell of sweat and dirt pervaded her nostrils.

"I asked you a question," Jason said in a tight voice.

Sierra shuddered to herself, feeling sickened that he intimidated her so easily.

"She told me," she said eventually, unable to think of anything else.

"Why?" he asked, his tone still a growl. "She hoping to fuck you?"

"Jesus, Jason!" Sierra glanced around, hoping that Colby wasn't around to hear that. "Do you have to use that kind of language? I don't need a call from the school saying that Colby is talking like that now."

"So? Was she hoping to fuck you or not?" Jason asked, as if she hadn't even spoken.

"Contrary to popular belief," Sierra said condescendingly, "not all gays are depraved degenerates that will sleep with anything of the same sex."

Jason made a sound that showed that he didn't believe a word of what she'd just said, but he let the other part of that question go. Sierra was relieved.

Later that night, as he continually did, he crawled into bed naked next to her, pressing his hard-on against her.

"Jason..." she sighed, shaking her head as she tried to read the brief she had in her hands.

"Put that shit down for a few," Jason said, pushing aside the brief and reaching for her hand. He guided it to his hard-on. "Do you know how much I missed fucking you?"

Sierra looked back at him, unable to formulate a reply. She wanted to inform him that talking like that did absolutely nothing for her. Another retort that came to mind was that his erection did nothing for her either. What she wanted to do was get out of bed and run away. She wanted to run to Kashena and never look back. But she knew it wasn't that easy. Nothing was ever as easy as it seemed.

In the end, she gave in and let him have sex with her. She never thought of it as making love anymore. Nothing about the sex act with Jason pertained to love. She'd known that long before she'd met Kashena again. The problem now was that she felt dirty after she'd been with him. That was something that hadn't been so prevalent before. Now she had something to compare it to, and it paled significantly.

Making love with Kashena was sometimes tender, sometimes heated, but she always felt like Kashena respected her. It sounded trite, even to her, but Kashena respected that she was more than a body to be used. Jason used her as he saw fit, never caring if she had an orgasm or not. Something she hadn't had with him in many years now. She'd mentioned it to him once a couple of years before. He'd snickered and said, "I thought that's what you women bought vibrators for."

Jason sensed Sierra's revulsion during sex. He'd always figured her for frigid anyway, but that didn't matter. She was a nice tight fit, so it always got him off. She was some overeducated suit, and he got to fuck her whenever he wanted to fuck her. That thought alone got him off half the time. She had a hot body, sexy, slim, even after having a baby, and long dark hair that fell all around her. He knew she didn't like sex, but tough shit. She was his wife, and he'd do her whenever and wherever he wanted.

Otherwise, what was the point in marrying her? Besides the fact that he'd knocked her up? One of the guys he used to consider a friend had told him that if he didn't marry Sierra, he'd report Jason. The last thing Jason wanted was to get ousted from the Marines. His dad, a good old-fashioned redneck of a Marine, would kill him. So he'd married Sierra.

His father, Jason senior, had been his usual charming self when Jason and Sierra had gone to the small farmhouse in Minnesota.

"You married a fuckin' breed?" Jason senior had sneered.

Sierra had stared wide-eyed at the man. She wasn't used to such treatment. Her family was one of the richest in San Diego. People in the community as well as the tribe had always treated her with respect and kindness. This was something totally foreign to her.

"Her family's got bucks," Jason junior had told his father.

"You knock her up?"

Jason had merely nodded, his eyes lowered.

"Dumb fuck," Jason senior had spat, then peered at Sierra. "You trap my boy, you little slut?"

Sierra's mouth had fallen open at such a crude, nasty accusation. She'd finally turned and left the room. She'd walked out to the rental car and sat in it until Jason had finally come outside. She'd told him she wanted to leave. He'd argued with her, but she'd refused to get out of the car. They'd never gone back to visit Jason's father again. Sierra could see why Jason's mother had left the horrible man years before.

The next morning, Kashena picked Sierra up but didn't go to the door as she usually had before. She was very aware that Jason was there, lurking somewhere, and the last thing she wanted to do was meet up with the man. She hadn't liked him on sight. There was also something she felt she needed to discuss with Sierra.

Unfortunately, Jason found it necessary to trail Sierra out to the vehicle and walk around to Kashena's side. Kashena had her window down, because she was smoking a cigar, so there was no avoiding the man. He gave her an appraising look, one she was used to getting from men. It was obvious he knew she was gay too.

"So you're a bodyguard, huh?" he asked snidely.

"Yes," Kashena answered, flicking her cigar pointedly over his head.

Sierra got into the vehicle and glanced at Kashena, once again sorry she'd told Jason that Kashena was gay, knowing her husband had a big mouth. Naturally that was the next thing he asked.

"Sierra says you're a lesbo," Jason said. "That true?"

"Is that pertinent to my protecting your wife?" Kashena asked, raising an eyebrow at him.

"Maybe," Jason replied, defensive immediately. "How do I know you're not cruising her for a piece of ass?"

Kashena's look could have frozen him. Her first instinct was to ask him if he was feeling threatened. In the end, she simply didn't answer him. She put the Suburban in gear and drove away, turning just tight enough to make him step back in order to avoid being bumped.

Kashena grinned evilly. Sierra glanced back to see Jason staring open-mouthed at the retreating vehicle.

"Kash, I'm sorry," Sierra said. "He was making snide remarks yesterday about your ability to protect me. I snapped."

Kashena shrugged. "I don't care if he knows I'm a lesbian. That's his problem, not mine."

Sierra nodded, noting the edge to Kashena's voice.

"But," Kashena said, "we do need to talk."

"Okay," Sierra said, looking worried.

Kashena drove to a coffee shop nearby, ordering them coffee and then leading Sierra to a private corner. She took Sierra's hands in hers.

"Now that Jason's back," Kashena said, "I think we need to talk about our relationship."

Sierra prayed that Kashena wasn't about to break things off, ready to beg her not to do that.

"In terms of what?" Sierra asked tentatively.

"In terms of sex," Kashena said, her tone direct. She could see that Sierra was nervous, and she didn't want her to feel like that. "I'm not saying we can't be together, honey," Kashena said, squeezing Sierra's hands gently. "What I am saying is that I need there to be some time between the times that you're with him and then with me."

Sierra looked at her for a long minute. "Like what kind of time?"

"Well," Kashena said, hesitant, "I think forty-eight hours is reasonable."

Sierra pressed her lips together. "So you're saying that if I have sex with him, you don't want to make love to me until forty-eight hours later?"

"Yeah," Kashena said. She'd noted that Sierra had referred to the act with Jason as "sex" and the act with her as "making love." She felt her heart tug at that. "I'm just a little funny about men in general," Kashena explained. "I don't want anything from them on me. Does that make sense?"

"So basically you want me decontaminated?" Sierra asked, smiling.

"Yeah, decon," Kashena agreed, chuckling, then her look became serious. "Do you think we can do that? That you can manage that?"

Sierra nodded, looking pensive.

"Are you sure?" Kashena asked.

"I can try, Kashena," Sierra said. "He's very pushy about sex."

Kashena's eyes narrowed slightly, but she said nothing. "All I ask is that you be honest with me."

"I can definitely do that," Sierra said, nodding.

"Good."

They both left the coffee shop feeling like there was a better understanding between them.

They found out quickly there was a big difference between "understanding" and being able to stand things. Many times on the way home from the office, Sierra would reach over to touch Kashena's hand. The first time was the day they'd talked in the coffee shop.

"Been deconned?" Kashena smiled wryly.

Sierra had pressed her lips together. Since she'd been with Jason the night before, it hadn't been forty-eight hours. She shook her head slowly. Kashena gave her an encouraging smile.

"S'okay," she said with understanding. "I'll just go to the gym and work off my aggressions."

Sierra laughed softly, nodding her head.

Chapter 6

Over the next week, things were much the same, and Kashena quickly found herself getting not only frustrated, but pissed off. A week and a day after they'd made the "forty-eight hours" agreement, Kashena drove to the river, parking the vehicle and getting out to walk. She'd asked once again about "decon," and Sierra had answered, once again, in the negative.

Lighting a cigar, Kashena did her best to walk off her anger. What the fuck was up with this? Did she really enjoy him that much that she had to fuck him every night? What did that say? That Sierra really wasn't into women, was what it told Kashena. That when Sierra had needed someone while Jason was away, Kashena had been a substitute, but now that he was back...

Sierra stood next to the vehicle, watching Kashena stride down the path, smoking and generally looking pissed off. She was nervous—she could sense things were coming to a head, and she had no idea how to stop them from doing so. Jason was relentless about sex, and it was making her crazy. She'd tried to stave off his attentions as much as possible, but he wouldn't leave her alone. It was as if he somehow sensed that in having sex with her, he was keeping her from something else. She hated it more than she could begin to explain.

In truth, too, she was afraid to admit to Kashena that she was unable to find a suitable way to reject Jason's advances without causing too much of a fight. It was a horrible situation to be in. She didn't want to fight with Jason, not while Colby was in the house, and certainly not about something so personal and private as sexual relations. And what excuse could she give Jason? "Sorry, I can't have sex with you because my girlfriend won't touch me for forty-eight hours after you have"? It just wouldn't work.

"This isn't going to work," Kashena said as she strode back to the SUV, echoing Sierra's own thoughts. "I can't keep on like this."

"Kashena, please," Sierra said, her tone pleading. "I know things are really hard right now, but I'm sure things will settle down with Jason soon. He's just... I mean, he was in the Middle East for so long..."

"You think he didn't fuck anything that wore a skirt there?" Kashena snapped, knowing male Marines better than most.

She regretted the sharp rejoinder a moment later when Sierra paled. But then she realized that Sierra was upset that her husband was sleeping with other women... The word *fuck!* screamed through her head.

Kashena moved toward the driver's side of the vehicle.

"Look," she said, her voice hardening significantly, "I thought I could deal with this, but I can't. So, we need to stop seeing each other."

"But..." Sierra began, getting into the vehicle as Kashena was. "I mean, what about this? The protection part?" she asked, stunned beyond reasoning.

Kashena nodded, feeling a little bit more of her ego get ripped away. "You don't have to worry about the protection part," she said icily. "I was going to tell you tonight—it's my understanding that Midnight has finally gotten your stalker picked up for just that. He won't be bothering you anymore. So you have no need of my *services* anymore."

222

The emphasis on the word "services" should have warned Sierra where Kashena's head was, but she was too busy trying to think of something to keep Kashena with her. Kashena didn't give her a chance to think about it too much.

Starting the Suburban with a roar, Kashena backed up and drove toward Sierra's house. She dropped her off without another word and merely a curt nod to Jason, who seemed to be waiting for them outside, a beer in hand.

Kashena drove home, changed clothes, and went to the gym. She spent the next three hours taking her hurt and anger out on the most readily available weight equipment.

"Pushing it a bit, aren't we, Marine?" came a familiar voice from behind her.

Kashena turned around and saw Sebastian standing there. He was dressed in gym clothes and was sweating, so he'd obviously been working hard too.

"Are you supposed to be out of bed, Ranger?" she countered.

"I'm supposed to be taking it slow," he said with a wry grin.

"Do they have any idea that what you consider 'slow' would kill a normal man your age?"

Sebastian laughed at that. "I doubt it," he said, "but let's not tell them that part, huh?"

Kashena nodded, curling her lips in a smirk.

"So what's had you here for the last three hours?" Sebastian asked, sitting at the weight bench next to where Kashena was working out with free weights.

"Checking on me?" Kashena asked, raising an eyebrow at him.

"Christie said you came in wound up tight," he said, gesturing toward the young blond receptionist.

Kashena narrowed her eyes. "Christie would grab any opportunity to talk to you, Baz, you know that."

"Yeah, well, you are wound tight," Sebastian said. "I can see it on your face. So what's up, partner?"

Kashena shook her head. "Not here," she said, glancing around them.

"Well, I'm done, so let's go have a beer," Sebastian said, nodding toward the door.

"I'll meet you out front in twenty," Kashena said.

Twenty minutes later, she was out front, having showered and changed clothes. She now wore jeans, a navy blue polo shirt with the Marine logo on it, and a baseball cap, her long hair in a ponytail at the back of her head. They went to a bar called The Monkey Bar, where they stationed themselves with their backs to the wall and ordered beers.

"So what's up?" Sebastian asked once they had their drinks.

Kashena shrugged, her expression jaded. "Just couldn't take playing second fiddle anymore."

"With Sierra?" Sebastian asked, surprised. "Second fiddle to who?"

"Her husband," Kashena said tightly.

"Oh," Sebastian said. "That bad, huh?"

"That bad," Kashena confirmed.

Sebastian nodded, unhappy that things hadn't worked out between them. Sierra Youngblood had certainly seemed very interested in Kashena. It bothered him that his friend had been pushed aside so easily by the other woman. *But is that what really happened?*

"So what made you feel second best?" he asked, casually taking a long drink of his beer.

Kashena looked at him for a minute, her face reflecting sarcasm. "Let's see, lack of sex with me, and a shitload of it with him."

Sebastian blew his breath out. Kashena had told him about her forty-eight-hour rule, so he suspected that was what was happening.

"He just got back from the Middle East, right?" Sebastian asked.

"Oh, don't fuckin' start with that, Baz, or I swear I'll bash your head in," Kashena said, her tone dangerous.

"You're not used to sharing," Sebastian pointed out.

"No."

"You knew she was married, Kash," he said, risking his head being caved in for him.

She let out a deep sigh. "I know," she said, sounding defeated. "But I didn't think it would hurt so much to know she was fucking him."

Sebastian looked back at her, not pointing out the obvious. He knew Kashena knew; there was no reason to say it.

"So, how are things going with your own lawyer?" Kashena asked, dying to get off the subject of herself—it was depressing.

Sebastian rolled his eyes. "She's fine," he said, his tone noncommittal.

"Uh-huh," Kashena said, nodding her head knowingly. "You nail her yet?"

"I'm not planning to nail her."

"Are you serious?" Kashena asked disbelievingly.

"Yeah, I am," he replied.

Kashena shook her head. "Never thought I'd see the day…"

"Don't fuckin' start," he growled.

"Don't tell me you went for it and she turned you down."

"I don't want to talk about it," Sebastian said.

Kashena raised an eyebrow at him. "So, what happened, Baz?"

"Nothing," he replied. "She's just putting all her gratitude about my getting shot instead of her on my shoulders. It's totally normal."

"Yeah, and you usually take full advantage of that kind of thing."

"How many times have I gotten shot for someone?" he asked her.

"Once, for me," she said, grinning.

"And you won't sleep with me." He grinned back.

"Damn right," she said.

"So, I don't 'usually' do anything in this kind of case, okay?"

"Okay," she said, sensing this was a sensitive subject for him and knowing it was time to back off.

That night, Linda came home to find her bags packed. She practically stumbled over them when she walked into Kashena's bedroom.

"What's up with this?" she asked, motioning to the bags.

Kashena, who was sitting on her bed, smoking a cigar, looked back at her for a moment, then shrugged.

"I'm cleaning house today."

"Cleaning house?" Linda said sharply.

"Yeah," Kashena replied, her eyes like ice.

"So, you're leaving me for that lawyer?" Linda surmised.

"Nope," Kashena replied. "I broke it off with her too."

"So why are you doing this?"

"Let's just say I'm tired of being used," Kashena said, her words more telling than her tone, which was stone cold.

Linda couldn't think of a reply to that. She had been using Kashena, especially lately. Things between them had been over when Kashena refused to marry her. Linda knew she'd lost then. So she'd been biding her time until she could meet up with one of her friends who would take her in. That hadn't happened yet, so this was not the time to let Kashena kick her out.

"Kash…" she said, putting on her best pout.

"Don't bother," Kashena said. "There's two hundred dollars in an envelope in that bag." She pointed to the black bag on top. "Use it and get out."

Linda's mouth dropped open at Kashena's attitude. She couldn't believe this was the same woman she'd had wrapped around her little finger just a year ago. Kashena had changed totally. A thrill went through her at Kashena's renewed strength. This time, Linda didn't want to leave her. Linda wanted her more than anything. It drove her crazy that she'd lost her, to a fucking lawyer, no less. Some married bitch lawyer!

Walking over to Kashena, her look seductive, she touched Kashena's shoulder.

"What if I promised never to stray again?" Linda said. "You're who I want to be with, Kashie, you know that…"

"Well, that's a damned shame for you, Linda," Kashena replied sardonically, "'cause I'm not interested."

Linda curled her hand into a fist. Kashena merely raised an eyebrow at her.

"I wouldn't trust my level of control at this point," Kashena said casually.

"With what? Wanting to hit me or fuck me?" Linda asked, her eyes glittering with excitement, though her look was haughty.

"I was thinking more along the lines of either killing you or just beating you senseless," Kashena replied coolly.

Linda stepped back involuntarily. This was not something she wanted to test. Moving back to the bags, she hastily picked up her things, looping both bags over her shoulders. She turned and looked back at Kashena.

"You're going to regret leaving me," Linda said confidently.

"Don't count on it," Kashena replied. "Oh, and leave my key on the dresser."

Linda did as Kashena told her, her movements angry. She left without another word. Kashena sat on her bed, smoking another cigar and staring at nothing. It was shaping up to be a shitty night.

***

"As you can see, the mezzanine is lovely," the woman rattled on.

Kana did her best to look interested, but the place was bad. It looked like the Chapel O' Love in Vegas or something. One glance at Palani confirmed that Palani agreed with her. That was all she needed.

"Yeah, thanks," Kana said. "We'll call you."

With that, Kana took Palani's hand and led her out of there. In the Navigator they both burst into laughter.

"Oh my God, I can't believe I just took you into that place," Palani said, shaking her head ruefully. "I'm sorry, Kana. I thought it would be better inside."

Kana grinned. "The fake marble on the outside should have been a giveaway, babe."

"I guess a name like Le Chateau was for effect, huh?"

"And to get suckers down here."

"Am I a sucker?" Palani asked.

"Only when I want you to be," Kana replied smoothly, leaning over to kiss her.

"Good save," Palani replied, winking.

Kana glanced at her watch. "What time do we have to be at the next one?"

"Not until three," Palani said, noticing by her watch that it was just noon.

"Great," Kana said, smiling, as she started the Navigator.

She drove them to La Jolla and through the rich beach community. After taking a series of small back streets, she parked near a set of stairs. It was a spot the Gang knew well. Each of them came here when they were having a difficult time in their lives, or simply to be alone, or alone with someone. Palani smiled when she saw where they were. Kana had brought her here once before, when they'd been together the first time.

Kana led Palani down the long wooden stairway until they got down to the huge rocks positioned just above the crashing waves. Kana was wearing jeans, her customary boots, and a black cotton shirt. Palani was wearing a long white skirt with a slit up her thigh, and a silk tank-style top in a rich rose color. They were a definite contrast. Kana sat down Indian-style, gently settling Palani on her lap. Palani leaned back against Kana, Kana's arms around her small waist.

"I love it here," Palani said, sighing.

Kana kissed Palani's temple. Palani's arms were over Kana's, her hands caressing. Kana loosened her hold on Palani's waist enough to let Palani's fingers lace through hers. They reveled in being close. The ocean breeze was just enough to keep the sun at their back from being too warm. Waves crashing below and the cries of seagulls were the only sounds.

Palani turned in Kana's embrace, looking up at her.

"I love you," she said, her tone emotional.

Kana smiled softly, her eyes shining.

"I love you, too, honey." Kana leaned down to kiss Palani, her hand reaching up to touch her cheek.

Palani pulled back suddenly, looking around them. Kana was about to tell her that this was a fairly private area, that she didn't need to worry about people seeing them, when Palani turned back to her with a brilliant smile.

"Here," she said.

"Huh?" Kana replied, perplexed.

"I want to get married here," Palani said, her eyes glowing with excitement.

Kana started to shake her head, indicating that she didn't understand how that was going to work.

"It will be perfect," Palani said, her voice as excited as the look on her face. "We can be out here, with the priest, and the guests can be up on the staircase. We already decided it would be a short ceremony. Oh, Kana, it would be perfect. You love this spot. Everyone you know understands its significance... Please, Kana..." Palani said, her voice trailing off as she stared up at Kana.

Kana was going over everything Palani had just said in her head. "You said I love this spot, that everyone I know understands its significance," she said.

"Kana," Palani began, her tone softening, "we both know that although our parents will be here for the wedding, they won't be the ones with us most of the time. The people who will be are our friends."

"Okay, that's what I mean," Kana said. "Do you consider the Gang your friends too, Palani?"

"Of course I do," Palani said, sounding surprised. "You didn't think that I did?"

Kana shrugged. "They aren't exactly the kind of people you grew up with, or would normally hang around with."

"They're like your family, Kana," Palani said. "I love them, like I love your family. Because they are part of you."

Kana gazed at her girlfriend, unable to believe she'd ever lived a moment without her. She looked around them, seeing the bright blue sky, the ocean stretched out before them, the monolithic rocks around them. It was perfect. It was them—it was her, and in a way it was Palani too. The ocean was something they had in common, both of them coming from Hawaii. You couldn't grow up on an island without either loving or hating the ocean. They both loved it.

Finally Kana nodded. "Then this is where we'll get married," she said, leaning down to kiss Palani again.

They kissed for a few minutes, then just sat and enjoyed the time together. They talked about arrangements for the wedding. Palani swore she'd handle everything.

"Can I ask one favor?" Palani looked abashed, which always warned Kana it was going to be a big favor.

"What?" Kana asked, her tone mockingly stern.

"Can I pick out your outfit for the wedding?"

"Why?" Kana asked, her voice deepening slightly.

"Because I want to surprise you," Palani said, smiling brightly, as if hoping to influence Kana's own countenance.

"I don't like surprises, babe," Kana said, her tone not changing.

"Please?" Palani said with an ingenue smile.

"Don't do that," Kana warned.

"Please?" Palani repeated, her dark eyes upturned to Kana's, her expression sweet.

Kana squeezed her eyes shut, lifting her head away from Palani's face. Palani started laughing, knowing that Kana was resisting with all her might.

"Please, honey," Palani said, going for the kill. "I just want to show everyone how beautiful my girlfriend can be. I was right with the *Cosmo* article, wasn't I?"

Kana exhaled deeply. "Fine, you win, but I swear to Pele that if you pick out a dress, I'm tossing you off this rock."

Palani laughed out loud. Kana would never do anything of the sort, but it was funny to hear her threaten it all the same.

"Well, you do have incredible legs, Kana," Palani said, sliding her hands along Kana's jean-clad thighs. "They'd really be accentuated by a lovely pair of three-inch heels..."

"Do it and die, little one," Kana said, her smile menacing.

Palani chuckled, enjoying teasing Kana.

When they left the rocks, Kana took her to lunch at a local restaurant that overlooked the ocean. They continued to discuss ideas for the wedding.

"We still need to find a place for the reception," Palani said.

"As long as it has a bar, I'm all for it," Kana said, lifting the beer she'd ordered to her lips.

Palani gave her a sour look. "You are not going to get drunk on our wedding night, Kana Akua Lee."

"If you buy me some scary-ass outfit to be stuck in all day, I just might," Kana said.

"That was a threat, I heard that," Palani said, smiling.

"That was indeed a threat, babygirl," Kana said.

The waitress walked up just then and cast a surreptitious glance at Kana. It was obvious she'd heard the term Kana had just used. She looked at Palani, then back at Kana. Kana's look back at the woman was direct and challenging.

"What can I get y'all?" the woman asked, her Southern accent thick.

Kana and Palani exchanged a glance. Kana raised her eyebrow at Palani; Palani, holding back a laugh, nodded slightly.

"Oysters for two," Kana ordered pointedly.

The woman's mouth dropped open.

"Welcome to California," Kana said, in a far from welcoming tone.

The woman scurried away, and Kana lifted the bottle of beer to her lips again, a look of vindication on her face.

"Feel better?" Palani asked, her smile soft.

"Much," Kana said.

Palani glanced over her shoulder and saw other people watching them. It was something she'd always been used to. Being a model, she was recognized all the time, so she was used to people watching her every move. Kana attracted a lot of attention herself with her mere presence. Police officers usually had what was called "command presence"—Kana had it in spades. Everyone noticed her.

Palani took Kana's hand in hers, her left hand on display. The engagement ring Kana had given her the year before sparkled on her ring finger. It was delicate petals of gold studded with tiny emeralds, then the intricately carved petals of a hibiscus flower in beautiful peach-colored coral, with a round diamond at its center. The hibiscus was detailed with tiny slivers of black. The hibiscus was the state flower of Hawaii. It was them.

"My, we're reckless today, aren't we?" Kana commented as she lifted Palani's hand to her lips, kissing it softly.

"I'm feeling far too happy to care what anyone thinks right now," Palani said, indicating the people watching them. "All I care about is what you think."

Kana looked back at her, their eyes connecting. "And I think you are beautiful," she said, smiling down at Palani.

Palani smiled back. "I think you are too."

"And I think you need glasses," Kana said, widening her eyes.

"Don't make me hurt you, Sorbinno," Palani said, narrowing hers.

"So tough," Kana said with a smile.

"My girlfriend's tough," Palani said. "I just pretend."

"I know."

"Hey!" Palani replied, balling up her tiny fist and hitting Kana on the arm gently.

Kana laughed, shaking her head.

The people in the restaurant watched with varying degrees of thought. Some couldn't help but notice the two women that were alike but so different. One so delicately beautiful she was breathtaking, the other so obviously powerful but with a strong beauty of her own.

"Oh my God, Helen, that's Midnight Chevalier's bodyguard," one woman said to her companion.

"It is not," the older woman said.

"Yes it is," the first woman said. "Don't you think so, Georgia?"

"I think she's right, Helen," Georgia said, a light of excitement in her eyes. "She's the gay cop who was shot while Midnight Chevalier was running for office. And that's Palani Ryker, the woman she was just in that article in *Cosmo* with… Oh my God!"

"Go talk to her, Cindy," Helen suggested to the first woman.

"No way!" Cindy shook her head. "What would I say?"

"Something stupid probably," Georgia said, grinning.

"Shut up!" Cindy said, giving her a sour look. "Okay, I'll go talk to her."

With that, Cindy stood up and walked toward where Kana and Palani sat. Kana, who was as usual sitting with her back to the wall, saw the woman walking up and tensed. Palani glanced over her shoulder and saw a young woman approaching them.

"I'm sorry to bother you," Cindy said, her hands clasped nervously together in front of her. She was looking directly at Kana. "But aren't you Kana Sorbinno?"

Kana nodded slowly.

"It is such an honor to meet you," Cindy gushed, putting her hand out to Kana, who regarded it for a moment, then extended her own hand slowly. "I'm Cindy," the girl went on, not noticing Kana's hesitation. "Those girls over there are Helen and Georgia. I just knew it was you."

Kana looked amused now. "This is Palani, my fiancée," she said, feeling weird at having to introduce Palani. Usually it was the other way around. People usually recognized Palani, not her.

Cindy nodded excitedly, extending her hand to Palani too. "Georgia said it was you," she said to Palani. "Your pictures are really gorgeous," she said, "but I have to say that the pictures of the two of you in that issue of *Cosmo* were just so hot." She shook her head. "It made me so desperate to find what you two have."

"It'll find you when it's meant to," Palani said wisely.

Cindy nodded sagely, like Palani had just given her a great gift of knowledge. Kana looked on, amused.

"Can my friends come over and meet you?" Cindy pleaded.

"Of course," Palani answered, happy that this woman had actually recognized Kana first and seemed just as excited to meet Kana.

Palani glanced at Kana, who rolled her eyes, a smile in place, however.

Cindy motioned to her friends. They walked over.

"It's really great to meet you," Helen said, shaking Kana's hand. "I think your boss is just amazing."

"So do I," Kana said, smiling.

"I think *you're* amazing," Georgia put in, her eyes on Kana. "Those pictures of you two in *Cosmo*. Well, that one, with you two and the white sheet—whew!" She fanned herself. "Hot stuff. It's up on my wall at home. It was a fantastic picture."

"Well, thanks," Kana said. "It was Palani's idea."

When the women went back to their table, Palani looked at Kana. "You really don't like fame, do you?"

"Not particularly," Kana said.

Their order came soon after that. The waitress set the food down without a word and walked away. Kana grinned; Palani shook her head. It was an interesting day.

***

Cat lay against Sable's bare torso. They'd just made love. It wasn't the first time that day. The sun was setting, the rays of orange, gold, and red playing throughout the room. Cat was drifting in and out of consciousness. She felt sated and relaxed. Sable stroked her hair; she sighed softly. Above her, Sable smiled.

There had been no end to the excitement she experienced with Catalina. All that Cat's body and attitude had promised had been realized. Cat was a truly sexual creature like herself. There were many women who weren't—Sable had found that in a lifetime of being with women. Some thought they had what it took to be sexual with her, but none were ever able to keep up. Cat was not only able to keep up, but able to excite her endlessly. It was a dangerous proposition, one Sable had no intention of denying.

"Cat…" Sable said softly, stirring Catalina from her languor.

236

"Hmm?" Cat murmured against her skin.

"I want you to stay," Sable said, her tone sure.

Cat lifted her head to glance up at the older woman. "Stay?"

"Yes," Sable said, touching her under the chin, stroking her jawline. "Stay here, with me."

Cat lowered her head, kissing Sable's skin. "I can't do that. You know that," she said softly.

"Why?" Sable asked entreatingly. "You don't have to work, Catalina. I can take care of you."

Cat rolled to her back, looking up at Sable as she did.

"I don't need to be taken care of, Sable," Cat said, her voice serious.

Sable moved down on the bed, sliding her arms around Cat and kissing her shoulder.

"I know you don't need to be, Cat," she said soothingly, "but I *want* to take care of you."

Cat said nothing for a few minutes. There'd been no way to stop Sable buying her everything under the sun. She'd tried anger, pleading, and downright refusing to accept anything. Sable just went right around doing as she pleased. And what seemed to please her was to buy Cat things.

"Anything you want, it's yours," Sable often said.

"I don't want anything," Cat would respond.

"Tell me your fantasies," Sable would reply.

It was endless. If Cat made the mistake of talking about a fantasy she had, whether it be driving a Lamborghini down the Autobahn, or going to the Moulin Rouge in Paris, or even getting to meet Gwen Stefani of No Doubt, Sable arranged it. Anything she wanted. It was like living in a dream world. It was an enticing place to live, but Cat knew it wasn't reality, and she needed to get back.

Thinking along those lines, she turned over on her side, facing Sable.

"This is a fantasy, Sable," she said, putting her hand to Sable's cheek. "A story in a book. And I appreciate everything you've done for me, I really do. But this isn't real, and I need to get back to my reality. My job, my life…"

"Am I not in your life?" Sable asked, her tone slightly hurt.

"You are," Cat said. "Yes, you are. I just… I have my job, my friends… I need to get back."

"Your job that almost gets you killed," Sable said, her voice filled with dread.

Cat sighed. "That's not what my job is, Sable. That just happened. Things like that happen sometimes. I'm not dead, because my friends rescued me. And I need to be there to rescue them if they need it. That's part of the deal. They need me."

"I need you," Sable said, sounding almost desperate.

"You don't need me," Cat said knowingly. "You have so many people here happy to worship the ground you walk on. You won't even miss me."

"Yes I will," Sable insisted, giving her a searching look. "Are you going back to her?"

"To Elizabeth?" Cat asked, surprised by the question.

Sable nodded slowly, her eyes staring into Cat's.

"No, Sable, I'm not going back to her," Cat assured her. "That's over. She made her choice."

"She's not going to let you go that easily," Sable said.

"Well, she's going to have to," Cat said, her voice stronger than she felt.

Sable said nothing, merely taking a deep breath and releasing it in a sigh.

"When are you wanting to go back?" she asked resignedly.

"My leave is up in two days," Cat said.

"Two days?" Sable exclaimed, horrified. "No, I can't lose you that soon. I'm not ready for that yet."

Cat smiled. The superstar wasn't shy about what she wanted. "And how long will it take for you to be ready for that?" she asked indulgently.

"At least a year." Sable's expression was serious, but her eyes glittered with humor.

"Try again," Cat said.

"A month?"

"Again."

Sable gave a long-suffering sigh. "A week and a half."

Cat raised an eyebrow at that. "A week and a half?"

"Yes," Sable said. "I have to be in San Francisco next week for three days. I want you with me. Then I suppose I could take you back to San Diego."

"San Francisco, huh?" Cat asked.

"Yes," Sable said. "Please come with me. It's a really beautiful city, and I could show you the sights."

"I've seen the sights," Cat said, grinning.

"No, I mean the ones that normal tourists don't see," Sable insisted. "Like the Castro District," she added, naming the biggest gay community in San Francisco.

"I spent my entire childhood in the Castro District, Sable."

"What?" Sable said, shocked.

"I grew up in San Francisco, born and raised there."

"Really?" Sable asked, surprised by this.

"Yep," Cat said. "My mother still lives there."

"In the Castro District?"

"She's a lesbian," Cat explained.

"Really?" Sable asked again.

"Yes, really." Cat chuckled at the look on Sable's face.

"Well, then maybe you can show me around," Sable said, winking.

"I may be able to show you a thing or two you've never seen."

"Mmm." Sable slid her hand over Cat's skin. "I can't wait."

"Mm-hmm," Cat murmured, gasping a moment later as Sable's hands caressed her. "God…" she gasped. "Sable…" Her voice was already breathless—Sable had that effect on her.

"I love it when you say my name," Sable said as she continued to touch her, bringing her quickly to the peak of orgasm. "You belong to me, Catalina," she whispered in her ear as Cat arched against her, moaning and crying out.

***

Elizabeth couldn't stop running things over and over in her head: what she'd done, how Cat had reacted, how awful she felt… She went over the moment when she'd had the choice to invite the bartender, or not invite him. Why hadn't she decided against it? She knew what she was risking, but she'd done it anyway. She'd give anything to change that moment, change that decision. A voice interrupted her thoughts.

"Elizabeth," Rick said softly.

She glanced over her shoulder and saw her uncle looking at her. She wasn't really surprised to see him. Her phone had been ringing a lot, but she'd seen that it wasn't Cat, and it didn't matter who it was after that. The fact that her uncle had shown up at her apartment didn't really faze her.

"Aren't you and Aunt Midnight still mad at me?" she muttered.

Rick kneeled next to her. "We weren't mad at you, Elizabeth."

"No?" she asked, not believing him.

"No," he said. "We were disappointed that things went the way they did."

"My fucking up," Elizabeth said, her words betraying her feelings clearly—she hated herself.

"The circumstances, Elizabeth," he explained. "The hideous timing of it all."

"I made a mistake, Uncle Rick," she said, feeling the need to push him away. "Not unlike one you made when Mikeyla was only three."

She didn't see her uncle's pained look, but she felt him tense. She knew her words had hit home, and she felt terrible for even saying it. It had been a horrible time in his and Midnight's history, a time when Rick had strayed from his marriage; it had almost had deadly consequences for Midnight. Elizabeth knew bringing it up was dirty pool, but at this point she just wanted to hurt others as much as she was hurting.

"You're right," he said. Elizabeth could hear the hurt in his voice. "And I'm sure that people around me were more than disappointed with me at the time it happened. What happened to Cat, though, was related to work, not you. There wouldn't have been anything you could have done to prevent it. If I'd been where I was supposed to be, then, I could have protected Midnight."

Elizabeth turned over, looking up at her uncle contritely.

"I'm sorry I said that," she said, wincing. "I just don't know what to think right now."

Rick's eyes searched her face. "Things will happen the way they will, Elizabeth. Nothing you can do at this point, other than taking care of yourself, will change them."

Elizabeth nodded slowly, thinking that the last thing she wanted to do was take care of herself. She wanted to just lie on her bed and let the life drain out of her.

"What's that?" Rick asked, pointing to the box Elizabeth held in her hand still.

Elizabeth smiled sadly, feeling sick again. "The ring I gave Cat. She left it behind at Kana's house."

Rick grimaced.

"Kana was kind enough to bring it to me when she came to get Cat's things from the apartment." She felt the bile rising in her throat as she thought of the confrontation. Kana had been very abrupt and seemed to relish hurting her by handing her the ring box.

Rick curled his lips in a wry smile. "Kana is one to be rather direct."

"Not unlike the threat to break my neck if I bothered Cat again," Elizabeth said.

Rick let out a deep breath. "She'd have to come through your aunt and me first."

Elizabeth didn't believe him. She still felt that he and Midnight weren't really on her side. Then again, she figured everyone hated her right now.

Rick tried to convince her of his sincerity for a while longer, but nothing he said meant anything to her. Eventually, he gave up and left. Elizabeth spent the next hour crying silently for everything she'd lost.

* * *

Sierra couldn't stand it. Not seeing Kashena was making her crazy. She hadn't realized how reliant she'd become on Kashena's presence until she no longer had it in her life. One day, a week after they'd broken up, Sierra got so desperate for just a glimpse of Kashena that she went up to their offices on the seventeenth floor. Kashena wasn't there. She was told by the secretary that Special Agent Supervisor Marshal was out of town on business. Sierra went back to her office, feeling both frustrated and foolish.

Things at home seemed to get worse. Without the balance of her time with Kashena, Sierra saw more and more what a pig her husband was. She still wasn't sure if he'd always been this way, or if being in the Middle East had made him worse. Either way, he was almost unbearable to her now. She couldn't stand the way he looked at her, the way he talked to her, even the way he smelled. Part of her knew that it was because she missed Kashena desperately, but she clamped down on that thought, because it was apparent Kashena had closed her out of her life.

It had been two and a half weeks since they'd broken up when Sierra finally snapped. Jason was being his usual pushy self. He'd come up to her while she was cooking dinner and pressed his hard-on against her thigh.

"Jesus, Jason!" she gasped in a harsh whisper. "Colby is in the other room!"

"So?" he said, his breath smelling of beer. "I'm leaving for Twentynine Palms in a little while. I'll be gone for two full days… I need something before I go." With that he rubbed against her.

Sierra turned around, looking him square in the eye. "Stop."

"And if I don't?" he asked, his tone amused.

"Jason, just—"

"When's dinner ready?" Colby asked as he ran into the room.

Sierra stepped back from Jason, turning to her son.

"Soon, babe," she said, smiling. "In fact, why don't you come here and wash up? Then you can set the table."

"Okay!" Colby exclaimed.

Jason narrowed his eyes at her but said nothing. A few minutes later he walked away, going to finish packing to check in at the base. Sierra breathed a sigh of relief—she'd thwarted him this time. She made a point of avoiding being alone with him until he left two hours later. After he left, she let out a deep sigh.

She cleaned up the dinner dishes, her mind reeling at all that was happening. Jason was already making noises about having to move. Twentynine Palms was where he'd received his orders for, and that was close to Los Angeles. He'd already started telling her that she was probably going to have to change jobs. She'd explained to him that as a Chief Deputy AG it wasn't that easy for her to just change. His response had been, "They need shark lawyers everywhere, babe."

He had no concept of what this job meant to her, nor did he care. His attitude was that she belonged where he was, no matter what hellhole that put her in. She'd been relieved when they'd been moved to San Diego and he'd been at Pendleton; at least she was home then. But when she'd gotten the chance to make Chief Deputy AG, Midnight had wanted her in Sacramento. Sierra had insisted. Fortunately, Jason had received his orders for the Middle East shortly after her promotion anyway, so it had worked out. But now, now it wasn't working out anymore.

She was going crazy. She needed to get out and think. She called the teenaged neighbor who often watched Colby for her and asked her to come over. Tammy was happy to have some extra money, she was saving for prom, so she came right over.

"I don't know what time I'll be back," Sierra said, "so feel free to make yourself comfortable."

"Great, thanks, Mrs. Youngblood," Tammy said, smiling.

Sierra grabbed her car keys and left the house. She drove her Mercedes aimlessly for a while. Then she found herself driving toward Club 21. It was a gay bar in Midtown Sacramento. Kashena had taken her there a few times. Walking inside, she looked around. Many women looked in her direction; she met their looks head-on. She'd learned that from Kashena. "Never look ashamed to be here," Kashena had told her. The same women looking at her began nodding as they talked to their friends.

Sierra made her way to the bar. Sitting down, she saw the bartender looking at her curiously.

"What'll it be?" the younger woman asked.

"White wine," Sierra said, smiling slightly.

The bartender nodded, picking up a glass and grabbing the wine. As she poured, she looked at Sierra.

"You looking for Kash?"

"No," Sierra said, feeling a sharp pain at the reminder.

"You were with her before, though, right?"

"Right," Sierra said, giving the bartender a quelling look.

The bartender, Gina, nodded, her grin impish. She handed Sierra the glass of wine.

"It's on the house, honey," she said as Sierra reached into her purse.

"Thanks," Sierra said, unsure of the woman's reason for buying her a drink.

"The reason I ask," the bartender said, "is 'cause Kash is here."

"She is?" Sierra asked sharply before she could stop herself.

Gina smiled. "Yeah, she's at the back bar." She reached out her hand, touching Sierra's. "And that scumbag Linda is making a play to get back with her as we speak."

"Linda?" Sierra asked, feeling sick. "Wait, get back with her?"

Gina nodded. "They broke up a couple of weeks ago."

Sierra wasn't sure what to do with that piece of information. Kash had broken up with Linda? Around the same time they had broken up? Now Linda was trying to get Kashena back?

"Linda's like a shark," Gina said, seeing Sierra's thoughts clearly on her face. "She smells blood in the water and she's going in for the kill." Gina paused. "On your woman."

Sierra's eyes connected with the bartender's. Gina inclined her head toward the back bar, and Sierra nodded. Gina handed her a shot glass with amber liquid in it. Sierra looked back at Gina, then drank the shot, feeling the alcohol burn down her throat. Gathering her courage, she walked toward the back bar, in another room of the club. Walking through the door, she looked to the left and saw Kashena at the bar. Her back was to the bar, her elbows against it. She had a beer in her hand, and her eyes were on a woman dancing in front of her.

The woman had waist-long dark curly hair. She was wearing a skirt that barely covered her legs and a halter top that barely contained her. She was pretty, Sierra had to admit that. Linda had a very sexy way about her; Sierra could see what attracted Kashena to her. Linda was a user, though, Sierra reminded herself.

Striding toward Kashena, Sierra got halfway there. She was ten feet away when she stopped. She stared at Kashena, unsure suddenly.

Kashena's face was composed in a bored, slightly amused look. The movement just behind Linda caught her eye. Glancing up, she saw Sierra standing there. Her eyes connected with Sierra's, and she found she couldn't look away.

Linda suddenly realized she'd lost Kashena's attention. Looking up, she saw that Kashena was gazing past her. Over her shoulder,

Linda saw a dark-haired woman with distinctly American Indian features, even a long braid down one side of her hair. *Oh shit,* was the next thought.

Sierra walked toward Kashena, as Kashena straightened from the bar. Sierra walked right up to her, staring up into her eyes.

"We need to talk," Sierra said.

"Excuse me," Linda inserted, moving toward Sierra.

Kashena didn't look away from Sierra, only holding her hand up to stop Linda's forward motion.

"Let's go outside," Kashena said to Sierra.

Sierra nodded and preceded Kashena out of the bar. Linda stared open-mouthed after them. Glancing around, she saw other women watching her. Many in the club knew all about Linda. Everyone knew Kashena and liked her a great deal. No one liked what Linda did to her on a regular basis. So it was with much amusement that they watched Kashena leave the bar with the beautiful dark-haired woman who'd been in her life lately. A few people knew the woman was married, but they were hoping that would change soon.

Outside, Kashena lit a cigar, leaning against the wall. Sierra shifted from one foot to the other, trying to decide exactly what to say. This wasn't something she'd planned on. She'd had no idea that Kashena was at the bar that night. Kashena never went out on weeknights. It was fate—fate had put them together once again.

Stepping forward, Sierra put herself right against Kashena, her face an inch away from hers. She kissed Kashena on the lips tenderly. Pulling back, she looked up into Kashena's eyes.

"I'm sorry," she whispered. "I love you. Please forgive me."

Kashena stared back at her. Flinging her cigar away, Kashena straightened and grabbed Sierra's hand, striding to her Impala parked not too far away. She opened the door for Sierra, and then got in on the driver's side. She drove directly to her house without a word. Kashena opened the door, taking Sierra's hand again and leading her inside.

Once in the house, Kashena turned to Sierra, kissing her deeply. There were no more words then, just the physical reunion they needed. Two hours later, they lay in Kashena's bed, both trying to catch their breath. Kashena settled Sierra on her side, her arms wrapped around her.

"Now," Kashena said, kissing Sierra's forehead, "talk to me."

Sierra snuggled closer to Kashena, reveling in the feeling of being with her again.

"I need to be with you," she said. "I'll do whatever it takes to be with you as often as I can."

Kashena nodded, her fingers brushing back long strands of black hair from Sierra's face.

"So what would be different this time?" Kashena asked, no accusation in her tone.

Sierra breathed deeply.

"Well, I know I can't live without you," Sierra said. "So I will just have to do what it takes to be with you."

"Can I ask you a question?" Kashena said.

Sierra nodded.

"Why do you have sex with him so much, if you love me?"

"Because he pushes me for it all the time," Sierra said, grimacing. "I never want to fight with him about it because I don't want Colby overhearing that kind of argument. But, if that's what it takes to keep you, I'll do whatever I have to."

Kashena winced. "I don't want you to have to fight with him…"

"That's what it'll take, to keep him away from me, though, Kash."

Kashena took a deep breath.

"Sierra," she said then, her tone changing slightly, "do you..." She hesitated. "Do you enjoy it with him?"

After a long moment, Sierra shook her head. "I haven't enjoyed sex with him since maybe the first or second time. Especially not now."

"Now?"

"It's nothing like this," Sierra said, gesturing to their bodies together. "Since I've been with you, nothing else compares."

Kashena grinned. "That's it, stroke my ego."

Sierra kissed her. "I'm not stroking your ego. I'm stating a fact."

"Mm-hmm..." Kashena murmured, leaning in to kiss Sierra again.

That movement was aborted abruptly when Kashena grabbed the gun from under her pillow, sitting up and pointing it at the person standing in the doorway in one fluid motion.

"Kash, Jesus!" Linda screamed, throwing her arms up in front of her face.

Kashena didn't move. "What are you doing in here?" she asked, her gun still pointed unwaveringly at Linda.

"You made a fool out of me at the bar," Linda said mournfully.

"I'm about to make worse out of you if you don't get out of my house," Kashena said.

"Kashie..." Linda began.

"I think she told you to get out," Sierra said, sitting up behind Kashena.

"Shut up, you stupid bitch!" Linda screeched.

"Not too stupid," Sierra said, her hand on Kashena's shoulder.

Linda narrowed her eyes.

"Linda, get out," Kashena said.

"You think you have her," Linda said, her eyes on Sierra. "You don't have her. Kash is in love with me."

"Guess again," Sierra said, putting her arms around Kashena's neck loosely, then pulling her back against her. Kashena's arm didn't waver; the gun was still pointed at Linda. Her look, however, changed to one of amusement.

Her dark eyes watching Linda, Sierra lowered her head and kissed Kashena on the neck.

Kashena closed her eyes briefly, making an "mmm" sound.

Linda narrowed her eyes dangerously. Kashena said nothing, merely watching Linda intently. It was obvious the moment Linda's tactics changed—Kashena could almost hear her mind click.

Linda dropped her arms, one hand resting on the dresser next to her.

"This isn't how things should be," she said ruefully.

"Yeah, well, this is how things are," Kashena said. "Now get out."

"Fine!" Linda yelled, tightening her hands into fists.

Kashena waited until Linda had turned and walked out, watching the indicator for her alarm system, which showed where Linda was in the house via the motion detectors. When the lights went back to green, Kashena got up and, setting her gun aside, she armed the system. Linda was getting into the bad habit of just walking in whenever she chose to. That wasn't acceptable.

Lying back down, Kashena glanced at Sierra.

"You okay?" she asked as she pulled Sierra back into her arms.

"Yes. She's definitely tenacious," Sierra said, indicating the spot where Linda had stood minutes before.

Kashena rolled her eyes. "And then some."

"You're very quick with that gun, Agent Marshal," Sierra said, smiling proudly.

"Quick where I need to be, slow everywhere else…"

"You're so worth fighting for," Sierra said.

"I don't want anyone fighting over me," Kashena replied, leaning down to kiss Sierra's lips.

Sierra wrapped her arms around Kashena's neck, kissing her back.

"How late can you stay?" Kashena asked.

"As late as you want me here." Sierra smiled. "He's down in Twentynine Palms for the next two days," she said in answer to the question in Kashena's eyes.

"Ah," Kashena said, nodding. "That's where his orders sent him now?"

"Yes," Sierra said.

"He gonna want you closer to LA then?"

"That's what he has in mind," Sierra replied, "but I'm not doing it."

"How's that going to go over?"

"He won't like it," Sierra said, "but I make more money, and it would be difficult for Colby to be uprooted from school and his friends, so I'll win for now."

"For now," Kashena repeated.

"One issue at a time, Kash," Sierra said, sounding like the lawyer she was.

"Ma'am, yes, ma'am," Kashena said with a grin, her deep blue eyes sparkling.

They kissed again and forgot everything else for a while. Sierra called Tammy and asked her if it would be alright if she stayed the night. Tammy happily agreed. Sierra promised to come home in time to get Colby ready for school and take him to day care.

251

Things worked for the next week. Jason came home from the base, wanting sex the minute he walked in the door. Sierra knew Kashena was out of town for the next two days, so she allowed him to have sex with her. She literally lay there trying to forget what was happening. Jason didn't even seem to notice or care. Afterwards she took a long hot bath, wanting to soak him out of her. The night he was supposed to leave again for the base, a day before she was to see Kashena again, he wanted sex; she managed to avoid it until it was too late and he had to leave. He left unhappily. She didn't care at all.

The next night she spent with Kashena, happy to be with her again. They spent most of the night talking about anything and everything. Sierra marveled at the fact that they could talk about so many things. Conversations ranged from their tribes, to what Kashena was doing down in Los Angeles, setting up new teams for security, all the way to where they'd travel if they got the chance. It was insane being so connected to someone, but it felt good too, and Sierra wasn't going to give it up, no matter what it took to keep it.

She found out what it would take the next time Jason came home. The timing wasn't as good this time. Jason came home on a Thursday. Sierra had a date with Kashena to go to dinner and the club on Saturday. So now came the test—she'd have to tell Jason no when he wanted sex.

He arrived home right before dinner. Sierra was in the middle of cooking when he walked in, so it was easy to avoid him for a while. Later, however, after dinner was over and the dishes cleared and washed, Colby went off to his room, and Jason came after her. Sierra had gone upstairs, hoping to avoid him for a while longer. She was sitting in her home office, working on a report for Midnight, when he came in. His hands slid down the front of her body, grabbing her breasts.

"Jason," she said, sharper than she'd meant to, because she was so tense, "I'm busy right now. I need to get this report done."

"Well, I need something too," he said, his tone far from endearing. He grasped at her again.

She turned her chair around, knocking his arms away with its high back. "I said I'm busy right now," she said more sternly. "You're just going to have to survive without me for a night."

"Bullshit," Jason said, his tone darkening. "Your shit can wait. I've been gone for three days, and I want to fuck. Got it?"

Sierra stood up, looking away from him. His language was getting worse. It was as if he had lost any semblance of respect for her. She was just some object to him now, something to be used when he needed it.

"Is that what I am to you?" she asked him evenly.

"What?" Jason replied, surprised by the question.

"Am I just something to be fucked and used?"

Jason stared back at her, obviously at a loss as to how to answer that question.

"You're my wife," he said finally, as if she should know that.

"Yes," she said, "but nowhere in the marriage contract does it require me to fuck you whenever you feel like it," she snapped, using his own language to try and get through to him.

"What is this?" he asked, his voice turning suspicious. "You think you're going to start holding out on me now?"

"I think I'm going to start having some say as to when we have sex," Sierra said.

"Tell ya what," he said, taking a menacing step forward and grabbing her wrists. "You can say where we fuck."

"Jason, no!" she yelled, trying to pull away from him, but his grip was like iron around her wrists.

253

Chapter 7

Kashena answered her door and was shocked to see Sierra standing there, tears streaming down her face. Sierra threw herself into Kashena's arms, crying harder then.

"What happened?" Kashena asked, holding Sierra close to her. "Tell me what happened."

Kashena walked Sierra over to the couch, sitting down and pulling Sierra down onto her lap. It was a long time before Sierra could calm down long enough to speak coherently. Even then, her speech was halting and half hysterical.

"Jason... came home tonight... he wanted... he tried... and I told him no, I tried, Kash, I tried... but he... he..." Again she began to cry, and Kashena knew exactly what had happened.

Kashena winced, closing her eyes for a moment. Sierra's husband had forced her to have sex, all because Kashena insisted on there being forty-eight hours between the times that she was with him and then with her. Damn it!

"Baby, I'm sorry," Kashena said, putting her lips to Sierra's forehead. "God, I'm so sorry..."

Sierra shook her head, her face against Kashena's shirt. "It's not your fault. He just wouldn't stop..."

"Did he hurt you? Maybe I should take you to a hospital," Kashena said, the cop in her kicking in.

"No!" Sierra exclaimed. "Please, Kash, no, no hospital, please. I don't want anyone to know, please..."

"Okay, babe, okay," Kashena said, tipping Sierra's face up to hers. "Did he hurt you?"

Sierra bit her lip; it was obvious that it was still sinking in. Finally she shook her head. "I knew he'd hurt me worse if I resisted, so I finally gave in and just lay there."

Kashena let out a relieved sigh. "Okay, then we won't worry about that part. But babe…"

"I can't believe he resorted to that," Sierra said.

"He's a bastard," Kashena said, her tone dark. "Personally, I think he and I need to have a chat, Marine to Marine."

"No! Kashena, no," Sierra said. "I don't want you anywhere near him. He thinks of me as his property—he'd kill you for trying to take me away from him."

"He'd try," Kashena replied confidently.

"I can't take that chance, Kashena, not with you, please?" Sierra begged.

Kashena took a deep breath, her desire to beat the shit out of Jason warring with the desire to allay Sierra's fears of a confrontation between the two of them. Although Kashena saw that confrontation as inevitable—she'd already seen it in her visions. They were never wrong.

"Okay, okay," Kashena said finally, pulling Sierra into her arms again, holding her close. "Stay here tonight though. I don't want you going home to that man tonight."

Sierra nodded, agreeing with Kashena on that.

Kashena got up, pouring Sierra a glass of wine and grabbing a beer out of the fridge for herself. They went out onto the patio and talked for a while. Sierra slowly but surely started realizing what had happened.

"He raped me," she said, her tone stunned.

Kashena's head came up a bit as she grimaced. She knew it would hit Sierra eventually, what her husband had done to her. Sierra looked over at Kashena, noting the grimace. She was looking for confirmation. Kashena nodded slowly, her expression unhappy.

"I can't stay with him, Kashena," Sierra said. "My God, he raped his own wife… What kind of monster is he?"

Kashena took a long drink of her beer, draining the bottle. "He's a Marine, Sierra. If the Navy had wanted him to have a conscience, they would have issued him one."

Sierra looked back at Kashena, surprised by what she'd just said.

"But you have a conscience," Sierra pointed out.

"Yeah," Kashena said, her grin wry, "and I've been out for over six years now. I got mine back on discharge."

Sierra smiled sadly, then shook her head. "I can't stay with him," she said again, as if trying to convince herself.

Kashena didn't say anything. She knew this was a decision Sierra needed to make for herself. She could, however, play devil's advocate.

"What about Colby?" Kashena asked.

Sierra nodded, accepting that Kashena was trying to help her work through this.

"I've stayed with him this long for Colby's sake," Sierra said. "But if this is the kind of man Jason really is… I don't want my son raised by him."

Kashena nodded in agreement.

"I have the more stable income and job in the household," Sierra continued. "No judge would award Jason custody. He could end up back in Iraq for all we know."

Kashena nodded again, thinking an air-to-ground missile up the man's ass right now would make her feel a lot better, even if it wasn't American made.

"The house?" Kashena asked, trying to cover all the bases.

"He can have it," Sierra said, her voice even, "if he can keep up with the payments."

There was an evil glint in her eyes. Kashena knew Sierra was now getting to the phase of being angry. It was a good sign. Sierra was a lot stronger than Kashena had realized. She'd been worried that this would really hurt her, but Sierra was pulling through it.

"I can get an apartment for Colby and me until the divorce is final," Sierra said, continuing that line of thought.

Kashena was surprised that Sierra was so completely calm. They talked about a few other things after that. Kashena was careful to keep Sierra's glass of wine filled, knowing it would help cushion her emotions. When it got late, Kashena took Sierra's glass out of her hand and then, taking her hand, pulled her gently up out of the chair. Inside, Kashena left the glass on the counter and led Sierra to her bedroom.

"Wait," Sierra said when Kashena would have laid her down on the bed. "I want to shower," she said. "I need to get him off me."

Kashena nodded, understanding that feeling completely.

"Go ahead, babe," she said gently. "I'm going to go lock up the house."

"Okay," Sierra said, walking into Kashena's bathroom.

Ten minutes later, Kashena poked her head into the shower to see that Sierra was standing under the streaming water, shaking from head to toe. Reaching in and shutting off the water, Kashena walked into the stall, picked Sierra up in her arms, and wrapped her in the towel she'd grabbed off the rack.

Sierra rested her head against Kashena, feeling enveloped in her girlfriend's warmth. Kashena gently dried Sierra off, then led her over to the bed and laid her down under the covers. Kashena had changed into sweats and a tank top. She climbed into bed next to Sierra, pulling her into her arms immediately. Sierra snuggled close, her lips against Kashena's neck.

"I'm leaving him tomorrow," Sierra whispered to Kashena.

"I'm coming with you," was Kashena's reply.

Sierra kissed Kashena's neck, then moved her lips to Kashena's ear.

"I love you," she whispered softly.

Kashena kissed Sierra's temple. "I love you too, honey."

They fell asleep with Kashena holding Sierra. They woke the same way.

When Sierra opened her eyes, she looked up at Kashena, who was already awake. Kashena moved her head to look down at Sierra.

"This is how I'd love to wake up every morning," Sierra said, smiling softly.

Kashena smiled back, her dark blue eyes shining. "Me too." She kissed Sierra's lips gently.

Sierra's hand reached up to Kashena's cheek as they kissed. Kashena deepened the kiss slowly, pulling Sierra closer. Sierra moaned softly, responding to the kiss. When they were both breathless, Sierra pulled back, her eyes searching Kashena's. Kashena's response was to kiss her again, her hands sliding upward to cup Sierra's breasts gently, caressing her.

"Ohh…" Sierra moaned softly. "Kash, what about the rule…"

"To hell with the rule," Kashena said, continuing to kiss her.

"But, Kash, I don't want you to think—"

"Babe," Kashena said, putting her finger gently to Sierra's lips to quiet her. "You need emotional healing right now. That's more important than my stupid rule."

Sierra bit her lip, tears in her eyes. Gratitude had her kissing Kashena back, forgetting everything else for the moment. Kashena made love to her that morning; she was extremely gentle and loving, and Sierra found it a wonderful counter to the evening before's occurrence. It steeled her resolve to leave Jason that day. Kashena was who she was meant for, not Jason. It was over.

That morning was spent hiring a divorce lawyer. Kashena was astounded at Sierra's resolve. She had no hesitation whatsoever, now that the decision had been made. It was amazing to watch Sierra in action too. Kashena, introduced to the divorce lawyer as her bodyguard, watched Sierra discuss legal matters with the other attorney. She was in her element, and Sierra was fantastic in her element. Every angle was touched on, every possible issue looked at and resolved. When it came to legal grounds, Sierra was on her game. She cited irreconcilable differences as the reason for the divorce, but gave the lawyer supporting issues such as Jason's long absence, change in behavior since returning from the Middle East, violation of her privacy and intimacy levels. Kashena had never heard "rape" put so eloquently. It took all she had not to grin constantly at how amazing her girlfriend really was.

The minute they left the lawyer's office and were in Kashena's car, Kashena made a point of telling her that.

"My God, you're amazing," she said.

"Why do you say that?" Sierra asked, smiling.

"You're one helluva lawyer," Kashena said in an awed tone.

"Is that a good thing?" Sierra asked, raising an eyebrow.

"At what you do, yes, it is," Kashena said, dying to kiss her but knowing this wasn't the time or the place.

Sierra smiled brilliantly, unaccountably happy that Kashena thought that she was good at what she did. Jason always treated her like some secretary. He had absolutely no respect for what she did, or how hard she'd worked to get where she was. He didn't care. It was yet another difference between who she was married to and who she wanted to be with.

Kashena insisted that they stop and eat before they went to the house. She could sense Sierra getting anxious and thought she could use a relaxing lunch first. She was, as usual, right. They ate at Isabella's, a Mexican restaurant located in the front part of Club 21. Kashena ordered Sierra a couple glasses of wine, and herself a beer.

"Are you sure he'll be home?" Kashena asked, hoping to avoid dealing with the man if she could.

"Yes," Sierra said. "He doesn't do anything when he's not on duty. He takes care of the yard and that's basically it. He'll be home."

"Then maybe you should practice what you're going to say to him."

Sierra picked up her glass of wine and took a drink. "I'm just telling him that I'm leaving. That I'm going to go pick Colby up from school and we're leaving him. That the divorce papers have already been filed, that he should receive them within twenty-four hours. I'll tell him there is a temporary custody order on a judge's desk as we speak, requesting full custody be given to me before the divorce."

Kashena nodded. "Sounds great, but you know it won't be that easy."

"I know," Sierra said. "I wish we could just turn him to stone, so I could say everything I need to say, grab my stuff, and run out."

Kashena laughed. "Yeah, me too."

"You know," Sierra said, reaching across the table and taking Kashena's hand, "if you don't want to come with me, you don't have to. I know you don't like to deal with him."

"With his propensity for violence all of a sudden," Kashena said, her tone serious, "and the fact that what you're about to do is not on his agenda, I'm going to be there."

Sierra bit her lip. "I really don't want there to be a confrontation between you two."

"I know you don't," Kashena said, "and I'll do everything I can to avoid it, but if he lays a hand on you, all bets are off. As far as he'll know, I'm there in an official capacity. And as far as I'm concerned, I am."

Sierra nodded, understanding that Kashena meant that she was acting as a peace officer for the state in protecting her from Jason. She hesitated to think about what that could mean. She didn't want to start worrying about something else now.

They left the restaurant a little while later. It was 1 p.m. when they drove up to the house. Jason's Jeep was in the driveway. Sierra looked over at Kashena; Kashena only nodded.

Walking inside, Sierra led the way, glancing around, wondering where Jason was. Kashena looked around, doing her best not to be shocked at how big and beautiful Sierra's house was. It was a mansion compared to Kashena's house, with cathedral ceilings and an open, airy feel to it. The house was very much Sierra, right down to the terra-cotta entryway tiles. Very earthy.

Sierra walked into the kitchen, setting her keys on the countertop of deep hunter green. Kashena looked around. Everything was pristine, and very expensive looking. It was another dimension to Sierra she'd never seen. The woman had incredible taste. Kashena knew, beyond a shadow of a doubt, that Sierra had decorated the house. It was very much her style. Elegant, tasteful, understated, but with just a touch of flair that spoke of an American Indian influence—including some incredible Remington bronze statues, all of Indians in traditional war dress on ponies. Sierra's house, from what little Kashena had already seen, was nothing shy of phenomenal. She wanted to give this up? Anything to get rid of Jason.

Sierra heard Jason in the backyard and decided that it would be easier to go and start packing a few things while he was outside. She led Kashena upstairs.

Upstairs was even more opulent. The master suite had double doors that opened into a huge bedroom. There were French doors that led out onto a balcony, and a huge walk-in closet. The carpet was a warm beige, the bed iron and bronze with sheer curtains draped around it. Everything had an expensive look to it—Kashena couldn't begin to imagine how much everything cost. She stood back, keeping her back to the wall next to the door. She wanted to see Jason coming when he realized they were in the house.

Sierra pulled out a suitcase and started putting clothes into it. She also packed an overnight case with things like her makeup. She knew she couldn't possibly get everything, but she'd come back when Jason was on base and get the rest and box it up. In the meantime she'd find an apartment. Kashena had already said that she and Colby could stay with her until she found a place. It was important that she get out of this house.

She was just finishing packing when Jason walked into the bedroom. He didn't notice Kashena—his attention was on Sierra and the suitcase she was closing.

"What do you think you're doing?" Jason asked in a derogatory tone.

"Leaving," Sierra said simply. She turned to him. "I'm leaving you, leaving this house, and leaving this marriage."

Jason's mouth dropped open, then his eyes narrowed. Colby came bounding into the room.

"Mom!" he said excitedly. "I got to use the edger thingy and—" He stopped as he saw the suitcase. "Where you going?" he asked, assuming she was going on a business trip.

"We're going," Sierra told Colby. "Why don't you go pack some clothes for the next few days at school, and I'll—"

Jason hit her then, backhanded her.

Kashena cussed at herself for not being ready for that. She came off the wall as Jason screamed at Sierra, who was now on the floor.

"Stupid cunt! Think you can take my son, think you can leave me?" he yelled. "I'll fucking—" he began as he brought his fist up.

In one move, Kashena grabbed his fist and twisted his arm up around his behind his back, and then slammed him into the nearest wall face first.

"You won't do anything else," Kashena said to Jason, glancing down at Sierra.

Colby, who'd screamed when his father hit his mother, was on the floor next to Sierra, holding on to her in complete terror.

"Let me go, you fucking dyke bitch!" Jason yelled, straining against Kashena's hold.

It took all of Kashena's strength to hold on to him, but she was used to suspects struggling.

"Not gonna happen," Kashena said. "So calm down before I break your arm." As if to back that statement up, she lifted his arm higher.

Jason let out a yell, but then stilled.

"Sierra," Kashena said, taking command of the situation, "get on the phone, call 911, and have them send out a black-and-white. Colby, I need you to do what your mom asked you to, okay? It's okay, your mom's okay, but you need to get your things. Can you do that for me?"

Colby stared up at Kashena with saucer-sized eyes, but he nodded slowly. He was responding to the authority in her voice as well as the kindness. Sierra pulled herself up off the floor. Kashena glanced at her, her face pained. Sierra nodded, as if affirming to Kashena that she was right, she was okay. Sierra picked up the phone and called 911. She identified herself as Chief Deputy Attorney General Youngblood of the criminal division and asked the dispatcher to send a car to her house. Kashena smiled. Sierra knew how to get a response.

"What the fuck do you think you're gonna do?" Jason taunted. "Think you're gonna arrest me, bitch?"

"No, I think the officers that arrive in the black-and-white are going to arrest you," Kashena said calmly. "I'm just going to tell them what I witnessed, and show them your wife's cut lip and bruised face."

"She won't press charges," Jason said confidently.

"She doesn't have to, moron," Kashena said. "In this state, the cops only need to see evidence of domestic violence. And I can assure you, considering who your wife is and who she works for, the DA will be happy to take your ass to court for it. You just made a big mistake, pal. A very big mistake."

Jason started to struggle again. It was obvious he'd been convinced that Kashena was very serious. Sierra screamed and jumped out of the way. Jason managed to get one arm free and twisted around, grabbing Kashena by the throat and literally picking her up off the ground. Knowing that he was ready to kill her, Kashena had to think fast. She kneed him in the groin. When he doubled over, letting go of her, she brought her fist through and slammed it into his face, knocking him out cold.

"Are you okay?" Sierra asked, her voice worried.

Kashena nodded, touching her throat gingerly. The guy had a grip on him, that was for sure.

"Go," Kashena began. Her voice was hoarse; she cleared her throat and started again. "Go tell Colby to hurry up with his stuff. I want to be ready to get out of here when the cops arrive."

Sierra looked worriedly at Kashena.

"I'm okay, babe," Kashena said, sparing a moment to touch the already darkening bruise at Sierra's mouth. "Are you?"

Sierra nodded, tears in her eyes. "I'm sorry."

"Shhh," Kashena said. "It's okay. That's why I came."

Sierra moved past Kashena to go and help Colby pack.

By the time the police car arrived, Kashena had cuffed Jason's hands behind his back and had him lying on his stomach on the living room floor. He hadn't regained consciousness yet. The officers came in, and Kashena explained what had happened, showing them the darkening bruise on Sierra's face as well as the split lip.

"So you've got him for domestic violence," Kashena said, watching as Jason began to stir as the other officer pulled him up off the floor. Her eyes were on him as she said, "And you can add assault on a peace officer to that too."

"You fucking bitch!" Jason screamed. "Fucking dyke bitch. Come into my house, think you can beat me up? I have rights!"

"Yes," Kashena said as they came face to face. "You have the right to remain silent, and if you're fucking smart, you will," she said, her voice deep and threatening.

With that, the officers took Jason away. It didn't stop him from screaming threats and obscenities all the way to the squad car.

Kashena looked at Sierra, who looked down at Colby. He was watching his mother with wide eyes.

"It'll be okay," Sierra assured him.

Colby simply nodded, the usually boisterous child very solemn.

Kashena helped Sierra put her suitcase and Colby's in the trunk of the Impala. She drove them back to her house. A few hours later, they'd ordered pizza and gotten Colby set up in Kashena's extra bedroom. Sierra put Colby to bed, still a bit shaken by everything that had happened that day. Jason's violence had somehow surprised her; she wasn't sure why. It had always been there, just under the surface. She'd just never really given him a reason to hit her before.

"Mom?" Colby said as she was holding him before he went to bed.

"Hmm?" Sierra asked, her thoughts a million places right then.

"Is Dad going to jail?"

"Yes, he is," Sierra said.

"Because he hit you?" Colby asked.

"Yes, and because he attacked Kashena too."

Colby nodded, assimilating that information.

"Are we going to live here now?" he asked a few moments later.

"Long enough for me to find us an apartment," Sierra said.

Again Colby nodded, glancing around him. It wasn't the room he was used to, but he understood that things were all confused right now. He was doing his best to comprehend what was happening.

Sierra felt a pang of guilt. It hadn't been her wish to have Jason arrested in front of her son. It had never been her wish to have Colby witness his father hit her either—Jason had made that choice. She only hoped that Colby would be able to understand someday that things weren't always black and white. Although she had no idea how he was feeling at that point. She didn't want to push, knowing that her son was the type of boy to think things out thoroughly. Once he had, she knew he'd ask the questions he needed to ask.

Once Colby was in bed, Sierra made her way back to Kashena's room. She hadn't explained to Colby why she was staying in Kashena's bedroom, but it had been Colby who'd brought her overnight bag to her there. He hadn't asked, so she hadn't said anything. There was no point in confusing him more this night.

Standing in the doorway, Sierra saw Kashena at the window, smoking a cigar and blowing the smoke outside. It was a concession to the fact that there was now a child in her house. It warmed Sierra's heart. She walked over and wrapped her arms around Kashena's waist.

"Thank you," she said softly.

"For what?" Kashena stubbed out her cigar and turned around to face Sierra, leaning back against the window ledge.

"For everything," Sierra said, looking up at her.

"You mean like letting Jason nail you while I was standing right there?" Kashena said, her tone self-castigating.

Sierra's mouth opened in shock at what Kashena had just said. She reached up to touch the light bruises on Kashena's neck. "You had no way of knowing he'd get violent so quickly. God, even I didn't think he would ever out-and-out hit me, especially in front of Colby."

"What made you think that?" Kashena asked.

"When I was pregnant, he used to talk about how his father always beat his mother in front of him. That he'd never to do that to his child."

"Guess he changed his mind," Kashena said wryly.

Sierra shook her head. "I think he just knows he's losing control of me, and that's making him crazy."

Kashena still looked unhappy.

"Kashena, you stopped him," Sierra said, touching her cheek. "He would have done a lot worse if you hadn't been there. I'm afraid he would have turned on Colby too, because Colby would have defended me."

Kashena narrowed her eyes at the thought of Jason hitting a defenseless child.

"So thank you for being there," Sierra said, "and thank you for letting us stay here, and—"

Kashena's lips on hers stopped her litany.

"I got it," Kashena said, smiling when their lips parted.

"Good," Sierra said, smiling back.

Later, after they'd showered and had gone to bed, Kashena wearing her usual sweat pants and a tank top and Sierra wearing her silk pajama shirt and shorts, Sierra lay on her back, Kashena on her stomach. They were close together on the bed, but their only contact was Kashena's arm across Sierra's stomach. Their faces were turned toward each other.

It was something Colby noticed that night when he creeped into the bedroom. He stood staring down at his mother and her bodyguard. Tilting his head, he looked at the tattoo on Kashena's upper arm. He touched it lightly with his forefinger. His eyes widened as he realized it was a Marine tattoo like his father's. When he glanced at Kashena, amazement still written on his face, he saw that her eyes were open.

"You're a Marine like my dad?" Colby asked, unabashed.

Kashena nodded. "Honorably discharged, but I was a Marine, yes," she whispered.

Colby took in that piece of information, then he looked at Kashena again.

"Why did my dad hit my mother?" he asked, his voice tremulous.

Kashena didn't answer for a moment, then gave Colby a sympathetic look. "He was angry that your mother was leaving and taking you."

Colby nodded.

"He shouldn't have hit her," he said a few moments later.

"No, he shouldn't have."

"I'm glad you stopped him," he said, his voice tinged with anger.

Kashena nodded.

"Does he love my mother?" Colby asked, his expression almost concerned.

Kashena wasn't sure how to answer that. "I don't know, Colby. I assume he does—that's why he was angry that she was leaving him."

Colby looked directly at Kashena. "Do you love my mother?"

Kashena stared back at him. This child was very perceptive. There really was no point in lying to him, and the fact was, Kashena didn't want to.

"Yes, I do," Kashena said softly.

"And you'll protect her?"

"With my life."

Colby nodded. Kashena could see his mind was churning over everything. It amazed her that someone so young could assimilate so much, and still take in more.

Sierra stirred then, glancing up at Kashena and seeing that she was looking at something else. Turning her head, Sierra saw Colby standing next to the bed.

"Colby, are you okay?" she asked, turning over to face him. "Did you have a bad dream?"

"Mom, she's a Marine too," Colby told Sierra.

"I know, honey," Sierra said, smiling and glancing back at Kashena, who was grinning.

"So she can protect you," Colby said, his tone satisfied.

"And she has," Sierra said, nodding.

Colby's look slid between his mother and Kashena, and then back to Sierra.

"I like it here," he announced.

Sierra smiled at him; Kashena chuckled. This was an easy transition.

***

At San Francisco International Airport, Sable, Cat, and the rest of Sable's entourage were whisked through customs in no time. Cat shook her head. She'd ceased to be amazed at how Sable was treated. The woman wanted something, she got it, no questions asked. That was why Cat wasn't surprised to see a brand-new SUV parked curbside with a man standing next to it holding a sign with Sable's name on it.

Amidst the paparazzi taking picture after picture, Sable walked over to the man next to the vehicle. He pulled out a clipboard and had her sign in a few places. Then he handed her the keys. Cat watched it all with amusement written on her face. She watched as the rest of the group climbed into a black SUV that was at the curb as well. The black SUV pulled away, and Cat looked at Sable again.

"Don't tell me you just bought an SUV to drive around San Francisco in," Cat said, as Sable handed the porter the keys so he could load their luggage in the back. "You know they have rental agencies that rent out luxury cars?"

Sable only shrugged, smiling at Cat. Cat rolled her eyes. Even so, she checked out the vehicle, while studiously ignoring the men with the cameras behind her. It was habit now.

The SUV was a Porsche Cayenne, their answer to the sports utility vehicle trend. It was nice, Cat had to say that—Sable had excellent taste. Naturally, Sable had gotten top of the line, the Turbo model, which held a 4.5-liter, 8-cylinder engine that put out 450 horsepower. A very powerful engine indeed. Starting at $90,000, it should be. Sable had chosen the blue with the steel-gray leather interior.

When the porter had finished putting the bags in the vehicle, he went to hand the keys back to Sable. Sable shook her head.

"Give them to my girlfriend, please," she said, handing the man a hundred-dollar bill.

The porter tipped his hat to her, and then walked around the vehicle and handed Cat the keys.

Cat looked around the vehicle at Sable.

"It's your town," Sable said, smiling. "You drive."

Cat got in on the driver's side, and the porter opened the door for Sable.

Cat looked around the interior of the vehicle. It had everything, including a Bose surround stereo system. Top of the line all the way, that was Sable. The woman was no slouch.

Starting the vehicle, Cat closed her eyes for a moment. It definitely had a powerful engine. She breathed in the scent of the rich leather, combined with that new-car smell—it was heaven.

Sable watched Cat, smiling. The woman could definitely appreciate quality. She'd spared no expense for this vehicle. Everything was perfect; she was very happy with it.

Once they were on the 101 headed for San Francisco, Cat glanced at Sable.

"Are you sure you want to do this?" she asked, not for the first time.

"Yes, I want to meet your mother," Sable said, her tone flabbergasted.

Cat grinned. "You're probably going to give her a heart attack, you know."

"Why?" Sable asked, looking worried.

"Ah." Cat looked a bit contrite. "Because she happens to be a major fan of yours."

Sable stared open-mouthed at Cat. "You little brat, why didn't you tell me that?"

"Because I didn't want to pressure you into meeting my mother," Cat said, rolling her eyes.

"Well, now I really want to meet her," Sable said. "Someone who appreciates good music."

"Hey now," Cat said. "I have some of your albums."

"Some," Sable repeated, pressing her lips together as she shook her head.

"Yeah, yeah," Cat said. "You like that I'm not a slobbering fan."

"I like that you're beautiful, sexy, smart, and exciting as hell," Sable said. "Being a fan would only be a plus."

"I'll work on becoming a fan." Cat smiled.

"That's what I like to hear," Sable said, chuckling.

Cat was set to meet her mother in a popular restaurant/bar in the Castro, as it was called. The bar was called The Café. Cat figured that if Sable changed her mind, she could drop Sable at the hotel, and her mother wouldn't know that Cat was in San Francisco with Sable

Sands until hopefully it was too late. Of course, Cat would never hear the end of it from her mother.

"So, you haven't told your mother that you're dating me?" Sable asked as Cat exited the freeway onto Mission Street.

"Uh, no."

"Why not?" Sable asked.

"Trust me," Cat said as she took a quick left onto Market. "You'll understand when you meet her."

Sable narrowed her eyes, then looked around her. "Well, you definitely know your way around," she said. "I'd have been hopelessly lost by now."

Cat smiled. "This is where I learned to drive, babe."

Sable gave Cat a sidelong glance. "So, how does the Cayenne handle?"

"It's nice," Cat said, grinning.

"You like it?" Sable asked pointedly.

Cat glanced over at Sable, and saw it in her look.

"You didn't…" Cat said in disbelief.

"Guilty," Sable said unapologetically.

"Sable, no."

"Cat, yes," Sable countered, shrugging delicately. "I bought it for you. It's in your name, and it's yours. Do with it what you want."

"Sable, it's a ninety-thousand-dollar vehicle!" Cat exclaimed.

"Actually it was one hundred and ten, but who's counting?" Sable grinned.

Cat stared at her for a moment, then sighed, shaking her head.

"You spoil me way too much," Cat said as they arrived at the Castro and she found a parking space, thankfully close to The Café.

Leaning across the seat, she touched Sable on the cheek, then kissed her lips. "Thank you."

Sable smiled brilliantly. "You're welcome."

Cat got out of the vehicle, glancing over at Sable as she got out. There could be no missing Sable Sands, even if she weren't extremely famous. She wore skintight black leather pants with high-heeled black leather boots. She also wore a black lace bra with a sheer leopard-print blouse over it, and a gold chain belt that looped around her tiny waist and slim hips. Her rich brown hair, shot through with blond highlights, was a long silky mane down to her waist. No, no one could miss Sable Sands—that's how she wanted it.

Naturally people started to stop and stare, simply because Sable was a beautiful woman. Then they realized who she was. Cat leaned against the driver's side fender of the Cayenne, watching people coming up to Sable, staring at her reverently. She was used to people's reactions to Sable and knew that it was best to stay back, lest she get between fans and their idol.

Oddly enough, people were very respectful of Sable. They didn't grab at her, or try to maul her in any way. Some would reverently reach out to touch her hair, but not to pull any out or anything so violent. Cat wondered at that—was it because Sable was one of their kind? She was a goddess to the gay masses.

After about five minutes, people started to back off. Sable looked over at Cat, who walked around the front of the vehicle to extend her hand to Sable. Sable took it, and they walked toward The Café together. A number of the older men and women in the community recognized Cat, calling hellos to her. Cat waved, smiling over her shoulder at them.

Cat had dressed more retro and conservative for this trip, in a jean miniskirt, beige calfskin ankle boots, and a paisley-print blouse of blues, browns, and beige with long flowing sleeves. Two small braids held the front of her hair off her face, while the rest hung loose around her shoulders. She was the classic beautiful hippy chick.

At the door to The Café, Sable was asked for her autograph by a few people who'd walked up. Cat glanced back at her.

"Go on ahead. I'll catch up," Sable said.

"Okay," Cat said, grinning and shaking her head.

Cat walked upstairs, looking for her mother, who was, predictably, parked at the bar. Walking up behind her, Cat put her hand on her mother's shoulder.

"Ms. Roché, I presume," Cat said.

Melanie Roché turned around, beaming at her daughter. Melanie was an older version of Cat with slightly darker blond hair. She had the same sparkling blue eyes, although she'd gained some weight over the years, so she wasn't quite as slim and lithe as Catalina was.

"Catalina!" Melanie exclaimed. She threw her arms around her daughter, then held her at arm's length, looking her over. "You're alright, aren't you?" she asked, motherly concern on for the moment.

"Yes, Mom, I'm fine," Cat said, smiling.

"Well, where have you been?" Melanie patted the barstool next to her for Cat to sit down

"Around," Cat said, nodding toward a table.

"Well, you haven't been at your apartment," Melanie said, getting up from the bar and following Cat to a table. She sat down across from her daughter. "I called over and over and finally got Elizabeth, who told me you no longer lived there."

Cat looked annoyed. "I don't live there anymore, Mom. We broke up."

"Why?" Melanie asked. "I thought you two were—"

"Yeah, so did I," Cat interrupted, "but I was wrong, and it's over."

Melanie looked at her daughter. Catalina had always been a free spirit when it came to romance. So much like Melanie herself. It was for that reason that she'd been surprised when Catalina had brought Elizabeth to meet her almost a year ago. Cat had told her that Elizabeth was her girlfriend, even showing Melanie the ring Elizabeth had given her.

Melanie looked for the ring on Cat's hand and saw it wasn't there.

"You gave back that beautiful ring?" Melanie asked.

"I left it behind, yes," Cat said. "It didn't mean what I thought it did."

"What happened?" Melanie asked, not understanding this. Catalina had seemed so happy with Elizabeth, and the young Englishwoman had certainly been besotted with Cat.

There was a ruckus behind them. Cat was saved from answering her mother's question as Sable walked up the stairs, people trailing behind her, still asking for autographs. Melanie looked to see what all the noise was about. Her eyes widened dramatically.

"My God, that's Sable Sands…" Melanie began. As she started to stand up, Cat's hand on hers stopped her. "For God's sake, Catalina, that's—"

"I know, Mom," Cat said. "Just wait."

As Sable managed to disengage herself from the crowd, she started walking toward the table Cat and her mother sat at. Every eye in the place was on her.

Cat stood, smiling slyly. Sable walked right up to her, and, taking Cat's face gently in her hands, she kissed her on the lips. Their intimacy was obvious to everyone.

Melanie could have been knocked over with a feather.

When their lips parted, Cat looked at her mother.

"Mom," she said, knowing what a shock she was giving her poor mother, "this is Sable. Sable Sands, this is my mother, Melanie Roché."

Sable was, as always, gracious and genuine in her greeting. Putting her hands out, she took both of Melanie's.

"It's great to meet the mother of such a fantastic woman. I can see where Cat gets her looks," she said with a wink and a sly smile.

Melanie was speechless, probably for the first time in her life. Her eyes jumped between Sable and Cat and then back to Sable again.

"I—" she stammered. "Thank you. Won't you please sit down?"

"Thank you," Sable said, smiling.

Cat stepped back, gesturing for Sable to sit next to her. Sable slid into the booth, smiling again at the still shell-shocked Melanie. Cat sat back down, glancing at Sable, then looking at her mother again.

"Mom?" Cat said. "You coming back down to Earth anytime soon?"

Melanie snapped out of her trance, giving her daughter a dirty look. "Shut up, you little sneak. You know you just shocked the hell out of your poor mother."

Cat grinned, rolling her eyes.

"So, is this where you've been?" Melanie asked, gesturing to Sable.

"Yes," Cat said. "I've been in Europe with Sable."

Melanie nodded, looking perplexed. "How and when did you two meet? I mean, a month ago you're in San Diego and get attacked and nearly killed. Now I find out you've been in Europe? For how long?"

"I was in Europe with Sable for three weeks, Mom," Cat said, glancing at Sable, who took her hand. "She kind of rescued me."

"Rescued you?" Melanie queried.

"What she means," Sable put in, "is that I showed up where she was staying and dragged her back to Europe with me."

"Dragged?" Melanie asked, raising an eyebrow at her daughter. Leave it to her ever difficult child to fight going to Europe with a world-famous rock star.

"She talked me into it," Cat said, smiling.

"Begged, is more like it," Sable interjected.

"Did not," Cat said, narrowing her eyes at Sable.

"Did so," Sable countered, narrowing her eyes too.

They both grinned.

"Okay, so she told me she wanted to take me to Europe and had to do a little wrangling to get me to go," Cat conceded.

"She was busy being depressed," Sable said, her features clouded with derision.

Cat said nothing, only sitting back and signaling the bartender for three shots.

"Over Elizabeth?" Melanie asked, knowing her daughter well enough to know she was avoiding the topic.

Cat said nothing, her face impassive. Melanie looked at Sable, who nodded, glancing at Cat.

Melanie took a deep breath, expelling it loudly as the waiter brought over the shots of tequila. Melanie picked up one shot and held it up.

"Well, here's to saving the day," Melanie said, smiling at Sable.

Sable picked up her shot, holding it up to Melanie's. Cat picked hers up and drank it, signaling for another. Sable and Melanie exchanged a knowing look, then drank their shots.

In the end, Cat drank, while Melanie and Sable chatted. At one point, Cat got up to dance to a song that she liked. The song was Savage Garden's "Tears of Pearls." There were other people on the floor, but Cat had a presence that had people watching her. She wasn't paying any attention; she was singing the words of the song.

The song itself was about how love could leave you bare, empty and crying. The bridge had Sable out of her seat and striding to Cat. When she reached Cat, she slid one arm around her waist from behind, brushing Cat's hair aside with her other hand. Leaning down, she kissed Cat's neck, moving with her during the rest of the song.

The DJ was kind enough to put on a slow song after that. Unfortunately, he'd grabbed one that hit far too close to home for both of them. The song was "You Won't Be Mine" by Matchbox Twenty. It talked about the damage a relationship had caused.

Sable found herself holding Cat closer, even when she felt the tears on her skin, Cat's tears. She caressed Cat's back, wanting so badly to take away the sadness that caused Cat's pain but knowing it was impossible. It gave her a sense of hopelessness—she wanted so much to heal all of Cat's hurts, and she couldn't do it. It was something Cat had to do for herself. Sable didn't know how much of it she could take, however. It hurt to be second best sometimes. Especially for a woman who was used to being desired by millions. Yet this one little girl, she couldn't make love her. Why was that?

Melanie watched, as everyone else in the bar did. She knew that her daughter was in turmoil. Catalina took things into herself very deeply. Her daughter was not one to cry about injustices or betrayals. Cat was one to do something about it, and when she did, she put it behind her. This didn't seem to be happening. Melanie suspected that her feelings for Elizabeth Endicott had been very deep, and she'd allowed herself to trust the girl. So what had happened? Melanie had to know.

When Cat went to the bathroom a little while later, Melanie asked Sable if she knew.

Sable was more than happy to fill Melanie in, as well as tell her what she thought of Elizabeth Endicott as a person.

"She really seemed to be in love with Cat, though," Melanie said, not understanding how Elizabeth could betray Cat the way she had.

"Well," Sable said, "if that's Elizabeth's idea of love, then I think that child has some growing up to do."

Melanie nodded, agreeing with Sable on that.

Sable and Melanie were only seven years apart in age. Sable was forty and Melanie was forty-seven. Sable frequently referred to Elizabeth as a child. Cat had commented that Elizabeth was only a little younger than Cat was at thirty. Sable's reply was, "It's all about maturity, babygirl, and that child doesn't have any."

"So you're performing at the Pride parade?" Melanie asked, purposely changing the subject as she saw Cat heading for the table.

Sable picked up the cue. "Yeah, tomorrow night."

Cat narrowed her eyes at her mother, knowing that she was covering.

"How long ago did this show get booked?" Cat asked, as if just joining the conversation.

"About three months ago, I think," Sable said. "But I'm almost always here for the parade. Why?"

Cat looked at her mother again. "Nice try, Mother. You would have known about Sable being here long before now."

"Why do you say that?" Melanie asked, knowing she was caught.

"Because you're one of her biggest fans, and you know whenever she's going to be in California at all. Remember you called me and begged me to get you tickets to her San Diego show while I was in college? And when I forgot, you wouldn't speak to me for a month."

Melanie rolled her eyes. "I don't think it was a whole month."

"At least a month," Cat said.

"You're exaggerating."

"And you're covering your ass," Cat countered, then looked at Sable. "She asked you what happened with Bet, right?"

Sable didn't say anything, shooting Melanie a glance.

"Well, it was obvious you weren't going to tell me," Melanie said, her tone hurt.

"Because I didn't want to relive it to tell you, Mother," Cat said sharply.

"So," Sable said, putting her hand on Cat's hand, "now she knows and you didn't have to relive it."

Cat looked at Sable, her expression displeased. Sable removed her hand. Turning to the bartender, she ordered another shot. The evening was over shortly thereafter. Cat dropped Sable off at the hotel, telling her that she was going for a drive. Sable didn't look happy about it, but nodded and walked inside. Cat gunned the powerful motor and headed for the Wharf, where she'd spent a lot of time as a child. It was cold that evening, but Cat didn't even care. She pulled on the beige leather jacket Sable had insisted on buying her.

Walking along the Wharf and smoking, Cat did her best to clear her head. So many thoughts kept crowding in regardless. She knew she was being unfair to Sable, but the fact of the matter was her heart was shut down. Elizabeth had held it in her hands and thrown it away. It was instinct for Cat to protect it now. How could she let herself fall for a world-famous rock star anyway? she reasoned with herself. She'd be yesterday's news before the end of the year. What was the point in that?

Still, Sable was doing literally everything she could think of to try and help Cat get over Elizabeth. It was so hard not to love a person who tried so damned hard. On top of that, the one trying was *the* Sable Sands, who, in truth, could have had any woman she wanted.

How stupid am I? Cat wondered. *Here's this beautiful, worldly, brilliant artist of a woman begging to save me from depression and heartache, and I'm pushing her away with both hands.*

Walking back to the Cayenne, Cat felt guilt weighing heavy on her. Sable had bought her so much, and although Cat had appreciated it, she'd fought her all the way. It made her seem ungrateful, whereas she simply didn't want Sable wasting good money on her. Why? So Cat could continue pining for something that no longer existed? How fair was that?

Cat climbed into the Cayenne, starting the engine with a roar. She intended to go back to the hotel and make it up to Sable. She parked in underground parking and took the elevator up to the street. She walked to the hotel, pulling her jacket tighter around her as she entered the lobby.

Elizabeth felt her stomach quivering as she waited for Catalina. She'd found out where she and Sable were staying in San Francisco and had made a point of flying straight there. At the hotel, she'd called the front desk and asked to be transferred to the room—fortunately Sable Sands didn't bother with fake names when checking in. Sable had informed her, in a very snide tone, that Cat wasn't there, and that she shouldn't have come. Elizabeth had decided to wait for Cat in the lobby; she didn't care how long it took. She was pacing back and forth, glancing at the glass doors every time they opened, then suddenly she saw Cat.

"Catalina…" Elizabeth began, but suddenly realized that she had no idea what else to say.

She watched Cat stop and look over at her, disbelief on her face, then Cat shook her head and turned around to walk back out of the hotel. Elizabeth panicked, running after her.

"Cat, wait! Please!" she yelled, running to catch up to the other woman, but Catalina didn't stop—she just kept walking. Elizabeth noticed a man walking toward Catalina. He appeared to be staring right at her and seemed menacing to Elizabeth somehow. She was about to call out to warn Catalina, who hadn't looked up to see the man approaching her, but someone grabbed Elizabeth from behind. Elizabeth's first thought was that it was security for the hotel. She screamed in frustration. Catalina turned around, and Elizabeth saw the other man shove her. Elizabeth screamed again, this time in fear. The man who held her was moving her toward a waiting van. Suddenly there was a cloth in front of her mouth and nose. She tried to yank her head away, but the man held it to her face with a great deal of force. She became lightheaded immediately; fear overtook her, just before the darkness encompassed her and she passed out.

"Why didn't you grab the other one?" the driver snapped at his companion, who was taping Elizabeth's hands together in case she woke up before they got back to the hideout.

"He only paid us to grab her," came the reply. "I don't know about you, but I'm not handing out freebies!"

The driver laughed as they sped off down the street. He cast a quick glance at the blonde lying on the sidewalk, but shrugged as he continued on.

***

Elizabeth woke up in a darkened room. She could see that the sun was coming up outside the shaded windows. Looking around her, she realized she was in a regular-looking bedroom, a bit bare bones, but there was a bed, a dresser, a nightstand, and a lamp. Her head was aching—she suspected it was from the foul-smelling cloth they'd shoved under her nose that had knocked her out. Moving slowly to sit up, she saw the door to the room open. She stared down the man who walked in and looked her over.

"Ms. Endicott, glad to see you're awake," the man said politely.

"Will you be equally grateful when my aunt puts you in jail?" Elizabeth asked in a superior tone.

"If she's still alive," he said smoothly.

"What?" Elizabeth asked, her composure gone suddenly. "What have you done?"

"Merely put into motion a plan to pull the great state of California back from the brink of poverty and depravity, a condition your aunt has seen fit to throw it into."

"Depravity?" Elizabeth queried.

"I'm sure you know all about that," he said, his tone darkening, "considering your own situation."

"You know nothing about me," Elizabeth said sharply.

"Don't I?" he asked in a condescending voice. "You sleep with women, isn't that true? The one you were chasing after when we arrived. The piece of garbage who herself should be dead right now."

"Cat?" Elizabeth asked, terrified now. "What have you done, you bastard?"

He merely looked back at her, his eyes cold.

"It was you," she said tonelessly. "You were the one that abducted her in San Diego, weren't you?"

"Had her abducted," he corrected. "If I'd done it myself, she'd be dead now like she was supposed to be."

Elizabeth jumped off the bed, bent on hitting him for what he'd just said. His longer reach got her first. He slammed his fist into her face, knocking her down.

"You bastard!" she screamed, moving back from him, but her eyes shooting venomous sparks at him.

"Here I was, going to give you a chance to repent your sins," he said, his tone completely reasonable again.

Elizabeth sat on the edge of the bed again and gave him a suspicious look. "Repent what sins?"

"The disgusting habit you have of sleeping with members of your own sex," he spat viciously.

"I've slept with one woman, halfwit," Elizabeth said, her anger coming to bear again.

"That is why I feel you may have done so in a show of poor judgment," he said, taking the tone of a scholar. "It is my feeling that people should be given an opportunity to repent their sins before they meet their maker."

Elizabeth's eyes widened at what he said, but then narrowed again.

"What is it you want to hear?" she asked.

"That you repent the sin of defiling yourself with that woman," he said, making the word "woman" sound like a curse.

"I happen to be in love with that woman," Elizabeth said, drawing herself up. "Does that count for anything?" Her voice was sarcastic on the last.

"Maybe she needs a chance to remember what men were like," a man's voice said from the doorway.

Elizabeth looked to the doorway, her eyes widening as she cringed inwardly. The man speaking was huge. He had the look of a criminal. His eyes, however, were all over her, his gaze lustful. Elizabeth did her best to look brave, but inside she was terrified. She looked to the man she'd been talking to, hoping he wouldn't want this. Certainly what the big man was suggesting was a "sin" too.

"Perhaps you're right," the first man said.

Elizabeth gasped in horror, moving back on the bed, getting as far away from the big man in the doorway as she could.

"You have one last chance. Repent now," the first man said.

Elizabeth looked from him to the man in the doorway, then back at him. Something inside her screamed to agree to anything the man said, but her heart wouldn't allow it.

"No," Elizabeth said, staring directly back at him.

The man simply inclined his head as if she'd just given him a drink order. Then he turned and walked out of the room. The big man walked in, and behind him walked in two more men, almost as big as he was.

Elizabeth's screams could be heard throughout the big house. Finally she quieted, but no one noticed. No one heard.

***

The next morning in San Diego, Kana, Tiny, and Midnight were headed for the airport. Midnight was on her way to San Francisco for the Pride parade. They had no idea what had transpired the night before. When they reached the terminal, Kana stood in line with Midnight to check them in; Tiny stood to the side with their bags, keeping an eye on things and the people around them, ever watchful. Kana looked at their tickets, making sure she had everything together. She always endeavored to make Midnight's travel as easy as possible, so ensuring they had their tickets, IDs, and gun letters ready was paramount.

"Couldn't get Sinclair's plane for this one, huh?" Kana asked.

"He's using it," Midnight said with a grin. "He and Randy went to Tahoe for the weekend."

"Lucky them," Kana said, grinning too, thinking she'd love to be in Tahoe with Palani at this point.

The incident with Cat had forced Midnight to postpone many of her trips—they were now rushing to catch up. They'd been traveling almost constantly since then. Kana had been sure Midnight would cancel appearing at Pride, simply due to lack of time. But once again, her boss had surprised her and staunchly refused to cancel. "I need to do this," Midnight had said simply. Kana had felt a swell of appreciation that Midnight wanted to support the LGBT community in such an open way. No one would have blamed her for canceling, and yet she still wouldn't. It said a lot to Kana.

"We'll get some time off soon," Midnight was saying, pulling Kana out of her thoughts.

"I know," Kana said, as her cell phone rang. Pulling out her phone, she answered, "Sorbinno."

"Kana, it's Rick! What happened? How the hell did someone get past you and Tiny? How did this happen? How could you let her get shot?" He'd said it so quickly that it took a second for Kana to catch up. She held up her hand as if to physically forestall the verbal onslaught.

"Rick, Rick, hold up, what are you talking about? She's right here, she's fine… Here," she said, handing Midnight her cell phone.

Midnight looked perplexed. Kana shrugged, having no idea what was going on. She looked over at Tiny and saw he was watching them. They both went on high alert though, as if telepathically discussing it. Something was happening—they just didn't know what.

"Rick?" Midnight said into the phone. She listened for a response, and it was obvious to Kana that Midnight was as confused as she. "What?" Midnight asked, clearly befuddled. "Wait, Rick, I can't hear you. Hold on…" she said as she stepped around the poles that

287

blocked off the lines for check-in. Kana watched as Midnight started walking toward the glass doors that led outside the terminal.

Just then the line moved and Kana was at the front. "Go get her," she said to Tiny, but he was already strolling behind Midnight, keeping a slight distance to give her some privacy.

Kana turned back and caught movement out of the corner of her eye. Then she saw someone reach up in front of her face. Something wet hit her eyes, even as she was pulling her gun and yelling for Tiny.

As she turned to look toward the front of the terminal, her vision blurred, she heard what she was sure was squealing tires and... were those gunshots? *Oh God!* was all she had time to think as she tried to move to get to Midnight and Tiny, but suddenly she was falling, and her vision was darkening. *No...* was the last thing she thought before she was unconscious.

***

Cat woke slowly, her head aching wildly, her mind in a fog. When she opened her eyes, she saw Sable hovering over her, a worried look on her face.

"Cat?" Sable queried softly.

"Where?" Cat asked, glancing around her.

"You're at the hospital," Sable said, putting her hand on Cat's shoulder to keep her from sitting up. "Just relax, you're okay."

"No." Cat shook her head. Something was nagging at her. "Wait..." she said, holding up her hand. "Fuck! Elizabeth!" she exclaimed, sitting up and instantly sorry she did. "Oh..." She lay back down.

"You have to stay down!" Sable told her. "You fell—you hit your head, hard."

"No," Cat said, shaking her head again. "Someone knocked me down, and... shit! Where's my weapon?"

"You had it in your hand when we found you," Sable said. "Jake took it back to the hotel."

"I need to get out of here," Cat said, her voice strong, as she sat up slowly this time. Glancing down, she saw that she wore a hospital gown. "I need my clothes, I need my gun. Where's my cell phone?"

"Cat, wait, wait!" Sable said, blocking her from getting out of bed.

"No, I can't wait. I need to find her, Sable," Cat said sternly.

"Find her? Why?" Sable asked, her voice angry now. "She came to San Francisco to see you—so what? That doesn't make her less of a lying, cheating—"

"Sable, someone grabbed her!" Cat said, wincing at the pain it caused to raise her voice. "Where's my cell phone? I need to call home."

Sable hesitated, still not understanding what was going on. She and Jake had finally gone downstairs to check on Cat when she hadn't come up. Elizabeth Endicott had called the hotel room an hour after Cat had dropped Sable off. She'd been looking for Cat; she'd said she was coming upstairs. Sable had told her not to bother, that Cat wasn't in the room, that she'd gone for a drive. Elizabeth had said she'd wait for Cat in the lobby then.

Sable had fumed for the next two hours. It had been 4 a.m. by the time she'd awoken her bodyguard, Jake, and dragged him downstairs to look for Cat. There had been a ruckus outside, and Jake had run out to see what was going on. Sable had been right behind him. She'd seen Cat lying on the ground half a block from the hotel. Cat had been unconscious, her gun in her hand. It had terrified Sable.

Jake had called an ambulance and checked Cat out to see if she was shot. The ambulance had arrived ten minutes later and taken Cat to the hospital. Sable and Jake arrived ten minutes after the ambulance did. That had been five hours ago.

"Cat, just wait," Sable said. "Your phone is back at the hotel; so's mine. I'll have Jake go get it in a while, but you need to rest. You can't go running off right now. You've been hurt."

"No," Cat said, her tone becoming all cop. "You don't understand—Elizabeth was kidnaped, and I need to get her back. This is family business now, Sable. It's not about us."

Sable stared back at her, then nodded. "I'll have Jake go get your phone."

"I'll use a pay phone," Cat said, moving to get out of bed and getting hit with a wave of dizziness instantly.

"Wait!" Sable said, holding up her hand. "Get into bed. I'll get you a phone."

Cat nodded, her vision already darkening. Jake had come into the room when he'd heard Sable yell "Wait!" so he was there when Cat passed out. He picked her up, putting her back on the bed gently, knowing Sable would kill him if he wasn't careful. This girl was different from the hundreds of others his employer had been with—he was smart enough to sense that.

It was another hour and a half before Cat came to again. By that time Jake had run back to the hotel and gotten her cell phone for her. Cat was on the phone minutes after she woke up. She called Kevin.

"Mace, it's me," she said when he answered, sounding rather harried himself.

"Cat! Where are you?" Kevin asked.

"I'm in San Francisco. Look, I don't have time for details—something's happened. I need to talk to Rick or Midnight."

"Well, that's going to be a problem," Kevin said, his voice serious. "Midnight was shot two hours ago. Rick is missing along with Mikeyla."

"Fuck..." Cat breathed, sensing that Elizabeth's being kidnaped was related here too. "Mace, Elizabeth has been grabbed," she said, knowing she was adding to the problems piling up. "Wait, Midnight was shot? What about Kana and Tiny?"

"Tiny took a round in the shoulder, Kana got knocked out, but they're all three okay—the wounds weren't fatal. But there's an all-out assault on the Debenshire household, and we're chasing our tails here."

"Okay," Cat said. "What have you got on Midnight's shooter?"

"Almost nothing," Kevin said.

"Okay, well, I have four numbers on a plate up here on the van that they put Elizabeth into. So maybe if we can find them, we can find Midnight's shooters, and figure out where Rick and Mikeyla are too."

"Got it," Kevin said. "I'll talk to the Gang and call you back as soon as we have a plan of attack. I'll be there, partner. You stick tight."

"Okay," Cat said, feeling calmer now, since she knew her backup would be there soon. They could handle this. They had to.

***

In Sacramento, Kashena was just getting up, moving to kiss Sierra good morning, when the vision hit. She jerked her head back as if she'd been struck, sucking in her breath sharply as the pictures flashed in and out of her mind.

Sierra watched, her hand on Kashena's leg, her eyes worried. When Kashena relaxed again, lying back on the bed, Sierra looked down at her.

"Are you okay?"

Kashena nodded, breathing shallowly as the headache started. She put her hand to her forehead and rubbed it.

"Was that a vision?" Sierra asked, recognizing the pained look on Kashena's face.

Kashena nodded again.

"Hold on," Sierra said, getting off the bed and going to Kashena's medicine cabinet.

Ten minutes later, she brought Kashena tea laced with the herbs from the healer and sugar. Kashena drank it gratefully.

"I need to call Baz," she said, reaching for the phone.

"Why? Was it about him?"

"No, the AG. Something's wrong," Kashena said.

Sierra handed Kashena the phone as Kashena got up and started pacing.

The story had led the news that morning. Sebastian answered his phone, knowing it was her.

"We need to go to San Diego," he said.

"I know," Kashena said, already heading for her closet to get her suitcase. "I'll meet you at the airport in an hour."

"See you there."

Chapter 8

Meanwhile, in San Diego, everything was going sideways. Palani had received a heart-stopping phone call from Dave.

"Midnight and Tiny have been shot," Dave had told her without preamble.

"Oh God… What about Kana?" Palani asked, feeling sick immediately, afraid he hadn't said at first because the news about Kana was worse.

"Something or someone knocked her out, but we think she'll be okay. But you should come to the hospital, okay?"

"I'll be right there," Palani said, her voice expressing the relief that flooded her veins, but as she got ready, her mind started going over it. What if he was lying to her to keep her calm? What if Kana was really dead? Or shot… What if… Her mind reeled as she picked up her keys and grabbed her purse.

Palani had done her best to remain calm, but it took every ounce of self-control she had not to break land speed records to get to the hospital. She kept remembering when Kana had been shot and had nearly died. It had been a nightmare time in her life, and she didn't relish reliving any of it. She also knew that Kana would want her to be careful—she could almost hear Kana saying "Babygirl, getting yourself killed getting to me wouldn't be productive at all." The thought of it made her smile.

At the hospital, she found Dave.

"How is she? Where is she?"

Dave put his hands on her shoulders, his face calm. "She's in a room. They're running tests, so you can't go in yet. She's still unconscious."

"But she wasn't shot?"

"No, we just know she passed out at the scene."

"What does that mean?" Palani almost screamed. "Kana doesn't 'pass out'! What happened to her?"

"That's what they're trying to figure out, hon," Dave said, his voice still calm.

"What about Midnight and Tiny?"

"They were both shot, but not anything life-threatening, as far as we know…"

"What?" Palani asked, knowing there was more.

Dave grimaced. She could see things were weighing heavy on him. "Rick and Mikeyla have disappeared, and we think Elizabeth is on the missing list too."

"Oh my God…" Palani whispered.

"Yeah…" Dave said, his tone indicating his worry.

Palani looked around and saw all of Midnight's people waiting for word on the three in hospital rooms. Walking over to a seat, she saw Joe standing by one of the doors. She knew without a doubt that it had to be Midnight's hospital room. Joe was always Midnight's knight in shining armor.

Sebastian and Kashena strode into the hospital where Midnight, Tiny, and Kana were an hour later. Palani heard one of the uniformed officers, of which there were many in the waiting room, say, "Who're you?" in a very authoritative voice, which had everyone looking up. Palani didn't recognize either of the newcomers. As she watched, however, the male newcomer pushed the officer aside. That was when Dave, Spider, and a few other officers drew their weapons, not sure who these people were, but determined that they weren't getting any closer to their fallen comrades.

Palani watched as the man and woman turned back to back; it was obvious they were used to handling dangerous situations together. They didn't draw their weapons, but their hands hovered near enough to do so if needed. Things were very tense for a few seconds, but then Joe Sinclair stepped into the circle that had formed around the two strangers. "Whoa, hold up!" Joe said, holding his hands up and gesturing for the other officers to put down their weapons. "They're okay. They're from the Sacramento AG's office."

Everyone immediately holstered their weapons, looking very relieved.

"This is Kashena Marshal and Sebastian Bach," Joe said, nodding to the blond man. "Good to see you healthy," he said to Sebastian, then looked back at Dave. "They're Midnight's Sacramento protection detail."

"Sorry, we're a bit tense right now," Dave explained to Kashena.

"I can see that," Kashena said.

"And we're here to do our job," Sebastian said, not appreciating the welcome.

With that, he started toward Midnight's room again.

"Wait, wait, we have it covered," Dave told them.

"We're her backup security team," Kashena said over her shoulder. "Nobody else."

"But we're her family," Joe said as they got to the door.

Sebastian looked back at Joe, obviously trying to decide if Joe could override him. Joe wasn't his boss—his boss was in a hospital bed. So, no, he couldn't.

"Look," Sebastian said, trying to remain reasonable, "it's our job to guard the Attorney General when her first detail is incapacitated."

Kashena saw Joe Sinclair's eyes narrow, and she jumped in before there was a fight.

"Wait!" Kashena said, stepping between the men and looking up at Joe. "You guys are worried about her, SAC Sorbinno, and SAS Ako. So are we. There's a serious cop convention going on here. Can't we come to some kind of agreement on who stands watch? We can trade off."

Joe and Sebastian were still eyeing each other. That's when Kyle Masterson stepped in.

"Joe, you've been here for four hours," Kyle said, clapping Joe on the shoulder. "Why don't you go get some coffee? I'll stay here with these agents, and we'll get a game plan together."

Joe looked at Kyle, knowing he was being managed, but finally he nodded. Someone had gunned down his best friend in cold blood, and his other best friend was missing. Two of his dearest friends were lying in hospital beds, and Midnight's niece and teenage daughter were missing. Things were spiraling out of control. Joe walked away. His wife, Randy, met him halfway with a cup of coffee.

Kyle looked back at Sebastian and Kashena.

"I'm Kyle Masterson," he said, extending his hand first to Kashena. "Chief of San Diego PD. And you are?"

"Special Agent Supervisor Kashena Marshal," she said, shaking his hand.

"Special Agent Supervisor Sebastian Bach," Sebastian said, looking calmer.

"Good to meet you both," Kyle said. "Sorry about that reception you got," he said, indicating the four men standing together down the hall. "We're all on edge right now. Midnight, Kana, and Tiny are family to us."

"We're just trying to do our job," Sebastian said.

"I understand that," Kyle said. "But when Midnight's extended family consists of almost nothing but cops, you can believe she's being protected."

Sebastian nodded, looking undaunted.

"Baz!" Kashena said, knowing her partner saw only duty at this point. "Relax, will ya? We're here, and we're going to do what we need to do to make sure she's safe. Okay?"

Sebastian looked at her, his eyes on hers as she gave him a pointed look. Finally he nodded.

"Now," Kashena went on, looking at Kyle. "How are they doing?"

"Fine," Kyle said. "Midnight was hit twice, but neither was serious. Tiny was hit once in the shoulder—he's fine. The problem is that Midnight's husband and daughter are missing, and one of her nieces is too. I've sent people to San Francisco to help locate her."

"Damn…" Kashena said, shaking her head, trying to fathom all that was happening and knowing it was all somehow connected. "Do we know anything about the people who attacked the AG?"

"Not much," Kyle said. "She was hit walking out of the terminal. Tiny was hit trying to cover her. Kana was sprayed with something that knocked her out—she's still out. Tiny got the make, model, and color of the car, but nothing on the plate. The airport police are interviewing as many people as they can, anyone who might have seen something."

Sebastian glanced at Kashena. "Anything there?"

Kashena shook her head. "It was a face, and a word, along with a smoke cloud, probably the gunshot."

"Excuse me?" Kyle asked, looking from Sebastian to Kashena, clearly lost.

Sebastian looked at Kashena, as she did him. He shrugged. "You could try telling him."

"Telling me what?" Kyle asked, sensing something was up here.

Kashena sighed, not sure how her information was going to be received. "I don't know, Baz..."

"If you know something," Kyle said, his tone changing to "chief."

"I don't know anything for certain," Kashena said. "I get, well, I get these visions."

Kyle's eyebrows shot up, telling Kashena that he wasn't one to believe in such things.

"Never mind," she said, reaching for a cigar and glancing around for a place to go smoke it.

"I'll cover you," Sebastian said, nodding toward the courtyard to the right of the corridor.

"Thanks," Kashena said, striding toward the exit and away from the San Diego Chief of Police.

Outside, Kashena got on her cell phone and called Sierra, feeling the need to talk to someone that didn't think she was crazy.

"How's it going?" Sierra asked immediately.

"It's worse than we thought," Kashena said, sighing as she smoked. "The AG's husband, daughter, and niece are missing right now too. Something big is going on, Sierra, I can feel it. That vision was vicious—my head is still ringing. This is big, but I can't explain this to them. The Chief of Police is already looking at me like I have two heads."

"Why?" Sierra asked, not liking the sound of all of this.

"Because I started to tell him about having visions. He thought I was nuts."

"Oh, Kash…" Sierra said, worried. She knew it had to be difficult for Kashena. Here she was, a hard-edged, well trained, disciplined cop and ex-Marine, and she had visions that made people think she was a nut.

"Don't worry about it," Kashena said. "I just need to figure out what the hell my vision meant, fast."

"Just be careful down there," Sierra said.

"I will be," Kashena said. "Sac PD has been told to let you know if Jason gets out of jail. You be careful as to where you go, and make sure the alarm is armed every night."

"I will, don't worry," Sierra said, astounded that Kashena was always thinking of these things. She missed nothing.

"I need to know you'll be okay, Sierra," Kashena told her, feeling weak for a moment.

"I will be, Kash," Sierra said, gripping the phone tighter. "Don't worry yourself about me. Just take care of business down there."

Kashena nodded, swallowing a few times to get her composure back. Things were a mess; this was not the time to lose it.

"Okay, okay," she said. "I better get back in there."

"Okay," Sierra said, knowing Kashena needed to feel like she was doing something right then. "Kash?"

"Yeah?" Kashena said, dropping her cigar and stepping on it with a booted foot.

"I love you," Sierra said softly.

Kashena smiled. "I love you too. I'll call you as soon as I can."

They hung up then, and Kashena went back inside. She wasn't sure what had been said to Kyle Masterson, but Sebastian was leaning against the wall next to the door to Midnight's room, and Kyle Masterson was gone.

"Better?" Sebastian asked.

"Uh-huh," Kashena said.

"We're on our own on the vision thing," Sebastian said, his tone slightly irritated.

Kashena nodded. "Figured as much."

***

Cat's team, often called Rogue Squadron, consisting of Kevin, Stevie, Christian, Donovan, and Jeanie, arrived two hours after Cat's call to Kevin. Kyle had used his status as Chief of Police to charter them a plane to get them there faster.

"Well, this is a fuckin' mess, huh?" was Christian's greeting to Cat when she opened the door to the room. He grabbed her up in a hug, lending his strength to her. Stevie, Jeanie, Kevin, and Donovan followed, each hugging Cat as they entered.

Introductions were made between the team and Sable and Jake, and then the team got to work. They needed to find Elizabeth fast, and were sincerely hoping that finding Elizabeth would lead them to who had shot Midnight, and where Rick and Mikeyla were being held. There was no time to waste.

"Fuck, where is she?" Cat said, pacing. "Blue, put the pictures back up. Let me look at them again." After running down every lead they had on the plates that Cat had seen, they were still nowhere. Cat's frustration level was through the roof.

Christian nodded, glancing at Stevie. She shook her head slowly. They were all feeling like it was hopeless at that point. It had been five hours since the failed attempts to find Elizabeth.

Cat sat down in the chair Christian vacated for her. She scrolled through each picture slowly, back and forth, praying for something, anything. Her mind couldn't stay away from the mental picture of

Elizabeth tied to a bed somewhere, beaten, or hurt, or worse... All she could picture was the house she'd been held in. Then something clicked.

"Nob Hill," she said, scrolling back to the original pictures and addresses. "Nob Hill, damn it!" she exclaimed, moving to stand. "That's where she is." She pointed to the address.

"That's major upper class," Jeanie said to Cat, shaking her head, her look sympathetic. They were all tired and very discouraged.

"Exactly!" Cat said. "So was the house I was being held in, remember? Midnight thought that was weird." She looked to Kevin, who was turning the possibilities over in his mind. "She's there, Mace, I know it," Cat said, her tone sure.

Kevin nodded. "Okay, let's mount up. We'll go for some surveillance and hit it if we need to."

"What about a warrant?" Donovan asked.

"Fuck the warrant," Cat said. "If they have her, I'm getting her back."

The members of Rogue Squadron exchanged glances, then shrugged, knowing they had to back Cat up on this.

A half hour later, they were parked in two SUVs a block from the house. Donovan and Kevin did some reconnaissance. They came back looking confident.

"It's possible," Donovan said.

"For a nice house, on a nice day, most of the shades are down," Kevin said. "Especially in that back room there." He pointed to the back of the house, which was visible from the street.

Cat nodded. "Let's try a knock and talk and see where we go."

Jeanie got out of the car. She wore civilian clothes, to act as the decoy. She had her gun at her back.

"Be careful," Donovan told her, leaning down to kiss her on the lips.

Jeanie walked up to the house and knocked on the door, waiting patiently for someone to answer, looking for all intents and purposes like she was selling something—right down to the clipboard she'd picked up from the front desk at the hotel.

The door opened, and a man stood in the doorway.

"Good afternoon, sir," Jeanie said, smiling brightly. "I'm in the neighbourhood today to give assessments on dual-paned vinyl windows. Would you be interested in a free estimate?"

When the man hesitated, Jeanie went on undaunted.

"You have a lovely house here," she said, moving to look inside. "Lots of windows. I'm sure, though, that your energy bills must be outrageous. These old windows let in far too much of a draft..." She went on talking, even as she leaned past the man to peer inside, pointing out areas in which he could save money.

"So," she said, smiling, "what do you say? anna give a girl a break, let me give you a free estimate? I'm sure it would be worth your time."

The man looked back at her, obviously moved by her looks, rather than her speech—he'd been staring down her shirt, purposely low cut, most of the time.

"Well," he said, reaching up to scratch his chin, unknowingly baring a very definite prison tattoo, and the fact that the heel of his hand had blood on it, "I can't really do it today, honey." He winked at her. "But maybe you can come back tomorrow."

"Sure," she said, smiling happily. "I can do that. What time would be good for you?"

"Say one thirty?" he said, licking his lips.

"I'll be here," she said, smiling again. "Thank you so much." Her eyes flicked behind him again, then back at him. "I'll see you tomorrow."

"Great," he said, his grin lascivious.

Jeanie turned and walked down the stairs; he watched her the entire time. When she got back to the SUV, she tossed the clipboard in the back and grabbed her bulletproof vest marked with POLICE and the Department of Justice patch.

"Definitely," she said, nodding.

The team started getting ready.

"I saw two men, plus the tree trunk that answered the door," she said, not mentioning the blood she'd seen on his hand, knowing it would only upset Cat. "I didn't see weapons, but my guy stood like he was packing, so let's assume yes."

Donovan nodded. "Okay, Blue—you, Stevie, Mace, and Cat take the back door. Jeanie and me will take the front. They won't be expecting much from the back. Blue, you're on shotgun. Let's go."

The operation took minutes. Christian heard Donovan's knock and notice, and kicked the back door open at the precise time Donovan kicked open the front. There were shots fired, and general mayhem ensued. Amidst gunfire, Cat and Kevin made their way through and got to the back bedroom they thought Elizabeth was in. Cat stood back, kicking the door open, while Kevin covered her. She pulled back out of the doorway, then spun back into it in a crouch, her gun at the ready.

She was stunned at what she saw. Elizabeth was on the bed; there was blood, too much of it, around her. She was bloody and bruised. Cat was sure she was going to be sick. Fortunately there was no one in the room with Elizabeth, because Cat couldn't see anything but the woman she loved on the bed, almost dead.

"Mace!" Cat yelled. "In here, now!"

Kevin moved into the doorway as Cat strode to the bed, dropping to her knees next to it. Kevin kept watch, glancing at Cat, then back out into the hallway.

Cat reached out and touched Elizabeth's cheek, cut and bleeding.

"Bet?" Cat queried softly, tears in her eyes, her lips trembling.

Reaching up, Cat touched Elizabeth's neck, feeling for a pulse, her hands shaking terribly.

"Bet?" she said again, her voice louder this time.

Elizabeth stirred, opening her eyes, although they were mere slits because they were so swollen.

"Cat?" Elizabeth said, her voice full of wonder.

"I got you baby," Cat said, moving to stand. "We're getting you out of here. You'll be okay."

Cat strode to the door, taking over for Kevin. Kevin holstered his weapon and walked to the bed, picking Elizabeth up in his arms as carefully as he could. It didn't matter—she'd passed out again by that time. Cat covered him as he strode out of the back of the house and down the back stairs. Everything had quieted by then. As soon as Cat was out of the house she was calling in the paramedics.

***

When Kana finally came to, she still felt like her head was filled with toxic fumes. She leaped off the hospital bed and into the bathroom, where she threw up, retching terribly. Palani was there, soothing her, holding her long hair back. Kana sat back down on the bed, feeling horrible.

"Are you okay?" Palani asked, concerned.

"I don't know what the fuck they nailed me with, but it's vicious stuff. How's Midnight?"

Palani shook her head. "She's getting worse, Kana. So is Tiny. He's not as sick, but Midnight seems to be in so much pain. The doctors are doing everything they can to figure out why she's so sick. They're wondering if it has to do with whatever was sprayed in your face. They drew some blood from you to analyze it. I told them it was okay, I hope you don't mind."

"No," Kana said. "They can take anything they want, so long as they figure out what's wrong with Midnight."

Palani knew that Kana was feeling like she'd let Midnight down, by failing to protect her.

"Joe says that this was an extremely well coordinated attack, Kana," Palani said. "That these men arranged everything right down to your cell phone cutting out intermittently, to get Midnight to walk toward the front of the terminal. He thinks there may have been a number of people involved."

Kana nodded, doing her best to deal with her failure in this instance.

"If you'd been out there, you would be in the same place they're in, Kana," Palani said. "And you wouldn't be here to help us figure out who did this and stop it."

Just then there was a ruckus in the hallway outside Kana's room. Kana jumped up, striding to the door and opening it. The hospital security guard was trying to stop someone from going down the hallway toward where Midnight and Tiny's rooms were located.

The sound Kana had heard was a woman's voice yelling, "Kashena!"

Kana glanced down the hallway and saw Kashena Marshal running toward the security officer standing two feet from Kana's doorway. Then Kana looked at who the man was grappling with—it was Sierra Youngblood.

"Let her go," Kana said authoritatively from behind the security officer.

The man was surprised to hear someone behind him. He turned his head to look at Kana. He also took his hands off Sierra momentarily, and that was when Kashena hit him full force. Kashena had him by two handfuls of his shirt, and she didn't stop moving, ramming his back up against the wall next to Kana's room. She held him two inches off the floor, her face not an inch from his.

"If you *ever* manhandle a woman like that in my presence again, especially her," she said, letting go of one handful of shirt to point at Sierra, her other hand still supporting the man's weight, "I'll take you apart piece by piece. You got it?" she asked, her voice low and threatening. Sierra stood staring wide-eyed at Kashena, astounded by not only Kashena's words but by the pure brute force she'd just exhibited very publicly in Sierra's defense.

Kashena let the man go, turning her back on him and stepping back over to Sierra, looking her over.

"Are you okay?" Kashena asked in a solicitous tone.

Sierra nodded, glancing behind Kashena at Kana, who still stood in the doorway to her room.

Kashena turned around, inclining her head to Kana. "I'm sorry you were disturbed, ma'am, but he was getting far too rough with her. I couldn't allow that."

Kana looked back at Kashena. She'd just seen how dangerous Kashena Marshal could be, and it had given her a new appreciation for the woman. Kana had also recognized the protectiveness of a lover, but she couldn't find blame with her for it. If any man had grabbed Palani the way the security officer had been grabbing Sierra, he'd have seen the dangerous side of Samoa pretty quickly too.

Instead of responding to Kashena, Kana looked at the security officer.

"I think we're pretty clear on that, aren't we, officer?" Kana asked pointedly.

"Yes, ma'am," the officer said, looking fairly intimidated.

Kana looked back at Kashena, a smile curling her lips slightly. Then she looked at Sierra.

"Good to see you again, Chief Deputy Youngblood," Kana said, smiling at the smaller woman.

"I'm glad to hear you're okay, Special Agent in Charge Sorbinno," Sierra said, smiling too.

"Palani," Kana said, putting her arm around Palani, "this is Sierra Youngblood. She's Midnight's Chief Deputy Attorney General in charge of the criminal division, and Kashena's girlfriend."

Palani smiled at Sierra, noting the way Kashena's eyes widened slightly at the way Kana had introduced Sierra.

"It's very nice to meet you," Palani said, extending her hand to Sierra.

"I'm sorry it's under such horrendous conditions," Sierra said sadly. She looked to Kashena. "How is Midnight doing?"

"Worse, not better," Kashena said, her voice pained.

Sierra pressed her lips together, very worried about the dynamic Attorney General.

"Kana, you need to lie back down," Palani said, noting the way Kana's hands were shaking.

Kana nodded. "Kashena, let me know if there's any change."

"I will," Kashena said.

Sierra and Kashena walked back toward Midnight's room. Sebastian stood to one side of the door, nodding to Sierra as they walked up.

"Good to see you, Deputy Youngblood," he said.

"Hi, Sebastian," Sierra said, smiling.

"Missed her, huh?" Sebastian said.

"And then some."

Sebastian smiled. "Kash, why don't you take a break and go grab something to eat?"

Kashena narrowed her eyes at him, knowing that he was trying to give her time with Sierra. Sebastian only grinned unrepentantly.

"I'll bring you something," Kashena said, nodding.

"A blonde would be nice."

"Tramp," Kashena said under her breath.

"And?"

"And nothing. That was it," Kashena said.

Sebastian grinned. "See you in a bit."

Sierra and Kashena walked across the street to a café.

"So, how's it going?" Sierra asked, after they'd ordered.

"To tell you the truth, I'm getting really frustrated," Kashena said. "I'm seriously starting to lose faith in this gift of mine."

Sierra chewed on the inside of her lip, looking concerned. "Kash, you know it means something, and you know that it will eventually show itself and its meaning."

"Before or after the AG dies?" Kashena replied unhappily.

Sierra grimaced. "Kash, you wouldn't have had the vision if you weren't meant to play a part in stopping this. You know it's true. You just have to have faith in your gift, and know that the spirits will show you the way."

Kashena took a deep breath and closed her eyes. Sierra was right. Her visions had always explained themselves eventually. She was just terrified that this was the first time it would fail her, and she'd lose the woman she was meant to protect. Opening her eyes, she looked across at Sierra. The gods had brought Sierra to her. Someone who understood not only her gift, but her culture.

"So, maybe you're meant to be here too," Kashena said, taking Sierra's hand in hers. "Maybe you're meant to keep me from losing my faith."

Sierra smiled, glad that she could be there to help Kashena. She felt that she owed Kashena so much, and finally she was getting a chance to be there when Kashena needed her most.

"So, have you worked with a sketch artist or anything to get the picture in your head out on paper?" Sierra asked a little while later.

"No," Kashena said, pressing her lips together in consternation. "That would have to come from San Diego PD's camp, and Kyle Masterson thinks I'm nuts."

"Well, maybe I need to have a chat with Mr. Masterson," Sierra said. Her tone matched the determination in her eyes.

Kashena couldn't help but smile. Sierra had a lot more clout than Kashena did. Course, Kyle Masterson could think Sierra was nuts too, but it was less likely.

An hour and a half later, Kyle Masterson had been "set straight" on Kashena's mental state. He'd also been informed that it was never wise to discount something simply because he himself didn't either believe in or understand it.

Kyle rocked back on his heels when approached by the small woman. She introduced herself, and he quickly found that her stature had absolutely no relation to either her determination or her clout. He was fairly sure she didn't understand his amused grin, since she found it necessary to remind him of the use of psychics in a great many police cases, but she truly reminded him of Midnight. It was obvious that Midnight was putting women like herself in power at the Attorney General's office. He knew he should have known that, but it was amusing, if not a bit off-putting, to have it in his face suddenly.

"So, what exactly would you require, Chief Deputy Attorney General Youngblood?" Kyle queried when she'd finished with her diatribe.

"A police sketch artist," she said, not lightening up a bit. "Kashena Marshal has likely seen the man behind all of this in her vision, and we'd like to find out who he is as soon as possible. Locating him may be key in finding a way to save the AG."

"I'll contact someone in my department right away," Kyle said.

"Good," Sierra said, her dark eyes staring up into his. "Thank you, Chief Masterson."

"So what have you come up with?" Sierra asked as she walked up to where Kashena and the sketch artist were sitting.

"Just about done," the sketch artist said as she made some final marks.

When she turned the sketch book around, Kashena nodded, and Sierra gasped.

"Oh my God, Kashena, I know him!" Sierra exclaimed.

"What?" Kashena asked, as Joe's and Kyle's heads snapped around in their direction. They strode over to them.

"You what?" Joe asked.

"I know him," Sierra repeated. "He was a Chief Deputy Attorney General in charge of the civil division—his name is Johnathan Weiskoff. Midnight made a point of getting rid of him," Sierra said, worried. "He was crazy. At least that's what I've heard. Very maniacal about his domain and civil rights and all that. A lot of people have said he's the type to go postal some day…"

"Lovely," Joe said, nodding. "Well, he's not going postal—he's doing much more damage than that." He looked at Kyle. "Let's run him."

Two hours later, they knew that Johnathan Weiskoff lived in a house in La Jolla, and a raid was quickly planned. Joe's private jet had brought Rogue Squadron back home that morning, and they were all too happy to take part in the raid, to go after the man that had created such havoc for their family. Kana, who was feeling stronger, was determined to take part. As she joined the team headed out of the hospital, Joe looked over at her.

"K, you're still not full strength," Joe said gently.

"Fuck full strength," Kana said, narrowing her eyes. "I owe this sonofabitch. Midnight's my responsibility. He fucked with that."

Joe made no further comment.

After a bit of a firefight with Weiskoff's men, Rick and Mikeyla were rescued. But the team learned then that Johnathan Weiskoff was dead. Rick told Joe he'd explain later; it was more important that they get to the hospital.

Weiskoff being dead, however, meant they had another riddle on their hands: they needed to figure what was killing Midnight and Tiny. Rogue Squadron and Kana searched the house and eventually found his journals, but there were many of them. They began going through them immediately.

While reading the journals and discussing what they knew, Joe mentioned that Kana, Midnight, and Tiny had been infected with a virus.

He also said the name of the virus and that Weiskoff had many versions it. He then mentioned that Weiskoff had mixed the virus with Dimpraline to tame it. That's when Kashena's head snapped up.

"That's it!" Kashena said. "That's the word I saw!"

"It is?" Kyle asked, looking over at her.

"That's it," Kashena said, standing up and starting to pace, glancing at Joe. "What is it?"

"It's some kind of solution that he used to tame the virus a bit, so it would take longer to work. He wanted it to be a slow painful death," Joe said, grimacing as he realized that was exactly what was happening.

"Slow and painful…" Kashena said. Her mind was telling her she was close.

"He tested it on rats?" Sierra asked. "How did he know how much to use on a human?"

"He could have calculated based on the size of rats in proportion to humans," Jay Mark said. He was from the crime lab.

"Or he could have tested it on a human…" Kashena said, her voice trailing off as she looked over at Sierra.

Sierra's look was perplexed.

"What?" Joe asked, knowing something was catching on here.

"How are things like anti-venom made?" Kashena asked Jay, wanting to confirm her theory before she got too excited.

"In the case of snake bites, it's made from the blood of an animal immunized against the venom," Jay said.

"Okay, so they have the cure for it in their bloodstream?"

"Yes, essentially," Jay said. "But in the case of this virus, the AG and Mr. Ako haven't been cured yet. So they cannot provide the anti-venom."

"But I can," Kashena said, her tone sure.

"What?" Joe asked, sounding shocked and excited at the same time.

"The fever..." Sierra said, realizing what Kashena was talking about.

Kashena nodded, then looked over at Joe and Kyle. "He tested it on me," she said, pulling up the sleeve of her shirt, showing the thin red scar on her arm. "From the scratch I mysteriously received in the Los Angeles airport. The one I received right before I came down with a very bad fever."

"One that didn't break for four days, and only then with the help of a healer," Sebastian put in.

"Healer?" Kyle asked.

"An Indian healer," Kashena explained.

"Our doctors," Sierra told them.

Jay Mark looked at both women, his face hopeful. "I think you might be right."

"Kashena Marshal, can we borrow some of your blood?" Kyle asked.

"Take whatever you need," Kashena said seriously. "I swore to protect her with my life. If I can save her with my blood, I'm more than happy to."

It took a lot of blood, and Kashena was feeling lightheaded by the time they managed to get the serum so that Jay was happy with it. Sierra fed her orange juice to keep her strength up. Every time Sierra suggested that they allow Kashena to rest, it was Kashena who refused.

"We don't have time, Sierra," Kashena said, her tone as lifeless as her face.

With a lot of work, and a team of doctors working alongside Jay, an anti-serum was developed. They administered it to Midnight and Tiny.

"Is this going to work?" Rick asked the doctor as he inserted the needle into Midnight's IV.

"The test we performed gives it a very good chance of working, yes," the doctor said, nodding.

While everyone waited, Joe had time to question Rick.

"So how did Weiskoff end up dead?"

"Well, apparently my daughter learned a lot from you on the range, including all about the safety on a weapon."

"Huh?" Joe asked, glancing over at Mikeyla, who was sitting with them.

"Weiskoff tried to have Keyl shoot me to save herself. The gun he gave her had the safety on—he didn't think she'd know. She switched it and shot him. It was brilliant," Rick said with a wicked smile.

"The red dot means it's hot." Mikeyla repeated something Joe had said to her over and over again at the range, her tone apathetic.

Joe's mouth dropped open, surprised at both the statement and the way she'd said it, but then he began to nod, understanding that she'd saved her father's life by killing someone. It was a very serious situation, and she'd handled herself well.

It was another five hours before Midnight finally woke, but her first words to Rick held her usual sense of humor.

"So what happened this time?" she asked, her voice a hoarse whisper.

"Oh, you know, the usual—people getting shot, people almost dying." His words were light, but Midnight could see that he was very serious.

"Who? Who almost died? Is everyone okay?" she asked, worried instantly.

"You, Midnight, you almost died. We almost lost you," he said, "and Tiny too, but he's okay, and so are you, thank God."

Midnight breathed a sigh of relief, nodding. She'd been more worried about one of her people almost dying than herself.

Kashena Windwalker-Marshal had saved the day in more ways than one.

***

Elizabeth slipped in and out of consciousness. When she was awake, she didn't speak much. Cat spent a great deal of time at the hospital, sitting next to the bed. At one point, Elizabeth was sleeping, and the nurse came in to check her vitals as well as the IV in her hand. When the nurse picked up Elizabeth's hand, Elizabeth reacted violently, letting out a strangled cry and yanking her hand away from the woman. That in turn ripped the IV out of her hand. Cat was out of her chair in an instant and at Elizabeth's side.

"Bet! Bet!" Cat called, taking Elizabeth's face in her hands. "It's okay, babe, it's okay. Relax," she said soothingly. "You're okay, babe. You're okay."

Elizabeth calmed at the sound of Cat's voice, her blue eyes staring up into Cat's as Cat talked to her. Her breathing was fast—it was obvious she was terrified. Cat knew she'd been having a nightmare before the nurse had touched her. There'd been a few of them, from which Elizabeth had awoken screaming. Cat had been there every time. Always calming, always soothing.

It was taking its toll on Cat's health too. She hadn't had a decent night's sleep for going on four nights. Sable came to the hospital, having stayed in San Francisco to be of assistance to Cat if she needed it. Sending Jake in to get Cat, Sable waited outside in the quad. When Cat walked out, Sable was shocked at her appearance. There were dark circles under Cat's usually bright blue eyes. She looked completely exhausted.

"My God…" Sable said, reaching out to touch Cat's cheek, her eyes reflecting her shock.

Cat pulled out a cigarette and lit it with shaking hands. "I know, I look like shit."

"You look tired, Cat," Sable said, her voice concerned. "Are you sleeping at all?"

Cat shrugged. "Hard to do in a hospital room."

"I have a full suite back at the hotel," Sable said.

"I know," Cat said, "but…"

"But what?" Sable asked, putting her on the spot. "Is this the part where you break it off with me, Cat? Because she was hurt?"

Cat looked back at Sable, her face reflecting the conflict going on inside her head and her heart.

"Sable, I know that this sucks," Cat said tiredly, "and I'm not expecting you to understand. But Elizabeth is someone I was in love with for two years. Yes she screwed up, but when someone you love is hurt this badly, this traumatically, it's impossible to abandon them."

"That's the thing, Catalina," Sable said, stepping forward and cupping Cat's cheek with her hand. "I do understand why you need to be here for Elizabeth right now." She kissed Cat's lips softly. "I just need to know where we stand, and if you can't give me that right now,

I'll wait until you can. In the meantime, I'm worried about you. You're going to make yourself sick doing this without sleep."

Cat looked back at Sable for a long minute, then shook her head. "I don't know why a woman like you would put up with shit like this—"

Sable stopped Cat's words with her lips, kissing Cat until she was breathless. Sable pulled back. "Because I'm in love with you," she said, her tone matter-of-fact. "And because I won't give up the idea of having you for my own simply because things happened that couldn't have been foreseen or controlled. I'm not one to give up that easily, Catalina, so don't expect me to. I didn't get where I'm at in the music business by sitting back and letting things happen to me. I make things happen. I want you more than I've ever wanted anything in my life, so I'm willing to hang in there and fight for you."

"I'm going to need to take care of her, Sable," Cat said. "Susan, her sister, has a baby, and her mother lives in England. I'm all she's really got."

Sable nodded. "I understand that, and I know that you still love her, despite what she did. I just don't want to lose you totally," she said, touching Cat's face again. "Unless you want me to leave you alone."

Cat closed her eyes. Her head was telling her that it would be better and more fair to Sable if she let her go, but her heart didn't like that idea at all. She opened her eyes. "I don't want you to leave me alone," she said softly.

She was rewarded with a smile so brilliant it was almost painful. Sable kissed her again, her hands sliding through Cat's hair and pulling her close.

In truth, Sable had known she was taking a chance telling Cat that she loved her. It could have sent Cat running in the other direction.

But Sable was always willing to take a risk when something she wanted was at stake. At eighteen, she'd left her good, stable home in Tallahassee, Florida, and gone to Los Angeles to "become somebody." Today she was one of the richest and most successful women in the country. Sable took chances—it was her way of life.

Pulling back again, Sable slid her hands down Cat's arms. "Please come back to the room and get some sleep," she said. "I'm sure that Susan or her mother can sit with her long enough for you to get some rest."

Cat breathed in deeply and let it out in a sigh.

"Cat, you're going to make yourself sick. You'll be no good to Elizabeth then, will you?"

"I know," Cat said.

"Just come back to the room for a few hours," Sable said entreatingly.

"Okay, okay, you win," Cat said, holding up her hands in surrender. "I'll go talk to Susan."

"I'll wait out here," Sable said.

Cat gazed at the superstar for a long moment, then she put her hand to Sable's cheek, her look tender. "You are the most incredible woman I've ever met," Cat said sincerely. "Thank you for everything you've done for me, and for putting up with all my shit."

Sable laughed at the last statement. "You haven't had to deal with any of my meltdowns yet," she said, winking. "I can be a real pain in the ass sometimes—ask Jake."

Cat laughed. "Oh, I'm sure."

Cat went back inside, talking to Susan and then leaving with Sable and Jake. Jake escorted them to the room, then went back to the hospital. He was doing double duty at Sable's bidding, keeping an eye on Elizabeth until things were safer for all of them. Cat appreciated his help and told him so often. The quiet Irish bodyguard had turned out to be quite a help and a fairly nice guy too.

In the room, Cat decided she needed to take a hot shower to unwind. While she was in the shower, Sable ordered her some dinner. By the time Cat got out of the shower and dried her hair, Sable had the table set with food and wine.

"You didn't have to do that," Cat said, her tone pleased.

"You need to eat too," Sable said, taking Cat's hand and leading her to the table to sit her down. "And I know you're not eating anything decent at that hospital. From what Jake tells me you live on bad coffee and stale donuts."

"Jake's been spying on me, huh?" Cat asked, raising an eyebrow at Sable but grinning too. "Didn't know that was part of his job description."

"Of course it is," Sable said, chuckling as she perched on a chair, watching Cat eat. She held up her hands as if captioning words on a page. "'Spy on Sable's girlfriend when needed.' It's right at the top next to 'Serve and protect.'"

"Is that close to 'Go get the boss Starbucks whenever she wants it, no matter where you have to go'?" Cat asked.

"Of course!" Sable said, laughing.

Cat ate while they talked. Eventually, Sable could see that Cat was getting tired, so she pulled her up out of the chair and led her into the bedroom. Lying down, Sable pulled Cat down with her, kissing her temple as Cat settled against her. Cat fell asleep with Sable holding her.

Sable was still holding Cat two hours later when Jake came in quietly. He stood staring at his boss and her girlfriend. Sable's mind was far away; she didn't notice him standing in the doorway for a while.

He could see that she was deep in thought and that those thoughts were troubling.

Eventually, Sable realized he was there, and she looked over at him.

"What?" she asked in response to the speculative look on his face.

"This one is very different, isn't she?" Jake said, gesturing to the blonde lying asleep next to Sable.

Sable took a deep breath and released it slowly. "Yes she is," she said softly.

Jake nodded, having known that was the case.

Sable saw his look. "She's going to break my heart, isn't she?" Sable asked, showing a weakness she rarely exhibited.

Jake grimaced slightly. "I kinda tend to think so," he answered her honestly, his Irish brogue a little thicker because he was tired.

Sable sighed, looking down at Cat and kissing her temple. "Women always break your heart much harder than men do," Sable said wearily.

Jake said nothing. He knew Sable had been through a few rough relationships, but she'd always had the upper hand in those. He didn't think that was the case this time. Cat was calling the shots on this one, and that was going to be very difficult for someone like Sable, who was used to being in control, to handle.

"Then again, she could be the best thing that ever happened to you," Jake said, seeing how hard the conversation was on Sable.

Sable smiled sadly. "She already is."

Jake had already guessed Sable felt that way. Cat was the first woman Sable had wanted that wasn't readily available to her. It was a challenge, and challenges were often dangerous to one's emotional health. He knew he'd have to watch his very deeply feeling, intense superstar close over the next few months. Things could and probably would get rough.

"Well, I'm headed to bed," Jake said, rubbing his eyes.

Sable nodded, putting her head back down to Cat's, then she looked up again, seeing him give her one last long worried look.

"Hey Jake?" she called to him as he turned around to go into his room.

"Yeah?"

"Thanks," she said, smiling at him. "You've been great with all of this, and I really appreciate it."

He smiled, even white teeth showing against tanned skin. "You pay me well enough. I figure I can go out of my way now and again," he said with a wink.

Sable laughed softly.

Jake left, and Sable snuggled back down next to Cat, savoring the time she had left with her.

In the end, it became a routine. Cat would get up early in the morning, and Jake would take her to the hospital. He'd bring her back to the room around ten at night. She'd take a shower, have a late dinner with Sable, and crawl into bed to sleep for a few hours. Jake also started picking up lunch and Starbucks for the beautiful blonde his boss was dating.

"So, is Elizabeth happy to hear her aunt is getting better?" Sable asked Cat the night after they'd found out Midnight was going to be okay.

"We never told her about Midnight," Cat said, moving her head to get more comfortable against Sable's shoulder. "Deborah didn't think Elizabeth could handle hearing that at this point in her recovery."

"What if Midnight had died?" Sable asked.

"Elizabeth had no control over what was happening—it would only have worried her. If Midnight had died it would have been difficult for Elizabeth whether she knew Midnight was sick or not, but at least this way she didn't worry herself into a worse condition in the meantime." Cat looked up at Sable. "Does that make sense at all?"

"Yes, I guess it does," Sable said, ever amazed by these people. "You all look out for your own, don't you?"

Cat shrugged. "They're the big family I never had. I feel the need to protect that."

"They're amazing people, Catalina," Sable said, touching her cheek. "And so are you."

Cat shook her head. "I'm not amazing. Midnight Chevalier, she's amazing. Kana, Joe, Dave, Tiny, they're amazing. That whole group. I'm just part of them by association."

"I don't think that's true," Sable said. "I don't think they'd consider you part of their family if they didn't feel you really were. Besides, I heard Dave Dibbins tell you that you were one of his best narcs."

"All of Rogue Squadron are his best, as far as he's concerned, because we're all family to him."

Sable sighed. There was no convincing this woman of anything she didn't want to believe. "So, when are they releasing Elizabeth?"

"Tomorrow," Cat said. "It looks like I'm going to drive her back down to San Diego."

"Drive?" Sable asked.

"Yeah, the doctors don't think she should fly just yet. Something about the pressure or something, plus she's feeling really self-conscious about the bruises and stuff that haven't healed yet."

Sable did her best to clamp down on the jealousy that surged through her. Cat was going to chauffeur her ex-girlfriend, the one she was still in love with, back down to San Diego. Lovely.

Cat saw the flash of jealousy in Sable's eyes and waited for the comments to begin. To Sable's credit, she said nothing. For that Cat rewarded her with a lovemaking session that left them both exhausted the next morning.

Sable was flying back to Europe that morning. Cat drove her to the airport, while Jake got the rest of the entourage together and got them there. Cat walked Sable to the gate, where they met Jake. At the gate, Sable turned to Cat, wanting to say a lot of things but not sure what to actually say. She took Cat into her arms, kissing her lips, then hugging her tight.

"I love you," Sable breathed, closing her eyes and hoping Cat didn't freak out at that admission.

Cat's face, buried in Sable's long hair, creased in a wince. It wasn't something she'd wanted to hear. It made things harder. She took a few extra moments to compose herself before she pulled back to look at Sable, her eyes searching the other woman's.

"You don't have to say it back," Sable assured her. "I just felt like I needed to tell you that before I leave."

Cat flinched slightly, but then she nodded, looking both unhappy and apologetic.

Sable reached out, touching Cat's cheek with her finger. "It's okay," she said softly. "I know you need to figure things out right now. Just call me when you do."

Cat took Sable's hand and kissed her palm, then looked back at Sable. "I will, I promise."

Sable smiled brilliantly, as cameras flashed. The paparazzi had been taking pictures from the moment they'd spotted them pulling up to the airport. As usual, Sable ignored them. Jake extended his hand to Cat, smiling at her.

"We'll talk to you soon," he said, winking at her.

"I'm sure," Cat said, grinning back at him.

With that, Sable was escorted onto her plane. Cat stood by watching for a few minutes, then turned to leave the terminal.

"Are you Sable's new girlfriend?" one reporter asked.

Cat ignored him.

"Why aren't you leaving with Sable? Didn't you come here with her?" another man asked.

Again Cat ignored him, continuing to walk toward the exit. She wore dark glasses and had put her blond hair up in a hat, doing her best to hide her features. No one had gotten her name. She was an undercover cop—her information was strictly confidential. She'd always had it that way. Even people in the Castro who knew her knew never to give out her name. The reporters had hit a stone wall time and time again. She never talked to them, and she wouldn't start now.

After making her way out to the Cayenne parked in secured parking, she drove to the hospital to pick up Elizabeth. Susan and Deborah were there to see Elizabeth off, and then they were flying back to San Diego. Elizabeth had said very little the entire time she'd been in the hospital. The few words she'd spoken were mostly to Susan, whispered requests. She'd spoken to Cat very little. Cat hadn't pushed it at all, knowing that she was dealing with a lot of nightmares and trying to get past what had happened.

Cat had spent a lot of time simply sitting next to the bed while Elizabeth slept, which she did most of the time in the hospital, especially, Cat noticed, when Cat was there. Cat tended to think it was contrived, but she didn't say anything. Things between them were still very much at odds, so it was awkward enough without trying to talk too. It was, assuredly, going to be an awkward long drive to San Diego from San Francisco. A five-hundred-mile stretch.

Cat had already arranged a hotel in San Simeon, assuming that Elizabeth wouldn't be able to travel too far in one day. She'd also planned the trip so that the drive would be scenic. Elizabeth had once told Cat that she'd never seen the shoreline along Highway 1, by Big Sur and San Simeon, so Cat thought it would be a way to take Elizabeth's mind off things for a while. It was a concession for Elizabeth's benefit, since the drive would take much longer along the scenic highway versus the most direct route.

At the hospital, Cat helped get Elizabeth down to the car. She'd wanted to walk, but the hospital staff insisted that she be taken in a wheelchair. At the entrance where Cat was parked, Susan and Deborah hugged Elizabeth, and Cat helped her into the SUV. Elizabeth had become extremely frail to Cat suddenly—gone, at least temporarily, was the fiery Englishwoman she'd known. She'd been replaced with a quiet, almost timid human being. At least Cat thought so.

It didn't take Elizabeth long to disabuse her of that notion.

They'd been on the road an hour; Cat had just gotten onto Highway 1 going south. Elizabeth had been thus far quiet, keeping her eyes closed, huddled in the passenger seat of the Cayenne. Cat had deliberately kept her music low so as not to disturb Elizabeth if she was trying to sleep. She had no idea that the younger woman wasn't sleeping—she was seething silently.

Finally, Elizabeth couldn't contain it any longer. Opening her eyes, she sat up, making a point of looking around her, then over at Cat.

"This is nice," Elizabeth said, her tone edged ever so slightly.

Cat caught it and knew they were about to fight. Pressing her lips together, she nodded, saying nothing.

"It's new, isn't it?" Elizabeth's voice was light, but Cat could tell it was forced.

Cat curled her lips in a displeased grimace, then she nodded again. "The Blazer was totaled. I cracked an axle and bent the frame when I went off road."

Elizabeth's look remained unchanged. "I see," she said. "And the insurance company saw fit to replace it with a hundred-thousand-dollar Porsche. How interesting."

"Bet," Cat warned, "don't start."

"Don't start?" Elizabeth queried, her voice rising slightly. "Because you'll let Sable Sands buy you a hundred-thousand-dollar vehicle when you wouldn't let me buy you a damned thing?"

Cat exhaled slowly to rein in her temper. In truth, she could see that Elizabeth was more hurt than angry—she was just using anger like a shield.

"There's a big difference between you and Sable, Elizabeth," Cat said, stretching out her fingers on the steering wheel and looking down at them. "She's worth millions, and she has more coming in all the time. You, on the other hand, have a trust fund—a fixed amount that you are, for all intents and purposes, supposed to live on for the rest of your life. I didn't want you spending your money on me because of that."

Elizabeth wasn't sure if she wanted to accept that answer. "So she has more money than me," Elizabeth said, sounding dejected suddenly. "She wins."

Cat looked over at her open-mouthed, unable to answer.

"Since when have I been about money?" she finally asked.

Elizabeth looked back at her, her blue eyes sad, her face indicating concern that she'd said the wrong thing. Finally she shook her head, slowly. She was silent for a while, staring out the window at the scenery. The ocean was blue-green; the sky was just brightening as the morning fog burned away.

"Are you in love with her?" Elizabeth asked, not looking at Cat because she had tears in her eyes at the very thought.

Cat said nothing for so long that Elizabeth finally glanced at her to see if she'd heard. When she did, Cat shook her head.

"I'm not in love with anyone anymore," Cat said quietly, her tone defeated.

"Including me," Elizabeth said sadly.

Cat narrowed her eyes a little. "You made your own choices, Elizabeth."

"I made a mistake, Catalina."

"And mistakes have consequences too," Cat said.

"I know that," Elizabeth snapped, angry at herself for being so weak. "It sent you running to someone else. Is she so much better?" she asked then, her lip trembling.

Cat pulled herself up short. This was not a discussion she wanted to have right now.

"Bet, look," she said, touching Elizabeth's hand. "I don't want to talk about this, okay? Not now. Things are too hard at the moment. Can't we just…" She paused to hold her hand up in a show of futility. "…not, for now?"

Elizabeth blew her breath out in a sigh. "You're right," she said. "I'm sorry. You've been so wonderful about all of this, and I need to just…" She shrugged, looking back out the window.

They were silent for a while. Finally Elizabeth made a comment about the music Cat was listening to, and they talked easily for a while. The rest of the drive was without incident.

That night in the hotel room, they had two queen-sized beds and a nice view of the ocean. Cat stood out on the balcony for a long time, smoking. Elizabeth made a point of leaving her alone. She took a long bath, soaking as the doctor told her she should. She sat in the comfortable chair, reading a book Susan had bought her while in San Francisco. Her mind kept trailing back to what Cat had said that day: "I'm not in love with anyone anymore." It played over and over in her head. One thing Elizabeth had clung to was the hope that because Cat had come for her, she still loved her. That hope was still hanging in there, despite what Cat had said, but it was growing dimmer by the minute.

Later that night when they were both in their respective beds, Elizabeth had a hard time sleeping. When she did fall asleep, she woke with the nightmares that had awoken her frequently in the hospital. Hands touching her, grabbing her, hurting her—she'd scream, but nothing stopped them, nothing. After forcing herself back to sleep twice, and waking the third time in a cold sweat, Elizabeth got up, pacing the floor, trying to will herself to get back into bed.

Glancing over at Cat's sleeping form, Elizabeth felt the pull of the security Cat's presence promised. Cat had always made her feel safe from everything. Now, Elizabeth saw Cat as her savior, the woman who'd rescued her once again, but this time from actual tangible danger. Fighting with herself, Elizabeth hesitated, squeezing her eyes shut to try to force herself to have some control. In the end, it didn't work.

Cat lay on her side, one arm out, the other on her waist. It was just too inviting. Elizabeth meekly crawled into bed next to Cat, gently laying her head in the crook of Cat's arm. Cat stirred immediately, opening her eyes, even as the arm under Elizabeth moved to curl around her shoulders automatically.

"What is it, Bet?" Cat asked, reaching up to touch Elizabeth's cheek gently.

Elizabeth shook her head, then lowered it to rest against Cat's chest.

Cat stroked her hair, pulling her closer.

"Okay," Cat said softly, pulling the covers over both of them. "It's okay, I've got you. It's okay," she said soothingly as she continued to stroke Elizabeth's hair.

They lay that way for a long time. Cat felt Elizabeth relax against her. She kissed Elizabeth's forehead gently, feeling the weight of all that had happened pressing in on her again suddenly. Her fingers brushed Elizabeth's cheek.

"I'm sorry we didn't get to you sooner," Cat said, sounding aggrieved.

Elizabeth raised her head. "No, Cat, you saved me," she said, her voice reflecting her surprise that Cat felt any sort of misgiving about the previous events. "They were going to kill me—they made sure I knew that. You saved my life." Her fingers curled around Cat's hand, which was still at her cheek.

Cat said nothing, looking like she was considering that thought. "I wish I could have spared you the rest too, though."

"I could have spared me that," Elizabeth said, her eyes haunted suddenly, "but I just couldn't bring myself to do it."

"What do you mean?"

"All I had to do was repent," Elizabeth said, her voice even.

"You said that in the hospital," Cat said gently. "What does that mean?"

Elizabeth was quiet, her eyes dropping from Cat's, her thumb moving rhythmically over Cat's hand that held hers.

"That man was crazy," she said softly. "He wanted me to repent my sin."

"What sin?"

"The sin of loving another woman," Elizabeth said, raising her eyes to Cat's again. "Of loving you."

Cat stared back at her, her mouth open in surprise but unable to formulate a response.

"I couldn't do it," Elizabeth said. "I wouldn't."

That's when it clicked in Cat's head. "You mean, they…" she began, unable to say the word "raped." She touched Elizabeth's shoulder as her eyes conveyed what she meant.

Elizabeth nodded in response.

"Oh my God, Bet," Cat said, feeling sick. "Why didn't you just tell them what they wanted to hear?" she asked, near tears now.

Elizabeth shook her head again. "I couldn't," she repeated. "I wouldn't deny you again. I'd already lost you because of my stupid pride. I wouldn't lose you again, even if just symbolically."

"They could have killed you…"

"They were going to anyway," Elizabeth said, sounding stronger than she had in a long time. "I wasn't going to let them take you away from me too."

Cat felt her heart ache. Saying nothing, she pulled Elizabeth into her arms, holding her close. Her heart was as confused as her head was now. She had no words to explain it. She prayed that Elizabeth wouldn't ask her to. Thankfully, Elizabeth didn't. They spent the rest of the night with Cat holding Elizabeth close. They eventually fell asleep.

When they woke the next morning, Elizabeth looked up at Cat, reaching out to touch Cat's cheek. Cat opened her eyes, looking down into Elizabeth's deep blue eyes. Elizabeth moved her finger to Cat's lips and kept it there as she began to speak. She'd lain there for a half hour going over it in her head. She wanted to say it now before they got up and forgot the closeness of the night before.

"I know I've hurt you," Elizabeth said in a tremulous voice, "and I know that you may never be able to forgive that. But I love you, more than I ever realized before. I was a stupid fool, thinking that because people said or thought that we were wrong, that we really were. I ran after something normal, to try to put my own doubts to death. And in doing that I hurt the only person that's ever truly loved me for me. I'm so sorry," she said, tears in her eyes.

Cat looked affected by Elizabeth's words, reaching out to brush away the tears that spilled over then. But she said nothing, partly because Elizabeth's finger still touched her lips, and also because she couldn't think of anything to say.

"When we get back to San Diego," Elizabeth began tentatively, "will you be staying? Or are you going back to Europe?"

"I live in San Diego, Bet," Cat said gently, when Elizabeth moved her finger. "My job is in San Diego."

"And the apartment?" Elizabeth asked.

"Once you're back to full strength," she said, her tone still gentle, "I'll get my own place again."

Elizabeth nodded, looking like she was doing her best to accept that.

"Will you at least see me?" Elizabeth asked, throwing all pride aside.

"Let's take it one step at a time, okay?" Cat said, smiling softly.

"Okay," Elizabeth said, smiling tentatively too.

***

Colby Youngblood knocked on the bedroom door and waited obediently for the words "come in" before he opened it. He wasn't surprised to see his mother sitting up on the bed reading a report of some kind. She was wearing silk pajamas. Kashena was lying on her stomach next to his mother, her arm over Sierra's abdomen. Kashena wore sweatpant-style shorts and a tank shirt. It was a common scene. His mother had explained that it was the way she and Kashena unwound at night. He'd often come in to find them talking about something, but in the exact same positions. Kashena often went to the gym at night after they got home; she'd come home, shower, eat dinner with them. Then Colby would go to do his homework, and they'd go to Kashena's room to "unwind."

He liked that there was never any arguing, never raised voices. His mother laughed often and smiled all the time. Somehow Colby knew that had everything to do with Kashena. Kashena too was very warm and kind. She never treated Colby like a stranger; she also didn't hesitate to correct him when he did something he shouldn't, like the time he decided to try to brew hot cocoa in the coffee pot. She'd informed him that if she was unable to fix the coffee pot, the money to buy a new one would come out of his allowance. Colby was sufficiently cowed, but happy that Kashena wasn't the type to hit. She never threatened violence of any kind. It was something Colby was relieved about. The time of violence seemed very far away now.

Jason was still in jail for his attack on Sierra. Colby had gone to see him a few times, but Jason's anger about being arrested was so tangible that even Colby didn't want to be around it.

"Uh, Mom," Colby began hesitantly.

"Yes?" Sierra asked, recognizing her son's oops-I-forgot-something look.

"I, uh, well, I kinda forgot to give you this," Colby said, walking forward and handing the green paper to his mother.

Sierra read it over, then looked at her son. "This field trip is tomorrow, Colby James Youngblood."

"I know," Colby said, lowering his eyes from his mother's. "But we got lots of parents going, and I knew you couldn't go, and I just… I forgot to give you the permission slip. Can I still go?"

"Lots of parents?" Sierra questioned. "Like whose parents?"

"Like Tommy's mom, and Sarah's mom, and both of Jane's dads, and—"

"*Both* of Jane's dads?"

"Well, yeah," Colby said, shrugging. "Jane's mom and dad got divorced when she was a baby, and Jane's dad married a man."

Kashena lifted her head and smiled at Sierra, then looked over at Colby. She moved to sit up.

"What do you think of that, Colby?" Sierra asked, glancing at Kashena.

"Of what?" Colby asked.

"Of Jane having two dads," Kashena said.

Colby looked thoughtful for a moment, then shrugged. "I think I'm luckier."

"How so?" Sierra asked.

"'Cause everyone knows two moms is better than two dads," Colby said with an impish grin.

"Oh really?" Kashena raised an eyebrow at him, hiding her surprise at his statement well.

"Since when do you have two moms?" Sierra asked, her tone serious.

333

"Well," Colby said, "I have you, and Kash is just like a mom—she tells me to brush my teeth, take my shoes off, do my homework, stuff like that. So I have two moms."

Sierra looked at Kashena, her eyes widening slightly, then looked at her son again.

"And would it bother you if Kashena and I got married?"

"It's just like a party, right?" Colby said.

"Kind of," Sierra said, rolling her eyes at the over-simplification. "But it would mean that Kashena would be a permanent part of our lives."

"Isn't she permanent now?" Colby asked, looking a little alarmed at the idea that she might not be.

Kashena chuckled at that. "Yes, Colby, I am," she assured him. "But I think what your mom is wondering is how you'd like having me as a permanent part of *your* life."

Colby looked down, suddenly shy. His lips pressed together boyishly, then he looked up at Kashena and his mother with eyes so innocent. "I'd like it," he said quietly.

"Well, good," Kashena said. "'Cause I think you're stuck with me."

Colby laughed as Kashena poked him in the stomach. A round of tickling ensued. The three of them wound up laughing and lying on the bed trying to catch their breath.

Later, when Sierra returned from putting Colby to bed, Kashena noticed she had a pointed look on her face. Kashena watched her as she sat on the bed in front of her. She raised an eyebrow at the smaller woman.

"That wasn't your idea of a proposal, was it?" Kashena asked, a smile playing at her lips.

Sierra chewed at her lower lip, her eyes sparkling.

"Oh my God, it was," Kashena said, her tone aghast as she rolled her eyes.

"Stop it," Sierra said, pouting.

Kashena laughed. "If that's the best you can do," she said, putting her finger under Sierra's chin and tilting it toward hers, "then leave it to me."

She kissed Sierra's lips softly, then pulled back and looked into her eyes.

"Sierra, will you marry me?"

Sierra bit her lip, her eyes bright as she smiled. "You know I will."

"Well, no, I didn't until just a little while ago," Kashena said.

Sierra stared back at her. "Really?"

"Sierra, I know that Colby means the world to you, and that you need to know he's going to be okay with everything. So until I heard that he was okay with us being together, I didn't know if we'd ever be permanently together as we are. You know?"

"You never said anything," Sierra said, shaking her head.

"Sierra, I'm with you. It doesn't matter to me if there are rings on our fingers to represent that or not. If it never came to that, I'd be fine. I knew it would take time. I expected it to take a lot longer than this for Colby to come to understand what we are to each other. But I wasn't about to push."

Sierra shook her head. "You're so amazing to me," she said, her voice soft. "For someone who's never been a mother, you understand what it means so easily."

"I love you, and you're a mother. I know what Colby means to you," Kashena said, shrugging. "I respect that."

Sierra smiled, still astounded at Kashena's way of thinking.

"Speaking of marriage," Kashena said, "you did RSVP for Kana's wedding, didn't you?"

"Of course," Sierra said. "Kana called me and asked that you and I be there—how was I going to say no to that?"

"She's not your boss," Kashena pointed out.

"No, but she's yours," Sierra said.

Kashena chuckled. "Blackmail always works best."

"Stop, you respect her much more than you'll admit."

"Yes, I do," Kashena said.

"I knew that."

"Yes, you did."

***

Kana and Palani's wedding was the topic of yet another conversation that evening. Cat lay in her bed, sleeping. Elizabeth, who had a key to Cat's apartment, stood in the doorway to the bedroom watching her.

"So you are home," Elizabeth said finally, her voice loud enough to wake Cat.

Cat's head snapped around, then she relaxed visibly.

"Hey, Bet," she said, tiredly. "Yeah, I'm home."

Elizabeth walked toward the bed. "I didn't know if you were going to make it back in time…"

"For K's wedding? You know she'd kick my ass if I missed it," Cat said, turning over onto her back.

Elizabeth stared down at her. Catalina Roché had no idea how beautiful she was, with her long straight blond hair, bright blue eyes, perfect face, and body that could stop a Mack truck. That body was eloquently on display, since she was naked and barely covered by a sheet.

"Did you have a good time?" Elizabeth asked.

"Do you really want to know?"

Elizabeth made a face. "Not really, no."

Cat chuckled. "Why do you ask questions you don't really want the answers to, then?"

"I have no idea," Elizabeth said, sighing. "I've missed you."

Cat smiled. "I've missed you too, Bet," she replied, patting the bed next to her.

Elizabeth kicked off her boots and lay down next to Cat.

Cat had been gone for two weeks. Sable had sent her a ticket to London, and Cat had taken the time off to go. She hadn't been sure when she'd be back, so it had been a waiting game for Elizabeth.

"So, you are going to the wedding," Elizabeth hedged, trying to ignore the fact that Cat's body was far too close for comfort.

"Yes," Cat said, grinning, noticing Elizabeth's discomfort.

"I don't suppose Sable is coming here to go with you, is she?" Elizabeth asked.

"No," Cat replied. "She's going to be in Germany about that time."

Elizabeth nodded, biting her lip.

"So, would you mind going with me?" she asked.

"You don't have a date?"

Elizabeth narrowed her eyes at Cat. "You know there's no one I want to see except you, Catalina. Don't play coy with me."

Cat laughed at that one. "Always to the point, aren't you, Ms. Endicott?"

"Always," Elizabeth said with a smile. "So will you go with me?"

"Yes," Cat said.

"Lovely," Elizabeth replied, sounding very English.

"Mm-hmm," Cat said, nuzzling Elizabeth's hair tiredly.

"Did you just get home?" Elizabeth asked, suddenly realizing that was quite possible.

"Uh-huh," Cat said, sounding distinctly tired now.

"Oh, Cat, I'm sorry," Elizabeth said. "I just... well, I wanted to make sure... Never mind, I'll let you get back to sleep," she said as she moved to get up.

Cat's hold tightened on her waist. "Uh-uh," Cat murmured, sounding like a stubborn child.

Elizabeth pressed her lips together, as if physically suppressing the thrill that went through her. Cat and she hadn't been together physically in quite a while, since before the breakup months before. Since getting back to San Diego from San Francisco, they'd gone out a few times, hung out watching movies, and had dinner at the restaurant, but nothing physical had happened. Elizabeth had every intention of waiting until Catalina made the first move. This was all up to her now; Elizabeth knew she'd given up that power when she'd foolishly cheated on Cat. Now she was willing to wait for Cat, no matter how long it took.

"Do you want me to stay?" Elizabeth asked softly.

In response, Cat snuggled in farther, holding her closer still. Elizabeth wrapped her arms around Cat, happy to have this moment at least. She did her best not to overthink things. Cat ruined what little reserve she had left when she slid her hands under the linen blouse Elizabeth wore, touching bare skin. Elizabeth sighed out loud. Cat snuggled with her, not moving to do anything more. Letting Cat set the pace, Elizabeth simply held her, stroking her hair while she drifted off to sleep. Reflecting on it, Elizabeth realized that even this was heaven to her. She missed the closeness she'd shared with Cat. No one else made her feel the way Cat did, safe as well as protective. It was an odd combination. But when she was with Cat, she felt she would take on anyone that would hurt her, and she knew Cat would do the same. She had done the same—she'd come to rescue her, and that was something Elizabeth would not soon forget.

***

"You're dying for a cigarette, aren't you?" Palani asked as Kana pulled into the airport parking lot in Los Angeles.

Kana grimaced. "That noticeable, huh?"

"Your hands are shaking, and you're chewing on anything you can get your hands on," Palani said. "So either you're craving a cigarette or you're teething," she added, winking at Kana.

Kana chuckled, shaking her head and sighing. "Yeah, I'm kinda wishing I'd waited to quit."

"You could have," Palani said, knowing Kana was dealing with a lot of stress right now without her usual outlet.

"I know," Kana said, finding a parking space and parking the Navigator. "But since we decided to keep Nat here to work on that whole baby thing, I knew I was going to need to quit soon anyway. Now was as good a time as any."

Palani bit her lip. "Yes, but are you going to end up killing someone before the wedding in two days?"

"Possibly," Kana said as she got out of the car and walked around to open Palani's door for her. "But I promise, I'll only kill Tiny."

"Oh, good," Palani said, rolling her eyes. "Kill your partner, that'll be great."

Kana chuckled, taking Palani's hand and leading her toward the terminal. They were there to pick up Palani's parents. Mika and Anone Malifa had flown into Los Angeles, as Mika had some queries to make the following morning before they drove back down to San Diego with Kana and Palani.

Anone Malifa was all for her daughter marrying Kana—she felt that Kana made Palani very happy, and that was all a mother could want for her daughter. Mika, however, being a very traditional Samoan male, wasn't so sure about all of this. He wanted Palani to be happy, but he wasn't altogether sure about marriage to another woman. On top of that, his daughter wanted to have a baby, and raise this baby with Kana. They intended to use Kana's brother as the sperm donor, so the baby would have both Kana's and Palani's DNA. It was all a bit too much for Mika.

Kana leaned against a pole outside the gate as they waited for Palani's parents' plane to land. Palani watched her mate, knowing Kana was nervous about seeing Mika and Anone again. Their last meeting had ended amicably, but Kana had sensed Mika's hesitation, and it put her on edge. The last thing Kana was used to was seeking anyone's approval of her lifestyle. Having to seek Mika's was really difficult for her, but she was doing it for Palani.

Palani was close to her parents but had intended to marry Kana whether they approved or not. It was Kana's edict that Palani not only tell her parents about marrying a woman, but also that she ask for, rather than demand, their approval. Kana knew the way of a Samoan family, and she knew that Palani being disowned by her parents wouldn't be the right way to start their life together.

Palani walked over to Kana and stood in front of her. Kana grinned on seeing the way Palani was searching her face.

"I'm fine," Kana told her.

Palani smiled in response. The paparazzi clicked away, always interested in these two if they got a chance to see them together. World-famous Palani Ryker and her lesbian girlfriend, Kana Sorbinno, bodyguard to Attorney General Midnight Chevalier.

"Don't you people ever get bored?" Kana asked over Palani's head.

"Not with you two," one photographer said.

"Go bug DeNiro or someone, huh?" Kana cajoled.

Palani leaned in, hugging Kana, not caring if anyone took pictures of the two of them together. She wanted the whole world to know that she loved this woman, and let them think what they wanted about that. Kana's arms wrapped around her, one hand coming up to caress her neck, the other at her back. Palani snuggled into Kana's embrace, forgetting everything and everyone else.

"Palani?" Anone said from behind her daughter a couple of minutes later.

"Mama!" Palani said, smiling as she turned in Kana's arms.

Kana let her go as Anone stepped forward, smiling first at her daughter, then up at Kana as well.

"It's good to see you again, Mrs. Malifa," Kana said, inclining her head to Anone.

"It is good to see you too, Kana," Anone said, smiling, as she hugged her daughter.

"Can I take that for you?" Kana asked, reaching for the small valise Anone held.

"Thank you," Anone said graciously. "You're looking well," she observed. "I hope everything is settled down from that terrible business a few months ago."

"Oh yes," Kana said, smiling. "We're all back to normal again."

"Very good," Anone said, nodding.

"Mr. Malifa," Kana said, inclining her head to Palani's father as he walked up.

"Ms. Sorbinno," Mika Malifa said, extending his hand to Kana. "You're looking well."

"Thank you, sir," Kana said. "How was your flight?"

"Fine, fine," he said. "Long, but fine." He smiled.

Kana chuckled, and she and Mika turned to follow Palani and Anone down the passageway toward baggage claim.

Two hours later, they'd checked into the hotel they were staying in for the night in Los Angeles. Kana and Palani had their own room. Kana lay on the bed, trying to avoid thinking about wanting a cigarette. Palani climbed onto the bed and reached out to touch Kana's back. Kana was lying on her stomach, her arms wrapped around a pillow under her head.

"You are so tense," Palani said, straddling Kana's waist and starting to massage her back.

"I know," Kana groaned. "Mmm…" she said when Palani hit a particularly tense spot.

"Okay, that's it," Palani said, moving to get off the bed. "You," she ordered, "off that bed, and into the shower. I want you to soak for twenty minutes, then I'm going to get rid of all that tension if it kills me."

Kana turned over onto her back.

"And if I have a better idea for getting rid of the tension?" she asked in a suggestive tone.

"Kana Akua Lee!" Palani exclaimed. "You get up and get in that shower. If we use *your* method, you'll only twist yourself into more knots."

Kana laughed out loud at that. "True," she said, sighing as she got up off the bed. "You win. I'll take a shower."

"Good," Palani said, leaning in to kiss Kana's shoulder.

The shower was followed by an hour-long massage, with Palani using her arsenal of massage oils infused with essential oils to help relax Kana's tight muscles. By the time they went down to meet

Anone and Mika for dinner, Kana was very relaxed, and it showed. She expressed her gratitude for Palani's ministrations by being extremely attentive and openly affectionate. It was something she wouldn't normally have been in front of Palani's parents, considering their not being used to their daughter's rather new sexual orientation.

Anone saw the affection in every look, every gesture, and heard it in every word Kana spoke to Palani and about her as well.

"So, what will you be wearing for the wedding?" Anone asked Kana.

Kana glanced at Palani. "You'd have to ask your daughter that, Anone." She smiled warmly. "She's reserved the exclusive right to pick out my wardrobe for the wedding."

"Really?" Anone said, looking to her daughter.

Palani waved her hand. "I can't tell you right now, Mother," she said, smiling at Kana, "but trust me, it's fantastic."

"You trust her to buy you clothes?" Anone asked Kana.

"She knows me pretty well," Kana said, canting her head to the side and looking at her girlfriend. "I trust her not to make me look too weird."

"No dresses," Palani assured.

"No dresses," Kana echoed, winking at Palani.

"Have you seen Palani's dress?" Anone asked, curious if this wedding was going to follow tradition.

"Nope," Kana said. "Palani's forbidden it."

"Good," Anone said. "It's bad luck."

Kana smiled. "We don't want any of that."

"Kana, will anyone give you away at the wedding? Your father?" Mika asked.

Kana looked at Palani for a moment, then back at Mika. "No," she said. "I'm giving myself to Palani alone."

343

Mika looked dismayed by this answer. "But surely your father would want the honor…"

"I'm sure he would have," Kana said, "but this is something that I chose to do for myself. I chose this path, this lifestyle. So I'm going into this on my own."

Mika nodded, looking like he was trying to understand. "But you still wish me to give you away, Palani?" Mika asked, looking at his daughter.

"Yes, Father," Palani said. "This is how I want to go into marriage to Kana."

Palani and Kana exchanged a look and a smile. They'd discussed this at length. Kana didn't feel the need to be given away by anyone—she was too independent for such an antiquated ideal. Palani, however, still felt that she wanted her father's approval and that by giving her to Kana, he would be approving in front of everyone at the ceremony. Kana had explained it to Mika in a way that left his dignity intact, as well as her independence.

"Are you having bridesmaids?" Anone asked, interested in how this wedding would go.

"No," Palani said. "Midnight Chevalier is standing up for me as kind of my maid of honor, and Kana's partner, Tiny, is standing up for her."

"Tiny?" Anone asked.

"It's a nickname," Kana said. "He's a true Samoan, size and all." She grinned.

"Oh," Anone said, laughing softly, getting the irony of Tiny's nickname.

The following day, Kana drove them back to San Diego. On the way, Palani could see that Kana was getting tense again. Reaching over from the passenger seat of the Navigator, Palani put her hand to the back of Kana's neck, rubbing it gently. Kana made a contented sound in the back of her throat. After a few minutes, Kana took Palani's hand, kissing her palm and then holding it, her elbow resting on the console between them. Palani slid her other hand and arm around Kana's upper arm, and she leaned against Kana's shoulder, sighing softly. Anone smiled from the back seat. It was easy to see that the two made a good couple. It was also easy to see that they were very much in love.

The night before the wedding, there was what would have traditionally been a rehearsal dinner. However, since the wedding ceremony was very casual, what would have been a rehearsal took only minutes and had everyone in the Gang encouraging its end so they could party.

At the dinner, Kana and Palani gave Midnight, Tiny, and the officiator of the ceremony baseball-style caps to designate who they were in the wedding.

"Keilani, your hat designates you as the 'Kahuna,' the priestess of our wedding," Kana said, her voice serious. Palani handed the Hawaiian woman a pink hat with white stitching.

"Midnight," Kana said, as Palani handed her the black hat with bright yellow stitching, "yours says 'Big Kahuna.' Kahuna in Hawaiian means a skilled person, an expert in your field. So you're our Big Kahuna," Kana said with a wide smile.

"Now, Tiny," Kana said as Palani handed him his hat, also black with yellow stitching. "You're the 'Other Kahuna,' only because 'noho mau ma ka hale o 'ilio' wouldn't fit on the hat."

Tiny laughed, as did Kana's family as well as Palani's. But of course no one in the Gang understood that, so he explained.

345

"That roughly translates to 'a permanent resident of the dog house,'" he said, narrowing his eyes at Kana, but grinning all the same.

Kana laughed.

"Now, before the party gets out of hand, and before Tiny breaks out that bottle of Patrón he's promised me," Kana said, winking at Tiny, "Palani and I want to thank all of you. Without your understanding, support, and overall putting up with our shit, we wouldn't be here today."

"We've put up with your shit for a long time, K," Tiny put in, smiling sarcastically.

"Palani makes it worthwhile," Spider added.

"That and watching you get caught finally," Dave added.

Rick made a face at Dave. "You just wanted to be last."

"Just because you were first," Dave countered.

"Excuse me, I was first," Spider put in.

"Oh yeah," Dave said, glancing at his long-time best friend.

"Yeah, thanks for forgetting," Tammy said, narrowing her eyes at Dave.

"Oh, you're in trouble now," Spider said.

Dave winked at Spider's wife. "Nah, Tammy loves me."

"Not that much," Tammy replied, grinning.

Kana smiled. "Can we get back on track?"

"Sorry, K," Dave and Spider both said, looking like naughty schoolboys.

The rest of the group chuckled.

"Anyway," Kana said, looking at the two pointedly, "let's eat."

The party that ensued involved all the usual Hawaiian luau cuisine—roast Kalua pig, teriyaki chicken, macadamia nut-crusted coconut shrimp, long rice, potato-mac salad, traditional Hawaiian poi, and fresh fruit, including pineapple, papaya, mandarin oranges, bananas, and watermelon. They also drank mai tais and enjoyed a fully hosted open bar.

Tiny did indeed have a bottle of Patrón tequila for Kana. He'd promised her that he'd make sure she had a good time and was fully relaxed the night before the wedding. As always, he didn't let her down—neither did her extended family.

The Malifas as well as Kana's parents, Aveolela and Kao, looked on as Kana and the rest of the Gang drank shot after shot, toasting whatever came to mind.

"I still can't believe Kana held out the longest," Spider said between shots, shaking his head.

"Well, she cheated," Tiny said, giving his partner a narrowed look.

"I didn't cheat." Kana grinned, feeling the beginnings of a good buzz.

"You cheated," Joe agreed.

"Definitely cheated," Rick said.

"Don't you get into this," Midnight said, poking Rick in the ribs. He laughed.

"Listen to your woman," Kana warned Rick.

"Why? You never listen to yours," Palani put in.

Kana turned to her open-mouthed; Palani only smiled.

"I thought you loved me," Kana said.

"I do," Palani said, getting up from the bar stool she was sitting on to Kana's right and standing in front of her, putting her arms around Kana's neck. "But you don't listen to me."

"Ohh…" many of the men in the group said, grimacing and laughing too.

"I listen when it's important," Kana said, looking down at Palani.

Palani kissed Kana's lips, then pulled back, looking her in the eyes. "It's important that you don't get too wrecked tonight," she said, leaning up to kiss Kana again. "Because if you do"—she kissed her again—"and you're hungover for our wedding"—another kiss—"I will kill you," she concluded with a big smile.

The whole group let out an "Ohh!!" as Kana and Palani laughed.

Palani held up her hand. "Before you get my woman any more trashed, I have something I want to give her."

Palani pulled out a small box, wrapped in silver paper with a navy blue ribbon around it. She handed it to Kana. Kana took it and kissed Palani again, smiling down at her.

Kana untied the ribbon and unwrapped the paper, opening the box to find another velvet-covered box inside. She gave Palani a reproachful look.

"What did you do?" she asked, her tone chiding.

"Just open it," Palani said, smiling.

Kana opened the box and stared down at the necklace within. It was a pendant on a chain. The chain was a silver color—platinum, Kana suspected—and Byzantine style. The pendant was about the size of a quarter, with a diamond in the center and tiny black diamond baguettes set in a sun pattern around it. At the edge of the pendant were symbols carved in black. Kana examined them closely, then looked at Palani with a warm smile on her face and a great deal of moisture in her eyes.

Palani took the box from Kana's hands, showing it to the group and explaining the symbols carved on the four points of the pendant.

"This symbol on top represents Ele'Ele, who was the first Samoan woman. This," she said, pointing to the symbol on the left side, "represents Afa, the Samoan storm god, and this on the right is Pele, the goddess of fire and the volcano. And this last one on the bottom,"

Palani said, looking back at Kana, her eyes shining, "represents Alalahe, the goddess of love."

Palani handed the box back to Kana. "Read the inscription on the back," she told Kana softly.

Kana turned over the pendant, having to squint to read the tiny print there. It was in Hawaiian. "It says, 'Aka'aka loko i ka ike a ke aloha,'" Kana read out loud, her voice breaking on the last as she looked at Palani.

"It means," Tiny translated for everyone, "'the secrets within me are seen through love.'"

Kana pulled her into an embrace, kissing her lips, then cheek, then ear, and whispering, "Aloha au ia 'oe." It was "I love you" in Hawaiian.

"I love you too," Palani said, so everyone would know what Kana had just said.

The Gang looked on, smiling and enjoying Kana's happiness.

Kana reached for her shot glass, holding it up to Tiny. He obliged by pouring her a shot. Kana knocked it back, then set the glass aside.

"Okay, my turn," Kana said, reaching into her jacket.

"Kana Akua Lee..." Palani said, her voice reproachful but her smile warm.

"She got that habit from you, Nathan," Kana told Tiny, giving him a stern look.

Tiny just smiled back at her, his look saying "So?"

Kana handed Palani a box covered with navy blue velvet. "I had some help with this," Kana said, winking at Joe.

Joe grinned, inclining his head to Kana.

Palani looked from Kana to Joe, then back at Kana, trying to determine what she meant. When she opened the box, she understood. She stared in awe at the creation nestled inside.

It was a necklace and earring set. And Palani had never seen anything more beautiful in her entire life.

"Oh, Kana…" she murmured in awe.

Kana smiled at Joe, thrilled at Palani's reaction. Joe nodded approvingly and winked at Kana.

"I used Joe's jeweler in London to design this," Kana said, putting her arms around Palani's waist.

Palani nodded, tears in her eyes now. "It's incredible."

And indeed it was. The pendant, on a gold chain, was a hibiscus flower, created in the most delicate pearl and mother-of-pearl. The petals of the flower were outlined in tiny sapphire baguettes. The earrings were smaller versions of the same hibiscus flower. Palani had never seen anything like it before.

"You had these created?" she asked Kana.

"Yes," Kana said. "I wanted you to have something just for you on our wedding day."

Palani smiled brightly. "Thank you, Kana, so much. They are so beautiful."

Palani hugged Kana. Then she turned to Joe and hugged him as well.

"I just put them in touch," Joe told Palani. "Kana came up with the design and worked with him on every step."

"A lot of long phone calls to London," Kana said, "plus emails and faxes."

"Oh my," Palani said, widening her eyes.

Palani walked over to where her parents and Kana's sat, while Kana did another shot with the Gang.

"Good job, K," Joe said, smiling.

"Definitely," Rick said with an approving nod.

"Might have to talk to Joe's jeweler next," Dave said.

"Like bloody hell," Susan muttered, shocking everyone.

When she saw everyone was looking at her, Susan realized that everyone had heard her. Her eyes widened dramatically, and she put her hand to her mouth. Everyone burst into laughter then. It was a fun night.

The morning of the wedding dawned bright. Palani, who had absolutely refused to do the traditional thing of spending the night away from Kana, woke first. Lying next to Kana, she looked up at the woman she was to marry that day. It seemed almost unreal. Things in her life had changed so much in the last two years. There were no doubts, not even a second's worth. Kana was who she was meant for; she knew that beyond a shadow of a doubt. In truth, she couldn't wait to start their lives together. She loved that they were actually committing to each other. It meant so much to her.

Palani knew that Kana was basically placating her by going through with the marriage ceremony. It wasn't currently legal in California for people of the same sex to marry. Palani also knew that it went against Kana's grain to do something that wasn't legal. It wasn't that it was illegal, but to Kana, if it wasn't binding, what was the point? There was a point to Palani—it was a commitment to stay together and work things out when they went wrong. It was what Palani needed from Kana, and she loved Kana all the more for compromising her beliefs to make her girlfriend happy.

Palani touched Kana's cheek softly, then leaned up to kiss her on the lips.

Kana's eyes were open when Palani looked at her again.

"Good morning," Palani said warmly.

Kana kissed her tenderly. "Good morning," she murmured in reply, caressing Palani's cheek. Kana's lips covered Palani's again, intensifying when Palani moaned softly.

Within minutes they were making love, taking the time to enjoy each other before the craziness of the day started. Afterwards, Palani stretched languidly.

"Promise me we'll start every morning like that on our honeymoon," Palani said, her tone warm and sated.

"That sounds like a perfect idea," Kana said, smiling.

They were honeymooning in Hawaii, at her parents' hotel. Mika and Anone had offered them the honeymoon suite, and Palani had accepted after discussing it with Kana. Palani hadn't wanted to impose her parents on their honeymoon if Kana didn't want that. Kana had always said that if it would make Palani happy to stay in their hotel, then it was just fine.

"I'll make sure my parents don't plan any breakfasts with us," Palani assured her, smiling.

"Good," Kana said with a grin.

After they'd gotten up and showered, Palani dried her hair. Kana put on the clothes that she usually worked out in, walking back into the bathroom to braid her hair.

"You have an appointment at eleven thirty," Palani told her.

"For what?" Kana asked, looking worried.

"Don't do that," Palani said, reaching up to smooth the worry lines at Kana's brow. "I already told you that I'm leaving you alone on the hair and makeup thing."

"Good," Kana said. "So what do I have an appointment for?"

"A massage," Palani said.

Kana's mouth dropped open. "How long will that take?"

"Around an hour for the massage, maybe an hour to travel there and back. Why?"

"Don't you need me for anything?" Kana asked.

"Everything is taken care of," Palani said, putting her arms around Kana's neck. "I want you to feel totally relaxed for the wedding."

"That's probably going to depend on what I'm wearing," Kana said.

"Well, then," Palani said, walking over to her side of the closet and pulling out a garment bag, "you should probably take a look at this."

Kana gave her a narrowed look, then took the bag from her, hanging it on the top of the closet door and unzipping it. She pushed back the sides of the garment bag and stepped back, staring at the suit that hung there. It was black with a tiny white pinstripe, with a crisp white collared shirt. The material was wool, but it felt incredibly lightweight and smooth. Kana read the label—it was a Dolce & Gabbana suit. And it was incredible.

Palani handed her a box that said Prada on it. Kana opened the box—inside tissue paper nestled a brand-new pair of black leather Prada boots. They were ankle length, the leather was butter soft, and they had a two-inch heel, like Kana always wore. They too were incredible.

"My God, babe, do I even want to know how much you paid for this stuff?" Kana breathed, her face alone telling Palani she loved it.

"Probably not," Palani said, grinning.

"How much?" Kana asked.

"About a thousand for the suit and six hundred for the boots," Palani said, grimacing at the shocked look on Kana's face.

"Jesus…" Kana said, shaking her head, her eyes going to the suit again. "It's fantastic, babe, it really is."

Palani bit her lip. "I do need you to go to the tailor this morning and make sure the suit fits just as it should."

Kana nodded, still gazing at the suit. She glanced at Palani then, and saw her unsure look. Turning to her, Kana took Palani's face in her hands and kissed her deeply.

"I love it, babe," she said. "You know me so well."

Palani beamed at Kana's words. She had felt that the suit would be perfect Kana. It was totally her style—sleek, strong, but with an innate style that was beyond description. When Palani had seen the suit in the boutique, she'd felt it had been made for Kana.

Later that evening, Palani found out how right she was. When she walked down the stairs to the rock landing at the beach, she saw Kana standing waiting for her. Palani couldn't believe her eyes. Kana looked so incredible. The suit fit her perfectly, her dark skin showing starkly against the crisp white shirt. At Kana's throat shone the pendant Palani had given her as a wedding gift. Platinum hoop earrings mingled with jet-black hair that fell unbound past Kana's shoulders. Even Kana's makeup was darker than it usually was, making her face more exotic and beautiful. Palani could only stare wide-eyed at Kana as she walked toward her.

Kana, too, was having a hard time believing how beautiful her partner was. Palani wore a dress in the style of a traditional sarong, but that was where the similarities ended. The sarong was made of ivory silk mingled with lace. It molded Palani's perfect shape and flowed down to her ankles. She wore delicate ivory silk sandals that laced up her slender ankles. Her hair was a cloud of silken black curls, her flowered wreath a mixture of ivory roses and small purple orchids, with ribbons of ivory and tiny orchids trailing down to mix with her waist-length hair. Her makeup was perfect, making her eyes practically glow and her face seem ethereal. Around her neck was the necklace Kana had given her, and at her ears were the earrings.

Mika took Palani's hand from his arm and guided her to Kana's outstretched hand. The two women smiled at each other. Mika stepped back, nodding to Midnight and Tiny. Midnight was dressed in a sarong of white with a delicate purple Hawaiian print on it. Tiny was dressed in white slacks and a shirt of the same material as Midnight's sarong. It was a classic Hawaiian wedding.

The wedding proceeded, with the priestess explaining to everyone that "aloha" was the Hawaiian word for love, and that Palani and Kana had come together today to join themselves to each other in love, in aloha.

"Kana and Palani, you are entering into marriage because you want to be together. You are marrying because you know you will grow more in happiness and aloha more fully as life-mates. You will belong entirely to each other, one in mind, one in heart, and in all things. No greater blessing of happiness can come to you than to have this devoted aloha, which you now publicly avow. Keep this understanding of your marriage alive in the days ahead. May your aloha continuously grow truer and more wonderful with each day you enjoy together."

There were the vows, which were the usual wedding vows. However, when Kana said her vows, she added a phrase in Hawaiian. "Ua ola ae nei loko i ko aloha," she said, smiling down into Palani's eyes.

"Life is once more alive within me for my love of you," the priestess translated.

Palani repeated her vows and added her own phrase as well: "Ka'u ia e lei a'e nei la."

"I pledge my love to you alone," the priestess once again translated.

After that, Kana's parents stood up, walking to the rock landing. They each held a lei made of green tea leaves and white orchids. Kana turned to her parents and bowed her head to them. Kao put his lei over his daughter's head, then Aveolela did the same, leaning up to kiss her daughter's cheek. Once Kao and Ave were seated, Mika and Anone stood, repeating the ritual with Palani. Kana and Palani turned back to each other again. There was a ring exchange, where they gave each other wedding bands. Kana's was platinum to match the engagement ring of platinum and black diamonds Palani had given her. Palani's was gold, matching the engagement ring in the shape of the hibiscus Kana had given her.

The ceremony ended with the priestess saying, "May you create a home that surrounds your family and friends with warmth, laughter and love. Pili olua e, moku ka pawa o ke ao—you two are now one, the darkness is past."

Kashena looked over at Sierra, hoping that was true for them too, squeezing her hand gently. She loved the woman beyond all reason, so she knew she'd fight for her, no matter what, but she did indeed hope that the darkness had passed.

You can find more information about the author and other books in the *WeHo* series here:

www.sherrylhancock.com

www.facebook.com/SherrylDHancock

www.vulpine-press.com/we-ho

Also by Sherryl D. Hancock:

The *MidKnight Blue* series. Dive into the world of Midnight Chevalier and as we follow her transformation from gang leader to cop from the very beginning.

www.vulpine-press.com/midknight-blue-series

The *Wild Irish Silence* series. Escape into the world of BJ Sparks and discover how he went from the small-town boy to the world-famous rock star.

www.vulpine-press.com/wild-irish-silence-series